RECONSTRUCTION OF THE FABLES

RECON
OF THE

STRUCTION
FABLES

A Novel

James D. McCallister

ISBN: 978-1-946052-42-1

For more information:

Mind Harvest Press
PO Box 50552
Columbia SC 29250-0552
www.mindharvestpress.com
www.jamesdmccallister.com

In Loving Memory of

Allyson Ray
Larry Campbell
Doug Dawson
and
Dr. Franklin B. Ashley

There is no such thing as memory: the brain recalls just what the
muscles grope for: no more, no less; and its resultant sum is usually
incorrect and false and worthy only of the name of dream.

— WILLIAM FAULKNER

The grim rumors were true. When I saw the corporate earnings report last week, I knew heads would roll. But, mine? Really?

Bigger people than me would fall, too—Ward Bentham, my mentor and the editor-in-chief. A massacre. A nasty, ruthless, moneysaving bloodbath at our newspaper, the once-leading voice in local media here in our small, Southern city.

Glory fades. Sometimes upon entire professions, all at once. Or so it feels inside my reality bubble today.

I'd come back from the lavatory to find a pall over the room. Where before there'd been camaraderie and laughter, a discussion of what to order out for lunch, a beloved Friday afternoon tradition, instead a sea change of mood. The blood, draining from faces already cursed by the pallor of late nights and deadlines endured in trying to report the news. An editorial board about to shrink by half.

Only one suffused with boundless naiveté couldn't have seen it coming. With his eyes on the rearview, not ahead. When—not if.

Downsized. As if any other papers will be hiring a man in his 50s. My career—it's over. And the season of what-now breaks like an angry wave breaks over the stooped shoulders of a twenty-first-century newspaperman; former, his new appellation. Awesome-sauce, as the kids might put it. If I had any children to mimic, that is.

THE TEAM HAD BEEN ASSEMBLED in Editorial receiving petitioners. The burnished wood paneling, the oblong conference table and plush chairs, low-lighted like an elder council's inner sanctum, all normal as could be: meeting first with the police chief and a city councilperson to discuss a proposed youth curfew, followed by a presentation from a neighborhood association suing the city on behalf of local merchants seeking redress over a sewer upgrade that had improved the aesthetics of the commercial district near the campus of Southeastern University—an area folks called the Old Market, a familiar haunt to college kids as well as reporters like me—but had done precious little to alleviate a pernicious flash flooding problem.

A typical day. Interests agitating for our attention, our words in support of, or else against, some particular injustice or outrage. I miss working the beat, sometimes. Chasing down crime stories, political shenanigans, breaking a story, which I did on a couple of big State House corruption cases.

All ephemeral. The publisher came in. Throats cleared. "Sit back down, everybody. I have some news."

Oh, the irony.

Ward and I, trudging out to the parking lot together. No tears, no real anger either, only a grudging acknowledgement we tried to perceive as shock, or surprise. I don't have the energy to pretend to feel any of that.

We all knew it was coming.

"There's always teaching." Ward, stooping his lanky frame into a BMW, the same one he's been driving for almost as long as I've known him. Leaning out the window. "Karen Feitch," the Dean of Journalism at Southeastern University, beside whose football stadium our newspaper building sits. "I've been guest lecturing for her for years. It makes sense."

Ward saw through my tight smile.

"You?"

The weather, so beautiful. An endless dome of blue sky curving away from me in marked contrast to the storm clouds within me. Envy as a migrating flock of waxwings decamped from the trees in the parking lot, on their way to who knows where.

Wherever they wish.

"I'm not sure I expected this to happen quite so soon."

"It's here now, pal. But look—you're still young enough." At least showing enough decency to elide the platitude *You'll land on your feet.*

Feeling like my gut had turned to granite. "Young enough to panic about not having much put back for retirement."

I can't take this personally—what paper isn't laying off?

I suggest to Ward a facile, non-lucrative plan of action: "Blogging? A novel? Freelancing—it's all DIY now, right?"

"Exactly. In other words—now you can start writing your own history."

A ghastly idea. But my reaction, withheld behind another forced smile.

Ward, a mentor to me in this trade that I've grown to love, announces that working with me is one of the aspects of this job he'll miss most. He clasps my hand, slaps the side of his automobile. He waves and drives off, pretty much like every Friday afternoon.

After almost twenty years at the paper, you'd think I'd feel more angry than I am. Maybe this is all unavoidable. The time of newsprint senescence, it's upon us all. An inexorability. Nothing lasts, as Ken Kesey said.

YEAH, here's some news—my life as a journalist employed by the *Columbia Record* is over. And with papers laying off experienced, longtime writers and editors the world over, hard to imagine starting over. The bulb in my professional projector has fizzled out, with no plans to replace it.

What a washout—a committed bachelor with no immediate family to speak of, and any highfalutin dreams I might have enjoyed sputtered out long ago. Vices? A few. Under control. Mostly. Been some time since I had a drink. But that can always change. Except, it shouldn't. This much I know.

Thoughts of struggling with addiction invariably lead to Levon Kunkle, Kunk to me and others who knew him in college, and my original writing mentor as much as our professor had been. I think of Kunk now because his death—rather, his suicide, now almost fifteen years in the past, a decade or so after we'd become college buddies—constituted the prior existential crisis of identity for me, though at the time I didn't realize its magnitude. I'd been too angry. Too disappointed in him to think straight. Disappointed in myself.

Like I feel right now. Fifty-two years-old, and I've failed to keep myself employed. At least I don't have a kid in college.

A couple questions, scribbling in shorthand across the lines pages of my notebook, one of a thousand I've filled over the decades:

Who am I? And how did I arrive at this sorry state of being?

All right. It's a start. I know this much: A good investigative reporter would address this story not from the beginning, but by first reconstructing the timeline of precipitating events—by working backwards.

On my way to becoming a reporter and editor in a Southern city, Columbia, South Carolina, a place on nobody's radar of cultural importance except perhaps its own inhabitants, I worshipped at the altar of movies. Film provided an escape from rural Edgewater County, to the north of the city, where I grew up.

I wanted to touch film.

Breathe it in.

Eat it.

And yet, after studying cinema and making a short movie and planning to set out on the Great Highway for the Promised Land, I stayed here in South Carolina. Became a newspaperman. Served my community, or so I have tried. Life often gets in the way of the dreams, as they say.

This big idea—filmmaking—had come halfway through my senior year in high school. My folks seemed troubled.

"People like us don't do that," a grandparent said in admonishment. "You should study engineering. Go to work at the power plant like your daddy."

Not encouraging. But as lifelong working class people, mill village shift workers who lived an enormous cultural and economic distance from New York or LA, who could blame them for feeling this way?

While studying the art form as a Mass Comm major—not simply theory or criticism, but actual production—this movie freak also worked at a theater, an eight-screen multiplex at the old mall on the freeway heading north out of the city. All the blockbusters; even the occasional foreign film. Heaven.

With so many titles playing, though, sometimes on a slow weekday afternoon no one attended a particular showing. No tickets sold, no screaming headlines in *Variety* about the stellar grosses.

But in case a patron showed up late or halfway through, the projectionist would still run the print to an empty house with the bulb turned off, an act of conservation to save on those expensive suckers.

When I would usher those theaters, however, hearing the soundtrack burbling along without any images to accompany, it would give me such melancholy—like the ghost of a movie's soul had been left to haunt its forgotten house of exhibition. A feeling sad and empty as the lonely auditorium. An artistic tree falling in a deserted forest.

The camera's eye, blinded.

Movies.

Made-up crap.

In the movie of my life?

Our protagonist, a callow, middle class kid, suffers grandiose dreams, and would be played by a youthful, burgeoning matinee idol—perhaps not the dreamiest of them, but handsome enough. Its soundtrack, all mid-80s cuts dominated by REM, superstars who got their start only a couple of hours from where I grew up, and would lurch from tune to tune, setting the scene.

A golden age, one's youth. But also a time for me of enormous heartbreak and confusion.

I hate to come off stuck in the past, but it strikes me how, at least until today, my significant life drama—all the real action—happened thirty years ago.

Right: Trouble is, standing in the parking lot of the major metropolitan paper at which I've worked and written and played ball and often toted political water for my whole adult life, the melancholic hollowness of those empty afternoon auditoriums has crept back into my heart.

BITTERNESS THREATENS: slumping in my own luxury Korean sedan, deep cherry red and with a glovebox full of unpaid parking tickets, this job, as I remind myself, whether as beat reporter, columnist, or more recently associate editor, has always felt as though it might be my true calling. After a tumultuous college career spent on more creative endeavors, I fell back on reporting what I saw of the world rather than trying to interpret it with the eye of an artist. Just the facts, ma'am, although the real world as it is reported upon is rarely so straightforward.

'Novel'—the word stuck in my craw when I said it to Ward. Who am I kidding? I was never a literary genius.

Another creative outlet—screenplays, baby.

As a kid I may have had dreams that never came true, but being from Edgewater County—the sticks, as far as I've always been concerned, Nowheresville—how could a kid know who or what he should be? Movies —they provided an escape. A depiction of how the rest of the world lived. I wanted to add my two cents. Put my fantasies up on the screen like Lucas or Spielberg.

T'wasn't to be.

No biggie.

Once I came to accept my career path, the way of the fourth estate always felt straight and true and right. But correct life path or not, however, the time of change has arrived.

As I mentioned to Ward, for some time now—in my free time, not while at the paper—I've been writing in a medium vastly different from what my career entails: Screenplays. I've tried my hand at such work, a pastime for which I have some degree of training and that I've re-cultivated to augment the writing I do by day, which I enjoy, but indeed seems like the job that it is. Everybody needs a hobby. I happen to have chosen writing, which I also do all day long.

Not the sharpest knife the drawer, am I?

Literary achievement has always been a dream of mine, but in the last year I've been looking back not out of ambition but nostalgia: back in my media arts days, I fell in love and made some of the best friends of my life —that's when I first met Levon 'Kunk' Kunkle, had become friends with a seasoned jazzman twice my age. Kunk, a guy getting his college degree with punks like me, half his age, was for-sure a real cool cat, one who stood out among the fresh-faced children.

How we became such good friends I can only imagine, now. How callow I must have seemed. He'd been around. A big city dude. Looked and acted like it.

He scared me, Kunk. Maybe that's why I was so attracted to him as a role model.

What a fool I was.

Him, too.

In fact, my relationship with Kunk and his eventual suicide inspired the screenplay that I've been writing in relative secret for the last few months.

But the work, it's only a lark.

A hobby.

When I decided to try writing a script, I blew a couple of hundred bucks on software, dusted off my old college notes, and even, with much courage, leafed through my one completed prior attempt at a movie script, called *Night Driver* and long collecting dust in my old, pale blue filing cabinet in which all my college papers rest.

For good measure, I also took a spin through Kunk's student screenplay. At the behest of his ex-wife Camille, I've been designated caretaker of that document, along with all his other classroom work.

This cave-dive, it's a harrowing class of spelunking. Take it from me.

Back in the saddle, though, I found I took to the writing process. Made an outline, did the little 3x5 cards for each scene, did character biographies —easy enough—and thanks to the formatting software, only took a couple of weekends to finish a hundred-page draft. Revised it a couple of times. Much easier than back in the 80s, when Kunk and the rest of the scriptwriting students pounded out our work on electric typewriters.

Hard to imagine. Only a generation ago, but several technological lifetimes.

A moment of clarity: I have no job, but I have no fear. This is a sign. This is a big day. Day one. Time to print up my screenplay. Make it all real again.

s I drive toward downtown I get caught by the slow traverse of a hundred-car freight train—that's right, Columbia is still that much of a cow-town, with major thoroughfares blocked by train crossings. It's still the twentieth century around here, in some ways.

I glance at my laptop case, consider the screenplay resting comfortably inside on the computer's hard drive, which used to spin fast back when I used to look into the darker corners of the internet in search of facts. At times, sitting for hours at night writing this script, I have felt childish. An adolescent affectation, here revived as a way to pass the time, else a way of keeping oneself from having unstructured time only to find my old spot at any number of local taverns. Taking effort and thought away from my quote-unquote real work, all this extra writing.

So much for that problem.

Trying out the sound of the next phase. "Hi. I'm a downsized free-lance independent blogger-journalist."

On the other hand, I have resources. I own my house, as well about ten acres back home in Edgewater County, family land to which I'll be retiring sooner, it seems, than I may have anticipated. Have decent money in the 401k. An austere life—on whom should I have spent these earnings?—about to become that much more. Who am I kidding? It's a place of extreme privilege compared to most folks these days. My ego is just wounded because I got fired. And I'm a young man, still.

As I PULL into the narrow parking lot of the campus Kinko's only a block from the building where I took those Mass Comm classes, the memories gather like storm clouds.

Where I met Kunk.

Where I fell in love with Camille Grahl.

Where, on an emotional and often physical level, I had my ass handed to me.

The copy clerk accepts a thumb drive with only one file on it, a PDF I exported while stuck at the crossing.

"It's a screenplay." I say this hoping she'll be impressed. "A hundred-eleven pages."

"How many copies? A hundred?"

"No, that's the page count. Only one for now. Three-hole drilled and fastened with brads. If you have them."

"Brads? I think so. With our wide variety of more permanent binding choices," with expectant, up-selling eyes, "nobody much asks for those."

"Not surprised. But brads it must be. May I wait?"

She says that I may, gives me a flat, phony smile, takes my drive and pulls the PDF over to the server.

Meanwhile I lean against the counter, clean my glasses, examine the Post-its and envelopes and printshop doodads for sale. Catch a reflection. Suck in my gut. Finger my waddle. Try to regard my situation as a beginning and not an ending. Plenty of time now to work out. Get fit.

The clerk clatters keys and clicks a mouse. Her face, brightening. "A screenplay? That's sweet."

"Yep."

"Can't say we print many of these."

I tell her about how I used to be a student right down the hill writing such documents for actual course credit. That I'd bet money folks were doing so right now—this minute—in one of the same classrooms.

"Do you teach, now?"

"No, more of a hobby."

Now seeing me for the dilettante I am, she utters a singular, cynical, biting epithet: "Understood."

Feeling foolish, I blurted how I was killing trees for no good reason probably, but still proud enough to want to hold it in my hands. Birthed, like the bundled morning edition thrown from the back of a van in that hoary old movie cliche. "But other than columns and stories at the *Record*, I haven't finished anything in a long time. Not like this."

Excited anew, the clerk, at this earth shattering news of my journalism, says, "I thought you looked familiar. You're one of the columnists my dad always reads. He gets mad, sometimes."

I beam with pride, eliding the fact of having been sacked. "It's been quite a career. Hell of a ride. Time to write something different."

"Writing a movie. You probably have so many cool newspaper stories to tell."

"Yeah. Sure. I know where some bodies are buried."

"Oh—a horror movie. I dig those." She spins on her heel, a set of bundled, manicured dreadlocks flopping, to check on the progress of my printing.

As she collates and binds with the brads, I gaze out the windows at the tall columns of Collegiate Coliseum. Memories of both innocence and high crimes stalk my impressions of that building. Acknowledging, and remembering.

A shudder—time, turning elastic.

I return to the world at hand. "You just want to escape reality sometimes."

"Excuse me?"

"The movies. It's like a waking dream for a couple of hours. That you can lose yourself in. A good movie, anyway."

She smiles, sly and secret, behind the copier. It's noisy—she didn't even hear what I said. Her fake interest in our conversation is without sincerity.

Who can blame her. Working here isn't her dream job. People who get dream jobs are lucky. I should know—I had one.

In the Sonata with my pages tucked into a paper sack, I note how they still feel warm.

A screenplay.

The sunlight through the windshield, the same light that fell upon me thirty years ago. I acknowledge the living essence of a time of dreams and youth settling over me like mist, suffused with sense-memories of a personal epoch long passed, but far from forgotten.

To do otherwise?

To forget?

No—a disservice to those who didn't make it. To the family, friends, and lovers who helped me become who I am. Who passed on and left me, but whom I have never forsaken. However lonely a person I may seem, I always carry those folks with me.

Who needs money and a career and a family? Who needs colleagues, or stories to edit? Not only do I have characters in a screenplay to keep me company, I maintain a passel of clanking, caterwauling ghosts too recalcitrant to remain sequestered in Our Father's many magnificent mansions. No shortage of buddies with whom to chill with all the spare time I'll now enjoy.

It's no big deal, those ghosts hanging around. They have their reasons. One of these days I'll have to write about it all. If I can stand to tell the whole story of how I ended up a journalist instead of a famous movie director.

Oh, wait—the script, which is called KUNK, kinda does that. The old trope about how, to tell my friend's story, I must also tell my own.

Maybe I'm on my way to figuring out this life of mine after all.

See, universe? I'm still ahead of the game. It's early yet, and rush hour traffic hasn't hit. Downsize that.

The afternoon I learned of Kunk's death—late 1990s but Before Lewinsky, as a political reporter like me thinks of those days—I got the grim call not from Camille, Kunk's ex-wife and the real, more or less, the love of my life—still—but from Connor Rush, the third of my filmmaking partners alongside Brenda.

Connor and I had been tight as college buddies, but despite both still living in Columbia—a city, but in some ways as limited in scope as Mayberry—we'd nonetheless lost touch, and at the time hadn't seen one another in several years. These days we manage lunch a few times a year, run in some of the same Columbia tastemaker and power-broker circles; he's an ad man, a successful one with his own agency.

Kunk, Camille phoned to tell Connor, had killed himself. I made a barking sound. Felt kicked in the groin.

"She asked me to call you, and a few other people."

Remembering my reporter's instincts, I recovered. "He OD'd."

"No." Connor described the circumstances. "A much more direct and messy action."

"Shit."

I knew he was bad off, Kunk. When I'd last seen him he'd seemed one notch above a street bum. Had taken a long fall, a decline precipitous on a shockingly short timeline.

But to eat a .45 in the basement?

The news, settling into my gut. "So this was yesterday."

"No."

"When did he do this?"

"Camille last spoke with him on Saturday. He'd gone to their old house to get more of his stuff out."

The timeline nagged. "Saturday—?"

"Yes."

"Three days ago."

"That's right." His voice came strangled, like something had gone down the wrong way. "But—they only found him this morning."

"They?"

"A realtor."

I'd heard enough. I arranged to meet Connor at D'Alessandro's for a drink and rang off. I went on with my business for a bit. Finished writing a story, about a suspected gang shooting at a notorious nightclub outside the city limits. I felt empty, but fine about my dead friend.

Until: I pitched forward and wept, explosive and brief, into my hands. Kunk, dead. Another fallen icon. Not quite Jerry Garcia to a Deadhead, but nonetheless like a member of my family. Once considered a brother. Or else a father.

I finally reached Camille. She sounded matter of fact, perhaps a touch annoyed by all this foolishness. "I lost him a long time ago," her succinct summation. "And now he pulls—this."

Good for her, I thought. She's handling "this" well.

Connor arrived at the restaurant owned by another of our old comrades, Opal D'Alessandro, but she didn't seem to be at work that afternoon. Probably hadn't heard about Kunk.

Awkward, we hugged. Cursing and shaking our heads, we rued Kunk's downfall.

Connor and I went on to speak of happier times, such as the evening of the Ten-Scene victory—in particular of the triumphal feeling we shared, that of anything now seeming possible: our scriptwriting work had been judged by Max and two of his colleagues, one from the theater department, the other a mid-list novelist who'd been teaching in the English College for years, all of whom judged our work as The Best. Still, one of the greatest nights of my life.

And not only for me. Connor's eyes sparkled. "What a night that was."

"Indeed. A high point, honestly."

"For me as well."

He sighed. "You know, I keep trying. Just finished another script a few weeks ago. A rom-com."

"Those things sell." Drinking much heavier in those days, I knocked back a shot of Maker's and chased it with a summer ale. Thought I'd get potted in honor of Kunk, who could drink his weight in liquor. But at the time, I didn't need many excuses to order a neat bourbon. "I'm glad you're still chipping away at it."

He shrugged. "It's something to do."

Nothing to be said, it seemed, about the Huge Misunderstanding all those years ago, on the very night in question. For which I felt duly grateful.

Connor cut his eyes around the room, pursed his lips, waved the server over. With curt insistence, he urged her to turn down both the music and the air conditioning, ordered himself another Gibson—but this one not as dry and with extra cocktail onions—and sent her on her way with tiny, shooing motions of his slender fingertips.

"Are you still writing?"

"Of course."

"Besides for the *Record*. What about scripts?"

I felt my cheeks redden. I described a desultory string of movie and novel ideas, a short story attempt. "I still jot down notes, get ideas. But scripts? I can barely watch movies anymore."

"Not even arthouse stuff?"

I considered how I hadn't been to the Main Street Bijou, our town's lone, independent film society screen, in ages. Before becoming a reporter I'd managed one of the multiplexes in town, moving up the ladder there after I got my media degree, at least until I realized I was wasting life and talent by being a popcorn salesclerk. Maybe that's why I don't go to the movies—after working in theatrical exhibition, I can hardly stand the smell of those places. "I have a hard time losing myself. All I see is the artifice."

"Me, too—except in the good ones."

"'That's what makes them the good ones,'" quoting a Max de Lisle truism. "When you can't see the puppeteer and the wires. Nothing like getting lost in a great film."

"Suspension of disbelief."

"Perhaps *the* key element."

A warm, nostalgic laugh; a further sigh.

"Well, notes and ideas—that's writing, too. A part of the process. So then the answer's, 'Yes, I'm a scriptwriter.' Remember how Max told us to call ourselves screenwriters from day one, to make our ambitions as real as we could in our minds first, so that it could manifest in reality later?"

"I remember. 'If you're a writer, then say so.'"

After the second round and feeling foolish at what sounded like a morbid joke, I said, "This wasn't the first time Kunk died."

An arched eyebrow to do Nimoy proud. "Well, don't keep it under your hat, journalist-man."

"When he found out Camille was pregnant. After she'd said she wanted to keep it."

"How is that a death?"

"Kunk said to me: 'My life is over; my life is over,' this sad chant." Sipping a fresh Maker's an acidic bile lapped at the back of my throat, a brackish tide. "I tried to talk him out of marrying her."

Connor cluck-clucked, a staccato chuckle. "I can only imagine you did."

My eyes bulged. My voice cracked. "You and I never talked about how I felt about Camille."

"No, we didn't." He smiled over the rim of his Gibson. "But now I know for sure—don't I?"

I'd been made. "What I wanted didn't work out."

"A lot of that went around back then."

At last. I forced a wink. Connor peered down his nose with pursed lips. "You think he knew? About how I felt?"

"Who?"

"Kunk."

Connor squinted into his cocktail. "How. The hell. Would I know."

Kunk and Connor, never the closest of friends. "Fair enough."

I wondered, too, if Connor somehow knew about my one night with Camille. I decided not to bring it up.

Ah—the secret mercy screw. A private, serendipitous, emotionally complicated clusterfuck of an occurrence. It hadn't been love on her part—Camille's main reason, to be honest, had been her anger with her man over suspicions of infidelity: Kunk, a rake, a wolf, which she ought to have known before they started dating, I thought. In any case, the next day, after the elation of being with her had worn off, I felt used and more broken-hearted than before we'd slept together.

"Here's one way to look at all this tragedy," Connor said, more weary than snide.

"Do tell."

"Now's your chance with her."

I dared not think that way. Kunk wasn't even in the ground yet. Yes, by then they'd been divorced for over a year, and I'd yet to manage a successful relationship with any particular woman. *Why start now?* I remember thinking.

Connor sipped his drink and waved the server back over. The young woman, unable to conceal a sour look—*oh, now what*. But this time, he only asked for the check.

"I don't want to be rude. But I have plans tonight I should keep."

"Someone special in your life these days?"

"Always—he's waiting for me right now. So," again fluttering the fingertips. "I should go."

"That's fine. It's—what else is there to say?"

Recount every self-inflicted tragedy that'd befallen Kunk? The worsening, impossible-to-deny alcoholism. Getting fired from the insurance company, right around the time their son turned six. How Kunk had started playing bass again, gigging with a jazz combo out of Charleston to make money, driving back and forth from Columbia a few times a week. How he'd been fired from that decent paying musician's gig for showing up too polluted to play. A couple of months later, how he'd wrecked his car, totaled it and got slapped with a DUI, his second. How it had all piled up—sudden, a culmination.

Worst of all? How I'd done nothing to help him.

Not true. Camille had given me the address of a boarding house where he'd been staying since he came back from Charleston. I'd gone, begged him to get cleaned up. But rebuffed. I'd tried. Our last words not cordial.

Finality—but as hopeless as he seemed, at the time I hadn't guessed how final. I considered making Connor stay long enough to hear about all that, but he had bigger fish, as they say.

We parted on the cracked dirty sidewalk out front, both sad we hadn't seen Opal, for whom I had scribbled a note the maitre'd pledged to put on her desk in the office. Swore to do better at keeping up. Planned to at least see one another at the funeral.

As I watched Connor drive away I toyed with going home, but instead went back inside to start a new tab, called Camille again, finally catching her. We had ourselves a good long talk, and this time she wept like a properly bereaved spouse. Like my old buddy at least halfway deserved.

I continued to drink and drink, trying to kill the anguish and crippling feeling of waste and futility. But for all my dyspeptic profligacy, I found it impossible to forgot anything about my relationship with Levon Kunkle, and all he'd meant at a time when I had needed someone—anyone—to believe in me and my dreams.

The next day I met Camille outside her office to ride over to the house together. My role? To finish what Kunk had started—the removal of the last few personal items from a corner of the basement, those scripts and other papers of his from back in the day, as contemporary kids would put it. She wanted no part of her ex-husband, not even his schoolwork; not even reminders of the happy times. That bad.

She picked me up at the paper, a two-story building around the corner from where she worked as a producer at the PBS affiliate here in town. I emerged from the smoky, tempered glass of the *Record's* lobby to see her in black exec suit and low heels, leaning on the car, the sun dropping behind Redtails stadium, an imposing, silhouetted edifice looming over us.

The grief and pain, etched into her face. But still beautiful. Despite everything Kunk put her through, Camille, aging with grace. We were both still young at the time, when Kunk died. He'd been twenty years older than both of us.

We drove over to Forest Acres in silence, until Camille asked with startling suddenness, "What is suicide?"

"You really need a definition?"

"No. I'm asking: do you know what it is?"

Since this couldn't be literal, I said I needed to understand the rhetorical angle. "Some kind of joke?"

Impish, a sneaky crinkle crept in around eyes smudged by teary mascara. She waited.

"I don't know. Why don't you tell me."

As it turned out, she had no deep revelations, only a comic's punchline. "Planned obsolescence—get it?"

"Rimshot."

She wagged a finger. "A good one. Now that—that's a good one."

Camille continued to laugh all the way through the neighborhood overhung by tall oaks, well-appointed older houses lined up one after another with manicured lawns. She kept chortling right up to her old driveway, into which she couldn't pull straight because her eyes streamed with tears, makeup running, sucking wind. She screamed with laughter, mad gales.

Patting her on the arm, I put the car into park and allowed her eruption to peter out, which it did, ebbing at last into quiet sniffling.

"Oh, goodness gracious *me*," a Southern girl through and through. "I didn't know how to help him. How to make him happy."

"Yeah, well—at least you tried harder than I did." Gagging on my words.

"He wasn't your responsibility. Nor was he mine. Not in the end."

"No? Neither of us? His wife and his best buddy from college?"

She shook her head. "Someone with his addiction issues—and ego issues—can only help themselves. He had so much—baggage."

"More than we knew."

Nodding. "More than even his wife knew. That's right."

Before becoming a mass comm undergrad among the kids at Southeastern, Kunk had led a colorful life, or so he claimed. He'd experienced "the 60s," for god's sake, as a working musician when the rest of us had still been in diapers. A baby boomer, he had been almost as old as my parents.

"Let's get this over with," unhooking my seatbelt. "My gut's as tight as a stone."

"I'm sorry to ask you to do this, but I can't go down there."

"It's the least I can do. For both of you."

Due to her long-delayed plans to get the house on the market, as she'd explained on the phone, she needed someone to gather up any heirlooms from Kunk's possessions worth keeping, which is what he'd supposedly been down there doing when he pulled this stunt.

Kunk's possessions. I wanted only to get my hands on the powder-blue, two-drawer filing cabinet, a place he kept his important papers, the records of achievement in Act II of his life, his college coursework: saving all of it, he said—the short scripts, his screenplay along with others he'd started but never finished; a half-baked play he'd attempted at Max's urging—to make sure he got his freaking money's worth. I am no stranger to such literary skeletons dangling their dry bones in secluded closets. I would add his pages to mine, a forgotten hall of records into which no explorer dreamed of spelunking.

"You sure you don't want the pages from the scriptwriting class?"

"What I'm keeping of him I already took a long time ago—mainly our son. The only furniture and junk left in there's what he had stored."

"And then?"

"Take you what want. The rest is going to goodwill, or in the trash. I—I don't have time to deal with sorting through it."

"Not his guitars."

"No—those I'll keep for Artie," by then about eight, an all-American kid with his father's crystal blue eyes and his mother's auburn hair. How would she explain it to him, I pondered. "I can't go *down* there. You understand?"

I hushed her. I did understand.

An exclamation point appeared over my head. "Has anyone called Max?"

"I don't know," she said of our old professor, still alive then and retired up at the lake. "Someone should."

I hated to have the chore on my shoulders. Maybe he'd heard already. I didn't want to be the one to break the news.

Max and Kunk, such buddies. The last time I'd talked to our old writing mentor had been a call I made after a scathing letter to the editor had come in from him, a witty screed decrying some corrupt aspect of our local government, which would be worth describing if such corruption weren't so endemic to South Carolina politics. Max's voice had come through chipper but frail. Said he'd gone back to the novel he'd always dreamed of writing—sound familiar?—also how he missed teaching, but had suffered his fill of the pernicious bureaucracy at Southeastern, in his words.

Kunk's decline had come up. Our professor already sounded heart-broken over him, even before this grim turn of events. An old man's tears lay in my future.

"Again: Whatever you want of his, take it today. I don't want to drag all this out. I want this over."

I assured her I'd be expeditious.

We got out, walked up the drive covered in leaves. The whole yard needed raking—a family home, abandoned by its patriarch. But much worse would be what remained inside of that father-figure.

※

AFTER RUSHING BACK out of the basement, I went down on my knees in the side yard, my stomach convulsing with dry-heaves. Hungover, I'd barely eaten anything that day, and my nausea at what I'd encountered in the basement felt like an animal ripping apart the lining of my stomach. Camille held my forehead until I stopped retching.

"What's wrong?"

Standing up, shaky. Sweating. I couldn't look at her.

"Say it."

"The smell," I managed to croak—three days, a long time for wet bloody meat to sit rotting. Brando whispering in my ear: *the horror, the horror.* "It's devastating."

"Oh—oh, god."

"You're going to need to call somebody who specializes in fumigation. Restoration."

She nodded, her face a mask of revulsion and grief.

"I'm okay, now. I can go back down there," convincing myself. "I'll— soak a handkerchief in Old Spice."

Her voice came tender. "You don't have to worry about it, hon. It's not that big a hurry. I'm just overreacting. Rushing things." She touched my face. "Are you all right?"

"Tell you what. Let's find a ginger ale nearby for me to sip on."

"Do you want me to go inside and see if anything's in the fridge?"

"No, don't do that. Let's go."

Camille pulled into the drive-through of a burger joint around the corner. I ordered a Sprite, large, lots of ice. Then as now I chew ice, especially when I'm writing. Teeth latticed by a network of cracks in the enamel; a bad habit over which I've been warned through the years by various dentists. Gurgling, a burst of cold relief exploded in my empty gut. "Oh—that hits the spot."

"Feel better?"

"Not really."

"I'm so sorry."

"It isn't your fault."

"No."

We pulled over into a space and talked for a while, watching as a steady stream of fast food junkies moved along the curbed horseshoe of the drive-through lane. The light turned gloomy. Kunk's diseased spirit hovered around us. Writer bullshit.

I reached across and held her warm hand; she allowed this.

"How's our boy?"

"Angry, confused, what have you. You don't know how much they understand, what they really feel. He's like you always were—keeping it inside." She punched me in the arm. "Hard-to-read."

I nodded. People tell me it's difficult to get close, that I keep the door partially closed. "And how's the girl?"

Perplexed. "The *girl*?"

"You."

Distant, she pondered and cogitated. Finally Camille uttered another laugh, this one minuscule and bitter. "I lost my husband once already. If I ever had him. Something that's irrevocable can't be any more irrevocable than it already was."

"Except in death."

"Yes."

Arrangements to finalize, she said. I offered to go to the funeral home, to help make decisions. I knew him well, after all.

"Artie's going with me. He wants to. He knows his father was sick, and understands that he's gone, and that life has to go on."

"Amazing. Imminent manhood, but in a pint-sized package."

"And so, it's time he learned about dealing with this part."

"Everybody has to." I thought of my mother, and how my father had asked me if I would come help him pick out a casket. "No better time— and besides, he'll only lose his father once."

Dropping me back off at my car, I leaned on her door, had more to say. She could see it on my face. But with a caution in her teary red eyes, I thought better of expressing what welled in my heart. Too soon; too much to unpack.

"I'll call you later," an edge to my voice. "May I call you later, I mean?"

"That would be good."

I couldn't help my next words: "I love you."

She smiled—but sad, so sad. "Love you, too."

She reiterated how I should call Max, a reminder I didn't need. Camille, a working mom, capable, competent, good with the details, in control. Strong. She and Artie would get through this fine.

"Here's a key. Go back whenever you're ready."

She placed the key in my hand, our fingertips lingering.

"There's something else," she said, rummaging in her purse. "Here."

A black and white wallet-sized print, a familiar image now matted and framed in my study at home; a version of it has been displayed in all the offices I've ever had. Taken in the spring of 1987, on a trip to New York with Max and all the other scriptwriters in the advanced class that semester, it's the three of us—Kunk, me, Camille—lined up against the fence on the observation deck of the Empire State Building, affecting Serious Faces: Kunk, in a leather jacket with aviators and a butt hanging out of his mouth, Camille all dolled up with a high frizzy mid-80s hairdo, and me sporting dark Ray-bans and a tweed sport coat with turtleneck sweater. The image made us look, everyone said, like a badass new wave band.

A brown smudge had soaked one corner of the photo. I pulled my eyes from the image of my young face back to hers in the car.

"He had it in his hand," she said.

"In—the basement?"

"Yes."

The brown stain—I emitted a sharp squawking noise, felt as though I'd lost my wind. "*No.*"

Her face said it was true.

I slipped the photo into my pocket. I broke down, leaning against the roof of the car. The sorrow passed, quick and humid like a tropical rain shower. "My brother."

Camille got out and held me tight. Kissed me, said all would be okay.

Watching her drive away, I wondered about Kunk's wandering consciousness, diffused into the ether. I hoped if he could see us now, he'd approve of a long gestating love affair coming—maybe—to fruition.

Thinking: yes, he might.

Or else simply awash in rationalization, and my desire to indulge an aching adolescent yearning forever unfulfilled, perhaps then as a bulwark against the grief I felt.

Kunk. A lost cause; suffering a personal conflagration as destructive as the one that'd befallen Columbia at the end of the Civil War.

Columbia had lived, though, lives to this day; Kunk, my pal, my mentor, my friend, does not.

I have to force myself, now, to think not of how he ended up but of a time before, when an innocent, a babe in unfamiliar woods, a sheltered college kid from a podunk town in rural South Carolina, got to become best friends with a Yankee jazz musician twice his age, and fifty times the life experience. How callow I must have seemed. And how right Kunk would have been to think of me that way.

The scriptwriting track in Southeastern University's Mass Comm program, which I began in the autumn of my sophomore year, included two official classes: Intro to Scriptwriting and Advanced Scriptwriting, but also Max de Lisle's special section called Feature Screenplay, open to students who'd excelled in the two prior courses. A moviemad child of the 70s and 80s, I was the only kid at my high school who seemed to care about the Arts and Leisure section of the *New York Times* that arrived via the mail every Thursday. Who lusted to see all the art movies and other cinematic esoterica that never played the Palmetto Grande, the theater in my hometown. Who had already tried his hand at writing scenes and dialogue, without ever finishing anything.

It'd been a shock to my system to cruise into Intro to Scriptwriting and see someone like Kunk, an older guy who'd been around; who hadn't been a teenager for nearly twenty years; and who, with his high widow's peak and wispy blonde hair reminding me of William Hurt, sat across from me at the conference table looking as though he ought to be teaching instead of taking notes.

All my other classes, they'd been populated by kids my age. What was a guy like him doing here?

My experience in the Intro class was a good one, but with stars like Kunk hogging the spotlight, my workmanlike scenes fell into the middle— I produced solid B work in the earlier exercises, but the final, five-scene project, maybe 20 pages total, had been judged the best in my group, but only the second best in the class.

That honor had gone to Kunk, who'd become the teacher's pet in a way I could never be—the professor and his favorite student seemed more like peers: Max, a Hollywood screenwriter for almost forty years, and Kunk, a working musician before his college career, one who'd gigged for almost quarter century, since, he said, his teenage years. Longer than I'd been alive. Even my fellow students made me feel like I hadn't accomplished anything of note in life yet.

Which I hadn't.

What I did possess? Literary and movie knowledge, however, which Max recognized right away, endearing me to him in a different way than Kunk. Unlike quite a few of my classmates I'd seen all the movies Max cited as examples, including the black and white ones from his time in Hollywood. I could reel off the names of not only directors, but cinematographers, composers, and most importantly, screenwriters: Ben Hecht. Joseph Mankiewicz. Robert Bolt. Wally Salt. Robert Towne, who'd written *Chinatown*, which Max felt might be the best screenplay ever. Trivia could only carry one so far, however, especially with cats like Levon Kunkle spinning his stories:

One scene Kunk wrote in class, he explained, had come directly from his prior life playing in joints as a pro musician. He described to the class the incident that inspired his work, which Max had read to us as an example of writing having what he called a strong voice, as well as verisimilitude:

"So I'm seventeen years old, in this club that faced a park, with these glass windows—the band set up sort in the window facing the club, so our backs are to the outside. This was in DC, not the best part of town, but I never cared about that—I wanted to jam, and these cats I'd been gigging with were smoking hot. But anyway, we're cooking, it's clicking, yadda yadda. It' summertime, so when we start at eight it's still light as hell outside. The way I'm angled with my bass, I can turn my head a bit, see all the way out into the park.

"And so I noticed these cats running—chasing each other, heading straight for the club. Next thing I knew, I see these flashes—one-two-three, just like that!—and the guy, bleeding like a stuck pig, comes staggering into the doorway of the club. The guys chasing him had shot the mother-fucker in the back, turned tail and bolted back across the park."

Everyone in the class, Max included, were leaning forward.

"The band stops; it's quiet for a minute. Then the guy screams I BEEN SHOT, Y'ALL, and everybody in the club goes apeshit. Cats go every which way, but I run over to check out this guy. To try to comfort him until the EMTs got there."

Kunk cleared his throat, traced a finger along his jaw. "Dude died, though. Right there in the doorway. Looking him in the eye. I didn't realize, at first. Thought he was looking over my shoulder at something. But that guy? He wasn't looking at nothing. Not anymore."

We all gasped.

This other older student, an army vet named Hoyt Bollard, asked, "Damn, Kunk—what'd you do?"

"Me? I'm playing it cool. Until I go back up on the bandstand and look over, and there's this perfect little bullet hole through the glass. Three feet from where my head had been."

Don't get me wrong, I loved to jam, his character's dialogue in his fiction- alized scene had read. *But I ain't gonna get shot for it.*

"Weren't you scared?" an enthralled Camille asked.

"Sister, I was so young, I didn't know enough to be scared. That," he said with a sardonic chuckle and shake of his head, "would come later."

Being in that first class with Kunk constituted my introduction to the slings and arrows of the writing life, of being poked and prodded and humiliated, but also enjoying moments of epiphany: the lightbulb turned on after someone pointed out a line or word that, in writing, had rolled right off the fingertips and which I thought had some snap and spice, only to find in the open classroom reading that the work fell flat, or otherwise felt deficient in conveying what I'd intended. A gut-wrenching process— laying oneself bare before a room full of strangers.

Before the blue piercing eyes of Kunk, no less.

Occasional embarrassments aside, though? I'd go back to those days in an instant.

Time of my life.

You never glean such wisdom in the moment, of course. Be here now, as the sage taught. It's all you've got.

"Nobody would say this crap. Not this way, anyhow."

Kunk made this trenchant and cutting pronouncement one day about a line of dialogue I'd written. The scene had been about a breakup, the boyfriend telling the ousted lover to get out of his apartment, to 'leave this place,' as I'd written.

"'Get out,'" he said. "That's the line." He snickered. "Or maybe, 'get out, you fucking bitch.'"

Nervous titters and stares from the female students, rightful. Max asked Levon Kunkle to tone down the sexist language, if he could.

Sitting in my hard chair and glaring slit-eyed across the classroom at Kunk, I felt three inches tall. "I don't see what's wrong with the line," I said in a drawling Edgewater County bleat.

"Because that's not how people talk, champ."

Camille, whom I didn't yet know, came to my defense. "But dialogue can't be how people really talk," one of the key tenets behind the construct of made-up people communicating with one another. Camille winked at me. "Right?"

I shot a look to Prof. de Lisle for confirmation. Max stood in his suit jacket and tie—always dress for success, this old man taught us—behind a lectern and in front of a white board on which he'd scrawl nearly unintelligible notes and phrases and important ideas. His arms folded, an impassive face taking in the discussion prompted by Kunkle's blunt critique. He also winked. "You bet."

"Here's the news," Kunk said. "The rule is that it has to seem natural even if it ain't. And what you wrote, bub, doesn't cut it."

Defensive, I felt desperate to offer a rationale. "But the character, he's in a state of—distress."

Kunk beamed a look of bemusement around the classroom."'Leave this place, knave!'" he proclaimed, booming, a theatrical voice. "Leave us be with our nettlesome scriptwriting!"

Laughter all around, including Max. Kunk got a coughing fit, his blue eyes streaming.

I fought back. "But it's high drama. *He's telling her to get out of his life.*"

Hoyt Bollard, a balloon-popper like Kunk: "I'll high your drama. Gimme a break."

Kunk recovered, sipped coffee and fixed me with a withering, hard-case stare. "Fine. Make it a line I can buy, though."

"Like what," I all but shouted.

"Anything that feels real, man."

Demonstrative murmurs bubbled up. My entire head felt hot. I noted that Camille, such a gorgeous, sophisticated young woman, watched Kunk with fascination.

"All right." Cracking and thin, my words compared to Kunk's seasoned croak came out like a mosquito's buzzing. A whining little shit, me. I felt six years old. "I'll rewrite it."

The teacher interjected, at last offering his opinion: "Well as they say, there's no such thing as good writing," fuzzy, gray eyebrows working overtime, "only good rewriting. So in that spirit, there's no shame to be felt. Give your pages another pass. Think about what we've said today. Accept or reject the criticism. It's a process," giving me an encouraging thumb's up, a gesture he offered all students in these moments of abject humiliation.

"But Mr. Kunkle here is right," Max continued. "Dialogue should replicate the actual rhythms of speech between individuals, but because normal discourse is simply too banal and filled with repetition and extraneous words, the substance of the language must be carefully chosen, on both a textual as well as subtextual level. But, too, must it feel real! And in this case, 'leave this place,' indeed, sounds like something out of a nineteenth century play rather than a contemporary scene. All right, who's next?"

Steamed.

But after I got over the hurdle of raw embarrassment, I knew they were right. When I went back to read the pages I saw what Kunk meant, and about more than that one line—this was the moment I learned to read things aloud to myself to see how they flowed. You'd think that part to be a no-brainer, reading dialogue you expected actors to themselves one day speak, but at that age you often can't see the trees for the forest, or however it goes. A process.

I had begun to miss writing articles for the high school paper. With journalism, you wrote up what happened and reported what people said. You didn't have to *decide* what happened, and put people's words into their mouths. Who knew that loving movies wasn't enough to make every description and line of dialogue shimmer like the gold of kings? I'd have to try harder, if I were to impress writers the caliber of Max de Lisle and Levon Kunkle.

WHEN THE TIME came at the end of the semester for me to present my five-scene project, in a crude staging of our work using class members as would-be actors—it constituted our final exam—the reception told me I'd not only improved, but arrived: my story about a guy trying to be a writer but hamstrung after being heartlessly spurned by his longtime girlfriend Nicolette touched hearts and resonated with the class, most especially Kunk. Instead of applauding at the end, he wrapped his knuckles against the table and said with an air of admiration, "God-*damn*. That hit me where I live."

Later, Max de Lisle, standing in the hallway with Kunk like friends rather than teacher and student, shook my hand. "Yours was the strongest piece in your group, you know. I certainly hope you're planning to take 521," the advanced class, "in the spring."

I turned to my fellow scriptwriting student. "Well, gosh—you taking it, Levon?"

Max and Kunk looked at one another and grinned. "What, *what*? Course I am, champ."

"Wouldn't miss it for the world, then," I said.

"Wonderful! Wonderful!" Max put his arms around both of us. "My day is made."

I'd done well in video production, in the b&w photography class, in one they called Previsualization, about planning and preparing media productions. But scriptwriting was, in the end, where I'd most excelled in the mass comm program, and truly found my sea legs. Why else would I stand there enjoying such approbation from the two men—the two writers—in the world for whom I now held such respect, if it weren't true?

Arrival, indeed. Or else, as I hoped, a precursor to liftoff.

"Hey, big-time." A couple of days later Kunk called after me, his voice echoing in the long, curving hall no longer bustling with mass comm students. "A word, if I could."

Adrenaline squirted—from his taciturn manner, I worried about lingering energy from our disagreements earlier in the semester. He still wasn't Kunk to me, not yet. "Hi, Levon."

He caught up. Sized me up. "So—your five-scene."

I panicked. Had no clue what to say. Felt humiliated, for no good reason. My throat clicked and clacked. "What about it?"

"It had snap. Showed a beating heart under the skin, brother."

Oh. "What—or rather, that means a lot."

Now late in the final exam week and with the holiday break incipient, we strolled outside and found a campus already beginning to empty out— a lonely feeling.

"Feel like grabbing a frosty mug or three?"

In those days I didn't drink much beer, but here was this cool cat giving me the time of day. Lying: "I was on my way to grab a cold one just now."

His theatrical voice bounced back to us from the wide, glass face of the hotel across the street: "Then let us leave this place and be off!"

After punching me in the arm, we crossed the six lanes of Convocation Avenue and made small talk about the class and the advanced section next semester, Max and his Hollywood career, competing students, attractive women we passed on the street, all the work ahead of us next year.

I'd never felt more grown and mature than that moment, walking alongside Kunk. Gray skies, autumn leaves swirling in the gutter, the afternoon traffic—dramatic. I wished I had a camera to shoot the scene. Not that I need a photographic record. It's all like yesterday.

He produced a pack of Camels and offered me one. I'd smoked all of two or three cigarettes in my life, those cadged from my mother's pack of gin-scented menthols, but hadn't cottoned to the habit. Despite having an inclination to decline, I instead heard myself saying, "Sure—you bet."

He lit it for me off a Zippo, cupping his hands close to my face, a gesture that felt bizarrely intimate. The smoke drew hot and bitter against the palette, raw across my vocal cords. Going easy, I managed not to cough.

The bar: A mainstay hangout and watering hole a block off campus with more character than charm, Upstairs West—an Upstairs East sister-establishment plied students from the opposite side of campus—sat empty but for a few afternoon warriors: refugees from the law school across the street, or the arena down the hill, the nether regions of which held not only the media classrooms and studios but also the College of Journalism, which I'd almost majored in, yet didn't—not then, anyway. I found the joint to have a sleazy vibe like out of 70s exploitation movie. In short, I loved it the moment I walked in, and not only that, but fantasized about shooting scenes in here for the student film I'd one day make. Low ceiling. Red vinyl booths all cracked and duct-taped. Dark corners.

His eyes twinkling like diamond chips, I watched Kunk order beers, crack wise with the bartender, work his eyebrows at some happening babes down the way, take his first foamy sip, inhale on the ever-present smoke colored his fingertips yellow, all in one rolling, elegant motion. Jesus, did he have charisma, personality, presence. He had a big handsome head, an older Mickey Rourke or maybe a younger Humphrey Bogart, and while his frame wasn't large, he nonetheless walked around the way guys do who know they own a room, that no one can beat them, who is wise beyond words and is calling the shots whether you like it or not. If nothing else, he had those blue eyes, so clear and shining. I'd been watching Camille get lost in them for weeks, now.

He called for his second beer already, but I nursed mine, early in the day for me. I supposed he didn't have any more classes or work to get done.

When our small talk dried up, I asked how he'd ended up in undergrad later in life than most of us currently enrolled.

He chortled and cut me a sidelong glance. "Long in the tooth? That what you're saying? Yeah. No doubt. But I had to try something new. Become someone different from who I was."

"Why?"

"Cause who I was, my friend, was-not-working."

I asked what had stopped working.

"What—you never get tired of 'you,' pal?"

I couldn't relate; I was too young. I hadn't *been* anybody yet, much less 'someone' from whom I desired to escape.

The only change I wanted to make to my life? Leave for good the tiny world of Edgewater County, the butt-end of the universe as far as I was concerned, and, like a Kinko's clerk would later say, a long, long way from Hollywood.

A MUSICIAN BY TRADE—HE'D been gigging almost 25 years, since his mid-teens; I'd had to ask what he meant by 'gigging' which blew his mind, but the only gigging I'd heard of was frog-gigging—Kunk explained how he'd never been much of a writer, neither of his own music, nor lyrics nor poetry nor prose. "And yet, all of a sudden. A writer."

To my ear, his scenes in class possessed gravitas and interesting, authentic language, made all the more dramatic being read in that smokescarred, lived-in voice of his.

I told him a version of that. He nodded. Drank in the compliment.

In retrospect, how hard was it for someone of Kunk's experience and street-smarts to shine? His peers, but shavetails and greenhorns.

In other words: Like me.

Kunk produced the Zippo lighter and flipped it open and lit the flame by snapping the tiny wheel with his long guitarist's fingers. He noticed my Walkman and soft foam earphones on the bar. "Whatcha listening to?"

I told him: REM, *Fables of the Reconstruction*. Or was it *Reconstruction of the Fables*? Side A read one way; side B, the other. Inscrutable, these modern rock stars. "I've seen REM twice now, including before they broke out."

"Whoa—that's really something."

Unimpressed, he ignored REM and expounded about jazz and improvisational music. How he had no use for punk and new wave and whatever you called it. How he'd been a musician since he was "old enough to know better," which made him bust a gut and have a coughing fit.

"So why mass comm?"

He met my eyes. Smiled. Seemed to appreciate my forthright question. I'd honed my interviewing skills on the school paper back home in Edgewater County.

"Figured getting out of Atlantic City," where'd he been living for years on a salary of steady gigging in the clubs and casino lounges, "was one good way to find myself. On one hand, I'd been there too long. Since like '71."

"You were sick of it. You felt held back by your surroundings."

"Hell, I always felt like that about AC. But you get stuck places, sometimes. And the reasons why, they ain't always clear."

He raised his eyebrows, dropped the volume on his voice-box full of sand and glue. "But in the end, getting out was also a good way to not find myself in pieces, if you know what I mean."

"You owed gangsters money?"

"Not exactly. But I had accrued a debt. Yeah."

"Really, now."

"I got the hell outta there, didn't I?"

I know I sounded dubious. *People getting cut up into pieces, huh? Cement shoes? The stuff of mobster movies, of imagination—of fables.*

But fable enough to make me all tingly—could I steal Kunk's story? Or borrow, rather, from Levon's life as fodder for my own narratives?

Was that allowed?

I didn't have anything else. I hadn't lived. An inner debate for later, much later.

"That's crazy stuff. Like in a movie."

"So maybe there's your answer as to why I'm here, making little movies."

Camel smoke pluming from his nostrils and in a confidential voice, the storyteller—after all, we fancied ourselves writers—continued his narrative about a boss's girl, a warning from a friend in the know, and a threat to get his ass out of town before the shit hit the fan.

"And I don't mean tomorrow, my boy CC tells me. He means like, five minutes ago."

"Dang."

"Dang is right. I had enough time to get some shit together, hit this guy up who owed me fifty bucks—which I didn't fucking get," shaking his head like *Can you believe that?* "And then I hit the slab running. Four on the floor. Not a dry eye in the house. And et cetera."

As connections and synchronicity reared into the foreground of my consciousness, my forearms broke out in chicken-skin: The first movie I'd driven myself forty miles to Columbia to see, five years before when I'd gotten a learner's permit and my father's reluctant permission, had been Louis Malle's *Atlantic City,* running at our city's one small art-house theater, the Main Street Bijou. I'd felt so alive and adult that evening. The movie, praised to the high heavens by Siskel and Ebert, had played moody and atmospheric and captivating. They served coffee at this theater near the university, which I'd never encountered at the mall cinemas; all the moviegoers appeared so sophisticated. The next spring I'd been the only kid on my block rooting for the Malle to win Best Picture over *Raiders of the Lost Ark.*

"You ever see *Atlantic City*?" I asked.

Kunk looked at me like I had three heads. "What the fuck you think? I lived there for years."

"No—I mean the movie. Louis Malle?"

"Louie *who*?"

I felt stupid. "The—uh—movie. With Burt Lancaster?"

At the mention of the actor, Kunk lit up. "Oh yeah yeah yeah, I remember when they were shooting that around town," sounding like he didn't, not really. "My granddad, damn if he didn't take me to movies all the time. Burt Lancaster, he always said, now that's a real man right there. Never seen it, though. Was it good?"

"It's an amazing movie." Was it, though? I backed off a bit. "Well— solid script, anyway."

"What's so great about it?"

I felt put on the spot. I wasn't sure how to articulate why Atlantic City seemed so accomplished—it had been the first movie I'd driven to Columbia by myself to see, so of course the experience had been memorable. But I couldn't tell him that.

Instead, I bullshitted my way through by talking about mood and atmosphere and certain cool shots I halfway remembered. I felt fraudulent —I didn't yet have the chops. I loved movies, could sense when they were great, but lacked enough of the language, the mature ideas. I fell back on lessons from our professor. "Strong story. Strong sense of place and, and conflict."

"Does it resolve?" This element, Max emphasized, was crucial to a successful and memorable stories.

I nodded. "You bet it does."

"Terrific, champ. So anyways: I shoved my basses in the old Malibu, my suits, shaving kit, two boxes of animal crackers, gassed up and pointed the hood ornament south. To my brother. Where else was I gonna go on short notice and way low on cash? Family. Thank god," he said, "I hadn't burned any bridges with Douggie."

"And so you ended up here." I couldn't get my mind around some-body moving here from somewhere else. All I wanted to do was leave.

"Am I here?" Amused, he belched and called for the check. "Yeah. It's certainly starting to seem that way."

TAKEN with Kunk's baroque narrative of romance with a mobster's doll and the threat to cut him into pieces, a fast decision to bolt the place in which he'd lived and worked for years—what a life he'd had, like a char-acter in a story!—I strolled, lightheaded, back to my dorm room.

Once there I tried writing up his anecdote as a short scene: A guy on his last leg, standing on the windy Atlantic City boardwalk, being told that his ass was on the line because he'd banged the girlfriend of a still-living, quite real Mafia capo I'd heard of named [REDACTED].

When the time came early in the next semester in 521, I felt afraid to read my scene aloud—Kunk would see how, bereft of my own ideas and experiences, I'd mined his life as a source of drama.

That day I lied to Max. Said I hadn't completed the assignment. Both he and Kunk shot me through the heart with their looks of pained disapproval.

"I'm so disappointed in you, Mr. [REDACTED].[1] You'll have to make this up to the class, yes?"

"I will, Prof. Max."

Their mutual disappointment in me, worse from Kunk than Max, seemed to hang in the air for the rest of the session. Everyone else's work that day sounded amazing.

I felt so angry and annoyed with myself for not having had my own cool life experiences on which to draw, as well as the courage to read what I'd stolen from Kunk, that I stuffed the pages I'd chickened out on reading into the square metal wastebasket beside the stairs leading to street level from the Mass Comm basement concourse of classrooms. I peered down at the crumpled work, which in those pre-PC days I'd typed on a hand-me-down Smith-Corona that vibrated on my scarred wooden dorm room desk as though powered by a lawnmower engine.

The only copy. I'd never get those pages back short of recreating them from memory.

Morose, I retrieved the crumpled ball of paper and stuffed it into my backpack.

Using his material felt like stealing a girlfriend. But what do you want? Dude made a hell of an impression on me, even when I might have doubted either his veracity or sincerity, which generally wasn't too often. Not then, anyway.

The doubts, they'd come soon enough. Not as many as later. But some.

---

1. Like the criminal referenced above, my own name, for reasons perhaps less obvious, is also redacted to avoid facing culpability for the various emotional crimes as described in this manuscript; otherwise, in a journalistic sense, perhaps the idea of 'anonymous source' comes into play as well.

Over Christmas break, I packed up a duffle of clothes and moved home to Tillman Falls, as it turned out for what would be the last time. I didn't realize it then, but doors to my past had begun closing in ways for which I felt ill-prepared.

My high school sweetheart Nicole Braden, who'd so cruelly shredded my heart near the end of senior year, also came home from the College of Charleston. She called me a few days before Christmas to 'get together,' as she put it.

I did not welcome this.

I'd tried so hard to put her out of my mind. You never forget the first girl with whom you fall in love, with whom you make love that first glorious, awkward time. But despite not having any relationships since then, it hadn't been difficult to get over her: The women in Mass Comm seemed so interesting, diverse, and cosmopolitan. Nicole, lovely and sweet and intelligent as she might have been, didn't care much about movies. Not a good fit.

I still smarted, at times, over being dumped. Two years, now. I'd been on dates, but nothing had come of them. The right girl hadn't waltzed into my life, heralded or otherwise. Or actually she had, though neither of us realized it. One of us still doesn't realize it to this day.

On the first date with Nicole, which had been the year after the *Atlantic City* milestone, I'd taken her to see the Oscar nominee *The Verdict*, Paul Newman's grim acting triumph, a somber, visually dreary look at an alcoholic lawyer's last chance at redemption. The two sixteen year-olds holding hands dead center constituted the youngest viewers in the theater.

Nicole, bored out of her mind, especially despised the ambiguous ending, an undeniable professional triumph for the character, but at a personal cost. Newman, listening to the call from his former lover Charlotte Rampling to ask for another chance. Newman, conflicted, unable to answer.

The phone, ringing.

And ringing.

And ringing—until a smash-cut to black. Goosebump city. I swore that one day, I'd end one of my movies like this too. This act of theft would take place so far in the future, I rationalized, that no one would notice how brazen my theft from Sidney Lumet, David Mamet and Paul Newman.

"I've missed you," she said, standing in her front yard where we had spent so much time, had kissed, had declared eternal love. Her hair, different. A new set of frames. A different Nicole. "We used to laugh so much."

I agreed we had gotten along well.

A rush of emotion, raw and hot. An old euphemism: "Want to take a ride?"

"Yes."

I hesitated—this seemed too good to be true. "Really?"

"*Yes.*"

I drove her over to the rear parking lot of the James F. Byrnes High School football stadium, where hidden from view we could do anything we wanted. Within seconds we began making out like we'd done on innumerable occasions.

We'd lost our virginity to one another on a blanket in the woods instead of the backseat, an unforgettable afternoon—birdsong and pine needles and Nicole's supple, nude body beneath mine, her eyes flashing and her soft moaning, over so quickly and then lying with her until I was able to do it again. How we'd pledged our love that day, forever. How forever sounded far away, how only the moment at hand had meant anything in the end. We were kids.

"What a cool surprise." More naughty little code words. "You want to snuggle?"

"Here?"

"Sure."

"No—I don't."

"Oh."

"I mean—yes, of course I want to. I've missed you, like I said. But now I want it in a bed. Like *real* lovers."

"Yeah. Of course." We smooched some more.

But the vibe, it troubled me. "What brought this on?"

She smiled, shushed, kissed and slurped.

I stopped her. "Why now?"

"You ask too many questions." Demure, she pulled back and crossed her arms. "I just wanted to try again. I—I don't think we were doing it as well as we could've."

"Really, now."

"I've dated a few guys now—and—well."

All the times I'd fought not to think about her—my girl, my first lover —with others, and here she sat, rubbing it in my face.

Envy.

Sorrow.

Pain.

I blurted that I got it; I understood. "You dragged me out here to tell me how lame it was?"

She flipped dark hair, longer now and quite fetching, out of her dark eyes. "I never thought that." Now she turned huffy. "Did you?"

"No." A lie—I had no further experiences by which to judge our carnal grappling. "You still rate right up there," a line stolen from Barry Levinson's *Diner*. "I've been with lots of girls, now."

Silence.

The windows, fogging up.

Sitting there with a hardon for the ages, leaking fluid through my jeans, I wanted her both physically and otherwise. But would I serve as Nicole Braden's sloppy seconds. "But this, it feels weird."

She fixed her hair, barely mussed. "Take me back."

"Take you back? You must be kidding."

"I meant take me back to my house."

Regret surged into me—I'd turned down not only the first and only woman I'd had, but the only woman I'd known in this intimate way. "Wait —I'm sorry."

"You should be."

Tears welled, like the first time she'd broken up with me. My voice broke. "It's just—confusing."

"This was a terrible idea."

The curbside lined with vehicles, her family's home bursting to the rafters with aunts and cousins and kids running wild, we sat in the driveway with the engine running.

Nicole went to get out. "Have a good Christmas."

Should I try to salvage this? What have I done?

Casual, as though nothing untoward had occurred. "You want me to call next week?"

"Pardon—?"

"What's going on for New Year's?"

Nicole looked like I'd asked if she wanted to eat shit. "Do you *want* to call me?"

"Tell me about these other guys, first."

"Hey—high school's a long time ago now. Grow up, would you?"

This, the real goodbye.

I sat until the front door closed behind her, the Christmas wreath with its big, red bow wrapping it all up real nice and neat.

I drove home sighing and frustrated—but she had been right. Way past time to let go.

Back at my own house, also filled with folks, the thought of being with Nicole had been so comforting I didn't want to go inside. With Dad's people gathered for that side of the family's get-together, my mother had likely been into the single malt scotch for hours—well into it. Also, I didn't want to face everyone and field their questions about life in college at Southeastern. But I didn't have anywhere else to go.

After that interminable holiday break, I swore I'd never move back to Edgewater County again. Maybe long enough to pack up my movie poster collection, the rest of my books and videos. But after that? Moving on.

J anuary found me back in the dorm for what I'd hoped would be my last semester in on-campus housing, alongside a roommate, Chip, whose role in all this remains unimportant because for an entire year, I rarely saw him—picture a gray shape of a human with a huge question mark where the personality ought to have been.

But the next chapter and a new place to live lay months in the future. For now, the scribe, stoked and focused on getting back to the writing game—MACM 521, Advanced Scriptwriting, spring 1987. Compared to this course, all other classes printed on my schedule seemed limp and meaningless.

Using some Christmas money from an aunt, I prepped for Max's further scriptwriting tutelage by sending off for a boxful of screenplays, ordered from a place called Script Shack in the faraway land of Los Angeles: *Chinatown. The Deer Hunter. Body Heat. Network.* And yeah, maybe in a lingering echo of Nicole, *The Verdict.*

The morning of the first class I sat on my bed looking at the stack of scripts, these paragons and exemplars of the form. I opened *The Verdict,* paged to the end. I wanted to see how Mamet had written that striking, bleak, unresolved moment.

Disbelief—no ringing telephone at all. However *The Verdict* read on paper, and it read well, no ringing telephone and cut to black.

Stunned. That had all been Lumet, the director, as it came to me in a flash.

Never forget that movies are a director's medium, as Max taught. *The scriptwriter often only provides the framework. It is a collaborative art, to be sure. But the director has the final responsibility, and ability, and tools, to shape the art into its final form. The director becomes, then, the author—it's called the auteur theory.*

So I needed to be a director, in other words. To have control. Yet I had a great deal yet to learn about screenwriting. And all other aspects of the art and craft.

Maybe, a voice whispered—the faint, faraway call of maturity—all I needed to learn was patience. Hard to hear that voice at the age of 20, though.

AROUND THE CONFERENCE tables that subbed for desks in Max's classroom sat friends and comrades, but also a few unfamiliar faces—kids, I supposed, who'd taken 321 a year ago instead of last semester, or had otherwise gotten waivers on the prereq.

The first table featured Alice Faith Westmoreland, a scrubbed and shiny preppy girl who kept a smug and superior air about her, an ice princess; Jaime Marzol, a half-Hispanic class clown-type who was a theater major; Pran Thi Trinh, a taciturn Asian with English as a second language, but who in her serious demeanor seemed in the initial days to be the strongest writer at her table; and Digby Cathcart, dirty blond hair straight and limp hanging around her long face, a tall tennis jock majoring in MACM, she said, with an eye on a future media career after retirement from sports.

Other than Pran, I did not take this group seriously—not a film scholar in the bunch except perhaps for Jaime, with his cinematic knowledge seeming to begin and end with Eddie Murphy movies.

Table 2 featured the most eclectic and potentially competitive mix: As though 'Alice Faith' wasn't precious enough a name and personality, Cynthia-Anne Goforth, a J school senior taking the class as an elective, sported the blonde hair, heavy makeup and regal bearing of the attractive telegenic airhead TV anchors taking the place of the Wise Old Men of broadcast journalism, and as such was sure to go far in her impending newsreader career; Darren Scott Wojcinski, at six-five and 300 pounds, and years before Comic Book Guy on *The Simpsons* would culturally codify the stereotype, loomed as the resident genre geek, the kind who'd often wear a taut and nearly threadbare *Empire Strikes Back* T-shirt he'd owned since eighth grade, a sharp enthusiastic cookie and a delight to talk to; Thaddeus Blanchard, our lone African-American writer, a studious no-nonsense straight arrow who dressed in khaki and oxford shirts and Weejuns and spoke in a precise, affectless accent I couldn't place; Freddie Baumbach, a guy with a rep: one of those types who made 8mm movies in high school, one of which an Arts Commission grant had paid for—a grant awardee at the tender age of sixteen!—and a MACM star already, a David Lynch acolyte of unknown writing talent, with whom I'd discussed movies and found him to be a formidable and threatening rival to my own depth of knowledge; and Opal D'Alessandro, a rich rebellious bad-girl type whose family owned D'Alessandro's, the best Italian restaurant in the downtown area. Opal, who wished to be billed, so to speak, as just Opal, presented as a Sicilian New Wave chick draped in black and fishnets and who slathered on crazy eye makeup, but a true natural beauty underneath the affected persona, a lovely one-named cinnamon girl—"Like Cher, or Madonna?" Kunk had teased; "Fuck you, you creep," she'd tossed off in disaffected rejoinder—but whom I figured for a lesbian, and who would go on to write disturbing scene fragments I thought Mr. David Lynch at the head of her table ought to consider directing. An eclectic group, but they seemed to get along, with Thaddeus B later emerging as the standout writer.

In fact, after the first assignment Thaddeus's work had been read aloud to the class by Max as an exemplar of how-to-do-it-right. "Every element speaks of a sure hand on the typewriter. Bravo, Mr. Blanchard."

Last but far from least, the table of yours truly included Brenda LaRose, the 'pale princess' as Kunk called her behind her back, a quiet, shy red-haired girl I'd barely noticed in 321; Connor Rush, a tall, geeky handsome cat who seemed like a sophisticated, intelligent and refined guy, and who I'd later discover to be my first gay friend; a rakish raconteur named Levon Kunkle; and a sassy l'il gal with the name of Camille Grahl, a glowing goddess.

When I first walked in that class, no question at which table I'd sit.

Oh!

Camille!

She had been so fetching across the room in 321, beautiful and naturally glamorous in a way that a plastic fake like Cynthia-Anne could never equal. Camille's family had money, lived up at Lake Hollings.

In not so many words, she would relate one afternoon how she labored in the shadow of her brother, an accomplished dancer with the Alvin Ailey troupe in New York, a rising star who'd been featured in a *New York Times* Arts & Leisure spread. She explained how growing up she'd always felt like someone's younger sister instead of her own person. Wanted to pursue a career in media. Wanted to maybe write or produce, but in the sense of the Corporate Media track, as was Kunk's plan.

Corporate media? Fuck that. Westward ho, thought I. Hollywood, or bust.

The more I got to know Camille over the next few weeks, the further I fell for her elegant Southern sensibility, level head, and self-deprecating misapprehension of her own luminosity. Also, she possessed a terribly tender heart—she loved animals, volunteered with a privately owned shelter that adopted out stray pets, and said she performed other community service work. An angel, in other words, which I called her and that she denied with cheeks aflame.

Angelic or not, Camille Grahl provoked a stirring inside that transcended hormones and sexual attraction.

And after she whispered to me early in the semester how, as much as Max loved and praised Kunk, she thought I was the best writer at the table?

A goner.

❄

As for Brenda, until I got to know her better I perceived her as an odd duck. With kinky hair pulled back, always doodling on a legal pad, sighing and stealing glances at Jaime, an admittedly handsome kid with Latino features but fair skin and blue eyes—mom or dad must have been Caucasian—she did little to catch my eye.

Knowing we had the Ten-Scene project at the end of the semester, a group effort we'd stage to a higher level of professionalism than our five-scene work in the Intro class, I felt that between Kunk, Connor and I, our table held the writing advantage. I figured Table 1, on the other hand, had a real ringer in Jaime—not only an actor with some chops, but a comedian to boot. If they were wise, as Kunk and I discussed in private—like comrades—Table 1 would shape their material to suit his skills.

Hoyt Bollard, a guy who'd taken 521 last year and a MACM vet—again, a bit older than the rest of us, but not as much as Kunk—and another department personality by whom I felt intimidated, explained to a gaggle of us in the canteen: "How your Ten-scene plays in the room with the audience goes a long way toward a win," as his group's script had indeed accomplished the prior spring.

Kunk shot me a look over the rim of his paper cup of machine-dispensed coffee: *Remember that, kid.*

The first peak of that semester's writing class, however, came not in the writing of scripts or Max's lectures or the films we'd screen and discuss, but instead on a spring break trip to a place of fantasy for me: New York, where our professor would introduce us to the world of show business in a visceral and primary way—but a trip that would also alter forever any chance I might have had with the glowing goddess.

other, toasted on early afternoon cocktails. "'Going to
—*where?*"

"*Nuh*-New York," I said with a stammer. It happened in
moments like these. She could be unpredictable.

"For one of them classes of your'n?"

I tried to explain how we'd meet real scriptwriters, the executive
producer of one of the daytime soaps, and other important activities.

At her most dismissive and supercilious: "Ain't never heard the like in
all my life."

Done with classes for the week, I'd come home on a Friday afternoon
to do laundry for free and beg travel money only to find her with a few
already under the belt, like the early-bird frat boys chug-a-lugging at
Pappy's and the Upstairs West and every bar in the Old Market on the
other side of campus. My mom would have fit right in.

I had to stop myself from screaming, *It's a dream come true for me to go to
New York! Can't you see that?*

Instead, I explained how Max had connections in show business, had
been a writer for the movies and TV. Max's most notorious claim to fame
had been in co-creating an *Andy Griffith* imitator called *That Dog Don't
Hunt*, which had starred James Franciscus as a fish-out-of-water Yankee
sheriff trying to manage the quirky sitcom denizens of a fictional Georgia
town called Dogwaller. Remembered now only by TV trivia freaks and
connoisseurs of so-bad-it's-good entertainment, the show had lasted only
half a season. More than the writing, Max insisted a curse on Franciscus,
veteran of innumerable failed TV series, had been the show's downfall.

I left out all those details, of course. I admired Max, who'd grown up in
South Carolina but had left to take on Hollywood by storm. He'd had the
words *Written By* appear before his name on screens the world over. His
accomplishments, to me, stood tall.

"What's this really all about?" Lidded eyes slicing sidelong through the blue smoke, she clinked ice cubes and made a ring of lipstick around the filter of a freshly sparked Virginia Slims Menthol Ultra, the scent of which I'd forever associate with receiving my mother's kisses. "Teacher ain't queer, is he?"

The matronly, southern lilt on the epithet 'queer' made my skin crawl. Relations between us had been icy since the beginning of my adolescence, but for reasons different from the stereotypical teen against parent dynamic—in our case, more personal. "I'm going to ignore that—like I said, Max is a great man. A writer. And besides, he's married."

Scoffing. "That don't mean nothing to them Hollywood types. My heart is still broke about Rock Hudson."

I laughed *ha-ha, yes-yes, mother dear*, and loaded a set of stiff bedsheets into the washer while Mother puttered around in the kitchen, grumbling and mumbling.

Knocking a plastic cup off the countertop onto the tile floor, a clatter barely noticed, she said, "Truth be told? Your Daddy and me, we wish you'd quit with that foolishness and get into another major."

"Excuse me?"

"You ought to be in business school. It's what he wants you to do."

"Too bad," I all but shrieked. "It's t-too late."

Blowing smoke in my direction, stubbing out the slender white tube, she propped hands on bony housedress hips. "Who's paying for it all? It's him, ain't he?"

A sense of going nowhere, fast. I needed extra money for the trip to New York, not a lecture on what I should and shouldn't be studying. What did she know?

I managed to ignore her insulting invective, tried to further explain the importance of the trip, how we'd get exposure to a number of show business environments—backstage at a Broadway play, meeting with the producer of a daytime drama, having breakfast with a writer who worked on Letterman.

She rolled her eyes, slurred and sputtered and p'shawed, but in the end wrote a check to cover the plane fare and lodging. I doubted she remembered doing so the next day. I hoped she noted the transaction in her register.

Later, Daddy, in my corner: "I heard y'all earlier."

"You did?"

Nodding. "And if it'll help with your education, I'm all for your trip. For what it's worth."

"I've never been more excited about anything." Shaking his hand, I lowered my voice. "Appreciate your support, Daddy."

He seemed taken aback. "Son—what else are we here for?"

As we rose from the tarmac into the breaking Carolina dawn on an Eastern Airlines DC-10 that roared away from the minuscule Columbia airport bound on a direct flight to Newark International, a couple of the classmates, Jaime Marzol in particular, possessed the wide-eyed looks of human beings who'd never experienced liftoff in a jet—including me. I'd been a few places in my life, but not an iconic mega-city like New York—Nashville or Atlanta, I suppose, had been the closest.

Feeling unreal at the sensation of flight, I watched as the attendants served a light breakfast, some of which I could stomach. After they removed our trays, Kunk, Freddie and I unbelted ourselves and cruised to the back smoking section of the half-empty aircraft. A little queasy with motion sickness, I didn't want to huff any more tobacco than necessary, but I didn't want to miss any chance to hang out with Kunk.

I still looked up to him, thought him an elder. But something about what Camille had whispered about my writing abilities had stoked fires of competition in my young belly; it conjured notions of Paul Newman and Jackie Gleason shooting championship pool. *"I'm gonna beat you, fat man."*

I'd never even seen *The Hustler* in full, only bits and pieces on a late night television broadcast, but Scorsese's contemporary followup *The Color of Money*, on the other hand, I'd paid to see three times the weekend it opened—after *The Verdict*, I'd become a huge Paul Newman fan. Only years later would I finally see the original pool shark epic in full, and finally grokking the dynamic at play in both pictures.

A youthful, chipper flight attendant came by, smiling through our cloud of smoke. I'd taken to the habit, now puffed five or six cigs a day. Kunk and I, we would stand smoking together before class. Come in together, sit down together. Team Kunk.

"Are you gentlemen comfortable back here? May I get you anything?"

Kunk ordered a screwdriver. "Make it two," he said, winking at me.

"Three," Freddie added. "Let's get this party started."

"Very good."

It was now seven-forty in the morning. Seemed like I was in for a long weekend.

Another dude who unlike me seemed comfortable in his own skin, Freddie Baumbach sat kicked back with his Converse propped up on the seat behind Kunk, squeezing his eyes at the flight attendant. Freddie had already seemed high all morning, extremely stoney and silly back at the terminal, as though he'd stayed up all night. I couldn't imagine getting stoned in the morning—or drunk, for that matter.

As such, when the drinks came I only sipped mine—we had a long day, and weekend, ahead. No worries; Kunk finished my drink for me.

He spent the rest of the flight in gregarious conversation with a series of passengers, people known to him and otherwise. Kunk had worn slacks and a pressed Oxford shirt and a jacket. His manner, his dress, his voice—a monument, living and breathing.

A movie star.

Furthermore, Kunk and Max held themselves like men who understood how to travel in style to a place like New York—with class, insouciance, and above all, maturity. Among my peers—other adults—I lit up a cigarette after all.

WHILE KUNK AMBLED back to the lavatory, Freddie moved over into the seat next to me. Eyes bloody and slitted, a devious smile danced along lips he fought to keep pressed together. "So—[REDACTED]. That's your name, right?"

Terrified, I nodded. "That's what they call me."

"Hear you're planning to take sixteen millimeter in the fall."

I couldn't fathom how he knew this intimate personal detail. "That's the plan."

Nodded, sighed and went *mm-hm*, like a doctor assessing a patient's presentation of a boil in need of lancing. Patted me on the knee. "I see."

Freddie, like Alice Faith, came from money, and carried an air of privilege. I heard they were dating, though I hadn't observed any direct evidence of this. In any case, prior to this exchange Freddie Baumbach acted as though I hadn't existed, what he'd now asked me probably eight more words than he'd said in total over the last year spent knocking elbows in passing along the arc of the media college halls. Had introduced me and Kunk to his younger sister Marcy one afternoon on the street outside the coliseum. A raven-haired punk rocker and pal of Opal's, she and her yuppie brother made for an odd couple. Like Opal, Marcy had terrified me with her confidence and heavy eyeliner into silence, but I'd never forgotten her.

But the film production class, yes. Scriptwriting enjoyed current mission critical status, but once I got to make a film, I knew the many an Edgewater County nights spent dreaming about would at last come true: actors, a crew, a professional editing bay.

"Your concentration's film?"

I shrugged and nodded.

His cheeks bloomed with color. "As in—you want to direct?"

I sucked on my Camel and tried to let the smoke plume out of my nostrils the way Kunk would. Coughing, I said, "That's the plan."

A woman in business attire sitting in the row ahead of us waved her hands around and glared back over a padded shoulder.

"Aw, that's too bad. I mean—I don't want this to sound all arrogant? But I don't wanna get into some pissing contest, like, six months before the class even happens." He drifted off, leaning across me and peering down his nose through the tiny oval window at passing clouds. "Wait—what were we talking about?"

"The class. Sixteen millimeter. In the fall."

"Oh—right. Just saying, there's only room for one big swinging dick."

What an entitled prick. "Meaning what?"

"Just laying down the gauntlet. Fair warning, is all I'm saying."

MACM had been like this for me so far, the Freddies and Hoyt Bollards and Kunks, all of them so self-assured and worse, knowledgeable about cinema. I'd been James F. Byrnes High School's only certified movie nut, the only kid who dreamed about seeing movies, dreamed of making them, of filling audiences with wonder and awe like he'd experienced at, say, *Close Encounters*, or later at more esoteric, less crowd-pleasing populist fare —his awe extended to less populist fare, like the dark endings of DePalma's *Blow Out* and *Five Easy Pieces*, artsy fare like *My Dinner With Andre* and Werner Herzog's *Fitzcarraldo*, the first and second movies this young aficionado experienced at the Main Street Bijou. No one back home in Edgewater County loved movies as much as that boy—maybe a grownup or two, I guess, but he didn't know them. But now in MACM, students came complete with passion, knowledge and sometimes actual work under their belts, as in the case of Mr. Arts-Grant Freddie.

Instead of rejoining us, Kunk had moved a few rows up and squatted down talking to Camille, whose delicious golden buttery legs were crossed, one high heel dangling in the middle of the aisle. They both let loose with gales of laughter. Impish, he tickled at the instep of her foot. Camille slapped at him, playful.

Tending toward the conciliatory, I said, "Look—I don't consider the class a competition. In fact, aren't we supposed to all help each other?"

Freddie, pursing his lips in distaste. "A real Boy Scout."

I told him, yeah, I had been a Scout. "Order of the Arrow, in fact."

Snickering. "Hard to see what you and and a streetwise cat like Kunkle have so much to talk about."

"We're both writers, I guess."

"Ah-ha," snapping his fingers. "And I'm the filmmaker. Get it?"

"I wish you'd just relax. We can all make films. And be friends."

"I'm looking for good people to work with," he finally got around to saying. "I saw some of your photographs last semester at the Student Showcase. You've got a good eye, especially for black & white. Was hoping you were interesting in DP-ing on my shoot."

Glowing at the unexpected praise—the last role I anticipated for myself was as a Director of Photography—I nonetheless demurred. "I'll be directing my own movie. Thank you."

"Have it your way, sunshine."

As the attendants shooed us back to our seats for the descent into Newark, I felt troubled. I didn't care about competition, only to get the chance to work in the medium. To make a short film. A calling card. An entry for festivals. A culmination of all this school work and preparation, of a dream I'd had since I understood that movies got made by the hands of human beings, not hatched full-formed from a mysterious, unseen artistic continuum a young, inchoate intellect like mine could but imagine only in the vaguest and most unsatisfying of terms, and who felt great terror at the thought of being responsible for exposing expensive film inside a whirring camera body.

In fewer words? As I'd soon find out, the most trying competition would occur not with Freddie but myself, and my own expectations.

I don't know if it was the screwdriver I sipped on the plane as an eye-opener, or the first mindblowing hours spent in the pulsing breathing cacophonous city at the center of the known universe—a concrete and steel hive of color and smells and faces and bodies scurrying this way and that, autos and cabs and buses and trucks like platelets in the throbbing gushing bloodstream of some great angular beast lying prostate along this jut of land, this island—but as our first day wore on, my perceptions became scrambled, jumbled and, at times, all but overwhelmed. I felt as though mainlining New York right into my veins. Too much information.

The sight of the city on the horizon as the plane winged into the airport had itself been like a vision I could barely comprehend, but being inside its canyons offered another level of hallucinatory disbelief altogether. Once on the streets, Gershwin chimed in my ears—not Woody Allen's *Manhattan* opening sequence set to 'Rhapsody in Blue,' but rather 'An American in Paris,' my eyes dancing like Gene Kelly's feet across the myriad sights: the pulsating movement of the bodies and the vehicles, the wispy gray clouds across the sliver of sky visible overhead, an elegant slender woman all in black hailing a cab, street vendors, hustlers outside the strip of porno theaters outside the Port Authority bus station where we disembarked from our airport shuttle from Newark, the bigger than life ads ringing Times Square. Not like in the movies, though. All of it bigger than life itself.

"So this is New York," I heard Brenda say as we stood clustered with our luggage on the filthy worn sidewalk like an island amidst the flowing river of people. "Smells worse than I expected."

"At last, we have found El Dorado," I commented with a Spanish accent low enough that no one could hear, in case I sounded dumb or no one got what I meant or Jaime became offended.

"Train your eyes to find this color." Max, pointing to a jaunty blue beret on his head corralling his wispy crown of white hair, Doc Brown reborn as a scriptwriting guru. "Now let's get moving and try to stay together."

Our fearless leader trooped us five blocks down Eighth, taking a right on 47th to the Hotel Edison, home base for the weekend. As we trudged and weaved through the throngs on the sidewalk and bombarded by sensory input, it really did feel like the center of the universe, New York. No wonder they came from all over.

Crowded, though.

Too crowded, maybe. I grew up amidst pine trees and dirt roads. The thrill and juice of the experience so far had my gut at times teetering on the precipice of anxiety. I kept reminding myself to breathe. New York.

OPAL AND THADDEUS had home court advantage, to a degree: a branch of her Italian family had emigrated to South Carolina from Little Italy itself, and she still had 'people,' as she put it, living in the old neighborhood. Thaddeus, who'd lived in Brooklyn until the age of ten or so with a grandmother, had cousins he wished to visit. They both seemed so knowledgeable and relaxed about what trains to catch, how to hail a cab, where various landmarks were, as though they be-bopped up to New York every weekend.

Jaime, even more of a country bumpkin than I, also staggered around bugeyed with excitement. Convinced he could simply swing by NBC and wrangle an audition with Lorne Michaels, Jaime talked a mile a minute, fixated on the future and making sure not to miss any opportunities—who knew when he would afford to come back, as he kept saying.

A silly notion, I thought—we were kids. All the time in the world. Besides, Eddie Murphy might have been young, but Michaels wasn't going to sign some schmoe from Red Mound, SC, to write and perform for SNL. They'd laugh, all right. They'd laugh him out of there. But running on the heavy fuel of ambition, no one could dissuade Jaime. He'd have to find out the hard way—on his own.

I watched with interest as Brenda LaRose had begun following him around like a puppy. Romance seemed to be blossoming on all sides of me —Kunk and Camille, inseparable but for when Kunk and Max huddled to discuss which way to walk or where to go for lunch, or when to assemble later before we headed off to a Broadway show. Furtive handholding, here and there, between my main man and my fantasy squeeze.

Damn him.

Envy, simmering in my gut like a crock pot of pork chops, but competing with Levon Kunkle on the romantic playground? This, a fool's errand. Besides, this was New York—everywhere I turned, a beautiful woman. Camille, out of my league anyway. They all were.

"Did you see that shit? TV's 'Alice' snubbed us." Hours later, Freddie, roaring drunk, yelled on the sidewalk near the stage door of the Broadhurst theater, turning heads in the theater district crowd. "SNUBBED, I say."

"What an effing tool." Darren, potted as well. We were all tipsy, but they constituted the most egregious cases. Honking like geese, the two of them. "Take back her motherfucking Emmy."

We'd been backstage with Gavin Bouknight, an elderly character actors Max knew from his days working in the industry. The thespian, robust and broad-chested, appeared onstage in a current smash-hit Neil Simon play, an autobiographical one about the writer's Brooklyn boyhood, with, indeed, Linda Lavin starring as the matriarch of the clan. Bouknight had generously offered to visit with his old friend's class, also accompanying us to dinner at the legendary showbiz restaurant Sardi's.

The moment Freddie referenced had come when Lavin appeared at the actor's dressing room door, quite stricken to see a fresh-faced group of college students clustered in her costar's dressing room; most especially when Digby blurted, "Oh my god it's like, like *you*," after which the famous TV star turned tail and bolted down the creaky narrow old back-stage hallway as though the devil at her heels.

"Settle down, gents," Max said to Freddie and Darren. "Let's remember to put on our best faces for Sardi's."

Gavin stood nearby, grinning and amused by our youthful antics. "What an execrable hypocrite your teacher has become. Forty years ago, he and I drank this town dry. Sardi's will survive our onslaught of merriment."

"Thanks, Gavin," Freddie slurred. "You're all right."

"You're not driving anywhere later, I hope," the actor said, waving away a cloud of Freddie's whiskey breath. "God help us all."

My gaze caught that of Pran, a teetotaler who appeared mortified by everyone's behavior. We'd had a few good conversations in the canteen back at school. Working on a screenplay about her family's escape from her native country during the fall of Saigon, no wonder she seemed such a serious person. The idea of being a refugee from a war and having to settle in another culture? Might as well ask me what walking on the moon felt like. Freddie and Darren—and maybe all of us—must have seemed coddled, boorish, weak, and quite unserious.

At Sardi's I grabbed at my chance to talk to Bouknight about his career. I cited memorable film noir appearances in two 1950s classics, also extolled the virtues of his performance in the play, as well as a recurring role in the first and second seasons of *M*A*S*H* portraying a visiting general tormented, but in the end won over, by Hawkeye and Trapper John's anti-authoritarian antics.

Blustery and dyspeptic, Bouknight waved away the compliment. "Any old coot off the street could've played that. More about wiggling jowls than truly acting, as in the theater."

"So the play—that's a good part, right?"

A smirk, sardonic, faded. Max had said Gavin would likely be Tony-nominated for his work. His eyes shone. "Indeed, my boy."

"Do you have a favorite role?" I asked. "Or movie you did?"

"The part that pays the rent is the working actor's favorite. Is there romanticism in show business that's earned otherwise? Oh, most certainly, but it's also only a job. Perhaps the Hank Fondas and Jimmy Stewarts and Bogeys and Brandos see it differently than we background players. You think?"

"It's beyond my imagination."

He chortled, shook his head with bemusement, patted me on the forearm like Freddie had on the plane. They could all see through me, how immature and idiotic I truly was. "Nothing's beyond the human imagination. Take a look around at the grandeur of this fair city and tell me it isn't so."

"I've never seen anything like New York."

"No one has." A cloud sneaked across his face. "But never forget, kid—it's all bullshit. Write it down. Do you have a pen?"

I did, along with a small notebook I produced from the pocket of my blazer.

"Here." He took the notebook and pen, writing down IT'S ALL BULL-

SHIT on the first page. "Tack this up on the wall at home. Make it a mantra. You'll sleep better at night."

I had no idea what he meant.

Bouknight went on to describe working with a few of the great directors of the 40s and 50s, a couple I'd heard of like William Wyler, but hadn't seen the films. "I was fortunate," he explained, "to be cast in an Academy Award winning film at the very beginning of my career." He'd played the bit part of a soldier waiting for a plane ride home at the beginning of *The Best Years of Our Lives*, the title of which had always sounded to me like some dumb soap opera. I told him I'd have to check it out.

About that time Camille and Alice Faith sashayed over to command Gavin Bouknight's appreciative attention, and I was satisfied to yield; I knew had to share.

AFTER DINNER we bid Max and Gavin adieu on the sidewalk, and the students, raucous, drunk, and loud, staggered en masse back to our hotel a block away.

As we moved through Shubert Alley, I glanced back to see Opal dragging along in her Doc Martens and stylish leather jacket.

"C'mon, girl," sounding like the country boy I was, but sloshed enough to not care, for once. "New York awaits us."

A sweet, warm smile, a soft countenance on the normally crusty and cantankerous chick who, with her dramatic eye makeup and spiky hair and withering stares of condescension, so intimidated me. "You have such pretty eyes. For a boy."

"So do you."

She cocked an eyebrow. "For a boy?"

"Yeah," giving her a friendly slap on the forearm. "I mean, no."

She ran her hand with black fingernails over my smooth pink cheek and through my thick hair, a bit shaggy, me trying to look cool. Before the trip I'd gone to the mall to a hip urban clothing shop, gotten myself some duds like the collarless shirt I wore.

Sighing. "I wish you weren't such a dork."

"Um," I said. "Maybe I'm not."

"Hey," she responded.

I stole a glance over my shoulder, saw that the rest of the group had already jaywalked across 45th. "Hey, what?"

"Nothing." She draped her arms around my neck and gave me a quick little smooch, spun away and called after the others to wait for her.

Inside the Edison everyone seemed to scatter, leaving me with no running buddy. Alone on the elevator up to the room, I felt spun—Opal D'Alessandro had made a pass at me. I didn't consider her my type, but hell, it was spring break, right?

Back at the room I discovered Kunk had hit the Smiler's on the other side of Times Square for a six-pack of Heineken cans he'd left iced down in the bathroom sink. I thought of psychotic Frank Booth castigating poor Jeffrey Beaumont in *Blue Velvet*, which had been my favorite movie of the previous year, but which few people besides Freddie seemed to get. I cracked a beer, drank half of it in two swallows.

We had another full day ahead tomorrow, but drunk as I was, once the other roommates returned and we crashed—Connor Rush and I sharing a double bed, and Kunk and Camille the other, platonically of course, as they'd insisted to a skeptical Max—I could hardly nod off to sleep.

Being in New York.

Thinking about Opal.

The sweetness of her kiss.

It had all seemed so incongruous with the rest of her persona. Perhaps her attitude at breakfast the next morning would guide me.

Connor snored beside me, his long bony frame in a fetal position; I thought about the fact that he seemed gay, and for a while it freaked me out. Was I sophisticated or not, though?

On the other bed, a lump had formed from the spooned bodies of Kunk and Camille.

I seemed to snooze, but a spotty, shallow rest, my brain alive with images and a sound-choked dreamscape filled with all the sensory input of the day swirling around—voices, colors, the roar of jet engines, the honking of traffic, applause in the theater and the burbling laughing cacophony of voices that'd been the dinner crowd at Sardi's. Not a good way to recharge spent batteries.

I seemed to wake up, or so I thought, when I heard a rustling. I peered through the dimness. Shapes on the bed next to mine. Movement. Soft moans.

"Oh, I love to fuck," I thought I heard Kunk say.

Panicking, I grunted and flipped over, making something of a ruckus of sheets rustling.

"Oh, no," I heard Camille whisper. "He's awake."

All became quiet from their side of the room.

I made my self breathe in, deep, and release in a long slow exhalation. Then again. I faked a light snore. But my heart, thudding—Kunk and Camille were doing it. Right there. In the next bed.

I felt ill.

"They're both sacked out, angel face," I heard him say in a gentle hush.

"Hurry." Camille, breathless. "Come for me baby, and let's go to sleep."

Kunk, more like a sigh than a syllable. "Oh, yeah."

A siren howled outside as a cop or ambulance roared by on Eighth Avenue. The light from the city bled into the room, but I could no longer see them coupling beside me.

I didn't sleep a wink the rest of the night. Or, perhaps I did. All I knew? The most beautiful woman I thought I'd ever had the privilege of knowing and desiring had been ravaged on a bed not three feet from where I lay in a half-drunken stupor.

Well—so that's that with Camille Grahl, I guess. Maybe between this and the Opal overture, I'm being guided. I could only hope.

The wind on the observation deck of the Empire State Building blew stiff and crisp. My vision cloudy and doubling, Kunk, Camille, and most of the others possessed the bloody eyes of revelers in similar hungover condition. Nobody seemed to have slept much. Small comfort.

We'd met with the Letterman writer for breakfast. Max had been disappointed with me—hurting and sleep-deprived, I hadn't come up with a question. Despite being hungover, Kunk—of course—bantered with the guy as though old friends.

As for Opal, now shy and withdrawn. Wouldn't make eye contact over the rim of her coffee cup. Oh-well, I thought. She's a weirdo anyway.

Levon Kunkle, a wicked, knowing smirk, squinted against the sun. "Hating life this morning. You?"

"I still feel drunk."

"Yeah—there's that, too." He snapped his fingers. "But how'd you sleep?"

Camille glanced in my direction and forced a small, expectant smile.

"Like a rock."

"You did?"

"After Sardi's, it's—all a big blank." I layered in a few details. "Man, I was so unconscious, dead to the world, I didn't even dream. I'll bet I snored y'all out of there."

Kunk, nodding and satisfied. "Probably other way around, champ."

A theatrical shrug. "Wouldn't know."

Kunk and Camille, sharing secret smiles. The little sneaks.

"Like a rock. I slept. All night. Didn't hear a thing."

A flash of recognition on Camille's face—*he knows*. Then both of them laughed at me.

Suffused with self consciousness: "What?"

Kunk, waving me over. "C'mere."

I went to the two of them leaning against the cyclone fence, the great city falling away from us on all sides. The diffused light from a scrim of clouds creeping in across the sun fell gentle on the shoulders of our overcoats. Plaid scarf flapping in the wind, Kunk placed me on the other side of Camille.

To Freddie he said, "Hey, Scorsese—get over here. Capture an indelible image of the three caballeros for me, wouldja?" Kunk handed him a disposable Instamatic camera.

Freddie, ever the director: "I want to see dignity. You're feeling proud, yet pensive."

I had no idea what to do with my face, but I couldn't let him think I wasn't hip. Framing our faces with my hands: "A medium shot, I would think."

Freddie sneered at me like *yeah, yeah.*

Kunk, emphatic: "Serious faces. Smiles are for chumps."

Freddie peered through the cardboard camera. "Ready?"

"*Yes,*" we said in unison.

The caballeros. I felt so honored to be part of a clique. Had to admit that technically, I was as close as could be to Kunk and Camille—I'd been a part of their first time making love with one another.

Sigh.

Freddie snapped the photo. "Let me get a safety."

"Coverage," I prompted.

Camille asked, "Serious faces again?"

Kunk sparked a smoke. "Serious as can be."

Freddie snapped the photo right as Kunk blew out a lungful, which in the prints I'd later make would form a mysterious, spectral cloud around his head. Later I would slave, frustrated, in a darkroom all afternoon trying to dodge the fuzzy blemish until I realized what it was—a blurry, permanent mask covering the lower half of his lived-in face, never to be removed. When I look at the photo now, I don't even see the smoke. All I see are strangers from my past.

WITH OUR FLIGHT home in the evening on Sunday, the last afternoon in the city, without scheduled events, unfolded clustered and clique-d into groups allowing us to explore the city as each unit saw fit—museums and the park for us, The Strand bookstore for Brenda; for geeky Darren, a swing by some comic book and sci-fi store called Forbidden Planet; Freddie sought out esoteric video stores, and in Thaddeus and Opal's case, off on their own visiting with family.

So much for the quick smooch from Opal, who remained distant. It didn't feel quite like Camille redux, but still offered a confusing, perhaps missed opportunity on the trip to connect with her, a fellow filmmaker.

All parties must end: At five we gathered our pile of luggage on the floor, a group of exhausted college students slumped in the chairs, the Hotel Edison lobby like a microcosm of the great city outside, in a seeming eternal pitch of mild bustle. Tired, all of us, but most seemed sorry to be going back home already. New York's energy had grabbed us all by the throat. And in my case, the city seemed like a place—the place?—I should plan to be on a more permanent basis. But for now, goodbye.

I'd be back. Sooner rather than later. Once I got my thoughts and plans squared away, I'd break the news back home: NYU for grad school. And thereafter, only God knew how high I would fly on the auteur's path.

From the cold concrete of New York to that of my looming dormitory building: with classes again underway the scriptwriters now began discussing the final group project, the storied Ter-Scene. A thirty to forty-page script, this group effort with one's table mates offered a test of skills as well of fragile, nascent friendships.

A big deal.

Professor de Lisle, who also taught playwriting in the theater department as well as his scriptwriting sections, emphasized as Hoyt Bollard had the importance not only of the writing but the eventual performance of said work. This unusually stressful final exam, given in an auditorium across campus with judges and invited guests, happened in public.

In a flash, April arrived and left only weeks before the due date. Our group found itself still in the prewriting stage, lounging and spitballing in the canteen, drinking two-ounce paper cups of coffee that only cost a quarter apiece.

An idea I'd thrown out gained traction: a kind of meta gimmick wherein this lonely, sad and drunken writer, alone in his musty abode, begins interacting with characters who come to life and help him sort through his problems.

Traction, yes; but I had to sell this to the group.

"Writers writing about writers?" Kunk, unimpressed. "Sounds pretty lame."

After New York we all had a better sense of each other, and no one, especially Kunk, seemed afraid to shoot down my ideas.

But Brenda, with whom I'd become comfortable if not quite yet close, defended the pitch. "They say write what you know. We're writers struggling to come up with pages. It kinda makes sense in a cool way."

Kunk, having none of it. He didn't care much of Brenda. He thought her some shy dumb kid, had said as much to me. Also, he rued the nasal, valley-girl lilt of her voice; said it reminded him of the muted, mumbling teacher's voice in the Charlie Brown cartoons.

"You people need to get out and live some," he said. "That's what you want to write about—the real world, spinning around. This? It's an in-joke about process."

"So I guess it should be about a middle-aged Yankee bass player?" Connor, gay, the first such person with whom I'd developed a friendship, came loaded with a wellspring of sardonic attitude. His gayness, not quite openly acknowledged as of yet, didn't bother me, but his constant snark got on my nerves. His sensibilities and manner suggested a sensitive person at the core, however, and he could be funny as hell to boot. "Who goes back to college like Rodney Dangerfield in *Back to School* and —and—"

Kunk's eyes turned dark like a bulb blowing in a strand of Christmas lights. "Who're you calling middle-aged, pal?"

Connor pursed his lips, kept his sarcastic tone. "Why, you, dad-dad-*daddy*-o."

Everyone laughed.

Kunk, unperturbed, leered with a thin smile disguising what I took to be mild disgust. "Old enough to know better, Mary," which I knew to be an oldschool gay-baiting epithet.

Connor's face, shining and scarlet. "Go—kiss a duck."

"There's a signup sheet for that in the Dean's office."

Connor slammed his notebook shut. "That *my* name won't be on."

"Oh, *snap*," Kunk mocked. "My loss, I guess."

The girls sighed. Kunk leaned back with his arms behind his head, gazed to the ceiling. Brenda doodled. Camille opened a textbook from another class. Connor started shoving things into his backpack and making to leave.

"Gentlemen, please." I steered our listing ship back on course. "If my idea stinks so bad, let's hear some other pitches. Connor?"

"*What.*"

"Sit. Back. Down."

Reluctant, he did so, after sticking out his tongue at the back of Kunk's head.

"Now: Levon?"

"Not I, said he."

No one else had a better idea. "All right, then. Let's flesh out a story arc using my idea."

Not waiting to hear from anyone else, I tossed out possible story details and suggestions. Since we'd visited the production offices of soap opera *One Life to Live* while in New York and met with its showrunner for an overview of that corner of the industry, perhaps our writer could be working on a daytime drama, I mused, with his characters manifesting before his eyes and informing his own script and allowing it to come together, a script that's about the people who are writing the script—a kind of circular type-deal. The ideas now tumbling out unbidden, I described the shape and flow I thought the ten scenes could take, pausing only to drop a quarter in the slot and get another coffee, which I downed in one gulp.

Everyone sat in silence.

"Well?"

Kunk said, "I get it. I get it. It's good."

I started getting excited like when caught up in a strong, involving movie. "Sounds okay?"

Camille nodded, laser-beamed her bright, beautiful eyes around at the others. By far the weakest writer in our group and stressed about her load of other classes like Video Production and Editing, she remained content to coast along and let the rest of us do the heavy lifting. As far as I was concerned? Camille Grahl could coast along on me all she wished. "I like it," she gushed. "*I like it all.*"

Kunk, nodding and engaged: "We have this guy at one corner of the stage with his desk and typewriter, other action upstage from him. All takes place in his apartment, but the imaginary characters, off in their part of the stage, they could be anywhere. Does that make sense?"

"Exactly. In any case, with our limited resources it'll have to be the words that set the scene, and not the scenery."

"I was going to say the same thing." Connor's voice came strained and quiet, a residue of the earlier tension. "I took an acting class last year, and we played scenes on a bare stage in my class," he said. "They worked fine. Just fine."

Kunk grinned, shot him a *what what what* look. "You just volunteered to dress the set."

Connor, not making eye contact, scribbled on his legal pad. "I don't mind."

We went around the group outlining ten possible scenes until we ended up with too many ideas, whittling down until we all could agree. Feelings got hurt. Two of my original scenes got the axe, but I didn't fight for them. No time. It didn't matter—the work would be mine in a way none of them could say. Despite what I told Freddie on the plane, perhaps I suffered a touch of competitive spirit after all.

WITH FINALS WEEK UPON US, our pages began to come together as if by alchemy. Each of the group had written two scenes, which Camille volunteered to type into a nice, neat draft. We did a table-read as a group to tweak, revise, and finalize.

It played.

Happy and pleased with the work, rather than feeling competitive I enjoyed the camaraderie we developed in crafting this piece of interesting writing.

Our writer-protagonist confronted his come-to-life characters, all of which embodied physical manifestations of his various failures: an alienated relationship (Camille contributing her experience with an old boyfriend who'd betrayed her with another friend), an estranged family member (Kunk telling me one day about his brother and him not getting along, me saying, let's use it for the script, him firing up a menthol and saying, *yeah yeah, fuck yeah*, pounding the table so hard all our notebooks jumped), and finally a minor 'character' from the writer's script within our script, a dog mentioned only in passing as scene decoration.

But the dog turned out to be crucial: The dog walked in announcing his own list of grievances, a moment intended to be the huge laugh-line but also a raw emotional peak, and intended to make an already surreal scenario cross a new line—raising the stakes, as Max had taught.

About that time the writer's real girlfriend shows up at his apartment door (Camille, in a duel role), and their moment of rapprochement offers the redemptive quality any decent dramatic climax needs to be effective.

Curtain.

Simple, neat, circular, poetic, apt, and, in my esteemed opinion, quite a clever piece of student writing, if I may say.

The best part? Seeing the idea, my idea, coming to fruition. A powerful feeling.

I don't remember now what the inspiration might have been for the story conceit, but I thought that whatever its precedents or influences, we had concocted a jape with some not-bad jokes and a plot and character arc that paid off in simple but satisfying ways. I thought we had a hit, if not possibly the winner.

Our last hurdle? A title.

Suspension of Disbelief, a meta idea sure to impress our teacher, had been Brenda's suggestion. We all agreed that it dovetailed with the fact that we were being artistically self-referential anyway. Our Ten-Scene, now all set.

Two days before our performance, I met Kunk for lunch at Pappy's, a burger and wings joint up the hill from the media classrooms. Home of the two-dollar pitcher of draught beer that came with a giant green olive in the bottom—Pappy, a waggish paternal Marine veteran and all-around chiseled tough guy, called this drink special "the poor man's martini"—this venue offered a time-tested college neighborhood atmosphere in which to either relax or study, the efficiency of which depending upon the boisterousness of the other patrons and amount of alcohol personally consumed.

We tapped plastic cups and drank. My writing partner said he thought we should all get together the next night to do a last read-through in anticipation of our looming performance, but otherwise remained circumspect about our script.

Instead, Kunk wanted to lay on me in enormous detail how he'd already started thinking about his feature-length project, which those of us going forward on the writing track would complete in the fall semester, a special advanced section open to those with bona fides and credentials and prereqs. The elite. The Hoyt Bollards. The Kunks.

And me.

He described the plot of his script. At first I thought Kunk was joking, riffing on what Connor had said at our contentious session the week before: a guy, at age forty, decides to utterly and completely spin his world in a different direction by ditching his old life and career and starting over as a college student. Spinning his life around, which is what the individual plot points are supposed to do in a screenplay, but in his case he would use the concept as the jumping off point for his character; he'd working-titled the piece *Learning Curve*.

Pointed, probing curiosity. "Thriller? Romance?"

"What, *what*? I just told you."

"The conflict, I mean."

"It's—inherent in the concept."

"Fish out of water."

"Say what?"

"Guy goes to college with people half his age," clearing my throat. "And encounters—conflict."

"The conflict," stabbing at the table, "is that he's changing his life."

"Who—or what—is the antagonist?"

"I don't fucking know. He makes peace over the whatever, overcomes the obstacles, gets a grip on the problems, gets a great girl. And everyone lives happily unto eternity-like. You know the drill."

"Who's the girl?" I affected a snide voice this side of Connor's drawl. "'Camille'?

Kunk killed his cup of cheap beer. Eyeballed me. "You little buttmunch —*what do you care about Camille*?"

I couldn't believe the way I'd said her name, dripping with onerous and obvious jealousy. "Just busting balls," a phrase picked up from Kunk himself. "Nothing."

"Anyway—the conflict is the conflict, and the ending'll be what this character decides the ending ought to be. The theme is, if you want something bad enough, work hard enough, you get it. He's going to get what he wants. What he deserves," extending twinned yellow fingers in my direction. "Got it?"

"And if destiny or fate or whatever should decree otherwise? And it all *doesn't* work out?" Why was I pressing him? I suppose giving back the way I'd been given. Having worked up the courage to take on Kunk, I ran with it. "What then, sir?"

"Destiny can eat me. You understand?"

I didn't, but since this was Kunk asking, you can be sure as hell I nodded, cadged a smoke from his pack, and told him that all seemed clear; all made perfect sense. Only later would I realize how much of my challenging attitude sprang out of the deep, burbling tarpit of fear in my gut at the thought of writing a feature-length script. Whatever its merits, Kunk's idea existed as one more than I had.

The atmosphere in the auditorium, a former middle school near campus now used as a Southeastern University classroom building, sizzling and electric. More so backstage.

The judges sat in a cluster down front, with family members, friends and supporters arrayed around the curving rows of ancient, wooden fold-down theater seats, with the three writing groups sequestered in different classrooms of the repurposed facility.

Our group had drawn the long straw, so to speak, and won the coveted final slot—the berth of champions. Max knew we were the best—he'd read them all. I could see the truth of it in his twinkling, proud eyes. A big night ahead.

I wasn't alone. Brenda whispered to me in the hallway outside the auditorium, "I really think we have a winner." And gave me a sneaky peck on the cheek.

I'd grown to like her, but like the rest she already had a boyfriend, one who had the unfortunate luck to be a part of Group 1. Ah, Brenda. Cute enough, but Camille, the one for whom I still foolishly pined.

Everyone had family in attendance but me and Kunk. I hadn't asked my parents to come. The very notion of my mother blowing fumes into Max de Lisle's face and making a fool of herself was mortifying enough without seeing it happen.

"I'm losing my mind." Connor, getting into his outfit as the troubled writer and protagonist, a role I'd assumed would go to Kunk. But he'd wanted to play against type by assuming the brief role of the writer's agent, along with one of the fictional characters who come to life, both of whom, luckily enough, required the wearing of a suit. My dog costume had posed the most difficulty, but I'd gone to the Army-Navy store on Main Street, a source of Halloween accoutrements, and bought a Snoopy mask to portray my character with as much verisimilitude as possible.

Kunk, dressed in his best dapper gray suit, primping, slicking back his coarse hair, a widow's peak like Nicholson. "We'd better have a slug of liquid courage."

"Meaning what?"

He produced a fifth of vodka out of a backpack, along with a Jack Daniels bottle filled with iced tea instead of bourbon—a prop for the writer's desk. He broke the seal on the vodka, took a slug, grimaced, passed the bottle to me.

"Straight vodka?"

"Not as much odor."

I sipped, cold-hot on my tongue and in my stomach; a slight gag reflex. "That," I said, coughing, "ought to do me."

"Yeah, yeah," Kunk said. "A bracer's all you need." He took the bottle back, gurgled it once, then again, wincing. "One or two," he croaked.

Connor choked down a good swallow. "Lord have mercy. That burns like fire."

"I'll pass." Camille, nodding to Brenda in solidarity. "Save it for the after-party, boys."

Already a goddess as a matter of record, Camille had dolled up for her part. Looking at her I thought I'd faint, would have given anything to take her in my arms. And Brenda, a doll-face in her own way, wild red hair teased out and a gaze made mysterious and sensual by stylized, heavy eye makeup.

"Life is just a party," I heard myself say.

My dream-girl snapped her fingers at me. "And parties weren't meant to last. Now let's break a leg without getting so drunk first that somebody breaks a leg."

WHILE THE OTHER groups performed their works of art, we ran lines from palmed cheat-cards. These plays were expected to be slick, but with a rather limited rehearsal schedule, only as slick as could be faked. It's not like we all didn't have other classes.

The other scripts played decent enough, none with the basic idea or snappy dialogue or inherent drama—dramedy, rather—that ours possessed, though props to Jaime for an engaging performance in a funny-sad story about a kid struggling with questions of religious faith, a piece without much payoff or earned emotion.

Group 2's opus had been a short story adaptation and went off without a hitch, but the literary, Kafkaesque tale about a guy turning into a beaver simply didn't feel like a full meal, only a sketch stretched out to ten often inchoate scenes, with several lines intended to be crowd pleasers falling flat. An ambiguous, artsy ending featuring Freddie dressed in a full-sized beaver suit complete with an enormous, weighted tail wobbling behind him as he soliloquized lay in the room like a bad smell. I could see looks of disappointment ranging to mortification on the faces of the cast, and a shock of recognition on his before he'd even finished.

I chuckled—he would crap himself when he saw me parading around in the Snoopy head. I hadn't known. A coincidence, I would say, and it would be the truth.

"We are going to kill this thing," I said to Kunk while we waited for our brethren to clear the stage of their props. "Slay it to death."

Backlit by violet stage lights, vaporous in plumes cigarette smoke, he said in a low voice, "Nah, kid—not it. It's *them* we're gonna kill," gesturing out to the murmuring audience. "After these two stiffs, ours is gonna seem like a sitcom."

A peek out at the audience provoked a cold stab in the gut. "Should've had another drink after all."

Kunk chuckled. He'd been onstage thousands of times. Maybe not as an actor, but still. "Relax, champ. It's nothing. Nothing's at stake."

Was he kidding? "This class, it feels more like everything to me. Not nothing."

"You gotta treat it like the opposite. When nothing's at stake, you can get out of your own way. And let it flow." He mined playing a bass line, his eyes closed. "If you played music, you'd know. Writing, theater—it's no different."

Getting out of my own way. How much sense did that make? None—until it later did.

At last we got the all-clear and rushed to arrange the pieces of our sparse set. I put the writer's desk on a corner of the stage, the electric typewriter (mine), a lamp, the bottle of faux bourbon.

I shielded my eyes and glanced out at the audience—we didn't have the luxury of a curtain to hide our scurrying scene-setting. In full view, I twisted off the cap and turned up the bottle, gurgling sweet tea.

A gasp. Murmuring. Nervous laughter.

Max covered his face with a liverspotted hand. "Oh, lord."

"First of the day, boys." I took another slug. "Gotta lubricate the machine."

"Bullcrud," I heard a voice say, one belonging to Hoyt Bollard. "That's tea I brung y'all from Bojangles."

I held the bottle out to the audience, which now included the entirety of the class, all gathered to watch us. "To all the writers in the audience tonight—peers, comrades, worthy adversaries." And bubbled the tea again. "We're all winners tonight."

Applause, cheers, but also jeers broke out. One of the judges, F. Gordon Blake, an elderly novelist and professor of creative writing in the English department, leaned over to Max and whispered.

Max, nodding and beaming, pointed in my direction—what he said about me I could only imagine, but his face appeared pleased. Even proud.

I KNOW A STORY NEEDS CONFLICT, but here all unfolded as Kunk had foreseen. Gales of laughter at our antics and witty banter. A winning Ten-Scene. A badge of honor.

Afterwards, we received congratulations from most of our competitors, but not all. Photos were taken—the whole class, our winning group with Max, the group with Max and the judges, and one more of our group only this time with me wearing the Snoopy mask, which even thirty years later is still packed away somewhere in the attic.

Backstage, our victorious crew again passed around the vodka. Connor had been fraught with nerves, but still made a perfect straight man to the various outlandish characters we'd concocted, a stable body at the center of our swirling solar system of mugging and joking and slapdash slapstick verbal comedy; now relieved of the stage, he guzzled vodka, hooted and hollered. Best part? Laughing and now getting along fine, Connor and Kunk seemed to at last bridge the generation gap and sexual orientation gap.

Alone in the classroom that had served as our dressing room, I packed up the last of our props into a cardboard box and went to change out of my costume, white pants and a white T-shirt meant to suggest Snoopy's fine furry coat. The others had gone out to various vehicles with plans for us all to reconvene down in the Old Market for revelry late into the exam-week night, or so I thought.

I heard a noise and turned. Connor, having come back in, shut the door behind him with a quiet click. "Hey, now."

"Forget something?"

Connor, swaying. "We pulled it off, didn't we?"

"We did, buddy." I wasn't all that self conscious, not after rooming with him in New York, but with haste I slipped on my fresh T-shirt, navy blue with the *Back to the Future* logo.

"What a rush."

"No doubt."

A moment of silence. Connor stepped forward with a canted head and a curious expression. He draped his arms around my neck. Fell forward against me.

"I'm in love with you," he said.

"Dude."

Kissing me.

I staggered back, pushing him off me. "I'm—I don't do that. I'm not—that way."

He blinked, held out his arms, let them drop. "But I thought—oh."

"I assure you not, good sir knight. I mean—I don't care. But—no."

Bewilderment; a flash of anger; mortification all played across his face in rapid succession, as though an emotional color-wheel spun across my friend's slender features. Slurring his words, the alcohol gone to his head: "I must've gone *crazy* there for a minute."

Not angry, only surprised. "Don't sweat it. It's—it's our secret."

"Well—I'm gay. And I'm not keeping it a secret from anyone anymore."

"That's awesome. But I'm just not."

"No duh." He shook his head in distaste. "Like I don't see you oozing every which way over Queen Grahl."

My cheeks flushed, hot and sudden. "Not at all. She's Kunk's girl, anyway."

"Keep talking."

He grabbed his backpack and hurried out, shooting me a final aggrieved look. "Sorry."

"Dude. I don't care. Honestly."

I hesitated, though, and let him get some lead time on me so we wouldn't have to walk up the hill to the dorms together.

Alone again, the excitement—and weirdness—of the evening rang in my ears. The world outside our theater seemed torpid and dull, far too quiet. I wished for a life filled with ten-scene triumphs The mini-drama of

Connor's attempted seduction seemed only part of a larger tapestry of meaning. I hoped he wouldn't let this ruin the night for him.

Alas, Connor never showed up at McHaffie's pub where we'd convened to celebrate. I told the others, which included a smattering of good-natured fellow students, that I thought the vodka had gotten to him; how he'd seemed tired and wrung out. They believed me; no reason not to.

Joking and laughing with my crew plus Jaime and Darren, who seemed to be using their group's loss as an excuse to get roaring drunk, we had a wonderful, long, boozy night. From what I remember, a singalong to "We Are The Champions." That sort of celebration.

But I felt isolated from the others, still. Ran out of dialogue. At one point Camille saw me standing by myself in the corner, staring up at a TV screen playing a west coast spring-training baseball game. She came over and hugged me. "We make an awesome team," she said.

"Who?" I asked, trying to sound hopeful, but I suspect coming out bitter. "Us?"

She bussed my cheek, gave my backside a naughty squeeze. "All of us, silly."

I agreed, watched her stagger-step back over to her boyfriend Kunk, who grinned and raised his glass to me.

I returned the gesture, though doing so left me feeling empty, confused, and more than a little lost on what should have been the best night of my college career so far. I half-seriously reconsidered having spurned Connor —gay or straight, alone was alone, perhaps more so in the light of the otherwise celebratory mood.

O nce I knew for sure I'd have a place to live off campus—as I'd sworn months earlier, this would be the first time I didn't go back home to Tillman Falls over the long break—I decided to knock out a couple of dull electives in summer school. Lucking into an apartment close enough to bike or walk, an old brick duplex built God knew when, sealed the deal. Although a bit of a roach motel, the duplex possessed enough convenience and character to make up for the flaws.

I felt what seemed a transitional period upon me, a veil through which I had begun passing into adulthood. Happy now to have a kitchen, I looked forward to freedom from the SEU dining halls.

And, I got a more personable roommate in Neill Wiegle, a neo-hippie and Deadhead with whom I'd made friends in an American Lit class the previous year. I'd run into him one day in line at the student union cafeteria where he'd said, "Oh, hey, [REDACTED]—where you living this summer?"

"Haven't a clue."

"Got a lead on this place off-campus, but I need a roomie."

I felt a tingling in my belly I'd later come to understand was intuition. "Let me know the details."

"Sweet."

The whole stoner hippie act aside, Neill had seemed pretty sharp. I wasn't into the Dead or smoking dope, but I didn't want to go back to Tillman Falls to live in my old room, not ever again. No, to return would be ridiculous. Commence, thy cutting of apron strings.

As my new roommate and I moved our stuff in, I felt a twinge of nostalgia at leaving the dorms, my first home away from home, but only a brief one. They didn't call the institutional, concrete tower the Penitentiary for nothing.

I could only get to know my roommate so much, however, for about the time summer school started Neill bolted out the door for Grateful Dead tour, which would take him up and down the East coast and into the Midwest for almost a month. It was fine; in his absence, I wanted to take advantage of my privacy to write. Not only that, I longed for amorous female companionship, and wondered if having my own place would help in generating romance. Who was I kidding—between getting a job and toiling through the intensive, short summer school classes, there'd be no time.

THE FIRST WEEK after moving I got hired at one of the corporate multiplexes in town, an eight-screen shoebox setup in a mid-market mall an exit or two out of downtown. No question on getting a job; I'd need rent money. Ordinarily my parents paid for all my expenses, but my mother, angry I'd refused to move home for the summer, told me if I was so grown up now, I'd be on my own, at least until school started again.

I didn't mind. As a kid I'd held plenty of jobs—a summer working for old Burnham Sykes at his used car lot, another year as a gopher for Gaston Bundrick, the editor and publisher of the *Edgewater Advocate* local newspaper, and finally during my senior year at the Palmetto, the downtown movie theater in Tillman Falls where'd I'd experienced many cinematic thrills.

My dad had instilled in me a decent work ethic, one I knew I'd need to realize my dreams; the previous experience in the business had cinched the job with Hank Halvorsin, the manager of the multiplex. Besides a paycheck, I would also have free movies to enjoy. All set.

Wait—in my case not only to enjoy.

To study.

That was the rub—for me this wasn't a tedious part-time job, more like an internship. I was paid to usher, but there to to watch; to learn.

The Columbia summer soon overstayed its welcome, breezeless, humid air heavy and immobile over the modest cityscape. Downtown felt moribund, the Old Market with its beer bars the same-old, and campus a near ghost town. Excitement guaranteed. I was glad to have a job indoors.

Neill returned from tour, but only to hustle down to the post office to send away for the band's upcoming fall tour—it seemed the Dead sold tickets directly to their fans. After completing this all important mail order Neill again left, this time for a two-week family vacation on St. Thomas. His dad, some big shot lawyer, was doing quite well, or so it sounded. Neill acted as though this, one of many such luxury vacations.

The house creaked and groaned in its emptiness; the neighbors in the other half were elderly people who kept to themselves, except when I played the stereo too loud and the man pounded on the wall with a cane.

Whenever I thought about Nicole, or Camille, I felt worse than lonely— I felt ripped in half. So I tried not to think about either of them, or any woman. As I always had when life had been too awkward or uncomfortable to confront, I indulged thoughts and fantasies about movies, ones I'd seen, as well the epics I'd one day make.

BUT I WASN'T ALWAYS lonely: Wednesday evenings offered socializing and fellowship because Kunk and Max had pooled their mutual musical talents to begin playing a regular gig at a downtown club called Murdoch's on Main, part fine dining, part wine bar with live jazz. A gang of us, including Camille and Hoyt Bollard, kept our school connections alive through the summer break by meeting for Hump-day cocktails accompanied by smooth piano-driven tunes and serpentine bass lines.

"You reminded me of Ron Carter up there," I said to Kunk one night at the table. I'd been listening to more jazz, reading about it, in particular who were considered the best bass players.

"Gimme a fucking break, kid. You don't got a clue. But thanks anyway."

A frosty Kunk seemed different when in musician mode, more dismissive of me and the others younger than him. A pro, at work.

Not to Camille, of course. Watching him nuzzle and grope her at the bar gave me the achy-breakies.

One particular Wednesday featured a special guest, septuagenarian saxophonist Trip Newton, a local legend: Columbia's version of a famous elder jazzman. With Newton I saw yet another version of Levon Kunkle, this persona steeped in extreme deference. Kunk, with an attentive, piercing face, watched as the saxman counted off a tune Max told the audience was called "Softly, As In a Morning Sunrise."

Kunk played with a concentration that seemed pristine and diamond-cut, the years and the experience writ in the lines and hollows, the lattice of faint acne scars, the furrowed brow all bathed in magenta, a stupendous bass solo of such delicacy and poise that I hooted and hollered for my friend: a professional musician bringing his A-game in the presence of a master. Closing his eyes to play, standing with the bass held to his body and his fingers dancing up and down, an occasional glance at the drummer with his brushers or the pianist, a nod to Newton as he wound up the tune after a long jam. Kunk.

Sitting at the small tables in hazy pools of light, I felt like one of those French cats smoking and bopping along to Dexter Gordon in *Round Midnight*, a movie Max had ordered us all to go see the previous semester. Those Wednesdays at Murdoch's I got a feeling I'd never had before, not growing up in the sandy pine needle-strewn barrens of the Carolina midlands: I felt as though I lived in a real city among hip, educated sophisticates. Much of this emotion I owed to Kunk—his stage presence, his playing, his entire bearing and demeanor.

His friendship.

During the next Kunk solo, the Prof leaned over his piano keyboard, catching my eye and giving me an appreciative nod. This, a look when he wanted to make sure you were grokking on the music or the dialogue in the scene, the fine meals we shared in New York, or else his beloved jazz —*this is the good stuff*.

Max knew about movies and the theater, but jazz seemed to be his true religion. He kept a picture in his office, framed, a beautiful color shot of what they called Swing Street—52nd between Fifth and Sixth, the block where he'd claimed to have literally run from club to club trying to catch the marquee names of the day, Davis, Monk, Powell, and Parker, all playing at joints like the 3 Deuces, The Onyx, Leon & Eddie, Club Carousel and Samoa, names he would rattle off, wistful, pointing at the image on the wall of a time passed and never to return.

My writing professor's classic jazz war stories had already nudged my curiosity, but hearing the two of them playing live put the hook into me. Still today I scour used record shops for LPs, sometimes only to smell them and think about Professor de Lisle sprinting across his 1950s New York photograph, or else about Levon Kunkle gigging at Murdoch's, or joints like he'd played in AC or Philly, which I imagined to be atmospheric and a shade shy, at any given moment, of turning dangerous. Who could blame my pal for turning to his own experiences for story ideas—unlike me, he'd already lived an interesting life.

W eeks passed, and after getting my compressed summer school classes squared away—audio recording, a snap, and a Modern American Lit section that kept me nose-down reading and typing papers—I tried to come up with ideas for a short script to shoot that autumn.

In only a few weeks, it suddenly seemed.

No pressure. Or anything.

I found my ideas, however, either too grandiose, or not interesting enough—not that I shared them with anyone. But the challenge ahead loomed: Freddie Baumbach, and his gauntlet of competition.

Time enough. Or so I kept telling myself.

Except that I blinked my eyes, the calendar pages fell away, and now August had all but arrived.

When fall classes would begin.

Including sixteen-millimeter.

I tried not to panic.

AT THE RISK of grave understatement, a major, unheralded occurrence of the first order, life-altering and horribly sad:

My mother, killed in a car crash.

Just-like-that.

I'd come home from the first class of 16mm Film Production to an answering machine message from my dad. He sounded so unlike himself, wooden and faraway, with his news that my mother had been in an accident. How I was to call as soon as possible.

In that same voice, he warbled a breathy account of the circumstances.

How my mother hadn't only been in a wreck. "She didn't make it. Son—your mama didn't make it home." And breaking down.

"Did she—run off the road?"

He said, yeah. Didn't have to tell from where she'd been returning: The Dixiana, or else some dive in the boonies of Edgewater County with an even worse reputation.

"I know school's getting underway. But I was wondering if you could run home for a spell to help me get things decided—I'm a little confused right now."

"I'll be there. I'll be there in an hour." I realized sitting on the edge of my bed, surrounded by movie posters and dirty laundry, that my heart had begun racing. Sweating but cold. Full-body tremors. "Quick as I can."

My mother is dead. My mother is dead. A shocking mantra.

"We'll get through this."

"I know, Daddy."

But neither of us knew anything, and we both burst into tears, sudden and febrile.

IN THE KITCHEN of the duplex, I found Neill sitting with a bowl of rubbing alcohol and a pile of cotton swabs. He concentrated on cleaning an ornate glass pipe he'd brought back from one of his Dead shows, the piece caked with blackened, sticky resin from what I considered overuse.

Not looking at me, his voice faraway. "What's all that ruckus in there?"

Surreal words: "My mother—she passed away."

Neill's pleasant stoner smile crumbled into dewy-eyed shock and sympathy. "What the fuck? *Was she sick?*"

I shook my head 'yes' but said, "No. A car wreck."

He leaned back from the table and snagged a beer out of the fridge, cracked it, drank, belched. Drank again. "To your mom," he said. "Damn —that's heavy."

He had no idea how fraught with layers his gesture seemed. But that wasn't for him to know.

I felt more tears coming, but no. Not in front of Neill. Not in front of a mirror, either. Not for a long time. "It was like I knew something bad might happen, for a long time. Bless her heart."

"When my folks split up, it was like one of them died—I was six, and my dad, he was just like, gone off somewhere. But not like this. Not like died-died."

"A good way of putting it. Died-died. Double-underscored, double-down emphasis."

"Anything I can do? Want to get high?"

I told him, not now. "Got to hit the road home."

On the drive I kept slipping into shocked disbelief. Surely she would be waiting for me, cigarette and drink in hand. Hot grief, welling and ebbing and flowing.

I tried to let the feelings go as I drove, counting the mile markers until the Tillman Falls exit. I would be fine. I insisted this to myself.

I knew nothing, of course, about grief, or being an adult. I thought losing Nicole, a childhood sweetheart, amounted to grief. But this sudden gust of existential torpor into my soul—the motherless child; no one in line between me and my own brush with eternity—started to feel a bit more like what they called being grownup.

Her personal foibles aside, and nobody's perfect anyway, nothing feels like losing your mother. A special kind of grief—it never leaves you.

Yeah. If you still have a mom, go call her. Right now.

During the surreal funeral service, Kunk, who'd never met my mother, wept as though he'd lost one of his own. One of my aunts noted how we both stunk of the Maker's Mark he'd smuggled in an elegant flask engraved with his initials, LCK. Levon Carlton Kunkle.

"This sacred vessel was a gift from my grandfather, only to be used at the most solemn of occasions and exquisite of opportunities," he'd said behind the church as we swilled. "This qualifies."

"I don't want to be drunk like her."

A strong, warm hand on my shoulder. "Medicinal purposes, [REDACTED]. That's all this is. Got nothing to do with your mom. Well, it does, but—you know what I'm saying."

My throat flared fiery-hot as I pulled another drink. I did, in fact, feel better.

Daddy didn't mind Kunk's nurturing and comforting attitude toward me—the man, an emotionless cypher, seemed lost. From an older generation, a dozen years my mother's senior, skinny, weathered, to me my father looked like a Dust Bowl farmer from one of those old photographs. Drawn, wan, grieving.

During the service the pastor's words came to me as borderline incoherent, irrelevant niceties. I decided for myself, and on my own that my mother wasn't a bad mother, no. Ostensibly normal and pleasant enough, meals for the most part on time and edible; the laundry sometimes we sent out, because let's face it, the [REDACTED] family of Edgewater County has always had some money—Great-grandfather and Grandfather had been a part owners in a bustling upstate textile mill that got bought out by a bigger company, and back then that didn't happen as often. As appearances went, we'd for the most part avoided the depravity that often comes with addiction. Other than the occasional drunken confession about some past bit of behavior on her part, of course. Those I wouldn't miss.

No, we weren't rich, but well enough off. Besides the family money father had had his own career, having recently retired with a solid pension from forty years working for the power company, the last couple of decades in management at the Sugeree River Nuclear Station: not scads of money, but enough to have a nice large house and two cars—one now totaled.

Certainly enough money to afford mother the time she needed to get into her little bouts of trouble, sowing the seeds of mood swings and manias she suffered from the speed she'd take to balance out the three-too many G & T's, with an over-the-counter sleeping pill taken to help mitigate the creeping alcohol metabolization of the predawn darkness—liver o'clock, as I later heard the moment called—and then, oh, daybreak and the hammering hangovers she'd obviously learned to live with, the BC Powder packets opened and scattered like little wax-paper bindles of cocaine. Her day's routine. But never again.

After the service wound down, in which this preacher I didn't know spoke platitudes I was certain my mother never believed, we motored with our headlamps burning to the graveyard outside town, and looking at my gray-faced, bereft father on the bench seat next to me in the funeral home limo, I took a sacred vow: to never again touch another drop of alcohol.

My resolve wouldn't last, not a college student. But in the moment, I felt self righteous and defiant: I'd show her who knew how to control himself. I'd show my mother, if she could still see me, how her downfall would not be my own.

As the family and mourners assembled upon the well-tended green grass of the gravesite in memorial gardens outside of Tillman Falls, Kunk caught up and commented on the longstanding small town tradition of cops blocking the side streets and taking their hats off in deference to the passing departed.

"[REDACTED]," Kunk said, choked up, "I'm from Philadelphia, and I never seen any cops do that. Maybe for another cop."

I didn't know what being from Philly had to do with anything. I'd never lived anywhere else. I didn't know how people up north buried their dead. Apparently without as much reverence and pomp. "Probably a Southern thing."

"Maybe so." Moved by our community's genteel manners and traditions, he shook his head: "Like the way you guys will give a stranger a friendly wave. A different planet from where I grew up."

Simple Edgewater County courtesies I took for granted as being universal, I realized thanks to him, held no such commonality. I could always count on Kunk to remind me I still had much to learn about the world.

After the interment—at which my father, weeping and gasping, fell sideways from the folding chair on which the funeral home name, Karlaney, was stenciled in fading white block letters; Kunk rushed over and helped me pick Daddy up and comfort him—most returned to our house for the ritual gathering: well-wishers bearing condolences, yes, but also mountains of food for the bereaved and motherless family, sustenance to be eaten now and much more for later. Too much sustenance for any one family.

Except, perhaps, for a family missing its mom.

The growing cornucopia made me angry at her—at the waste and foolishness. Who was to eat all this, the two of us left alive? I didn't even live here anymore. The bounty would spoil, first.

Furious, too, at the fact I'd now be expected to pitch in and take care of my aging father—the door to my adult life not yet fully open, yet now blocked by the dead weight of my mother's corpse.

Looking for any reason I could to be upset with her, my emotions raged, but anger seemed better than grief. Felt hot and warm in my chest. Made tears seem like wasted water. Only later would I realize Dad would be lonely but fine; that, by necessity, he'd taken care of her much more than she of him.

My tie now loosened and sport coat draped over a wooden hanger in the hall closet hanging beside one of my mother's winter coats, I stole a moment to myself by the dessert table in the dining room, munching cookies and bite-sized brownies to soak up the bourbon I'd shared with Kunk. I flashed back to any number of unpleasant moments I'd shared with my mother, but in doing so felt only a vast and burgeoning emptiness.

Thought of her in the box; in the ground.

Cold, alone, dead.

All but choking on the sweets I gobbled, tasting nothing, I finally felt sad enough to almost-cry.

But I didn't. I made myself remember any number of happier moments, moments of innocence from before her drinking had gotten out of hand. It didn't help much. Maybe a little.

I skirted the throng in the formal living room and dining room—cousins, aunts, in-laws, kids, old folks I barely knew, all of whom being Southerners and as such having nothing to say, not openly, about my mother and her well-known travails—and ducked into the kitchen, every available surface containing Pyrex dishes and rectangular pans covered in foil and cakes under plates and an enormous stainless steel serving tub like you'd see in the high school lunch room, this one filled by what I recognized as my Aunt Esther's Madwoman Macaroni and Cheese, a holiday staple, the best anyone in the county had ever tasted, a mountain of baked pasta in the process of being strip-mined by a serving spoon sitting beside it on a plate. Mother had confided that Aunt Esther's trick had been to add a portion of creamy Monterey jack cheese to balance out the sharp cheddar. Heaven. She also made a championship-grade pimento cheese, no small feat in the American South. Finely-diced Vidalia onions were the secret in that one.

From among the cluster of chattering bodies in the dining room, Kunk caught my eye. I'd watched him and my dad huddling in close conversation, my father speaking and gesturing, unusual for him even under the best of circumstances, especially with a stranger. With laughter and a hearty handshake, Kunk clapped my dad on the shoulder and threaded his way over to me.

"Let's take ourselves a stroll," gesturing with his glass of sweet tea toward the back the door. "Stuffy in here."

We paused on the way out to let my cousin Donna pass—with twins in her stomach, we had to make way.

I watched as Kunk held the door, his eyes twinkling. "Hello there, gorgeous."

Under the ice-hot gaze of my dapper and charming companion, Donna appeared she might melt. She looked at me like *who is this*?

"When are you due, sweetheart?"

"Not soon enough." She turned and hugged me. "I'm so sorry."

"It's okay," I said.

"No, it ain't. But nothing anybody can do now." Donna touched my face. "You call me if you need anything."

So many had said these words they'd begun to lose meaning. "Will do."

"Best of luck to you and your family," Kunk said, charming as hell.

Donna, glowing at him, smiled and waddled away.

Once we were outside, though, Kunk's attitude turned frosty. "Pregnancy—it's a disease to be avoided," the opposite of the generous and complimentary attitude he'd displayed to my cousin heavy with child.

"Sounds grim."

"You want your life to get complicated? Have a kid."

I'd never considered whether Kunk had had any children. "Sounds like first hand info."

"Nah." He knocked knuckles against a tree trunk. "I been lucky—so far."

I wanted to follow up and point out how, without pregnancy, we're like, kind of finished as a species, and all? But instead I let it go, thinking the idea nothing more than an example of Kunk's acerbic street patois, his cocksman's talk, a guy who always kept rubbers on hand in a wallet or jacket pocket. I'd remember that pregnancy line later, and later again, both times for much darker reasons.

Kunk led me into the backyard. My father always kept the lawn immaculate, in a sense his life's work on display in the lush and landscaped tableau, the roses and hydrangeas and azaleas, the wooden swing where mother would drink and smoke and read books when the weather permitted.

A place of life, and now death.

"Here," offering the flask again. Carolina sunlight glinted golden off the burnished, aged metal. "You need this."

"Thanks." Burning, a hot-cold explosion in the gut, a temporary calm descending. "What was all that with Dad? I saw you talking."

Kunk, shrugging. "Nothing. Two guys shooting the shit."

"Looked like some heavy conversation. Not like him."

He hooked an arm around my neck. "Champ, all we were talking about was the Redtails. About football."

Something about this news came as a further palliative. "He does love his football."

I thought of my dad watching the big game on TV in a darkened living room, alone. I broke down, a couple of tearless dry heaves.

Kunk bundled me into his arms, bore me away from the house toward the thicket of woods along the property line. I caught a whiff of Camille's perfume coming from Kunk's coat. I'd barely spoken to her today, didn't know where she'd wandered off.

I calmed down, had another nip from the flask. Birdsong ringing out from all around, the scent of the food replaced by a peaty smell of earth and decomposing flora, the thicket felt peaceful.

"When I was growing up," pointing back to the house, "I'd be sitting on the back porch or looking out the kitchen window, and I'd see a deer appear out of these woods—a doe with fawns, that kind of scene. Really magical on a misty morning. Ethereal, dignified animals."

"Deer—like with antlers, and shit?"

"Antlers, and shit. Yeah."

"Freaking wild kingdom."

I didn't know how much the next words were going to make me seem like some sensitive emotive pussy, but I didn't care, the Maker's Mark giving me a fit of *in vino veritas*. "The idea of these damn rednecks around here hiding in deer stands picking those innocent, graceful creatures off has always really chapped my ass."

He went *mm-hm*. "Not a sportsman, eh?"

"Some 'sport.'"

"Never gave a thought to going hunting. Not growing up in the city." An aside. "Maybe some goombahs from the AC are still hunting me, though, ya dig?"

"After all this time?"

Dismissive. "Maybe if I showed up there and ran across the wrong guy. Could develop into a definite type of situation. But look, it wasn't like I owed money. That's what'll get you iced quicker than over some skirt."

"So—how is Camille?"

Offhand: "What, *what*—she's Camille. There's the good with the bad. She's young." He gurgled the flask. "Christ, I don't know what I'm doing, [REDACTED]."

I asked what he meant.

"Getting in too deep with this chick."

Bitter words. "She seems to really be into you—that's too deep?"

Packing a Camel against his Zippo: "Your cheeks are flushed a shade shy of purple."

Flustered, unable to think on my feet, I wanted to blurt out the truth— that I loved her, but now Kunk has her, and he's suggesting that that's not entirely a good thing, and I'm confused, and I guess I'm feeling jealous and pitiful and weak on the day of my mother's funeral.

But I didn't say any of that crap. "I'm just trying not to bawl."

A savvy guy, Kunk had to know about my feelings for Camille—I'm sure of it. He hit me with those steely blue eyes, neither a friendly expression nor not a hostile one, more like a granite carving that captures a face in ossified repose rather than the act of emoting. "It's like Max says—we're like family, the writers," walking me back in a one-eighty toward the house. "Don't you forget that."

"I've never been that big on family." I wasn't lying. An only child—a loner—I spent most of my childhood buried in books, long walks in these woods of solitude behind my home. Never a joiner, nor a social animal. "So that's good to know."

"You bet your ass it is. Now, let's go get ourselves some more of this here down-home funeral cuisine. That macaroni's *absosively, posilutely* out of this world."

"Won my aunt a few blue ribbons at the county fair."

"Fucking Norman Rockwell, this place." He stopped and grabbed me by the arm. "So look. We all got class tomorrow. Max knows you won't be there."

"Who says I won't?"

"You gonna be up for jumping back in the saddle? I dunno, pal."

I told him I didn't have any other choice. At least now I had acquired life experience about which to write. How an artist translated such dreadful feelings as grief for one's own mother into a short film, or a screenplay, or to even begin to make any sort of rational sense, however, I hadn't a blessed clue.

"M ise-en-scène," Hedda Gamble began her lecture on the first day of 16mm Film Production, "means more than deciding what to include in the frame. It means being aware and in control of all aspects of the shot—the blocking of actors. The placement of objects in the background and foreground. The costumes; the light as well as the shadows. And the *acting* by the actors often requires explicit direction in order to achieve a specific effect. In short, the director of a film suffers an enormous amount of responsibility— to the art, and to all the people helping achieve the vision."

But wait, there's more: "Some say *mise-en-scene* includes the tone of the finished piece, too. The subtext. The 'all' of the movie," making rabbit ears. "Mastering control of the elements of the shot, the arc of the story, the physical on-set production of the movie, the post-production and promotion, all the pieces-parts that make up every aspect of filmmaking, is how you become a successful director of motion pictures. You live and breathe not only the finished movies, but the process itself."

With the fall semester ramping up into high gear, I set aside personal troubles—not really; a mental construct in which I managed daily waves of grief over my mom by keeping it all at arm's length—to get through the year-long production class.

Salivating at the thought of actual shooting, I pictured myself in the director's chair stabbing my finger like the famous on-set publicity still of Hitchcock, calling—literally—all the shots. That my mother would not live to see me realize my ambitions stung and hurt in a different way. I would try to keep my dad engaged, especially since the film would cost several thousand dollars to complete.

❄

I HAD immediate trust in the three person film crew I gathered. We'd been through it already; we knew each other:

The pale princess, Brenda LaRose, along with Connor Rush, would be my partners.

It felt organic and natural for us to work together again. I didn't care about the Big Misunderstanding with Connor, and thought that asking him to partner on this project would go a long way toward healing our relationship. Since the incident that night, he had a hard time looking me straight in the eye.

All I wanted to say to him, in the parlance of Edgewater County, was: *Lookit, beau—it ain't no thang.*

Outside that first production class, Connor himself summed up our situation in a more succinct and direct manner: "Better the devil I know than working with Freddie," who'd rubbed everyone the wrong way back in the spring with his born-to-the-manor attitude about the 16mm adventure to come, and here had announced he'd written a new version of his short story adaptation to shoot. I scoffed—*out of ideas already, Freddie?*

Brenda, giving me a friendly punch in the arm. "We already know that if necessary, we can push you around."

"Har-har, it is to laugh."

Brenda held out her open hands. "Let's make a bond."

I put mine on top of hers, with Connor, after only the smallest of hesitations, placing his clammy palms on top of the pile.

"To our movie," Brenda intoned, reverent. "May it turn out worthy of our hopes, dreams, and best efforts."

"Our commitment," Connor said.

"Our mighty ambition," I added.

Huzzah! we all yelled, throwing our hands up to the low curving ceiling like a ball team about to take the field of engagement.

At that moment a knot of students, led by Freddie and Professor Gamble, came bustling out of class, catching us in the moment.

"You see this, budding cinéastes?" Hedda demanded of the students, thrusting one of her stubby, definitive fingers at our display of camaraderie. "That's teamwork—and teamwork is what's required to make a successful film, whether you're Hitchcock, Herzog, David Lynch, or Mr. [REDACTED] here."

I gave Freddie the biggest obsequious grin I could muster. In my best Sir Alec Guinness: "Yes, even dear old *Freddie* here, too. Isn't that so, my boy?"

He squirmed, shifting his book bag from one blue Oxford-shirted shoulder to the other. Beady eyes squinted amber with animosity. "Look who's all confident suddenly."

Riding a wave of courage, I continued in my smarmy British accent: "Oh, we'll all find out about confidence. Won't we."

"You little boys don't forget me." Opal, deadly serious, a cigarette tucked behind her short-shorn black hair, her mascara-lined, challenging eyes bouncing back and forth between ours. Already a teacher's pet for having been the only female wanting to helm her own film, Opal's entourage and future crew clustered behind her, the other kids in class draped in black and with garish makeup and hairdos, shod in Doc Martins, Vans, and other hipster footwear. "Wait till you see what my lens captures."

Freddie, his shirt untucked, started dancing and snapping his fingers in front of her and her friends. "An athlete, a princess, a brain, a criminal—and a basket case."

"Fuck you."

"'*Don't you, forget about me, don't don't don't, you . . .*'"

Darren, his man-boobs jiggling with laughter. "Ladies and gentlemen, the winner for Best Director is—Ally Sheedy, for *Breakfast Club Returns!*"

Opal, a tough cookie: "Eat my asshole, dork."

"Hey, *hey.*" Hedda, trying to suppress laughter at our antics. "Relax, guys."

I cleared my throat. All eyes fell upon me. "Look—this isn't a competition."

Freddie and Opal, turning their fiery ire back upon me instead of each other, snarled in unison: "*Speak for yourself.*"

Hedda, professor-*cum*-mediator, gestured for calm. "This is going to be a long process, and everybody's passionate. But let's all try to stay friends."

Everybody nodded, shuffling their feet and murmuring so-longs until the next class. I held my hand out to Freddie as he passed, but he pretended not to have seen the gesture.

OUTSIDE ON THE street amidst lunchtime traffic, Brenda took me aside. "So look. I have a script already."

"For—a short film?"

Nodding. Embarrassed. "I haven't shown it to anyone else yet."

I felt frozen—I had planned to write the movie as well. But wait: if Brenda's script were good? We could get right to work on preproduction. "Gimme," I said, eager.

Handing over the pages, she pitched a brief logline. Dark, dangerous stuff.

I said, "Whoa. I had no idea."

"I contain multitudes."

I stuff her script into my backpack. Winking: "Our people will be in touch with your people."

She turned red, waved and hurried off down the street.

Unlocking my bike from the rack outside the classroom entrance under the looming columns of the basketball arena, I thought the existence of her work a positive development, as well that we discharged weird energy among the three competing directors. Like I had long anticipated, my intuition assured me these next two semesters would be the peak of my life— so far, that is.

Biking home to the duplex I navigated a downtown, major university campus crackling with movement and activity. Squirrels foraging, leaves falling, traffic, pedestrians clustered and burdened by backpacks and briefcases, a roiling, the student body and faculty a cosmopolitan mishmash of humanity hailing from all over the planet.

Motion.

Bodies.

Faces.

Every point of view offered its own unique angle on the scene, all unfolding in a kaleidoscope of individual perspectives on the world. Developing an expansive filmmaker's eye, I filed away my observations of the passing world.

With a welcome, cool autumn breeze tickling cheeks rosy with anticipation, I quivered with excitement—*Directed By* [REDACTED] would at last flicker across a screen. Had fantasized about the moment for ten years, ever since I'd seen *Star Wars* at the Palmetto Grande in downtown Tillman Falls and had my life changed forever. And now—at last—I'd make my own movie.

Amidst the coffee shop baristas, beer-bars and boutiques of the Old Market, I met Brenda down at Maxine's Koffee Klatch, a college neighborhood fixture, to knock around our burgeoning narrative. Brenda's first draft of the script had come in at the right length, and while changing a few elements from a true-crime TV show source of her dark little piece of work, she indeed captured the horror of the crime in question, a college party gone wrong:

A couple having a small gathering devoted to drinking games kept going after the others had left, an argument ensued over matters unknown, and sudden, inexplicable violence followed—the male perp, smashed out of his head, did the same to his date's skull with a heavy glass vodka bottle.

As if domestic violence wasn't bad enough—it's a problem in South Carolina—to add to the horror he'd next dragged her into the backyard and attempted to bury the evidence, all while she still lived and breathed.

This premature burial, the creepiest part, is what'd stuck with me: As the victim pled for her life through mouthfuls of rich Carolina loam, the mad inebriate took up a cinderblock, dropped it onto her face, and finished her off.

Except . . . the girl's weak cries had been overheard by a neighbor, who called the police and found the fresh, shallow grave. They pulled her out of the ground, still breathing, but the victim perished on the way to the hospital.

Meanwhile, the murderer? Oh, you know—he had gone back inside and continued to drink and watch television. Said once he noticed all the dirt under this fingernails, shit had gotten real. That what he had done hadn't been some bad dream.

Booze. It made people crazy.

Brenda's version retained the gruesome details about the crime—the head-bashing, backyard burial and cinderblock shock-moment—but here with a fictionalized story of two feuding fraternity brothers, an amorphous, hinted-upon suggestion of a financial dispute behind the argument leading to the bottle-bashing bit, but otherwise the same scenario.

But I wasn't sure we needed to stray as far as she had from the source material. "I don't understand why you needed to change the basic setup so much. A tragedy, a date predicated on romance and attraction going so horribly awry—that wasn't interesting enough?"

Brenda, clasping her small hands like a pair of freckled, alabaster lovebirds nestled together on the cover page of the script, fixed me with a clear-eyed stare. "When I tried to literally translate this insane act, I found that I would not and could not write what amounts to a senseless depiction of outright *misogyny*. What is the narrative? There isn't one in the true story—only depravity."

She had a point. "I don't wanna make some exploitation thing that's just about technique, or the violence that's central to the story."

Brenda, definitive. The scribe, her eyes bulging with passion, deep-breathed and summed up the script I'd read: "Two fratboys, a pair of inebriated bulls in a contest of testosterone-fueled nonsense over some mysterious bit of business—money, or a woman, or whatever, like Hitchcock's MacGuffin—and with mayhem and death as the consequence. Which is the whole point of a short movie like this. Something memorable, and fast."

We'd talked in scriptwriting class about retribution and redemption, and the requirement, at one time, for wrongdoers in movies to be shown getting their comeuppance. I wondered about that part.

"It's a good script. But it could always be better." I called for a coffee refill. "What if we made it actual fratricide?"

"Fratricide?" Brenda's wheels turned. "Now you're onto something. Not frat-rats, but actual brothers. Delicious."

We went over a few details; Brenda took my suggestions with good humor.

"All right, so you have notes. Go forth and revise," I directed.

"I'll have fresh pages tomorrow."

WITH A FRESH DRAFT IN HAND, we now brought in Connor, whom we met the next day in the canteen.

After Brenda, demure, waved her fresh pages in his face, into his book bag went the latest *American Cinematographer*, the magazine featuring a cover shot of Peter Weller in heavy *Robocop* makeup. My DP and I had a big job—whomever and whatever the characters ended up being and doing, we had to depict it visually. This meant decisions achieved through storyboarding, which led to choosing lenses and stocks, color palettes and exposures, locations, equipment, and most of all, budgeting.

After reading it through, he seemed shocked but impressed. "I think this script's all but ready to shoot."

Brenda, relieved. "That's so kind of you."

"I'll start storyboarding this weekend."

"May I tell you both my vision for this?

I felt challenged—who was the auteur, here? And yet, I needed help with the technical aspects, in which Connor had found his MACM niche.

"Black and white."

"Oh," Brenda said. "My little arm-hairs are standing up."

I also loved the idea. "We'll need to get on with our test shots A-S-A-P. Look into where we can get it processed."

Connor, pleased. "I'll get the gear scheduled."

For our tests we'd be using so-called 'short ends' Hedda kept around, the last few feet of unused film at the end of a reel and often traded out for a full mag. We'd been using blank leader to practice loading magazines. I felt nervous about loading our own stock, which we hadn't yet acquired. We couldn't waste film on mistakes like misloading and fogging a whole reel.

I flipped through the script again. Lean, mean screenwriting, the establishing scenes deceptively free of foreboding, only ordinary conversations and interactions, making the shock of the murder and the subsequent aftermath evocative of the unsettling tone I wanted to achieve. Also, it was clear we could add the literal-brothers angle with only a few small changes to dialogue.

I grunted and nodded: in only a few visual cues, Brenda had conveyed much information—the essence of cinema. Maybe she should be directing.

A flash of insight: "We could underscore the family dynamic by having an insert of, say, a photo on the mantle: the two brothers with their mom, her seeming to favor one over the other." I'd watched a fuzzy VHS of Polanski's *Repulsion* a half-dozen times, and thought of the shot at the end of the family portrait depicting the younger version of the protagonist as different, disturbed, and set apart from her smiling family

—in other words, a brief image offering enormous insight into the character.

Brenda, nodding. "Visual shorthand in place of expository backstory. I get it."

"Terrific," Connor said. "Approved."

We wrapped up our production meeting and Connor hustled off to his next class. With Brenda bound for a long haul to the Business Administration building across campus, I offered to walk her, which she accepted. Tossing out ideas for shooting locations, we moseyed across the sprawl of the urban college campus in the middle of South Carolina's busy capital.

Strolling by the Humanities building and across the pedestrian bridge over Pinckney Street, I stopped her and said, "Hey—I'm psyched about this thing of ours."

"Me too. But I'm worried about the money, though. We have to be frugal."

"We will. Don't sweat it, little sister."

I reached over and squeezed her hand, held the gesture a little too long, maybe; our fingertips brushed as the handclasp was released, and for the first time I felt attraction to Brenda LaRose, which took me by surprise. Walking with her like this seemed like the first time the two of us had ever been alone.

Thoughts—and hormones—flourished inside me: Nothing had come of that Opal flirtation in New York, so maybe it was Brenda I should be pursuing? Camille, certainly out of reach.

I had to stop myself from leaning over and kissing my production partner—we were about to work together, and to my mind this left no room for romance. I wrote off these feelings as another symptom of inveterate horniness, an untamed tiger in my tank.

Brenda, her cheeks aflame, adjusted her glasses—she must have felt the charge in the air like I had.

But as we walked on, I found only the script on her mind: "I couldn't sleep last night worrying about what you would think of the pages."

"You needn't have. It's a fine script."

"I get anxiety real easy. It's something I need to work on."

Without overburdening her intimations with too much specificity, she hinted about having been in therapy. About working on this or that personality quirk. About having a weird childhood.

"Relax—you're one of the best writers in the program."

A smile from her like I'd never seen. "You really think so?"

"Yes," though to be honest I only felt she was the best *female* writer I'd encountered in MACM. At least I was smart enough not to qualify the compliment with that tidbit.

As we crossed the Ellipse, the old campus from antebellum times that survived Sherman's 1865 burning of the city, Brenda said, "So listen—there's just one more thing."

"What's that, Lt. Columbo?"

"It's about Jaime."

The boyfriend. Ah—the sensation of jets cooling. Dang it.

"I think he could be one of our lead actors."

Oh, boy. I hadn't thought much yet about casting. "But he's into comedy."

"True—but a real actor can play anything."

Uncertain and maybe a touch jealous, I told her to give him the script. "See what he thinks."

"You're a doll. So easy to work with."

"No, you're right—Jaime's a fine actor."

A quick hug. Brenda whirled her red hair around and disappeared into the small throng of students filing onto the Ellipse from the parking garage near the humanities campus.

Am I giving in to everyone's ideas too easily? Maybe I should've said no to her. Or to Connor's idea about the black & white. Or to the script, the changes, the setup, the characters, the whole project—!

As I remembered Hedda's mise-en-scène speech, I suffered a pang of terror—so much new territory ahead. The first of our team had now proven herself, and Connor seemed to be on top of his technical requirements. As director, I hoped I'd up to my own challenges.

Another day or so passed, and I found my confidence ebbing. I needed another seal of approval on our shooting script, so I biked over to Kunk's place to talk him into reading Brenda's work. He did, but only under a kind of duress.

As he welcomed me into the pigsty of a bachelor pad, he switched off a playoff baseball game. Reading through the pages, he nodded and grunted at this or that moment.

Then, Levon Kunkle cried out in surprise.

It turned out to be when *Assailant* bashes *Victim* in the head, as Brenda had called the otherwise unnamed characters, striking with what she described as

```
     . . .the business end of a heavy glass liquor
     bottle. The victim COLLAPSES like a poorly
     assembled HOUSE OF CARDS.

     A spray of VISCOUS, DARK BLOOD on the wall of
     the kitchen DRIPS DOWN behind the victim's
     head.

     DISSOLVE TO:
```

"Damn." Kunk smoked, poured himself a bourbon short and neat. I watched him sip the hot liquor, which made me think of standing outside my mother's wake hitting the flask. "That's a mean little script."

His compliment, I realized, seemed fraught with portent—Kunk appeared downright troubled. "You think it's good?"

"A lot going on. Like, with subtext, and all."

I hadn't considered notions like subtext, only the text itself. "The girl can write."

"No freaking doubt."

I described the true-story inspiration for the script and the changes she'd made, first to frat brothers, and in the next draft to actual brothers. "I thought it a page or two long for what we need. Otherwise, it's pretty sharp."

"C'mon," he said.

"What?"

"You wrote this. Or at least revised it."

"I'd tell you if I did."

"Bullshit."

"It's the truth." I didn't get why he was so upset. Her scenes in the scriptwriting class had always been solid. "The Pale Princess has got some chops. More than I realized, I guess."

Kunk looked like he'd swallowed a rock. I asked what was wrong.

"It's nothing. Girl's just got a helluva lot of talent."

Next, he said he wanted to bat around the idea for his feature-length screenplay project, a course I'd tackle in the springtime. Confessed he'd been floundering. "I feel stuck in the mud on this thing."

I found the news unnerving. Kunk made everything look so easy. "Having trouble getting started?"

Through a haze of blue Camel smoke: "[REDACTED]? I think you might be the only person in the program I'd admit that to. But, yeah."

I felt more confused than honored. "Why me?"

"You got a good head on your shoulders. For a backcountry Carolina redneck."

Cornpone accent, more pronounced than my real dialect, but only just-so: "Coming from a Yankee like you? Wellsir, I reckon that there's a real compliment."

Kunk shook off his concerns, seemed to snap out of a troubled reverie. "Listen, champ—forget my script. You got bigger crap on your plate. Let me know if you need any anything. I'll grip for you, pull cable. Anything you need."

"Production's still a few weeks off, but eventually, we're going to need a score."

He chuckled. "Dude, I can play, but I ain't much of a composer."

I held up a hand for a high-five. "You're the only musician I know, pal."

He seemed touched. Slapped skin. "Gonna be a great fucking movie. I can feel it."

Weeks later, deep into principal photography and surrounded by cast and small crew, the three friends—the filmmakers—stood conferring in the back yard of a bungalow-style home in an aging neighborhood near campus, an unoccupied, furnished rental property owned by Connor's father's golfing buddy. We had been fortunate to enjoy the run of the house, and had accomplished most interiors—everything but the actual murder scene.

Production of the now-entitled *Too Far Gone* had so far proved a gut-wrenching exercise in anxiety and head-butting among the over-the-line principals, as *Variety* might describe the brain trust at the heart of the crew: the writer with firm opinions about not only her story and dialogue but all other aspects of the production, writers not normally welcome on a Hollywood set in the first place; the DP—Director of Photography—who sputtered with displeasure at most every idea presented about angles and lenses and lighting, and who turned every small decision into a veritable production number of second-guessing and handwringing; and the first-time director, young, ambitious, but burning with fear over money and time and momentum and, as an auteurist, his chance to have more-or-less complete control over what would forever be known as "his" film. In short, a volatile stew.

Much of this conflict occurred while the actors—Jaime as the killer, with Marcel LeMoy, a politician's son and pretty boy as well as a scriptwriter taking Max's intro class, and in thrall of veterans like me and Kunk—stood around watching us bicker. Serving as crew, we had Darren as grip and sound guy to complete the roster of human beings observing, unfiltered, the sight of us us—of me—flailing.

Humiliating; a trial by fire. But we were getting shots.

At first I'd thought Darren's offer to pull audio made him a spy, until he said that trying to deal with Freddie Baumbach and his beaver suit was pissing him off so much he wanted to be a total dick by working on my film as well. Said that Freddie's script was good, but didn't have any elements nearly as cool as bashing someone's brains out and burying the still-living body in the back yard.

The property had quite a bit of atmosphere. Far from an example of the nicer, renovated bungalows in Herndon Hill, which in many cases dated back to the early part of the century, this one already looked a little haunted. One of Columbia's original suburbs and for a time connected to the city proper by an electric trolley system, the neighborhood had declined for decades before gentrification and campus-creep had taken hold.

I'd researched old Columbia for a paper in a Southern history class, and unlike most who might gravitate in such a document toward more dramatic events like Sherman's wholesale ransacking and destruction of the city, I'd chosen to explore the early twentieth century, the flowering of modern life following the inception of the industrial age and the end of Reconstruction: the trolley system; the 15-story Palmetto Building, the south's first skyscraper; the establishment of a short-lived, WWI era military camp that would later grow into massive Army training facility now called Fort Jackson; a long-forgotten age of numerous taverns on Main Street, with such drunkenness and assorted vices on display apparently enough to put the Old Market's current college ghetto watering hole vibe to complete and utter shame.

Speaking of vice: despite being busy, I'd been going out drinking almost every night of the week, either with my roommate, or else rousting Kunk out of his nest.

Kunk nights turned into raucous affairs—liquor, shots, licentious behavior toward female servers and college girlies alike, sometimes until last call. Like sailors on shore leave, or so I imagined.

And yet my mature buddy, he never seemed hungover. I didn't know how Kunk managed to seem so fresh on the mornings after one of those bacchanals. But he did.

And sometimes after leaving the bar with a girl. Women decidedly not Camille.

Not often. But a couple of times. This, a secret he expected me to keep, one I tried to keep my imagination from considering an ace in some romantic hole.

※

THE NIGHT before our first day of shooting had been such a night, both anticipatory and celebratory, the remnants of which contributed to the general sensation of bile rising in my throat all day—and never more so than during the latest and last argument of the day's shoot.

Brenda, Connor and I faced off while staring down at my storyboards arrayed across a gray, rotting picnic table, as everyone else examined their shoelaces. Jaime Marzol, to whom we'd given the part of the murderer, paced and checked his watch every five seconds—this guy, always broke and scraping along, needed to get to his bar-back job at McHaffie's Pub.

"Here's the news," I announced. "I storyboarded these shots this way because the visual information contained therein is integral to the telling of this story."

A red-faced, pouting Brenda flinched as I made a thumb-and-forefinger frame in front of her to mimic what the drawings depicted, a long shot of the murderous brother dragging his presumably deceased sibling down the back steps of the house. "I yielded to you on scripting issues, and now that we're on set, I expect a reasonable degree of quid-pro-quo."

"I understand," swatting away my finger-frame. "I just think it would be interesting to handhold this shot and slowly creep forward as he drags the body."

"I can do it either way," Connor said. "Somebody make a decision before we lose this light."

"Handheld?" I huffed and puffed. "So—a POV shot. Whose POV?"

She didn't know. "I just thought it would look cool."

I scoffed about wasting time. "We're locking down the camera. No POV shot."

A formalist at heart—you'd never have seen a handheld shot in, say, a Hitchcock masterpiece—I insisted that Brenda had become too entranced by the idea of moving the camera, which was prohibitive for us without using dolly tracks or some lesser method like being pushed in a wheelchair, which wouldn't work anyway through an overgrown yard full of leaves and trash—the property, as an unoccupied rental, had gone to seed. It was fine; I found the messy yard contributive to the general morbid atmosphere we'd hoped to convey with our little tale of filial malfeasance turned murder.

"I think the horror in this will be conveyed not through something like what you're suggesting." I peered over my shades at my collaborators.

"But from the fact it'll be presented unadorned by visual flourishes. Static, centered in the frame for all to see. Think of Kubrick, and *The Shining*."

Connor, exasperated. "*The Shining* is filled with glorious Steadicam shots, bonehead. Moving shots. That's what she's saying."

Brenda, going *hah*. "And yet Kubrick over here, he doesn't want to move the fricking camera."

"*But what I'm saying*," attempting patience, my voice shaking, "is that we don't have so much as a shopping cart or a Radio Flyer wagon or, for that matter, a goddamn fucking Steadicam at our disposal."

Directing a movie, and hanging around with Kunk, had coarsened my language.

Brenda threw up her hands. "Let's try it your way."

Connor snapped into action, firing up the key light from our Lowell kit, and the 1K to be used for fill. "Maybe we could try one of those oldschool shocking, fast zooms like Kubrick used."

"As part of what we'll term coverage," as I walk away to confer with the actors. "As an experiment. Sure. If we've got film left to waste."

Brenda, rolling her eyes. "Oh-my-god."

Her boyfriend, glowering. "C'mon, bossman. Try it her way too, it sounds cool."

I thought better of vocalizing another Hitchcock bit, the part about actors being cattle who ought to know better than to open their snouts. "We'll see, Brando."

To complicate matters we were attempting to shoot day for night, the success of which tended to be predicated, ironically enough, on having a bright day with a cloudless sky. In B&W photography such as ours, one could employ a red filter to render a blue sky darker in hue, which along with stopping down the exposure changed bright sunlight into quicksilver moonlight upon the shoulders of an actor, say, digging a grave in which to plant his murdered brother.

I craned my neck around. The sky looked clear, but not a hundred-percent clear-clear, as one might say.

Slapping my hands together, loud enough for all to hear. "We're got two factors working against us today, and that's light and weather. So let's get these setups knocked out.

Connor chimed in. "The sky to the East looks good."

"So let's get this long shot and make it count."

Despite our earlier friction, Connor and Brenda both leapt into action— their grade depended on the quality of the film too, and they had their pocketbooks on the line as well as mine. Wanting to inspire cooperation and efficiency was my only concern. Not the ego boost of being the boss. No, not that. The triumphant glory that would be my film would be shared by all who made it possible. And as hard as I was trying, and as much as I cared? Surely nothing, I thought, could go irrevocably wrong.

"All set?"

Everyone, cast and crew, nodded. Jaime readied himself, holding a limp and bloodied Marcel by the shoulders, ready to drag him through the leaves.

"Roll sound."

Darren did so. "Speed!"

I nodded to Connor. I didn't need to say, 'roll camera.' His eye pressed against the eyepiece; the motor whirred into life, exposirg film.

"And—*action*."

CLOUDS CREPT IN. The low angle shot of the killer dropping a cinderblock on the head of his still-living victim loomed as the last of the day, and although we couldn't catch a break with the sky over Jaime's shoulder, after the fifth take I called "Cut" and declared that we had what we needed.

According to the industry norm, insert material—a hand inserting a key; a spade breaking the earth—would be shot later, when actors, impatient and sighing, weren't standing around. We'd gotten sufficient coverage, including a couple of indulgences and sops to other opinions; I thought we were ready to break down and all go drinking, in my case for what they called hair of the dog—with every setup, my hangover had dug itself farther in. Fighting nausea and a swimming head, no way to do good work.

Brenda clasped her hands together and pleaded the case for soldiering on. "Let's hustle up and get a few more takes of Jaime dropping the block. C'mon."

"Pardon me? I say this is a wrap."

Connor, standing with hands on hips, looking to the sky, swiveling his head around. "She's right—those puffy, pesky clouds there have been sneaking into every take." He hopped over the shallow grave containing an uncomfortable Marcel half-covered in dirt. "You can get up, LeMoy," my cinematographer said. "We're done with you."

"Yeah, sorry," I interjected. "We're wrapped with you."

Now it was Connor's turn to take umbrage at my leadership. "As Captain Queeg over there said."

Queeg—what did that mean? Some gay thing? I'd have to follow up on that.

Marcel, annoyed and spitting dirt, clambered onto his knees. "You've all been standing around for ten minutes while I've got dirt and rocks in my ass."

Shooing the actor on his way, Connor ignored Marcel's precisely stated complaints. "This time we'll put the camera in the hole, point up at Jaime this way," bending down and twisting around, "and all you'll see is that tree and a patch of clear sky behind his head—if we hurry."

The clouds, as we'd established, would spoil the dark-sky effect of the red filter, but the angle he suggested meant a complete reversal of space, what they called crossing the axis—in those days it was unusual to see one of those shots spinning 360 around actors, as in the lunch scene in *Hannah and Her Sisters*, or also in the big 'Werewolves of London' sequence from *Color of Money*. Showy and cool, maybe, but crossing the axis, in formal cinematic tradition, a no-no.

"That's not going to match worth a damn. I want the roof of the house in the background. Instead of being in the grave, we can set up over here and put Marzol on *this* side of the grave."

"[REDACTED]—honey," Brenda said. "Look at the clouds from that angle. We've already burned off an entire mag trying to get a shot that isn't going to look as good as the others." She walked off whispering with Jaime, apoplectic at being held up. "And we need to hurry," she called over her shoulder. "He's late for work."

"I'd prefer to shoot it both ways."

Connor, mocking: "As 'coverage'—yeah yeah." He went to break the setup and move the sticks down into the grave. "We're doing it this way first."

I shrieked with frustration. *"Who's the goddamn director here?"*

"Don't be a drama queen—we've only got a hundred feet left on this mag. Let's go for it."

Connor's supercilious dismissal enraged me. Starting the day hungover and fighting battle after creative battle hadn't helped. I'd had a gallon of coffee, but my head, still splitting. My limbs tingled like a foot that'd fallen asleep. I wanted to puke.

A different sort of red filter dropped over my own vision.

A pulse beat behind my eyes.

I lunged for the camera.

"No, we shoot it my way first, while we have the light. Here—*ch!*"

I stumbled, taking a bad step into a hole hidden by the deep layer of mulch we decided to leave in place as a signifier of autumn, the season of decay, in keeping with the grim tone of our piece. Over I went, forward momentum pitching me onto Connor, the set of sticks—and the precious camera, the Eclair.

An undercranked slo-mo moment; skidding toward the big truck on the icy highway. Connor, twisting his body away from me, fell over and smashed the eyepiece straight into the ground with a telltale cracking sound.

Silence and stillness, but only for a few seconds.

A chorus of concern bubbled up; leaves crashed and the rest of the crew gathered round. I squawked like a wounded duck and rolled off Connor.

Cussing up a storm, he kicked at me. "You fucking nitwit."

Brenda fell to her knees beside Connor, her concern extending only to him. "Are you all right?" Noticing the camera. "Oh—my god."

Brushing myself off. "Hey, what about me?"

"You broke it." Connor cradled the French 16mm camera, the best the department had to offer, to his body. "You broke the fucking *Eclair*. And you've probably fogged this whole roll with light leaks," his voice breaking.

Cold in my gut. "Well—we'll just have to reshoot everything."

Connor burst into tears.

The Pale Princess turned whiter than normal, her face perhaps best described as now khaki in color, a Woody Allen joke. "We're going to have to pay to fix the camera, too." Brenda came from a low-income background. She'd barely gotten over the extra expense of shooting with B&W stock, which had to be sent off to a lab all the way in Seattle *"It's all ruined."*

I rolled onto my knees and climbed to a standing position. "It's fine, it's fine," a mantra like I'd always heard my father chant during one of my mother's alcohol-related dramas. "We'll fix it. We'll fix it all."

I watched Connor inspect the Eclair—the lens came off in his hand with unnatural ease. "You're nuts," sniffling and defeated. "It's fucked."

Darren lumbered over, crunching into a bruised apple from the brown grocery sack that'd served as our craft services table. Spraying bits of fruit flesh: "So—is that thing hosed, or what?"

I offered a limp witticism, one last direction made in a high, ridiculous voice filled with false good cheer: "Okay everybody, listen up: that's a wrap for today."

No one laughed.

Besides inconveniencing the rest of the class, who'd hoped to use the Eclair themselves instead of the CP-16—a capable but far older and more abused piece of equipment—the camera needed repairs that a disappointed Hedda Gamble said would run several hundred dollars. Southeastern University, a long way off the beaten track of film schools like NYU, had a decent equipment shed, but few pieces per capita for the MACM student population to use. Not a popular move on my part, and worse, bearing out all Brenda's fiduciary fears.

Hedda, pained by the damage to the sad, broken Eclair, castigated us as we stood in her office, Connor cradling the broken Eclair. "Oh, y'all," she said. "Never move a camera while it's still on the sticks. Always remove, reset, and lock that motherfucker *down*," the first instance of such language I'd ever heard one of my teachers use. "Damn it all."

"We weren't moving the camera on the sticks." Connor, his cheeks scarlet and eyes like daggers. "He—tripped and fell on me while I was holding it."

The instructor shrugged. "Be that as it may. To Chuck's we go."

THE NEXT DAY, I rode with Hedda over to Chuck's Camera Care in West Columbia. An old guy with gray, papery skin and burst veins in his nose, Chuck peered at the damage and sucked his teeth. Grumbling and unenthusiastic, he said the damaged eyepiece could be repaired; but he'd have to call with an estimate, a number the mystery of which settled in my stomach like a bad hamburger.

"Who dropped it?" he asked with a kind of bored curiosity. "You?"

I cleared my throat. "Afraid so."

"Smooth move."

"At least we'd gotten our shots for the day."

He snorted. "Wait—you process the roll in the mag yet?"

"No."

"And this viewfinder came off in your hand?"

"Yes."

"Son—that film's fogged."

I thought I'd weep in front of this old codger and my professor. "We're hoping for the best."

"Keep hoping."

On the drive back across the river, I turned and blurted to our film professor for about the hundredth time, "I'm really like, so totally sorry." I sounded like an average, inarticulate teenaged idiot. "It really was all my fault."

"Listen." We sat at a stoplight in her rumbling diesel Volvo across the bridge from downtown, the modest skyline of Columbia sunstruck and glowing red-gold as though we'd discovered El Dorado on the banks of the mighty Congaree. Patting me on the forearm, she said, "Stuff happens on set, especially on location like that. Mistakes get made. Accidents happen—sometimes where more than the equipment gets abused. It's how you recover from the mishaps, though, that'll show the true measure of your character."

"At least nobody got hurt."

"Right—this is make-believe, but injuries do do happen on movie shoots. And as for being sorry," she added, putting the car in gear as the light changed, "apologies are lovely and for the most part necessary, but aren't a solution to anything other than salving somebody's tender hurt feelings, and sure as shit don't get shots in the can. So get over this and move on—that's what you'd have to do on a real set, where it's about finding solutions to problems on the fly, all with one eye on the clock ticking and always remembering all the money flying out the door. Sometimes, that money's the only thing filmmaking's about, which is sad, but the way of the world. So—live and learn. Now, I'm all out of clichés."

She dropped me off at my car behind the coliseum, said she'd call when the bad news about the cost of the repair came her way. Her face spoke only of kindness and sympathy to my plight. I would remain forever grateful for Hedda's understanding.

❊

ONCE THE NEWS swept through the classroom of filmmakers, however, Freddie Baumbach appeared ready to kick my ass. "You've fucked everybody, shithead."

"Not like I did it on purpose—an accident."

"One that would never have happened on *my* set."

"Oh, get over yourself," Connor said in my defense. "It was just as much my fault."

I caught his eye. A tiny shrug of loyalty to the team, I supposed.

Almost everybody in Hedda's auditorium-style classroom of curving tables and swivel seats seemed to hate and deride me but Opal, whose documentary on the Columbia punk rock scene, such as it was, required a rougher edge to the images. "I didn't want to use the Eclair at a place like Slim Lupo's anyway," the Old Market's longtime grungy rock club where she planned to shoot a band called Choking Hazard that weekend, with a notorious frontman named Mucky Turnbull, she explained, who was known for antics that bordered on the scatological. "The CP'll be fine, so long as I wrap it in plastic."

How sweet, I thought, at one of the ostensible rivals downplaying my foolishness.

Contrite, I glanced around at a constellation of sour faces. "I deserve everyone's ire."

Opal, offering a succinct version of Hedda's speech in the car. "Shit happens."

"Thank you."

She came over and gave me a quick hug.

Freddie mimed a gagging motion. "You guys make me want to fucking hurl."

Opal, looking more embarrassed than me, sat back down in her seat. "Suck shit, you yuppie cunt," more of a mumble than an outright threat. "He didn't mean to do it."

"For heaven's sake," our instructor pled. "Decorum, please."

"Cunts," Opal repeated, as though the shock value of hearing it the first time hadn't been enough for Hedda Gamble, who again shushed.

Opal, a big personality in a small package. She knew how to get noticed. I wondered what her film would be like. Better than endlessly speculating if our shots on the last mag, due back from the lab in a couple of days, would be usable.

A quick run up the interstate to Edgewater County had become necessary.

Dad's pen went *scratch-scratch* in his checkbook; the money for which I asked was of course no problem, he said, so long as there'd be a tangible result to show for it.

"Just bring home an A on your movie, my boy. Let's make your Mom proud."

"We'll have ourselves not only a good grade, but a real film."

"You think you can get somebody to put it out after you're done?"

"Not like a movie anyone would go and pay to see—it's just a short. Maybe festivals, where important folks might see it."

He smiled and patted me on the arm. "I bet one day you'll make a million dollars."

"Let's not worry about that part."

"At this rate, I'd better be worried a little bit." He slid the check across the kitchen table. I noticed him sitting not in his usual chair, but the one where my mother used to take her coffee, sweet and almost white with cream, and smoke the first of her morning cigarettes. "Y'all would do well not to break any more cameras."

I promised we wouldn't.

Being back home felt strange, but in the time since my mom died—I still couldn't believe it; still cried into my pillow at night, missing her but telling myself I was grown now and didn't need her anymore anyway—I had called my dad often. I worried about him being lonely.

Happy memories kept me company: I remembered riding around with him in his pickup truck, taking trash out to the dump or going to the grocery store or taking Rufus, our black lab who died last year, over to the Mickey D's on Saturday mornings for the dog's weekly sausage-biscuit treat, all the while regaling my good-old boy dad with tidbits of Hollywood news gleaned from *Variety* and the Sunday *New York Times*—what filmmaker was making what. How much money thus and such made at the box office the previous weekend. How much this or that film meant to me. How high my anticipatory vibration for my own coming celluloid epics.

He must have been bored out of his mind, or perhaps thought me mad. At least he pretended to care.

One afternoon years ago we'd driven over to The Dixiana to see if my mother was inside yet again drinking away her life, and I had listened to my father talking with that crusty codger Rabbit Pettus, both men sitting at a weathered bench out front of the honkytonk covered in pen-and-penknife graffiti, cigarette burns, and old gum.

"My boy loves them picture shows better than about anyone I ever seen." My father, cocking a thumb across the green at the Palmetto Grande, the church at which I'd had first cinematic communion. "Man, I tell ya what."

I remember how Rabbit, a white-headed giant dressed in a flannel shirt and work pants, but who some people said had more money than he knew what to do with, squinted down at me. "Picture shows?"

"The movies," I said, correcting him. I had been twelve at the time.

He spat tobacco juice off the porch onto the sidewalk. "Yeah, we go and look at them things. Pictures talking to you, telling you what to think. Telling you *how* to think. Lord, don't let nobody do that to you."

At that young age, I had no idea what he meant. Thought him an old drunk talking gibberish. Much later, in my Media Studies class with its discussion of Marshall McLuhan and his theories, the professor, a young guy named Cullen Margrave, would remind me of Rabbit's words.

But at the time, I had other reasons for despising that old redneck man and his honkytonk than disparaging my beloved movies—my mother seemed to love being at the bar more than her own home. I wished the place would burn down, or maybe somebody would fly a plane into it or some other ridiculously destructive notion that no normal person ought to ever conjure in their mind.

WHILE MY FATHER made a fresh pot of coffee, I'd gone over into the laundry alcove to throw a load of black T-shirts, jeans, and briefs into a dusty washing machine that seemed to have been little used since my mom's passing.

"So, y'all bout done with it?" Dad asked, dumping Eight O'Clock brand coffee into his machine.

"With what?"

"Your movie, son."

I laughed at my dear sweet old father's lack of context and knowledge about the process. "It won't be done until spring. We'll get principal photography in the can next week, have a rough cut together by the holiday break. In the spring we'll do the fine edit, sound mixing, music—the whole bit."

"Dang. No wonder it takes so long."

"And costs so much."

"I hope you got enough son. Your mother's funeral expenses—we wa'n't expecting all that."

"Needless to say."

"No."

Dad said his stocks weren't doing well, but he didn't know anything yet, not until the next month: October of 87, and the mini-crash. He would go on in the 1990s to build it all back up, though he didn't live long enough to enjoy his money. I'm not sure he ever had fun again. Probably didn't have much when she was alive, either. "I had took good insurance took out on her, of course. But still."

The matter of fact statement about the cost of mother's final expenses stabbed me in the gut, a blunt reminder of her absence, both before and after her death.

I steadied myself on the edge of the washer in which she'd cleaned my clothes, an aging Whirlpool we'd had—she'd had—for as long as I could remember. I looked through the open louver doors at my father, sitting red-eyed at the kitchen table watching the coffee drip, legs crossed and thin gray hair at his temples making him look more like my grandfather than father.

"You okay, Daddy?"

"Yes," he said, emphatic. "All set."

"Are you sure?"

He smacked his lips a few times before blurting out the truth: "Lord, but I sure do miss her. I keep a Bible by the bed, and a picture of us on top of it, but sometimes it hurts worse to look at it than not. Makes me just start bawling."

"Do you?" I dumped in a scoopful of Tide and knocked the lid closed with a clangorous thud. I wrenched the dial around to the Ultra Clean setting. "I mean—really."

"Do I what?"

"Miss her."

His features hardened into stone. He asked what kind of a question this was.

"Mom wasn't much of a prize. Was she?"

My father twitched and his neck literally reddened behind jug ears. The hushed tone of an assassin: "Boy, if you ever say some shit like that again, *I'll knock your smart ass six blocks over onto queer street.*"

I hadn't heard Dad speak with such gravity since the time I jerked away from him in the mall parking lot when I was four years old, running right out into the fire lane in front of an old lady in a Lincoln Town Car who'd had to jam on her brakes with a squeal. I can remember the sound as though I'd only heard it yesterday, as well as the feeling of his hard, flat palm spanking my bottom and yelling.

"I'm sorry," in a tiny voice. "I didn't mean it like it sounded."

"Good. Because if you did, I think I'd slap the white off your teeth." The second violent threat in the last 30 seconds. "You hear me?"

"Yeah. Okay."

"Okay what?"

Now diminished in a manner difficult to bear, I mumbled, "I meant 'Yes, sir.'"

"That's more like it." He picked up the check from the placemat where I'd once taken my meals. "Now put your school money in your pocket before you forget it. And use it like you got some sense."

I sat down, flung longish hair out of my eyes. "I just get angry at her sometimes."

He cleared his throat. And again.

"Like, really mad."

"You don't think I get mad about it all, too?" My father crumbled like stale crackers. "Mercy on her soul."

My mother—his wife of twenty-six years—had died. The weight of it crashed down on us both.

He wept.

I wept.

Howling gales of weeping.

Two men, what remained of the immediate [REDACTED] family, gradually stopped boohooing like the survivors of a tragedy, which of course we were.

Afterwards, we got on with the day without talking about her again. Both of us felt lighter, a spring in our step. He asked me if I wanted to start going through her things, help him start cleaning out a few closets. I said we'd do it over Christmas break. He smiled and hugged me. Healing, underway.

A part from prosaic classroom assignments, worries about the film, and ushering shifts at the multiplex, I soon suffered another task at hand: I'd been pressed by Camille—oh, would that I be pressed by her in a literal way!—into helping with the planning for Kunk's upcoming weekend birthday bash. A big one—forty. I had a hard time imagining turning thirty. A lifetime away, such a milestone.

Backpack laden, my fantasy girl and I trudged up concrete stairs from the below-ground classroom level in the Coliseum to emerge into blinding sunlight; we became squinty. Camille's gorgeous eyes and angelic face tended to cloud my vision whatever the lighting scheme.

Fumbling in her purse for shades: "We owe him a good time—a man only turns forty once, after all." Camille's glowing smile faltered. "My boyfriend's about to be forty."

"Levon and your dad must have a lot to talk about."

"Hush. Not funny."

"Let me see." I drummed my fingertips together in front of my face. "What would a guy like Kunk want out of a surprise birthday party?"

"He said he wants to really celebrate—to do this one right."

Nodding, I cringed at the thought of the other women with whom Kunk had been dallying. "A man of appetites."

"He said you're only as old as how hard you can party. Or something like that."

Even with as much beer as I'd been downing, Kunk, without breaking a sweat, could still easily drink me sideways and seasick.

As if reading my thoughts, she said, "I worry sometimes."

"About what?"

"How much he parties."

"Dude like Kunk's got a liver like inch-thick steel on a battleship hull. He's fine."

"I see you've heard that line as well."

"Eh, fuck it," in a decent enough Kunk imitation. I shrugged and rolled my eyes. "What what *what.*"

She laughed. Said I had him down cold.

"Why do you think he drinks?" I asked in my own voice.

Her tone changed. "For one thing, I think his script is getting him down."

"That'll do it. What's the hangup?"

Camille Grahl sighed away into the middle distance, the afternoon sunlight shaded by a high overhanging roof supported by the columns of the arena. With her face half in shadow—a striking image, a striking woman—I wished I had my Canon AE-1 on hand to capture the moment. "He's writing. But I also keep hearing him cussing and ripping pages out of the Selectric."

"The clichéd scene of the stuck writer. As Max says, failure's part of the process."

"Tell Levon that."

"Sounds like y'all are pretty much living together now."

"Pretty much. We've been together six months, now."

"Wow—that's awesome."

I couldn't imagine Kunk, so self assured and cool, having one whit of difficulty—denial on my part, I supposed, despite having reports from both Camille and the subject himself. "His script, it'll come together. Hell, half of what I turned in for Max I wrote the night before. If not the same morning," which in a few cases had been true enough.

"No, you didn't—really?"

Far from exaggeration, Last Minute Larry is what I've always been, a quality ill-suited to a complex foray like filmmaking, the success of which being predicated upon meticulous planning. "Not a good habit to cultivate."

Her frustration bubbled over. "Why's everything come so easy for you smarty-pants guys?"

Ridiculous—I couldn't even make my movie without breaking the equipment. Quiet truth like a tickle at the back of my throat: "None of this comes easy for me."

"I think this party should be a boy's night out. Maybe that's what he needs."

"Don't we do enough of that already?"

"Think of something extra fun and different to do. *Within reason,*" she said, wagging a finger. "Know what I mean?"

"Of course, maiden." I said I'd call him when I got home, work out the details, get together a posse of scriptwriters and quote-unquote destroy this podunk burg. Maybe it'd be a sort-of working party, if Kunk wished to make it so, and we could bust his writer's block with our mutual mental kung-fu. "Just make sure you've got strong coffee for the morning after."

She beamed me with gratitude. Gave me a quick peck on the cheek. "You're the best."

Flooding with hormones at the brief touch of her lips, I didn't want to say goodbye to Camille, not yet. "What lily pad you off to now?"

"Self-paced Astronomy," groaning. "I'm falling behind already."

I proclaimed my own fear about taking any non-major class that depended on personal engagement and motivation, and wished her luck. Stopping myself from calling her *gorgeous* or *angel* or some other term of endearment, I watched her walk away with golden hair bouncing, a petite, voluptuous vision in chunky heels and tight jeans.

I swooned.

I made myself stop swooning, and castigated myself for pining after Kunk's girl with such urgency. *She's counting on you to make him happy, you big jerk—do as the queen commands.*

The first indication I got that Neill had returned home from Fall Dead Tour—yes, he had blown off a week's worth of classes to follow the band around the northeast; after Garcia's illness the previous year, in which the revered pothead guitarist had nearly died, my roommate said he'd take any risk to see as many shows as he could—came when I entered the living room after a late shift at the cinemas greeted by a wall of odor, like a muddy sheepdog had been hosed down and left to air-dry.

I noted a pair of filthy, crusty, scabby human feet sticking out from under a dingy Guatemalan striped blanket. Gagging in the back of my throat, I said, "The peripatetic Neill, back from never-neverland."

No response.

I poked at the lump under the blanket with the toe of my black penny loafer, part of my usher outfit of black slacks, white button-down shirt and black tie like one of those Mormon kids on the bikes. My roommate, an enormous lump under the blanket, looked as though he'd gained weight.

A rumbling came from beneath the colorful fabric. A bearded moon-face rose over the blanket—a scraggly man in his 40s. Not my roommate at all.

Bloodshot eyes bugged out at me. "Who the fuck are you? The heat?"

Oh, only the other tenant, stranger. "Why, I'm Nigel, Neill's gentleman valet. And you, good sir?"

"Name's Country Gravy," again covering his face. "Now have a heart and lemme sleep, wisely."

About that time Neill breezed through the back door, wrestling a red cooler covered in Dead stickers—dancing bears, rose-festooned skulls, swirling tie-dye like I imagined that Neill saw every time he closed his eyes—into our cluttered and dirty kitchen.

"Comrade." Happy as could be, Neill, slapping me on the back. "I have returned."

I whispered. "What's the deal with sleeping beauty over here?"

Neill, bobbing his shaggy, greasy hair and peeking over my shoulder. "It's all good—that's Country. I gave him a ride down from Providence. He asked if he could crash for a night—or two—so I said, shit yeah, dude."

"Wonderful."

"See—I figured you wouldn't mind. You're so busy these days, you're barely here anyway."

Ironic, coming from a traveling man such as Neill.

I grumbled, but said okay; indeed, I had quite an enormous amount of work ahead, including more shifts at the suburban shoebox multiplex grinding out its weekly mainstream movie entertainments, as well as assembling a rough edit of our film, at least the shots we had so far. I wouldn't be home much for the next few days.

It occurred to me: perhaps this Country Gravy, if that was his name, represented Neill's version of Kunk—an elder, a veteran, a grateful mentor to whom my roommate now gave back by providing shelter. As I'd be repaying Kunk's tutelage in matters streetwise by throwing him his birthday party.

"Help me with this shit, bro."

After he flipped on the floodlights, I followed Neill out back. The yard, weed-strewn and tiny. We never went out here.

I helped him dump out coolers, and put up his tent to air it out.

Manhandling the yellow fabric and spindly aluminum poles, dragging it over an old clothes line covered in black yard-mold, I gagged anew. "What a stench."

Neill, amused. "Yeah—had a li'l accident in there a couple nights ago."

Mysterious, but I bade him to spare the details.

Neill did a fair share of camping on Dead tour, a way for poor hippies who didn't work, I guessed, to afford all the traveling. He had one of those pop-up VW microbuses, all covered with stickers, in which he could live while on the road.

I couldn't fathom the risks these people seemed to take. For all the drugs my roommate did—the hippie one: weed, shrooms, acid, but no white powders—I wondered how safe it could be out on the open roads for an unrepentant, obvious Deadhead in Reagan-Bush America. Fish in a barrel.

I supposed therein lay much of the Dead's appeal to a kid my age, who, like Neill, missed out on the heady 1960s: a way to become unstuck in time, follow the circus, experience a little danger.

I'd have gone and checked out one of the shows myself, but despite adapting by necessity to tolerate hissy bootleg recordings of the Grateful Dead spinning on the stereo night and day, more tapes coming every time the postman dropped off another padded mailer—some kind of bootlegging ring, I surmised, in which Neill had gotten mixed up—I simply never dug the music. After living in such an environment I'd learned to tune out the aimless long noodling jams, the countryish ballads and polkas. A strange, strange act, with even stranger fans. Obsessive.

But I figured one could say the same about me, with all my VHS movies taped off cable, three to a tape on the six-hour slow speed, back when I was a kid with limited resources. The old film magazines. The soundtrack albums. The posters—the ridiculous poster collection. A box of my old ticket stubs, going back to *Star Wars* ten years before. Yeah. Deadheads like Neill didn't have anything on me in the obsession department.

IN THE MORNING, rested but still cranky, Country Gravy scarfed down three barbecue sandwiches from some local joint Neill knew about, showered for half an hour, stopped up the toilet, smoked an enormous joint about half a pack of Marlboros, after which he took another endless nap persisting through the many hours I'd be gone that day.

The next day Neill cajoled our guest into getting his shit together and motivating over to the Greyhound station, where this tour buddy would be off to Delray Beach, either the cat's home base when not on Dead tour, or else another crash pad. I didn't ask.

After Gravy had agreed it was time to go, now commenced a marathon session of bong hits that left the house cloudy and reeking. Forty-odd minutes later the aging hippy, older than Kunk, finally said with a yawn and a stretch, "Reckon I guess it's time to think about wondering if it ain't time to start getting onto moving on down the road, like." Or stoned verbiage to that effect.

Later, I'd learn that Country Gravy left a gift behind: a Murine bottle, one containing much more than eyedrops. Neill, reverent: "What a fucking dude, dude. Just laid it on me."

"His eyedrops?"

He whispered, awestruck: "It's liquid, bro."

"Liquid what?"

Neill, remembering my level of drug naiveté. "It's doses."

"'Doses'?"

"Acid, dude. Alice D. Millionaire. Vitamin A. Pure, clean and awesome." Neill gazed at the small bottle in his hairy, cupped hand. "Country: what an awesome dude. He's a real light-worker—he's true family."

Whatever all that meant.

In any case, I always heard LSD came on little pieces of paper. That's what a couple of the other ushers at the Enemas, a staff term of endearment for the Cinemas at the mall, took one night when we featured *Pink Floyd The Wall* on at the midnight movies. One of them had lost his shit and come running out of there during a particularly intense sequence of psychological horror. Another area in which I felt like a neophyte—how was this crap fun, exactly?

I considered the legal ramifications of having heavy drugs in the house. "Is that a lot? Of—doses?"

He tapped the bottle, held it up to the sunlight coming into the living room. "Naw, not so much. A good many trips, though. To be sure." He looked at me. "You want to try some?"

Dry, I arched a disapproving eyebrow. "Dude, I've got class in an hour."

"Ah," he said, grim. "Yeah. Class."

I realized I hadn't mentioned anything about Kunk's big birthday party, so I filled in Neill on the details—how I wanted to start here at the house, maybe take everyone out for drinks and dinner, end up back at Kunk's so we'd be able to walk with impunity, shitfaced, on an epic bar crawl of the Old Market. That I ought to get some decent bourbon for him as my personal gift. And so on.

"How old's he gonna be?"

"Forty—you believe that shit?"

"Damn. That's older than Country."

"I really don't know how to entertain the thought of being—" I started to say *a grown man like Kunk*, but realized how much less of a man it might make me sound. "Someone like him."

"Whatcha mean?"

"Someone—who's been around."

Without hesitation Neill said, "Y'all should totally dose, dude. Think about it—he was our age back in the 60s. And a fucking musician? He probably did more acid than I ever thought about. *Fuck,*" an emphatic epithet like a grace note. Neill often spoke of wishing to get ahold of a Doc Brown DeLorean and going back to have communion with what he termed 'primal Dead,' whatever that meant, and get some real 60s acid. "Suddenly I want to pick that boy's brain."

"Kunk did say some of the best times of his life were spent on acid, jamming all night with jazz cats."

"See?" Neill extended his forearm, with every little hair standing up. "You guys gotta trip."

"Something to consider."

"It's like, cosmic that Country Gravy left *these drugs* behind when he did. There's no question what we need to do. No doubt."

At that moment, I didn't give Neill's suggestion any credence. I nodded yeah-yeah, and made to leave for class.

Until I talked to Kunk, that is. After I announced that Camille had entrusted me to help him start the next decade of his life, as well as honor all the many adventures that had come before, he lit up with pleasure and affection, grabbing me in a bear hug. At the moment I mentioned Neill's 'liquid,' however, my mentor hooted, and a particular train left the station: The decision about what happened at Kunk's party, I found, would no longer be mine to make. Here, a man in control of his destiny—one of Kunk's qualities I admired the most.

A

t four on the afternoon of Kunk's birthday, I sat in my living room watching with trepidation as Neill placed drops of LSD onto a plateful of Dixie Crystals sugar cubes—"That's fucking classic, man," Kunk exclaimed in delight—before passing them out to the participants.

The players: Connor, who'd tripped before and liked the experience enough to decide to join our party, and two other guys from Mass Comm I'd invited—the estimable Hoyt Bollard and my other lead actor Marcel LeMoy, both of whom were taking the feature screenplay class alongside Kunk. He'd christened them the Oy Boys. A real crew of heavy hitters.

Legend had it the Oy Boys had dropped acid the night they performed their own winning Ten-Scene in the section of 521 the semester before my own, which made our own boozing sound like chickenfeed. Their project, a backstage comedy-drama about a troupe of actors in the *13th Week* of a stage show, in which relationships form and dissolve as they struggle to maintain their enthusiasm for the material, apparently killed with jokes and what Max called "trenchant subtext about the inherent phoniness of show business." Their group's work had been impressive enough that prior to beginning our own Ten-Scene, the Prof had suggested Kunk and I both read this impressive, winning script. It'd been tight, amusing, and in the end, even touching. The best gift our instructor could have given us—a hint at how high the bar.

We cracked beers and contemplated our cubes. Kunk checked his watch. "So this is the real deal?"

Neill, already pie-eyed and hippy-happy: "It's clean and kind as hell. Y'all are gonna be flying high. Bank on it."

"I knew this one Deadhead?" Kunk, nodding in sage remembrance. "Dude had some of the original shit, actual Blue Sunshine. That was the best LSD I ever had. I jammed so long that night," splaying open calloused fingertips, "my digits bled."

"Orange Sunshine," Neill corrected. "Not blue."

"Yeah, Kunk—*Blue Sunshine* is an exploitation film." I'd never seen the movie, but I had a poster of it in a box of old water damaged one-sheets I'd gotten off Mr. Sortwell, the owner of the Palmetto Grande theater back home in Tillman Falls. "Some low budget crap about murderous hippies."

"I dunno, man. Dude said it came from the lab where that guy who discovered it worked."

Neill, loading a glass pipe with stinky, sticky pot. "Zardoz Laboratories."

Idiots. I sputtered, "*Zardoz* is that John Boorman sci-fi movie with Sean Connery."

"Sandoz—he means Sandoz." Marcel, a rich kid who had been educated in boarding schools, continued in his precise manner of speaking, "I recently read a *Rolling Stone* article that described the whole affair, Dr. Hofmann and his famous—or infamous—bike ride home the day he first synthesized the compound. In any case, however, Owsley Stanley made all the Orange Sunshine."

"Enough of this history-lesson badinage." Kunk, working his knowing eyebrows for all they were worth, popped the cube into his mouth. "The only time is now."

Uncertainty flooded into me. Heavy hearts-blood thudded in my veins. But Kunk had done it, so… I had to join in.

The sugar cube, an incongruously explosive taste on my tongue alongside the cold longneck Budweisers we quaffed, two cases worth chilling in a fridge otherwise cleaned out to make room for the beer. Sweet and bitter, mixed together. The drugs. I tried not to panic at the decision I'd made.

Neill smiled and squeezed what was left in the Murine bottle into his mouth—a veritable, literal *glurt*. "That's how it's done."

"Christ H. Jesus." Kunk, laughing. "You kids are crazy."

Hoyt, in a solid imitation of Chong from the iconic *Up in Smoke* car scene: "Dude, I hope you don't got anything to do for like, the next three days."

Neill, frowning and dismissive. "I just got back from Dead tour. My toleration is like, fucking intolerable."

"'Tolerance'," I corrected.

"Whatever, Hollywood," puffing his pipe and passing it around. "Here we go."

UPON REFLECTION I ingested too great, or perhaps too grateful, a dose; after later looking into the matter, I better understood that the set and setting had not been ideal for a neophyte explorer of cosmic inner space.

Sure, I felt comfortable with all the players involved. High spirits. A party. But I had too much baggage—my mother's death, my expectations, my ambition, my lack of self-confidence camouflaged by knowledge tinged with arrogance—simmering on the stove.

Baggage. Simmering. A mixed metaphor, as Max would point out.

The day before, I'd asked Neill what to expect from the experience, and had also done some reading; hallucinations as described in the drug literature sounded scary, but my roommate assured me that such 'heady visuals' were to transport me on a literal trip, as he put it, through inner, and depending on what level of mysticism one subscribed to, perhaps outer space as well.

"My mind definitely left my body, once," Neill had explained. "It was at Cal Expo during a smoking hot 'Truckin' into 'Nobody's Fault But Mine'," which meant nothing to me.

I didn't get why all this hallucinating while listening to music passed the so-what test. "It's just songs, isn't it? What's the big deal."

He seemed less offended than piteous about my ignorance. "That night I coulda sworn Jerry looked right into my soul, man." Neill patted me on the shoulder, a piteous gesture. "If I gotta explain, you wouldn't understand."

Dissatisfied, I fretted and wondered aloud if I shouldn't stay sober to manage the evening's activities.

Neill, aghast, went *nah-nah-nah*. "When we get into this, I'll throw on some old school tapes. See if we can get you on the bus. I could use a new tour buddy. It'll all make sense then, [REDACTED]. You'll see."

Did I want to become a hippie? If so, from what would I be changing? I didn't think I had a persona to exchange.

Did I want Jerry—whoever the hell that was—looking into my soul?

Did I want my mind to leave my body?

Soon enough, I realized I wouldn't have any choice in the matter.

ESCAPE CALLED OUT TO ME.

From Kunk's apartment to which we'd journeyed before the intensity of the trip had kicked in.

From inside my head.

From myself.

From these crazy drugs, man. Getting stoned on weed a couple of times had seemed intense. But this acid—God help me!

A torrent of crying had started while I stood trying to pee in Kunk's bathroom. Despite a bladder bursting with cheap beer, I had been unable to make a stream. Instead, I stared at my own face in the mirror, in which not only did I see my mother's eyes looking back at me, but also a werewolf and a melting skeleton like at the end of *Raiders of the Lost Ark* and finally back, briefly, to my own tortured, teeth-gritted countenance rippling and changing from second to second.

Everyone else had seemed like they were having the time of their lives —Hoyt and Marcel at one point started wrestling like little kids in the front yard, the result being that Hoyt chipped a tooth on the curb, precipitating a brief, bleeding, laughing and tripping non-crisis. We'd listened to music—first a Dead tape to mollify Neill, then a Coltrane record called *Live in Japan*, a screaming wailing bizarre freeform jazz recordings that'd been deeply unnerving to all of us. Hoyt told stories about getting fucked up back when he was in the peacetime Army, stationed over in Germany. Neill told crazy Dead tour tales.

We drank. Talked about going down the hill to McHaffie's or some other bar, but never managed to leave the living room. Kunk, playing guitar. Marcel started tossing cards into a hat, which got us all laughing with much greater mirth than the situation deserved.

Everything got stranger. Grew quiet. Kunk and I kept looking at each other. I swore I could hear his voice inside my head. I started sweating.

Hoyt began flipping through the channels on the TV. This made Neill angry, precipitating a speech about mind control and Reagan and a government that'd used the War on Drugs to chip away at civil liberties, an idea with which no one had any serious disagreement. At that point, I had made the mistake of realizing I needed to trip my way into the bathroom.

"[REDACTED]'s having a moment," Connor announced after I came back out, eyes swollen and face soaking with tears. "Son, you look whiter than my great-granddaddy's KKK robe."

Struggling, sucking wind, trying and failing not to boohoo in front of them. My lips and tongue, rubbery and swollen-feeling, at last formed words. "I can't piss."

"Oh, my," Connor said. "Plugged up?"

"I don't know. Also, I can't stop crying."

My film partner screamed with laughter, as did Marcel. Merriment spread to Hoyt and Kunk. Everyone laughing at a joke I didn't get.

"Champ, just relax, stop thinking about it."

Neill, nodding. "Your body's signals are crossed. You know you need to pee, but it's coming out of your eyes instead." Ominous. "I've seen this before."

Kunk went in the bedroom, he said, to change his shirt. The rest of us sat looking at one another, smiles playing around everyone's lips but my own; Kunk seemed to be gone an inordinate amount of time.

My cranium, pulsing with hot, salty water that continued to run down my cheeks. Droplets fell like Neill's liquid LSD had earlier onto the cubes of sugar. I kept seeing my mom's face—not drunk, but from when I was little. Thought how I wanted to show her my movies one day. Thought of how I'd never see her again.

I began sobbing. Openly.

Nobody laughed this time. "Damn, dude," Hoyt said. "Pull it together."

I did.

For a moment.

The record ended. The sound of the tone arm lifting up and moving across into its cradle seemed louder to me than the music had. I tried wiping clammy palms on my jeans. I licked my lips. My mouth felt dry, but I was afraid to drink.

What if everything—even the air—was filled with LSD?

Hoyt, a beanpole with a mane of wild curly black hair and an Adam's apple that looked big—in that moment, too big—grinned at me with his broken incisor. His face turned into that of a dragon with bloody fangs breathing green smoke.

The dragon, with laughing malevolence. "You're freaking out—aren't you."

"Indeed," Marcel added, "I believe he is."

Neill, belching, cracked a fresh beer. "You gonna be okay, *bruh*. Keep your feet on the ground, but keep reaching for the stars."

Kunk came busting out of the bedroom in a loud Hawaiian shirt. "Time to go get some pussy, boys—oh." He lurched over and stared with those glimmering steel-blue eyes. "You're still all fucked up? *What gives.*"

Self-consciousness.

PANIC.

I sprang from the couch and bolted out of the creaking screen door, down the steps and onto the sidewalk of a neighborhood much closer to the center of campus action than mine with groups of students walked in clusters to and from the Old Market down the hill.

Now what? I couldn't mingle with these knots of alien bipeds, not with their gangly limbs and bulbous heads all turning to look at me like they'd all stepped out of the mothership at the end of *CE3K.*

Kunk appeared on his front porch. "Champ," he called, startling the shit out of me. "Con-man said you couldn't take a squirt."

A passing group of sorority girls, dolled up for a night out, snorted and snickered. "Do you have to tinkle-winkle, sweetie-pie?" one of them sang-spoke to gales of amused, distaff derision. "Well, you just go and tinkle, then."

Before I could respond, the girls sprouted fairy wings out of their Greek-lettered sweatshirts and fluttered on their way, chanting tinkle-winkle-winkle all the way down the hill to the Old Market. In their wake I saw sparkling fairy dust and dandelion fluff dancing in the air like wet snowflakes.

I rubbed my swollen eyes. *Fuck these drugs, man. Next time, just say no.*

Which made me panic even more.

Stricken and confused, I ran straight for a nearby railroad crossing and cut onto the rail line. I planned to walk until ending up wherever the train tracks reached their terminus.Where the tracks led, no one could say.

Such mystery sounded comforting to me—much as it could, what with the ties rippling and undulating like the planks of a pier disintegrating into a roiling black sea that fell away on all sides, as well the pressure turning to pain in my groin. I walked.

ut Kunk, calling after me, had followed onto the elevated railroad tracks running across the street from his apartment, a nearby line of demarcation between the university neighborhood and the Old Market commercial district. "[REDACTED], ya freaking nut. Slow down."

Sweating like a guilty bastard—but guilty of what?—I picked up the pace. Words I tried to shout over my shoulder came instead as rasping, papery wisps of language. "Leave me alone."

He pleaded for me to slow down. I tried to lose him.

My scalp pulsating, light bent around my peripheral vision into prismatic, even kaleidoscopic displays, and as the railroad tracks curved around past Modjeska Simkins Park and the campus area beyond, every surface vibrated with a discrete, crackling energy. The railway ahead stretched and writhed like a bronzed striped serpent slithering on flopping, rubbery legs like the pair I had to cajole to keep moving. A floating blob of protoplasm, I felt as a sea creature struggling to take its first slimy steps onto a beach.

Except no beach existed, no sea from which to emerge, only my real legs and the railroad tracks and the traffic streaming below me on Bloomwood Street, headlamps and taillights leaving trails like fireworks or streaking meteors. And close behind, a man I hoped to impress with my own maturity and acumen.

He couldn't see me like this.

He'd already seen me like this.

Terror.

Cool and weird at first, this trip, but as the hours passed, my head had filled with terrible thoughts. Self-recrimination over being an asshole to my mother for so long. Over her being an asshole to me, but maybe I deserved it for being so self-absorbed. Despair over Nicole breaking it off with me back in high school. Over missing my chance with Camille. Over damaging the Eclair. Over stealing a candy bar from the convenience store around the corner from my house when I was eight.

Over a niggling, persistent voice that liked to whisper:

Boy, you ain't never gonna go to Hollywood and make movies—you're from Edgewater County. Your uneducated, linthead forebears did not intend nor anticipate for you to be anything more than what you are, an ordinary 'beau' from out in the South Carolina sticks. You ain't nothing. You can't even keep from breaking the goddamn camera, you boneheaded idiot.

Kunk, sucking wind, finally caught up. "Champ, I'm an old man— remember? Stop, you freak."

"I need to be alone."

"What, ya gonna rub one out?"

I had no idea what he was talking about. "I'm fucked up. I may need to go to a hospital."

"Forget it, man." Arms outstretched to the heavens, he griped about his lungs. Despite this apparent condition, he sparked up an ever present smoke and let it dangle from his lips as we went on walking. "This too shall pass."

From our elevated position on the tracks, an opening in the trees gave us a view of the campus skyline, the high rise dorms and student union on a high hill like you'd find in downtown San Francisco. Beyond lay the capitol dome, and the skyscrapers—at twenty stories, the best we could do —of our downtown and its Main Street.

"Good evening, Columbia." Kunk hooted and whooped. "This here's the night of nights."

I flopped a leaden arm and squawked with fear about how I'd become acutely aware of my status as an animated meat-covered skeleton stuck by unseen forces like gravity onto a stony orb spinning through an endless and infinite space mostly devoid of matter, a sensation seeming not only new, but bizarre and untenable. I considered my place in the cosmos spinning up and away from me. I peered skyward, but thanks to light pollution could see no stars.

How high would I get? Where was the ceiling?

What was 'high'?

Who was I?

Still enduring a painful bladder, I had a hard time fixing my gaze on any one object for long—spinning swirling trails across my vision, a vortex of encroaching madness. I murmured again how I thought I might be dying. "I'm finished. I'm fucking gone, you understand?"

"'Gone'? Yeah, me too. This Zardoz is some heavy shit. I keep seeing cartoon characters jumping out of the tracks up ahead, and rainbows streaming outta the capitol dome. Shit's the real deal."

"I'm not talking about these drugs—I'm dropping out. I'm going back *home*."

That seemed to focus him. "All right. Stop right here."

"It's been decided."

"What, what, *what*?"

I kept walking. Faster.

"Brotherman—what the fuck ya talking about?" The traffic noise from Bloomwood receding with every step farther along the tracks into the park, Kunk grabbed my elbow. "What's all this horseshit about quitting?"

"You heard me. I'm done."

Kunk demanded a better answer. "Done? Forget about it. Champ—this stuff lasts all night." He stifled one of the omnipresent giggles. "We just need to pound more brews. Smoke some more of that hippie's grass. Take the edge off."

"I'm not talking about the acid." Though the idea of being able to stop all this seemed a sound one. "I said I was quitting school."

Further demands for clarification.

"I don't—it's not—I can't." I flailed my arms around at the material world. "It makes no sense anymore."

"This is news?" Kunk, pleading for me to stand still. "World's a fucked up place. Welcome to it."

"You don't understand. I'm not gonna be able to finish the movie. I'm not gonna be able to write any screenplays or have a girlfriend or ever know who my *mother* really was, and I'm not able to process my own feelings anymore, and what is this, what is all this bullshit—?"

Sobbing anew, I choked off and fell to my knees on the rough ties. Gravel dug into my kneecaps. I could barely feel it.

I felt a hand on my shoulder. Kunk's troubled eyes floated above me, two dilated spinning discs. "Champ—stand up."

I did as he asked. But for my heart pounding hard enough to make my chest hurt, I calmed down.

"Now."

"I'm dying. That's all this is."

Kunk snorted and put his arm around me. "Kid, we're all dying. We're fucking dying from the moment we're born. Get used to it."

"Helluva way to look at things."

Gentle as a meticulous empathetic caregiver ministering to a helpless hospice patient, he righted me and we again began walking. "It is what it is."

STILL TRIPPING HARD, yet my thoughts felt more ordered. I now perceived Kunk and myself as Zen monks strolling in peaceful discussion about the implacable nature of the universe; the careful steps we took over the ties and gravel provoked a stillness of spirit. My respiration slowed. The sweats dried up. I still had to pee, but somehow it didn't matter as much.

I tried again to describe my troubles. "Nothing's coming out perfect— nothing's going right. And I feel haunted."

"That little piece of redneck chicken still fucking with your head?"

My eyestalks twisted around and peered into his. "Excuse me?"

"The girlfriend from back in podunk."

"Nicole? A high school thing. Meaningless."

"Ancient history?"

"Might as well be. I meant my mom, actually."

"Like I told you before, I'm here for ya."

"It's just like it—it all sunk in on me. All at once."

"That's grief for you. It'll pass. You'll always miss her. Get used to that part."

My thoughts had now scattered like leaves from the oak trees back in the park we'd left behind; the tracks had carried us into the wing of campus that included the P-E complex, with its tennis courts and track and swimming pools, off to our left. I stole a glance at Kunk's craggy profile. He exuded a deep royal blue aura, his face glowing amber with every contemplative drag on a fresh cigarette.

His words, sagacious, came as Absolute Illuminating Truth: "You can't solve what was wrong with your mom. Drunks have to help themselves first—it's what I always heard, anyway. As for your movie, it can be what-ever you want, still. Relax and let it happen. That's how you make music on stage. You let it flow. Let all this flow—don't you feel it?" He spun in a circle like Neill listening to one of his precious psychedelic Deadhead cassettes. "Anything's possible."

Deep down, I knew Kunk was right about my mother and that fractured, forever unresolved relationship. But other problems festered, ones not necessarily unfixable. That's all I was trying to say to him, without being so obvious—like Max had taught us about dialogue—it had to be oblique. Had to come at the truth from an angle. Too on-the-nose and you end up with what our teacher called 'announcing,' hitting the audience over the head instead of ingratiating them into your messages through sharp dialogue brimming with mood and subtext. It's as hard to get right as it sounds.

Levon Kunkle froze and grabbed me by the arm. "Champ—you feel that? *A train's coming around the bend.*"

The glow from ahead, I now realized, was no LSD hallucination. A vibration through the rails carried up my legs. A horn, sounding.

Next, I thought Kunk had lost his mind: he began running in the direction of the oncoming locomotive.

Madness.

But a method to Kunk's insanity: dragging me by the arm, he hustled me to the next street the tracks crossed, near the engineering college and the campus infrastructure that existed back in this corner of campus. We got off the tracks in time to see the train engine, creeping slow and steady, down the tracks toward us.

Safe.

Kunk led me down the small slope of gravel past railroad warning arms and onto the sidewalk. Plumes of steam and giant machines and boxy strange buildings covered in ductwork and pipes running this way and that; the industrial part of campus. We watched as the train rumbled across Convocation Avenue, the six-lane main drag to Redtails Stadium. Powerful, the beast's great eye glowing, the dragon's breath animating its infinite snake-body stretching back into the darkness toward the river. Such power. Immense.

Kunk, ruminative, watching the train go by. "Old girl's rolling on through. No particular place to go. Not late in the night like this. No, sir."

"That scared the mud out of me."

We waved to the engineer. The call of his mighty beast split our eardrums.

The pain from the passing train horn eased off. The locomotive began to pick up speed.

"You feeling better?"

Nodding. "Thirsty as heck, now. Still need to pee."

"No doubt. Let's get back, have ourselves a couple of cold ones."

Kunk grimaced up the steep incline we'd need to scale if we were to follow the sidewalk back home instead of the tracks—as established, this part of Columbia, quite hilly. "One fuck of a hike back."

I rued this expenditure of energy as well.

"Wait—I got me an idea, champ. Follow my lead."

What could I say? In those days, following Kunk was all I knew how to do.

WITH THE TRAIN whistle screaming and Kunk hollering with joy, we dangled from the side of a boxcar.

I hadn't wanted to hop the train at all—surprise—but now, as it sped up through the park, I knew we'd made a mistake. *"We're gonna die."*

Kunk, hanging off the front of the graffiti-covered freight car we'd clambered onto, shouted over the wind, "By the time it gets to the Old Market, this heap'll be going too fast to hop off at the crossing. We gotta jump in the park, that one hillside."

The trip, already unreal, had taken on a life-threatening aspect: this is what they warned us about. This is how people on drugs *died*.

The train now going over 30 mph, I hung terrified to the handhold, my feet melting into the hard steel bar on which I stood.

We passed the PE complex and rocketed across Pinckney Street and the city pool complex. The train now skirted Simkins Park. I watched as Kunk, counting off in anticipation, leaned out. As the last of the huge live oaks passed, a brief expanse of grass running right up to the gravel rail bed appeared.

"Now." The birthday boy leapt, flinging himself away from the tons of steel on which we clung. I watched transfixed as he tucked in his knees, bounced and rolled down the hillside like a stuntman.

I hesitated. If I should have counted one-two after him and jumped, it was more like one-two-three, four before I pushed off from the boxcar like a swimmer diving into an Olympic pool.

Missing the edge of the grass, I bounced on gravel and rolled halfway down the steep but not quite shear wall of grass and shrubs. A face full of dirt, coughing and sputtering. Later I'd discover my knees and chin were scraped, but for the moment I had survived, nothing seemed broken, and I felt nothing but elation.

Wrenching around a wrist like he might have sustained his own injury, Kunk hurried over to me. "Champ—you okay?"

"I think so. One piece."

"*Goddamn.*" Kunk, exuberant, spun in a circle and bounced on his heels. "That made me feel like I was twelve years ago again. We used to hop trains in my neighborhood all the time." He threw his arms around me. "What a party, man. I got to give it to you."

Still too hyped up and high and completely totally freaked out, I didn't truly appreciate what a favor I'd done for my friend on his birthday. Only years later would I remember the delight in his eyes, the vibe of aliveness he exuded.

We duck-walked down the slope and took off our shoes to ford a small gurgling stream running parallel to the high slope of the rail bed. I finally emptied my bladder.

"I could drink a gallon of beer right now," Kunk said. "You?"

"Yeah—enough riding the rails for tonight. If you don't mind."

The trip had settled down, the adrenaline rush of the train adventure counterbalancing the acid. Or something. We talked more on the walk back to his apartment, this time on the sidewalk instead of the tracks overhead. I felt close to Kunk.

Back at the apartment other party members, concerned by our absence and now relieved, began peeling away one by one to go finish their trips in their own spaces and times. Kunk and I sat smoking pot Neill left for us, rapping and drinking cans of beer and laughing all the way through the night until dawn, when he seemed to drift off into a troubled, grunting sleep on the couch.

The trip at last ebbing, my mind felt sharp and clear. Greeted by the crisp morning dew, I walked outside and stretched. Shrill, melodic birdsong came to me, sounding as though the first day of spring had sprung rather than creeping autumnal senescence. The sunrise peeking over the tree line and the condo buildings in the Old Market came as quietly violet and beautiful as any I'd ever seen. I'd gone from feeling like the walls were closing in on me and being crushed by my hangups and problems, to staring up into the lightening sky and believing that anything—everything!—was possible for me: twenty years old, almost twenty-one. I had all the time in the world to mold life into any shape I desired.

I said to myself:

I don't need my mother, and because I can't have her, I don't need Camille.

I don't need anyone.
I can do this alone.
I was wrong.

"Cut, cut, CUT."

Breathless, I switched off the Eclair and pulled back from the repaired viewfinder and eyecup. After a long weekend of reshoots—yeah, our last roll of film from the accident had been useless—we were almost done.

"Let's do another one, boss." Seething with murderous rage, Jaime still loomed over me with a bottle gripped by its neck, a deadly weapon he'd used to 'kill' his own brother. "I'm into this."

"I think we have it."

"Let's go again."

"No—we got the shot."

"Okay. I feel like I need to go run around the block, now." He hooted and jumped to his feet, an actor in his moment.

In reality, what he'd been striking had been my fist held out of frame as I sat on the floor in the kitchen. Sweating, lights blazing, tilting the camera lens up into his scowling rage-face, I felt energized by the process of creativity, but satisfied with what we'd done.

Brenda applauded; Connor, ashen and nervous. "I hope the exposure's right."

Peeling the heavy work glove off my red, raw knuckles: "It's fine."

Darren, also on the floor running the Nagra and holding a shotgun mic —like Travolta's soundman in DePalma's *Blow Out*—switched off the tape deck, removed his cans. "Damn, y'all. That was intense."

My lead actor, menacing and enraged by a string of taunts, had stared down into the lens with burning, dark eyes, his face half-lit like a mad murderous demon loosed from the bowels of hell, striking my fist with abandon. So as not to break my fingers, we'd switched from the prop glass bottle of vodka to a similar 1.5 liter vessel made of plastic. Jaime, such a sweet guy normally, had transformed into a killer.

"You sure we don't need one more?" He paced back and forth in the kitchen, slapping the plastic bottle against his thigh and stepping over the snakes running to Connor's three lights. "I can go-go-go."

"We got it."

A gloved Connor, making some minute adjustment, fussed with a hot light. "Are you sure you weren't jostling the camera too much when he hit your hand?"

"Might've bounced too much once or twice. Otherwise, I was a rock." My shoulders and back would be sore for days, in fact, from keeping the camera stable. "I'm satisfied."

"The rushes will tell the tale."

"Granted."

Brenda hugged her thespian boyfriend, who'd indeed done a fine, fine job for us on this day, one of the last shooting days with our actors. "That's a side of you I've never seen."

"That's why they call it acting, baby." Jaime planted a wet one on the screenwriter. "You ain't seen nothing yet."

We struck the set-up and moved on.

LIKE ON A REAL MOVIE, by the end of the shoot all we had left were more inserts and pickups, as they're called: Marcel's outstretched feet after having his head bashed in, shadows of tree limbs dancing in the wind on the wall of the kitchen, two tumblers of vodka on the table.

After dismissing the actors, we had two bits left to shoot: an establishing shot from a small park across from the house, and a late idea from Connor, using a leaf blower off-camera to simulate Kurosawa-esque wind scattering yard debris across the top of the now-filled in grave, a POV shot as the killer stands over his malevolent work. With those images now captured, we called a wrap, at least until a moment in editing when we discovered a lack of coverage or some other arcane problem.

At last, *Too Far Gone* seemed in the can, as they say.

Thank god.

We all had other classes. The semester, waning, meant that final exams loomed. I faced long shifts at the theater on three weeknights coming up. Stuff hanging over my head. But our principal photography? Done.

On Monday we sent off our rolls of film to the lab on the other side of the country. Now I could finish the semester knowing that, despite my fumble-fingered foolishness, we'd gotten our project lensed, with round two—post-production, with all of its meticulous detail and expense—looming in the spring.

After a scattered requirement or two, I'd be done with undergrad.

With school altogether, if I chose. Or got the right professional break. Who knew just how good this film of ours would turn out.

❅

SPEAKING OF SPRING, Max's feature script class awaited me, one of many worrisome topics Kunk and I had covered during our long acid trip and bonding session. He'd spoken of breaking through his block and the excitement of building up pages, getting from Act 1 to Act 2, and the complicating plot points and character bits and dialogue—but Act 3, he'd said, had given him fits. "My fingertips are getting cold. And I can't figure out how to get out of this thing. Not yet, anyway."

So far he hadn't asked me to read the material, for which I was grateful. Not that I didn't want to help. But I had my own fish frying in the skillet.

Until I got home from class on the Monday before Thanksgiving, that is, and found a large manila envelope stuffed behind the screen door. At first I thought it mail, perhaps a copy of some famous screenplay I had ordered and forgotten.

Close, but not exactly. Inside, a sheaf of pages, with a title page like this:

BINGES
An Original Screenplay
by
LEVON C. KUNKLE

1st Draft
MACM 521, Fall Semester 1987
Instructor: Prof. Max de Lisle

I dropped my book bag, fixed myself a sandwich, poured a glass of iced tea, and sat down to read my best pal's first feature length screenplay. I knew it would rock. Had no doubt. This was Kunk.

After the first ten pages, and with my fingertips smelling of mustard and baloney, I understood why he was in trouble.

No, not bad writing, which, like Kunk himself, seemed sharp, had snap, created mood and atmosphere. He'd written active, succinct scenes that built narrative suspense, especially around the first plot point, when the musician who's shacked up with the rich woman agrees to help kill the brother who controls the family wealth and who, she explained in a harrowing monologue, had abused her as a child.

In the worst way.

Now: What, pray tell, signaled the problem with this edgy, noir-ish romance?

The issue, intrepid screenplay students, was that BINGES seemed more than a little too much like Lawrence Kasdan's *Body Heat*, a film we'd studied in the first scriptwriting class, and which for all its considerable merits was itself but a tip of the cinematic hat to such fare as *Double Indemnity*. Kunk's story seemed to me, in musician nomenclature, like a cover of a cover song.

I liked Kunk's characters, sufficiently different, I supposed, from those portrayed by William Hurt and Kathleen Turner. But from the sex angle in the beginning to the fact that the musician's a womanizing guitarist who's one gig away from being on the skids, not unlike Hurt's hapless mediocre horndog lawyer 'Ned Racine,' to the beachfront setting—a well-described Atlantic City standing in for the small Florida town of Kasdan's script—to the musician jogging along the Boardwalk to clear his head the way Racine would run on the beach, all the beats and details felt familiar. Too familiar.

At last the story finally began to have more of an original feel—it appeared the second half would be a cat and mouse game of wits between the protagonist and the *femme fatale*—but right as this conceit seemed about to develop, the script ended with a several-scenes-missing feel.

Incomplete, an ambiguous, tacked-on ending around page seventy left me bereft and confused.

After the last page I found one more sheet with a few handwritten notes, including one directed at me in his spiky, sloppy handwriting:

You see where this thing ends up, but for some reason I can't write through the scenes in the last act to get to that ending. Help, champ.

Nodding at the honor of being needed—at being considered an expert, even—I clicked a ballpoint pen a few times, grabbed a legal pad, and started scribbling.

BEFORE I COULD GET FAR, though, the phone rang.

I sat up straight off the couch—my dream girl, Camille. She'd called to kvetch about Kunk, about whom she had become more concerned.

"Kunk's still in a funk, eh?"

"Seems that way."

Camille described what sounded to me like depression, the polar opposite of the bright-brained feeling I'd enjoyed since the party and my wild acid trip.

"Ever since this birthday, he's been a real bear about stuff."

"Forty's pretty old. He's a cranky codger."

She hissed admonishment. "Don't say that."

"You realize, fair maiden, he dropped off his pages earlier today?"

"Do tell. He won't let me have so much as a peek."

I calculated how truthful I should be, for surely anything I might say would make its way into Kunk's ears. "It's got real suspense."

"From what he told me, it's dark."

"Not at first. But, yeah—there's murder and betrayal and a double cross."

"Sounds like *Body Heat*," said my fellow former scriptwriting student. "Doesn't it?"

Relief and validation—I wasn't alone in feeling the way I did about the story. "Some scenes felt a little familiar. Not like a ripoff or anything," downplaying my own reaction. "But a bigger problem, it's incomplete. Third act is a gaping hole."

"And after Thanksgiving, there's only another week of classes before the deadline."

Kunk had some writing ahead of him—thirty to forty screenplay pages. "I'm making notes. I wouldn't intrude, but he asked."

"He trusts you. Thinks the world of you."

"He's like my drunk uncle, watching over me."

Camille laughed. "So, this party y'all had—I've never done any of that acid stuff."

Stumbling and stammering over my words, I described how we'd watched a couple of movies, drank a river of beer, went on walkabout beneath the stars.

"And that's all?"

"Sure. Pretty much."

"[REDACTED]?"

"Yes, ma'am?" I said in a small voice.

She related a story going around the MACM department—that there'd been strippers and whores at the party. That Hoyt had been bragging about the wild scene that'd gone on.

I suppose our absence the next day in the halls of MACM—I could not function for many hours—had promoted a sort of urban legend, one lacking in truth.

"Preposterous—it was a regular sausage fest the whole night."

"You're the worst liar I've ever heard."

"I wouldn't lie to you."

She hung up.

Okay. So now I was in trouble with Camille. For what, I hadn't a clue. Of course the business with Levon's occasional drunken hookup floated in the aether, but I hadn't divulged such info to anyone. Certainly not her.

How little I understood back then about a woman's intuition. Or, for that matter, my own—rather, the lack thereof. No intuition could have prepared me for where this angle would lead, however: straight into heaven, yeah, before plummeting down toward hell.

AFTER SPENDING MOST of the next day going back through Kunk's pages and thoroughly marking them with suggestions, I went out with Connor and Brenda and Jaime for pizza and beer to celebrate the completion of the shoot.

Neill, totally blazed up, insisted on tagging along, which annoyed me. My roommate wasn't one of us—he was the Other, a regular student. Not a Media Artist like the chosen ones. A statement like, "I'm buying the first round," however, gained him access to this club of cash-challenged college students, foolishly engaged in making an expensive-by-our-impoverished-standards motion picture extravaganza.

We cruised over to the Pizza Joint Too, Pizza Joint prime being located across town and operated by the brother of the Greek man who ran the PJT. The pizza was excellent, the mugs of draught beer frosty, the ID checking loose—thanks to the recent raise of the drinking age to twenty-one, which I'd soon turn, PJT offered an easy place to drink underage.

Neill, despite my fears, sat at the bar engrossed in *Monday Night Football*—Raiders versus the Cowboys; who cares about sports?—while the filmmakers shot the shit and talked about doing post in the spring. How we hoped our final rushes, in this case inappropriately named, would arrive via FedEx by the end of the week. But Thursday being Thanksgiving meant our quote-unquote dailies would be delayed a day or two longer than normal. Agony.

"That shoot was intense. *Intense*." A little of the murderous fire blazed anew in Jaime's eyes. "Your hand okay?"

I told him it was, though my knuckles still felt sore.

"You proved you can do more than comedy, baby," Brenda said.

Jaime leaned over and kissed her; she glowed with affection.

I envied their relationship. I felt like I'd never known such love. Because, of course, I hadn't.

Feeling empty but putting on air of good cheer, I raised a cup of suds. "To our cast."

"And crew," Jaime added, smiling.

"*Cast and crew!*" Neill, yelling from over at the bar, downing his beer and belching. I hadn't even realized he'd been eavesdropping on us. "Fuck yeah, y'all."

We laughed, drank, poured ourselves another round.

A terrible mistake followed, however: lips loosened by the beer, as well as perhaps a feeling of slight superiority over Kunk and his script struggle, I started dishing on his details. Too many, as it turned out.

T hanksgiving at home with Dad, needless to say, unfolded with deep melancholy.

I finally admitted to myself I'd been hoping he would be relieved mom was gone; that he wouldn't ever have to bail her out of the drunk tank again; never sneak around ridding the house of the empties secluded behind sofas or books on bookshelves or in cabinets; never face the indignity of handling another DUI, perhaps one that ended up injuring —or worse, killing—an innocent motorist or pedestrian.

In any case, I couldn't know what it felt like for my father. What it was to lose a spouse, even one who'd been as flawed as my mother. Who despite her drinking, still put food on the table for us.

Kept up the house.

Cleaned our clothes and the rooms in which we lived.

Thanklessly, it occurred to me. At least on my part.

No wonder she drank.

My ribs quivering, I sat holding myself on my parents bed. I squinted through wet eyes at my mother's possessions—objects on her dresser, dresses hanging in the closet, a pair of ratty bedroom slippers she'd wear, bleary-eyed and hungover, as she shuffled around the kitchen. Like a thunderclap, it struck me that my father hadn't touched any of it. He said he didn't spend much time in the bedroom. He'd been sleeping downstairs in his lounging chair every night.

Her energy, lingering in the room.

I began to miss her so. This grief, it kept changing on me Slippery in the hands. Keeps you on your toes, trying to manage such feelings.

I wondered if it all went down easier when one's parents died naturally. When you were old, and they were like, really old.

All of it felt so pathetic—her death, my confusion, his bereavement. Hot silent tears, my throat on fire.

But the weeping didn't last, and afterwards I felt better.

A noise. My father, standing in the doorway, his own haggard cheeks also damp.

"After we go and eat at your aunt's house," where the Thanksgiving gathering traditionally occurred anyway, so we had that going for us, "what say we run ourselves over yonder?"

"Where?"

"To the cemetery."

I nodded. My insides stopped quivering and became warm, especially in the center of my chest. Sunlight from a break in the clouds streamed into the window.

It was all going to be okay.

"We could get some flowers from the grocery store."

"I reckon we could do that."

"Then I think we ought to."

He sat down on the bed. The springs sounded rusty, as though no one had slept on it for years. So skinny, my dad—he didn't look like he ate much anymore. Or else being eaten from inside, perhaps.

"You okay, Daddy?"

"I ain't doing too good, son," wiping at his eyes. "Not too good at all."

"If it makes you feel better—I guess I haven't been, either."

He asked me about school, about the film shoot. Did I need more money? Or pocket money, as though he'd forgotten I now worked at the theaters?

I said I was fine, and thanked him again for his understanding about my accident with the camera.

"Make your mistakes. But make sure you take in the lesson from your error."

"Max says every success is built on failure." I searched my memory for his exact words. "'Every mistake's a building block in the firmament of eventual triumph.' Kind of a necessary evil, I guess?"

My father made a sharp, guttural sound. Looking up to the dusty blades of the ceiling fan, he grabbed at the back of his neck. A tendril of cobweb hung fragile between one of the blades and the pull chain. A mausoleum, this place. "Your teacher's a smart man."

I didn't know why what he'd said made him react that way. Making mistakes? Perhaps acknowledging that some aspect of his life spent with Mother had been a mistake. One long error in judgement? A necessary evil, stuck here with me alone?

He started trying to tell me, but broke down before he could get out the words.

I draped my arm around my father's slight and stooped shoulders. He lay his head against mine and finally let go, weeping and gasping for breath.

When he calmed down enough to find himself again capable of speech, he confirmed what I'd been thinking.

"Truth be told? I made a whole mess of mistakes in my life. But I did some good, too. The fact that my son's sitting here next to me, a college man all grown up—you wasn't no mistake. Far from it."

"I'll try to live up to that."

We gathered ourselves. He went downstairs while I freshened up in my dead mother's bathroom.

Thanksgiving now became more of a pleasure, with the family supportive and loving, and my aunt's food some of the best I'd ever tasted. Afterwards, the men sat watching the Cowboys and Packers play during a Wisconsin snow shower. My relatives asked me what college was like, about the filmmaking. I went back for thirds on dessert.

By the time my father and I made our way to the memorial garden and laid a bouquet of bright happy flowers on the grave, I felt tired, cold, but pleased—cleansed, even.

My father, however, tried to convince himself. "I think I'm glad we did this."

"I feel better now than I have since it happened."

"Me, too." But I could sense his uncertainty. Raw—it was all too raw. I could only hope that time would temper our mutual sense of loss. We placed the flowers. Her granite marker, clean and new, the engraving sharp. It would outlast all of us.

I spent the night in my old room, had breakfast with Daddy, afterwards heading back to my 'real' and current home on what they now call Black Friday, biggest shopping day of the year.

That's a day also quite busy at the cinemas: everybody off work, and kids out of school, plus Hollywood always loads up the weekend with big releases. By the time classes would start again on Monday, I'd be one whipped puppy.

On Wednesday we had opened the year's big Thanksgiving movie now packing houses, another *Star Trek* sequel. Demand was such we ran the print interlocked on two screens, the film from the first projector running not to the huge take-up platter, but across a series of pulleys and runners where it would be projected into house number 2. The next set of shows? The reverse, back across the pulleys to the first projector. When ushering, one had enough time to walk the first house and get over into the next auditorium only to see the exact same moment of the film all over again.

I'd seen Earl the projectionist run a film this way only once before, the *Beverly Hills Cop* sequel that'd kicked off the summer movie season back in May. That had played on three screens, with its print, as Earl noted, scratched and beaten to death on all those pulleys after only the first weekend. "They don't call 'em grindhouses for nothing," he said.

This *Star Trek* episode, involving whales and time travel, seemed particularly silly—watching Shatner and Nimoy prancing around modern day San Francisco in those ridiculous naval-style epaulet-adorned uniforms, eh. Too implausible, too much goofy humor, and didn't Spock already die?

To me, movies were serious business. This was clearly a series being milked to death, like when they sent 007 into space in what amounted to a comedy with bad special effects. Me, I was always more of a *Star Wars* than *Star Trek* guy anyway.

But you know what? For the lack of anything better to do after my shift on Sunday, I collapsed on the front row of a packed house to watch Kirk and crew save the whales, and for all of my predisposition to dislike the farcical nature of it all, I got caught up in the story. By the end, I found myself downright roused by the triumphant ending with the crew back on board the Enterprise, heading into deep space on another adventure—and to veritable cheers from the rapt, entertained audience: whole families aged six to sixty, everyone stamping feet and happy and satisfied. I remembered what Max had taught about story being everything. About redemption and resolution.

I fretted and wondered if we had a decent narrative going in our little 16mm film. Also, of course, I thought of Kunk and his script troubles.

That night I called my buddy to arrange a time to talk through his script's issues, which I'd decided needed to be discussed with brutal honesty. I wanted him to succeed, to be happy with his work. I felt certain he'd be receptive to the notes I'd made.

"**S**on of a gun. Son of a *gun*."

My mentor? Furious.

Kunk shoved the sheaf of screenplay pages back across a pub table damp from our pints of beer. "You fucking little prick."

Stammering, I asked what on earth was wrong.

"Asshole."

"My notes are that hurtful?"

"No, numbness—this is my only goddamn copy."

"No."

"Yeah."

"No no *no*."

"Yeah, yeah, yeah, you putz. Everything but the pages I wrote over the weekend. The whole thing's got to be retyped now."

He'd dropped off his master original pages for me to read? When running off a copy at Kinko's would have cost but a pittance? "Why the hell would you give me your only copy?"

Kunk had no answer, only hot fury in his normally cool, ice blue eyes.

Finally he said, "Because you're a writer, champ. I thought you'd recognize an actual typescript and know better than to—than to—fucking write all over it."

He had me there. The smudges and smears, even the quality of the paper bond, none of it had registered.

I must seem like the biggest idiot alive to him.

We'd met at McHaffie's, the neighborhood Irish pub, for a beer and a chat. I hadn't begun to offer remarks yet, had only handed him the script, replete with numerous scrawled notations. We hadn't yet gotten to the meat of what I had to offer as actual criticism, and my best bud, already furious.

He flipped pages. Swaths of ink—all my little suggestions and criticisms. My entire head felt blazing hot with embarrassment.

We drank in silence. Kunk stared out the window at the passing college kids along the Old Market commercial strip. I cleared my throat, tried to find words to express the idea that he'd have had to revise at least part of it anyway, right? Surely he hadn't planned to turn in a first draft as the final project.

I couldn't bring myself to ask any of that. "Jesus—I'm sorry."

He cast glassy eyes askance at the loose, defiled pages on the table. Downed his beer, called for another.

As he skimmed my notations a range of emotions played across his face, beginning with anger, changing to curiosity, and annoyance. At one lengthy note I'd scribbled about the protagonist's backstory, which the script as it stood lacked in an egregious fashion, eyebrows of what I took to be insulted disbelief raised into his creased forehead. A lengthy, silent exhalation followed, this one portending a smidgen of acknowledgment.

I sipped my foamy draught beer and waited. His eyes again found mine.

I started to apologize, but he cut me off:

"This is all good, champ. All good. Maybe I can get Camille to retype everything—which needs heavy revision anyway." A grudging admission. "Like I didn't know that shit."

"There's no such thing as good writing," I said, quoting Max. "Only good rewriting."

Kunk, chagrined but conciliatory. "I appreciate what you did here."

We clinked our beer steins together.

I made a statement: "These notes, and the pages as they are—that's not the real issue."

"No. Finishing this draft is like a fucking stinking-ass albatross around my neck. It's like pushing a rope to get this bastard squared away."

"It can't be that bad."

Breathy, a whisper, shocked and shocking: *It all came so easy at first.*

This, no way to think about writing. School assignment or otherwise, such an attitude constituted the kiss of creative death. I said so.

He agreed. Explained how the pressure was getting to him. That maybe he was too close to the work. Too lost in the woods to see the trees, so to speak.

I flirted with the idea of coming right out and saying that *Binges* felt like a retread of *Body Heat,* only with a musician instead of a lawyer, but I felt so relieved that Kunk's anger had dissipated, I chose not to.

Instead I said, "Look—just write the damn thing. Knock it out. We're sweating over pages that don't exist."

"Yeah, but—" He didn't seem to know how to finish the script, or his sentences. "It's—eh."

We paid our check and walked outside. The day, all-but December, now, lay in gray repose, a cool breeze brushing against our faces flushed with alcohol.

"Now what?" Kunk, leaning against a tree and smoking, the same spot I'd find him years later, though by then in much worse shape than being under the gun of schoolwork.

I thought the answer obvious: "You should go get to it. Don't you think?"

He nodded, grim. "Suppose I should."

"Damn right."

"You don't want to get another round somewhere?"

I shook my head. "Don't put it off another second. In fact—why don't I help type up the new draft?"

"Let's let Camille worry about that."

"Think she'll do it?"

Grinning. "I'll talk her into it."

The script tucked under the arm of his leather jacket, Kunk pounded me on the back and went off trudging up the hill and across the tracks to his apartment.

I watched that jive-ass strut of his with admiration. Kunk might have been struggling with his narrative, but he still walked like an all-knowing badass. Which he'd remain, in my mind, at least, for quite a long time to come.

Our final rushes, in this case inappropriately classified as such, returned to us.

Breathless with anticipation, we sat clustered around the battered, sky-blue eight-plate Steenbeck editing table; we all felt pleased by what we saw. Relief as the POV shot of Jaime murdering my hand yielded a couple of decent efforts, one outstanding take, and a last, unusable version due to the force of his blows shaking the camera.

"I knew it'd shake like that," Connor said of the last take. "But I almost like it. The urgency of it."

I'd become tired, wasn't able to keep the Eclair steady enough. It was a mistake. I said so. "Forget it. Take three."

Brenda, however, preferred the first take. "His gaze is more neutral in that one. If this is a premeditated act on his part, maybe it makes more sense for him not to seem quite so angry—the cold, dead eyes of a calculating psychopath." Brenda shuddered, thinking, I supposed, of her sweet lover being capable of such a heinous act. "A less is more, type-deal."

"Makes sense," I said. "But it's take three. It's definitely the most stable shot. No question. It's the one I want. Now let's move on."

Brenda, frowning. "I thought this was a group project."

"Let's just move on. We don't have to decide right now."

We went back to watching our work, the rest of which consisted of the pickups and inserts. All looked fine, simply fine, in our silvery monochrome cinematography.

In the end I slapped five with my compatriots, and we all agreed it felt good to be done for fall semester with what was our main class, our huge project. With so much work left to be completed in the spring, being able to say, "We're done for now" felt liberating.

Besides, I now had an idea for what I was going to do over the holiday break—all the reading and talking about Kunk's script had gotten my wheels turning. The Christmas present I planned to give myself this year was to embark on writing my first real screenplay, mainly to be ahead of the game in the spring. No rest for the weary.

WHEN I CALLED to inform my dad I wouldn't be moving home for the holidays like I had when I'd lived in the dorms—he seemed to have forgotten that I'd stayed in the city all summer, too—he had a fit.

I explained I didn't mean skipping Christmas with him, only that I had work to get done over the break. That my boss at the cinemas, Hank Halvorsin, expected me to put in long hours over the insane holiday period, a huge moviegoing time. During the semester I hadn't worked as much as either I, or Halvorsin, had hoped.

Being immersed in the theatrical exhibition side of the industry hadn't been as thrilling as I'd anticipated. Not much interesting happened—people came to watch movies, we sold them snacks, and cleaned up afterwards. We got to watch movies ourselves for free. Got paid three bucks an hour. I'd stolen a couple of one-sheet posters for my collection, so I had that going for me.

More than all that, I tried to impart to my dad how I felt the concept of home now held dual meanings.

"This is a real place," referring to the duplex. "This is where I live."

He took offense, blustered and argued, but didn't become angry. Only sad, ringing off with a bleak bye-bye.

I now worried for my father's wellbeing, more than I'd ever been concerned about Mother. She barreled her way through life denting fenders, going on benders, and in the worst aspect—to me, anyway—she'd done and been things with other people that she hadn't been with me, or her husband. She thought we didn't know. But over the years, I grew to know the smell on her, that sour-sweet horror of a drunk's dragon breath on the morning after a binge.

What a title for Kunk's script. But what did *Binges* mean?

I knew in the context of my mother's behavior, that much for certain. But beyond that assurance, I wasn't sure to what Kunk's title referred, which in all the reading and thinking about his screenplay hadn't yet revealed itself. With thirty or forty pages to write, however, I felt certain what he intended would become clear.

❄

AFTER FINISHING my ushering shift in time to catch the last show, I found myself entertained but underwhelmed by *Broadcast News*. Maybe if I'd been on a date its romanticism might have struck me on a more effective level. But I wasn't on a date. I was alone.

And while its excoriation of the sorry direction taken by infotainment TV news had resonated with me, the ending blew, a non-resolution that, as a writer, had me struggling to figure out what James L. Brooks had in mind. I remembered how *Terms of Endearment* had kind of a soft ending as well.

Endings. I hoped Kunk had gotten his knocked cut. Hadn't heard a peep.

Mulling ideas for screenplays, I drove home from the Enemas and swore that I'd get started when my last exam was finished, only one to go. I wasn't starting from scratch, because I'd considered using one of my well-received scenes from last semester as a jumping off point, until I reminded myself those were exercises in exploring the various aspects of screenwriting—narrative, character, dialogue, et cetera. What I needed was an idea, a full-fledged one that could sustain the weight of ninety to a hundred-twenty pages. I don't know what inspired me to go in this direction, but like with our film project, I found myself thinking dark—way dark.

Why?

The year I'd had. The 16mm film, with its own bleak subject. My mom.

Who wanted to write about their own life?

Wake me when it's over.

After cleaning up a few beer cans and junk mail and Neill's Frisbee full of stems and seeds, sliding it in its appointed spot under the La-Z-Boy we'd found on the curb a few blocks over, I sat on my couch with a legal pad. I chewed the end of a yellow Bic pen and stared at the blue-white light of the TV screen tuned to HBO, the fiftieth time I'd stumbled onto *Tango & Cash*, an action movie so ridiculous it became difficult not to be pulled into its milieu of absurd kinetic explosions and macho bombast; a guilty pleasure movie. Mindless so-called entertainment. A trifle.

I surveyed the shelves of paperbacks I'd accumulated, the LPs and stacks of Neill's colorfully labelled Dead cassettes. An ancient Atari unit and a few games I still carried around and setup in dorms as a totem of my receding childhood had gone untouched for several seasons now. A picture, small, framed, of Nicole I'd yet to dispose of. The stuff of childhood.

The chocolate brown spine of one Atari box caught my eye: *Night Driver*, a POV driving game in which you, the Night Driver, maneuvered between a pair of guardrails until either increasing speed, an obstacle, or a sudden curve took you out. Simple as could be, the earliest of such trifling, 8-bit time wasters.

A video game, a voice said, *in particular such a basic model only a step above Pong and long before the age of immersive multi-chapter epic war and fantasy adventure games, offered no basis for a movie script.*

But the title—*Night Driver*. It conjured up evocative images and emotions—a purposeful solitude, foreboding, forbidding loneliness.

What was a "night driver?"

What was his mission?

What was his burden, his secret, his quest?

I'd only gotten as far as scribbling down the title and a question mark, and wondering if I needed a(nother) new typewriter ribbon cartridge, when the phone rang.

After I answered and heard Camille's dulcet voice on the other end, I forgot all about my script. I didn't know it yet, but what turned out to be the most significant night of my life had arrived, unheralded, on an otherwise ordinary Tuesday. A red letter day, this. A signpost to new space, as the title of one of Neill's heady books sitting on the coffee table suggested, but not, as I thought at first, to the future with Camille about which I'd dreamed. But somewhere, however glorious and ephemeral as it might have been.

S ounding as though she'd had a glass or two of wine, Camille, revealing frailties, phobias, and fears, spoke for over an hour.

We were becoming friends.

Oh no!

Most of all, though, she continued to probe with ever more leading questions about what Kunk and I did on our drinking nights. About Kunk and other women.

My resolve to refrain from answering in detail crumbled in the face of her fragile, pleading interrogatives. Loyalty to my mentor intermixed with a deeply held religious belief that I was in love with his girlfriend made for an emotional high-wire act. "Kunk's streetwise. He likes to flirt. How did it start with the two of you?"

"That's what I'm afraid of." She sighed. "[REDACTED], he hasn't been the same since that night."

Forced to revisit what I thought we'd settled, I offered the same answers as in my prior deposition: it was a hell of a party; I had a semi-bad acid trip for awhile; the worse thing that came out of it had been Hoyt having to get a tooth capped. No girls.

"But it's not the party or his birthday or anything that happened there," my tone definitive. "It's his script."

"It's more than that script."

"How's the last act shaping up?"

"Quit changing the subject. I just got through re-typing the first part."

I explained about Kunk's difficulties and worries and problems, the conversations we'd had. I left out how derivative the piece felt, only offering that I thought it wasn't bad. That he'd be able to finish in time. "None of this should be news to you. You guys pretty much live together."

She grumbled. "Sounds like he shares more with you than with me."

"We're writers."

"As if I wasn't in the writing group."

"Sorry. Of course. But you're in the corporate media track."

Camille, cursing my hole-digging.

But I didn't know about Kunk sharing all that much about his life otherwise—he seemed like a guy with secrets. I kept calling him my best bud, but I didn't know from shit compared to his life, all he'd seen and done and been through. He'd tried Blue Sunshine in the goddamn fucking 60s. Played the blues, swung onstage with jazzmen in smoky clubs full of goombahs. Had no trouble making time with women half his age. The coolest guy with whom I'd ever had the privilege of associating. A real character—a real man, compared to me. And really, too old for Camille.

The call waiting tone beeped; I ignored it.

"Do you need to go?"

"No, no." A wicked, red-eyed devil, sporting an erection tiny but no less tumescent, squatted upon my shoulder. "I think the biggest favor you could do for him?"

"Yes?"

"Get out of his hair for a while."

She said that Kunk, ensconced in the spare room hunched over his Smith-Corona typing away like mad, hadn't so much as said *boo* to her for days.

"For all that racket in there, you'd think he'd be done by now."

My face flushed. After scribbling all over Kunk's master copy, I'd had a nightmare about going to turn in pages to Max and finding them covered in crayon drawings, the symbolism of which had not been lost upon me. On some days the sense I was but a kid playing with adults beat like a second pulse.

A skeptically suspicious and flat statement from her: "So: you think I should get out of the house."

I felt a warm, pulsing bothersomeness. "A writer needs his space."

I could feel her thinking things through. "All right—granted."

"A lonesome trade, that of the harried scribe on deadline."

She laughed. "All right then. What are you up to tonight?"

My body convulsed on the couch. I nearly dropped the phone. "*Me?* Nothing. I've all but got this semester put to bed, I'm off work—I'm, I'm, I'm wide open."

What Camille proposed next made my heart skip a beat—a night out, the two of us, friends on a late semester bar crawl. I barely got the phone back on its base before tearing off my grubby lounging clothes and hitting the shower.

Camille appeared at McHaffie's dolled up like I hadn't seen her since New York, or maybe those Wednesday jazz-jams at Murdoch's on Main—a pink puffy shirt with padded shoulders accentuated the shape and form of her glorious torso. A short skirt, sheer hose; stilettos on her feet with shiny red toenails poking out. Big hair. Mysterious eyeliner. A fragrance about her like ripening blossoms on the first day of summer in the Garden of Eden.

As she approached across the bar, every male head glancing in her direction, I fixated on the shoulder pads. They made me wonder if Sean Young's costuming in *Blade Runner*, retro 40s-looking from the hair down to the shoes, had influenced the world fashion industry. I doubted it. *Blade Runner* had been a flop, a huge financial disappointment and an artistic one as well, especially not with that silly, drive-off-into-the-sunset ending.

What a dork. Get to the girl.

I'd gotten there early with my legal pad and had a draught already, but I'd taken not one note on *Night Driver*. At the appearance of Camille Grahl, of course, all thoughts of work vanished.

We moved from the bar to a table in the corner near the front entrance. A server, frecklefaced and peppy, came over to take Camille's order, a gimlet.

I had to ask what was in it.

"Gin, lime juice, soda."

"Make it two."

The joint, not very busy—a couple of tables for dinner, a half-dozen drinkers scattered around the L-shaped bar staring at college basketball games on the TV sets. According to Jaime, who didn't seem to be working that night, McHaffie's busiest time came on what they called Pint Night: one dollar draught and two-dollar pitchers of domestics, plus all you could eat chilled cocktail shrimp and other bar snacks.

Camille noted my legal pad. "You brought work?"

"A writer writes."

"Am I that uninteresting?"

I chuckled, a choking sound devoid of mirth. "Hardly. Besides, you can see that my paper remains unsullied by ink."

"What are you taking notes about? The semester's all but over."

"Thinking of taking the feature class. Thought about getting a leg up on something over the break." I dared not express my true plan, which was to knock out a draft in the three and a half weeks between semesters. That, I feared, would be a jinx of the first order. "I'll have a heavy load with finishing the film. I don't want to end up next spring like Levon."

"He came back from meeting you the other day really stressed out."

"I thought he wanted my help."

"Sounds like he really got it."

"What bonehead gives out his master copy?"

She shrugged, helpless. "Really."

The server arrived with the drinks. "Cheers," Camille said. "To the writers."

"The writers."

We clinked glasses. She smiled, so warm and loving and friendly and open. "Now—tell me about the script *you* want to write."

HOURS PASSED. Camille and I, drunker than skunks, had roughed out the idea for my screenplay, the details of which are relevant enough, but not compared to the rest of the evening.

"Let's blow this popsicle stand." Camille, her eyes drooping. "That was fun, but seemed like being back in class."

"I can't thank you enough for all those ideas."

Shrugging, she fumbled around in her purse for a compact and fixed her lipstick, much of which had been left on the rims of cocktail glasses. "I could've done that for *him*," almost more to herself than me. "If he'd only let me."

"He's kinda old for you. Ya know."

She shoved me in the arm. "I wish you and everyone else would quit saying that. It's—it's nobody's business."

We ended up hitting the Parlor, full of suits and cigar smoke, followed by the Red Tub, an artsy-fartsy joint up a flight of stairs where a group of hep-cats were having a poetry reading, and finally the Back Porch, a late night joint that sometimes went until daybreak, or so I'd heard. I'd always pictured it as a sketchy kind of dump, but inside it wasn't so bad—folks sitting around drinking, including our cute server from earlier at McHaffie's over at the bar getting roaring drunk with a group that included none other than my roommate Neill.

As Camille and I stagger-stepped our way into the bar, arm-in-arm and giggling like naughty sneaks who were up to something—but we weren't—Neill and the server, whose name I recalled as Abby or Annie, both saw us at the same moment and erupted with equivalent surprise and delight:

"It's my table from before!"

"It's my fucking roommate, with some hot chick!"

A chorus of approval greeted and welcomed us into the arms of this cluster of Tuesday night revelers. I glanced at Camille. She rested her hand on my forearm as I introduced her to Neill, who didn't normally get drunk except in dire circumstances but he'd been out of pot for two days, which happened at the end of semesters.

As Camille went to say hi to someone she knew, Neill's words in my ear arrived as a happy, gurgling string of sibilant syllables: "Jesus, Mary and Josephus, who's the special lady, broheem."

"Settle down. Camille's a friend."

"Yeah," hooking his arm around Abby-Annie. "So's my little gal over here."

The server leaned over. Nodding toward Camille she said, "So, I was watching y'all before?"

"Oh—were you, now."

"Dude, she's like so into you."

"You guys don't know what you're talking about," I said with a modicum of impatience. I felt surly, a little more drunk than I'd have liked. "We're just friends."

Neill pulled me aside. "Yeah, I'm real good friends with Ally, here," speaking of the waitress for whom at last I had an accurate name. "We're gonna have ourselves a sleepover—but at her place. So you go to town, pardner." He flung a hippie arm around my neck and gave me a face full of his Neill-funk, concealed, barely, by a slathering of patchouli oil.

"Thanks. Won't happen, though."

Camille came back. We extricated ourselves, but not before being forced to join in on a round of shots called Sweet Tarts, and which indeed tasted like the candy.

"That didn't even seem like it had any booze in it," I said.

"That's the idea," the bartender, an older guy with gray at his temples, informed me with an eye-roll. "Shave-tail."

My already flushed cheeks flamed hot.

We ordered beers and collapsed into an empty booth. A TV over Camille's head played an old *Twilight Zone*, the one with Burgess Meredith wanting to be left alone to read.

"I'm fucked up," I informed my so-called date. "Sloshing, at this point."

"I got a run in my hose." Camille, in a little girl's whine. "Look at it."

"Maybe you should take them off."

Looking down into her beer, she didn't respond.

My heart exploded. The words, unbidden, had slipped out of their own accord. My face must have looked like an aircraft beacon. "I didn't mean that like it sounded."

She sipped her beer, made hard eye contact. "A favor?"

Without hesitation: "Anything."

"I need to ask you some things. Again."

I told her I had the answers she sought.

Had I seen him with other women?

"Sometimes."

Had he confided in me anything she ought to know?

"Not really, but sort of."

What, she asked. That he sometimes saw other girls?

"Yes," I answered.

Saw them in some serious way?

"I really don't know the—but no. I don't think so."

"Bullshit. Details," she commanded. "Who is it?"

"It's nobody. It's nothing you should—he's done things when he's drunk. But again, it's not like I've been in on the action."

"Before, or after New York?"

"Well—both."

"*Bastard.*"

I gulped and related a few anecdotes about boozy nights and times when I'd left him in places like Murdoch's, talking up women who'd watched him play music, or here in the Old Market. By the time I'd finished, Camille Grahl didn't seem mad—she appeared satisfied.

"For what it's worth—I couldn't believe it."

"You couldn't? Well, wait—of course you couldn't. You're a man."

At least being called a man felt good. Not much else about her comment did. "I just wouldn't cheat on you. If it were me. With you."

"You—with me."

"Yeah."

"Thank you," she said. "Now: let's get out of here."

"Already?"

"That's correct," in an officious, dry tone. "I've had enough to drink."

"But we ordered more beers."

Camille, her eyes lidded and voice husky, suddenly reminded me of a sultry Kathleen Turner. "Somebody else can drink them."

I felt something moving under the table—her toes. Wriggling, inching, exploring.

Finding.

"Ulp," I said. "Gah."

"As I was saying." With a gleam in her eye, the toes nudged a little further. "When you're able to walk again, let's get out of here."

O peratic.
    Epochal.
    Eternal.

The greatest night of my life ended the next morning as it had begun, with me alone in my apartment and considering my looming screenplay project. In reality, of course, I lay consumed by all the wonder of the short night I'd spent making love to—and what's more important, with—the woman of my dreams.

My best friend's girl.

That I'd loved for all I was worth three glorious times.

For now.

The last had been the best. I hadn't gone to sleep at all, and I'm not sure Camille did either. The sun had finally crept in through the blinds, awakening her fully.

"Hey, handsome."

"Hello, my love."

"This is bad, you know."

"Is it?" I didn't think so, not at the moment. "Kiss me, and then decide."

She shook her head no, slid out of bed and padded toward the hallway bathroom, grabbing a towel off a stack I'd washed the day before. The door shut with a click, followed by the squeaking of the old faucet fixture and running water.

When I heard the screech of the shower curtain rings sliding, I got up and went into the bathroom.

"No, honey. We—shouldn't."

I shushed Camille and stepped into the cascading water. Her hair matted down by the steamy shower and what makeup she had left running down her face, her truest, natural beauty shone through the remaining scrim of cosmetics. From behind, my hands crept under her arms to her breasts, nuzzled her neck.

Hesitant at first—after what we'd experienced?—Camille finally responded. She slid her slick body against mine, tugged at me. She put her cheek against the wall, and one foot up on the side of the tub.

"Hurry," she said. "Just one more little time."

But there was no hurrying, and it got intense and dangerous in the slippery tub. After scurrying wet and excited out of the bathroom and tumbling onto the already damp sheets, she rolled me over and climbed on top.

Languid and bittersweet—though the latter emotion wouldn't become apparent until much later—Camille finally came, and came hard, the line of her jaw set with a grimace as though in pain; a pulsing inside that gripped me like a fist. My vision doubled and body convulsed and god, okay, thank you.

Delirious and exhausted she lay upon me, wet and sated, head on my shoulder. The sun had arisen on day one of the rest of my life.

"Look at me."

She did so.

"Camille, I love—"

"Don't." She moved off and my penis, sore, slid out. "I'll never forget it, not any of it. But this is all, sweetie. That was it. Okay? Do you understand?"

I thought I would cry. I held onto her, kissed her neck.

She pushed me away, rolled off.

I fell back and burst into tears. I couldn't help it. Hungover, sleepless, disbelieving all that'd happened. Fragile.

"Oh, honey—what have I done."

She grabbed at her clothes and ran into the bathroom for the second time. This time, the door locked with a definitive snap that would reverberate in my ears for several decades to come. The sound of failure.

For the rest of that finals week I avoided Kunk and Camille, which wasn't difficult—he'd had a few other classes to finish, including a Modern American Lit that'd been killing him with reading and essays, and of course the burden of whatever he could manage in the way of presenting Max with a completed screenplay.

Maybe Kunk wondered why I didn't check on him. I had my reasons—varied, nuanced, and insurmountable.

Now I felt no elation at having been with her—my unassailable feelings, physically requited, were burned into the fiber and stuff of my being.

In am emotional daze, I went through the motions of discussing with Brenda, Connor, and Hedda Gamble our post-production plan for the spring, tried to comprehend when and what benchmarks our instructor expected. Best of all, Hedda told us that, based on our work so far, we'd be getting an A for the fall class.

I ran into Camille only once, in the hallway outside Hedda's office, as my lover walked past with younger students from Margrave's Intro to Film Theory, one of the first classes I'd taken in the Mass Comm track. She gave me the sweetest, saddest smile one could imagine, and a single word, "Hey," that left me reeling in the wake of her shampoo, the smell of which still lingered upon my unwashed pillowcase.

The previous day I'd discovered her torn hose under the bed; this garment I stashed under my pillow, a weird, fetishistic behavior, perhaps, but the only piece of Camille I truly retained. I hoped against hope that, whether she remained with Kunk or otherwise, I also possessed a piece of her heart.

※

NEILL CAME BE-BOPPING in on Friday afternoon, the last day of exams, to find me sitting in the shuttered living room listening to Pink Floyd's *The Final Cut*, one of the most downbeat, depressing cries of injustice and existential angst ever committed to recording media.

Mocking, he sang along with Roger Waters' plaintive warble. I shushed him.

"Jesus, brother—forget that whiny nonsense." Neill handed me a bulging bubble-wrap mailer of his precious bootleg Dead cassettes. "I just got the Greek theater shows from this summer. That'll lighten your mood."

"I don't want to listen to the motherfucking Grateful Dead again."

"Whoa." He looked truly hurt. "What's wrong?"

"I'm under stress, all right?"

"But the semester's over," he said, sputtering. "I thought you were stoked about your movie."

I shrugged. "It's all meaningless."

Right as the background singers in "Not Now John" sang *"Bing-go,"* Neill's face lit up in recognition. "That chick from the other night shut you down, didn't she."

"Not exactly. Well—yeah. Kinda-sorta."

"Dude. You had some kicks. You got laid. You had fun, you had joy, you had seasons in the sun."

"It's more complicated than that."

Greasy hippy hair hanging down into his eyes, Neill wrinkled his nose as though he smelled mediocre weed smoldering. "Oh, no—*you love her.*"

"What, is this published someplace? Yes, guilty."

"Go march over there and tell her. Tell her about it."

"You are clueless, my friend. I wish it was as easy as all that."

"On the other hand," he said, "let her ass be the one to call. You think I've called Ally? Hell, no."

"I thought you liked her."

"I do. But let 'em twist, man. Twist around on your big old fishhook. Thinking about it. Thinking about the fact that you haven't called until they can't stand it anymore, and then—"

I shouted, "I can't because she's Kunk's girlfriend, you dumbass."

Neill blanched and blinked a few times. "You diddled Kunk's girlfriend? That's hardcore."

Hearing it said aloud made me feel gutted. "It just happened."

"Dude. This is major."

I held up my hands. "Newsflash. Who do you think you're talking to?"

"Kunk's a real badass."

"No duh."

"He's gonna pound you for this."

"Camille's not gonna go and tell him. It's our secret. That was the last thing she said to me."

"Still—awkward."

"She's the one, Neill. She is the one."

"A complicating element. Almost like—*you gotta choose between her, or your best pal.* Dude, it's like a movie."

I took offense. "It's nothing like a fucking movie."

Jutting out his bearded promontory of a chin, sagacious, he said, "Get over her. Cast thy net well and true and wide. Keep them both as friends."

"I suppose that would be ideal."

"Have you looked around this campus? Southeastern's ground zero for hot little mamas."

"I have eyes. But Camille—"

Insistent: "One out of fucking multitudes."

"But—"

"Multitudes, says I."

Satisfied and certain over his philosophizing, he lifted the needle on Pink Floyd in the middle of "Two Suns in the Sunset," sat down and produced a sack of bright green pot out of the kangaroo pocket of his faded Guatemalan baja pullover. Onto the Frisbee did his weed go.

"I guess you're right." Didn't believe it for a minute; felt heartbreak at the thought of giving up on her. "Maybe I should smoke some of that."

"I don't think there's any doubt," sparking up his filthy glass pipe, a dragon's head. "This is the dank."

A knock came at the door, startling us both. Coughing, Neill expelled the biggest, bluest cloud of smoke in history, a plume illuminated through the blinds by shafts of afternoon sunlight.

I got up and craned my neck from the living room into the small foyer. A shape outside the door—a familiar boxy head and big nose.

"Oh—shit."

Neill, turning white as Adluh biscuit flour. "Is it the heat?"

"Worse. It's Kunk."

My roommate collapsed back onto the sofa. "Thank god. I had a dream the other night I got popped. And I was in my underwear at the time."

Shaking, I went over to answer Kunk's insistent knocking. Greeted him with bulging eyes and a breakneck, racing pulse.

"Hey, buddy," I said, all genial and nonchalant. "Get those pages knocked out?"

The leather jacket, the black jeans. Eyes hidden behind mirror shades, he glowered from the other side of the screen door. Pitched a smoldering butt into the bushes. Tense body language.

Took off the shades. I could see it in his eyes. He knew.

She'd told him about us.

About me.

About us.

And what we did.

"Open this fucking screen door," he said.

I did so. The last I recall about Kunk on the porch is hearing him call me a son of a bitch, the blur of his fist, and an explosion of stars, followed by the sensation of falling backward onto the hardwood floor. Fade out.

My reaction after Neill picked me up off the floor and I found out the real reason Kunk had clocked me a well-deserved poke in the jaw?

Relief.

"That was like—uncalled for, bro." Neill, hollering as Kunk, having sucker-punched me, went strutting back down the sidewalk to his car.

Working my jaw, I eased down on the couch. Neill, bat-crap paranoid from smoking his high-test weed, hovered over me like a fussing grandmother. "He hit you. Kunk hit you."

"Be glad it isn't worse. Give me the cordless phone—quick."

I called Camille to find out why she'd done this to me. But, bless her heart, she hadn't told him anything about our night together.

"Of course I wouldn't tell him we did *that*, silly boy. Besides—his feelings were hurt enough already." Instead, she said she'd dished about my opinion of his script being nothing more than a warmed-over knockoff of *Body Heat*.

I felt spun, bewildered. My heart, still so full of her. Now that we'd been together, no turning back or away. How could she deny what had happened between us? "Maybe you should."

"Should what?"

"Tell him."

"Tell him what?"

"About us."

"No, honey. What I did—what we did—was shitty. Low-rent romance."

"Please."

"Don't. Just—don't."

Words like knife wounds. I pushed away Neill trying to shove an ice pack onto my jaw. "But I love you—please."

"No, you do not." She hung up.

Crushed. The phone felt as heavy as a brick in my hand. I dropped it onto the floor with a clatter.

I told Neill what she'd said, and he laughed about the source of Kunk's anger. "Writers, man. Y'all should really try to like, relax about it all."

Later, my roomie took me out and got me drunk, drunk enough that my jaw, and my heart, quit hurting. For the moment. With all this drama and nonsense—many things seemed to be going wrong—I wondered if I ought to get out of MACM. Not the strongest way to finish up the semester.

As for Kunk, now I felt free to seek rapprochement with him over my critique fail—icky, but not frightening like the idea of a Philadelphia tough guy, once mixed up with mobsters and assorted rough trade, gunning for me as a vengeful, cuckolded lover.

And Camille, she made it clear again and again that I had to set aside feelings. To file away memories. To get over it. In any case, Kunk and I would manage to continue our friendship.

But only barely.

Never the same again. Years would go by, the sharp sweet ache of the memories weighing me down. Resentment of him. Not admiration. The old glow of being Kunk's sidekick would be gone forever.

None of this was Kunk's fault—she'd fallen for him first. I couldn't hold that against my friend, much as I ached having lost my chance. Would never have her again.

No—not 'have' her. Be with her, together.

A couple.

Partners.

Simpatico.

We had chemistry. I'd known it from the first time I met her. It hadn't been that way with Nicole or what few others with whom I had gone on dates. Not by a long shot.

This was different; this was real.

But I had to let it go.

"C'mon." When I finally got Kunk to answer the phone a few days after exams were over, he sounded pained. "I'm fucking humiliated, here."

"I should have been straight with you. How did the draft end up?"

"I'm not talking about the goddamn script."

My gut turned to ice. "What, then?"

"About cold-cocking you."

A visible contusion below the zygomatic arch had faded. "Oh—it's nothing. Like out of a movie. Guy opens door, gets clocked, smash cut to black and then in the next scene, we find out it's all a big misunderstanding. Classic."

"It's some childish shit, is what."

"It's forgotten."

"But champ, I wished you'd've said it to my face. Don't send it through the chick, pal. That's—no. It ain't done that way."

Contrite, I admitted my failings. But we also had an elephant on party line with us: "*Did you finish?*"

A chuckle, rueful and small. "More or less."

"Max?"

"He gave me a B."

"But what did he think about the script?"

A thoughtful pause. "Said it felt a touch derivative of a lot of things. But on the other hand," switching to Max's voice, "*that comes part and parcel with the noir genre, now doesn't it, my boy.*"

"Here is wisdom."

"Nothing new under the sun."

"Happens by osmosis."

I'd been working all week on a treatment for *Night Driver*, which had evolved into an edgy, dark, violent story about a chauffeur for a gangster in Atlantic City who gets mixed up with the mobster's moll, who's way, way too young and trying to get out, get away; the driver, as we discover, isn't a lover but a father figure, the girl reminding him of his estranged daughter, and he says, fuck it, I'm going to help this girl. Whole thing turns into a cat and mouse chase between thugs and the night driver, who is caught and beaten and left for dead, the girl returned to the mobster, a sad story with a bleak ending.

But wait—the driver, risen from his watery grave, returns packing major heat, laying all to waste at the mansion. At the real end, bloodied, bedraggled, dirty but alive, he and the girl stagger out together into the sunlight, free. A montage with voiceover from the Night Driver tells us of becoming famous as the heroic mob chauffeur who saved a young girl from a Mafia-war shootout. How he'd been redeemed; how he could now drive in the (drumroll) daylight. Fade to black—or maybe to white, like at the end of the 1978 remake of *Invasion of the Body Snatchers*.

Most of which, I realized later, seemed like I'd lifted wholesale from Scorsese and Schrader's iconic *Taxi Driver*. Once I got it all down in note form and typed up a reasonable two-page treatment, the similarities hit me like a thunderclap.

Osmosis, homage, yes; but outright thievery? I felt sick to my stomach. Kunk, now more than forgiven for his own trespasses.

Frustrated, I paced and fretted: I had wanted to write a script in two weeks like Paul Schrader had with *Taxi Driver*, not steal all the basic story beats of his Jody Foster subplot. My guy, he was just a dad himself who wanted to help a young girl in trouble. A dad who missed his daughter.

That's a long way from Travis Bickle, I thought in my own defense. *Isn't it?*

Over lunch one day close to Christmas, I laid all this out to Kunk, who said it was fine to use some of the familiar story beats. That my treatment had workable elements and a decent enough spine, with enough meat to fill out a reasonable first draft.

"Something to work with feels good."

"That's what Max says about *Binges*—that whatever its problems, now I got something to work with. That the writing, it can always be better."

"Always."

He blew out his lips. "The Dean says I can get independent study credit for taking the feature class again in the spring. Do a revision. Maybe start another one."

Whatever the issues over Camille—an ongoing but private struggle— the two of us taking a Max class together for one more semester felt comfortable and familiar. "Like old times. Table 3?"

He laughed, coughed, fired up a Camel. "One last thing about this whole brouhaha—you know what hurt the most about what you told the old lady about the pages?"

Smarting on about fifty levels: "No. What?"

"It's not you thinking I was trying to cop Kasdan's licks. But it's like— that shit's my real life, man. That whole plot. Don't you get it?"

"Atlantic City."

"Yeah, baby."

"No shit."

"For real."

"You almost pawned your bass?"

"Almost? More than once, champ."

Hot blood rushed to my cheeks. I should have understood—he'd told me all about Atlantic City. Romanticized in my mind, dangerous in his real memories, it's no wonder I had also chosen the Jersey shore as the location of my story, a place I'd never been. "Sometimes I'm a little slow on the uptake."

"It's going around. I finally figured out why the last act seemed so rushed—it's because that's how I left the scene up there."

I asked what happened in the last scenes he'd written.

He smiled. "I finally had to start making shit up."

Laughter and warmth bloomed between us.

Much needed to happen in the upcoming semester—movies would be finished, screenplays written, and lives would change, though not quite in the way any of us in our circle could have anticipated. Camille would be a problem for me—no two ways about it. But Kunk and I were still friends, would again be classmates. It felt right.

Over the holiday break I managed to get more than half a script written, an impressive sixty pages in total. I felt like a golden god.

Had I not made major story changes necessitating a thorough rewrite of the first act—which was like just like starting over, as Lennon sang; getting rid of a character, adding in some backstory that'd come to me about how the Night Driver ended up where he was in his lonely alienated nocturnal life, and a new, exciting opening sequence as the driver drag races a fellow chauffeur on a deserted freeway deep into the night—I might have completed the entire draft.

I'd also originally made the protagonist, named DELANO, a drunk, but after much cogitation about drinking and driving and my mother's death, I 86'd that angle. I wanted him to be heroic, and to my mind, anyone driving around nipping on a flask—a silver flask like Kunk's, as I'd described the driver's ever-present liquor vessel—could never be seen as such.

About the time classes started back, some serious cold weather, by South Carolina standards at least, came roaring across the midlands. Heavy coats and scarves warmed us now as we trudged across campus, but of course what we called 'cold' around these parts would seem down-right balmy to anyone from places further north.

I abandoned the breezy bike riding and started walking the almost two miles from my duplex through the Old Market and uphill toward campus. Something about the crisp air, a frigid Arctic Express, searing my lungs felt bracing enough that it made me forget about Camille. Sort of. Passing by Kunk's place every morning didn't help, nor did my inability to realize I could walk a different way if I so desired.

In the case of Connor, Brenda and your humble director of *Too Far Gone*, going to class in January and February meant sitting cramped around the

Steenbeck and pulling together a rough cut. After a couple of weeks we'd completed the first assemblage, the screening of which played well for Hedda and the fellow students—Freddie Baumbach applauded, but did so looking over his rimless glasses with slitted, spiteful eyes.

His rough cut, which we'd screened earlier in the week, hadn't gone over as well. Freddie had serious pacing and story issues. The actor's badger suit's enormous tail swayed hilariously whenever the actor walked into or out of a frame, though, the way it had on stage last year. And truly, many of his shots looked amazing—Freddie, a pompous ass, but he knew lighting and lenses. As silly as it might have seemed on the surface, a magic-hour shot of the badger lumbering along a lonely set of railroad tracks had given me chicken-skin.

As for Opal's *Untitled Punk Rock Documentary*, her cut ran almost twenty-five minutes long thanks to its featured music performances, an epic by our classroom standards, and thereby making me and Freddie look like insufficiently ambitious also-rans. Hedda's rapturous reception to the footage caused both Freddie and I to slit-eye the short, dyed-black hair on the back of Opal's head.

Opal, who'd shot much of the visually exciting film herself, suffered sound issues, however—her crew hadn't pulled good audio tape at the shows. With the results distorted beyond reason and quite unusable, including key interview material of punk fans at the shows and musicians backstage, she didn't yet know how she'd surmount this problem-leaning-to-crisis. Damn film looked great, though—raw, handheld, immediate, exciting.

I cleared my throat. "I have an idea."

Opal whirled round. "Oh—really, now."

"Why don't you just re-shoot the interviews and dub over the music? Get those people into the production studio. Controlled conditions. Frame them against black, like Warren Beatty's 'witnesses' in *Reds*."

Hedda, nodding and smiling. "That's actually a very good suggestion."

Freddie, his sarcasm dripping. "That's the way to go. Shoot even *more* footage."

"I'll figure it out on my own." Opal, dejected. "But thanks."

To the class Hedda said, "You all did wonderfully; you all have your own problems to solve. There's a terrific amount of fine cutting to be done, sound to be mixed, et cetera et cetera *ad nauseum*. But these rough cuts, it's another milestone. Pat yourselves on the back."

Despite the beauty I saw in Freddie's images, Hedda went on to cite our cinematography for special praise: "The look of *Too Far Gone*, which feels the most complete of the three projects on a narrative level, is so wonderfully silvery, especially the day for night sequence. Bravo, crew."

Smiling and blushing, Connor clutched the reel of our cobbled-together rough cut to his body. "Thank you all."

Darren, snorting. "We like you, we really really like you."

But we couldn't bask, not with so much left to do, all that Hedda listed plus the most frightening task, the actual conforming of the camera negative—meaning, we had to cut and splice the original, irreplaceable master film from which all future elements would be made. A mistake in conforming, the details of which are germane but not worth recounting, could prove irrevocable.

It had to be perfect. It would be perfect.

I had a plan: To make sure my fumble fingers didn't ruin any shots, I'd let Connor and Brenda do it all.

Hoyt Bollard decided to take the feature class for a second time as well, and during the semester we became much closer than we'd been. Even talked about collaborating on a script one day. I lost track of Hoyt a long time ago, but in the spring of 1988, we were tight.

As for me and Kunk, however? Despite our ostensible reconciliation and mutual apologies, a touch of frost, now. He never asked me again if I'd read his revised pages, even after I'd requested the same of him.

Once he read my work, though, Kunk gave me a strong response. Said he loved the first act of *Night Driver*. Would only change this or that line of dialogue. "You were never too good with dialogue, champ. If I can be straight with you."

"You'd want it straight, wouldn't you?"

"You're damn right," he said.

We laughed, dry and brief.

I felt guilt about the night with Camille, about which I could never be fully honest with my friend. Not and risk what goodwill remained between us. Kunk and Camille seemed tighter as ever—I suppose they had worked through his infidelities. Meanwhile, I had to act like nothing occurred, which I did with relative ease.

Most of the time.

Except in moments like this: alone in the classroom hallway, Camille had noticed a new shirt I'd bought, deep royal blue with a wide collar. "Blue is your color," she said, adjusting the shoulder seam and picking at lint with her beautiful nails. "Handsome man."

My gut burned. I wanted to touch her and kiss her and hold her again. Thought I would die.

"Blue like my heart," I managed to bleat.

"Aw," she said, giving me a quick hug. "Don't say that."

"I wouldn't want to lie to you, of all people. Would I?"

With pity in her eyes, her fingertips brushed my face, and she was gone.

On Kunk's advice, I worked on the dialogue. All semester long I spent much time on this aspect of my work. Listening with full attention to the lines in the movies I saw; scrutinizing with great care how people spoke to one another; trying to concoct an amalgamation of the two.

Both Max and I felt my work was improving, as did Kunk, Hoyt, and Opal, too, who, on my recommendation, had also taken the feature-script class. She wanted to write a screenplay about a doomed New Wave rock star like Ian Curtis, she explained, the singer from Joy Division. I'd never heard of him, but encouraged her all the same—we had both loved *Sid & Nancy*.

The writers in the class, including a couple of other familiar faces like Thaddeus Blanchard, all encouraged one another, a true spirit of camaraderie. And after three classes with him, Max de Lisle seemed like a true friend, if considerably older than even Kunk. Rumors abounded that, in a year or two, he would retire from teaching. I hated to hear that. Couldn't imagine learning scriptwriting from anyone else.

A month into the semester, however, a seismic event occurred that shook up Max, Kunk, and me too, disrupting whatever wave of creativity we'd both been riding.

I'D BEEN SEQUESTERED with Connor in a recording booth—a closet, essentially—for three hours working on sound effects, going through all manner of library material looking for the right sound of a lock clicking or a spade striking earth or, for that matter, a heavy glass vodka bottle smashing into the side of a human head.

Tedious, yes, but another *Blow Out* moment: threading little reels of quarter-inch tape onto machines, I found myself ensconced in the warm and smothering bosom of minutia, of meticulous detail work, our body odor and breath from drinking cup after cup of bitter vending machine coffee all commingling into a fetid funk. When buried in such arcane, demanding, but creative tasks, I found I would lose all sense of time—and of myself. In a good way.

Until Kunk came knocking on the plexiglass of the recording module, a row of four freestanding units along a corridor where students did audio production and post work.

I opened the door to see my friend looking haggard, harried, and despite a chilly February day outside, sweaty.

"[REDACTED], baby—got a minute or three?"

I exchanged a bleary-eyed look with Connor, who'd started the session with a headache, he'd said, and welcomed the idea of wrapping it up for the day. "We should probably quit. Everything's starting to sound the same."

"Fifteen?" I said to Kunk.

"I'll be at the bar," meaning the venerable Upstairs West where we'd first bonded.

Watching Kunk shuffle down the hall, Connor unloaded the reel of tape we'd been reviewing. "Maybe you could remind him about the music," he said. "We don't have the rest of our lives to get this nailed down."

I'd pitched the idea to the group that we get Kunk and Max, too, to contribute a jazzy score to our ten-minute movie. "I'll give him a nudge."

Twenty minutes later I found Kunk at the bar a half-block up the hill. He'd started on his second beer, and sat smoking with the kind of deliberation you see in longtime puffers—intense, drawing on the small tube so hard you'd have thought he could suck a cantaloupe through a drinking straw. He had some schoolwork on the bar: a novel, a famous Updike: *Rabbit, Run.*

"What a schlub this guy is." Kunk, tapping the trade paperback on its cover, its cracked spine sporting a peeling yellow USED sticker. "This Angstrom bonehead shoulda kept running."

"I haven't read any Updike."

"Scarier than Stephen King. No shit."

I ordered a beer and plopped down at the corner so I could face my friend.

He had a hard time making eye contact. Kept tapping the paperback. Shaking his head.

I sat waiting.

"Champ." His lips worked, but little else came out. "Shit."

Finally: "So what's the big deal?"

"My life is over," he said. "Seriously."

Dumbstruck, I sat in silence. "—"

"Over," he repeated.

"But—why?"

"Shit's gotten realer than real. That's why."

"Sounds melodramatic." I cadged a smoke out of Kunk's pack. When I went out drinking with him, I always wanted to smoke. He made it look so cool. "Max not happy with the revised pages?"

"If only it was that easy."

I asked what, then.

"Camille—ah, god."

My voice cracked. *Did she break up with you?*

His laugh, low and rueful. "Far from it. She's pregnant."

Smiling. Nodding. Oscar-worthy. But inside, my guts squirmed like newborn snakes in a cold slimy knot. "Wow," I said with a squeak. "What —are you going to do?"

"Do? Nothing. She wants to keep the fucking thing."

All I could do was chug half my beer and snap Kunk's Zippo open to light my smoke with hands that betrayed a tremor. "That's a real situation."

"It's a definite type of situation, here."

After he told me he'd asked Camille to marry him—and that she'd said yes—I don't remember the rest of the conversation. I suffered a kind of buzzing in my ears, like when being plagued by mosquitos or gnats, a whining, high frequency through which my friend's words passed and were diminished, all but subsumed.

A question begged its way through my fog of shock and incredulity: "How does this translate to your life being over?"

"Don't you realize I've organized my future for the last couple of decades around the idea of *not* having kids?"

All I could think was, sure, it would be scary to have a kid. But marrying Camille in the process seemed a fair trade. "I hear you. A surprise."

"An unwelcome one."

I didn't let myself think about them being together—of course they were, before and after I'd made love to the goddess Grahl—but the idea that he'd made her pregnant gave me a sick feeling, like taking a shot to the nuts.

I made a speech about how this was all one more step on the path Kunk had sought, a different one from the life he'd led—as he'd said to me a year ago, a path of normalcy. A house, a job. And now, a wife and kid. "This isn't the end of life, surely, but a beginning."

Kunk told me he thought I'd misunderstood him and what he wanted out of this crazy ride called life. Faced with the enormity of what I'd been told, all I could do was agree. And while he later ended up writing and recording a few moody minutes of music for *Too Far Gone*, on that particular day, I never quite got around to asking him about it.

Over a bright, temperate Easter weekend at Max de Lisle's lake house, Levon Kunkle and Camille Grahl became husband and wife.

Numbness, coursing throughout my spirit.

The universe, so cruel.

If nothing else? The pain—maybe it would give me material.

Afterwards, they drove down to Hilton Head for their honeymoon. Lucky that we had spring break from school that week. Camille, citing the unappealing *kuh-kuh* repetition, declined to take Kunk's surname as her own.

I'd seen her only once since hearing the news, or rather, only once when we had a chance to talk, on an afternoon walking across campus when I lied and said I had an errand near the garage where she parked.

"This is incredible. That y'all are getting married."

"I don't believe it yet myself. But—it feels right."

Halfway across the Ellipsis, with the sagacious facades of historical architecture and ancient live oaks whose judgement I could feel, I half-collapsed onto a bench, overcome.

"Oh, honey—what's wrong?"

"Don't marry him. Please."

Shaking her head with pity. "I have to."

"But I—I haven't stopped thinking about you and us and our night together, and I can't sit by and just, just not say—*how much I love you.*"

At last. The words. To her ears.

Shushing me, she sat down. "Angel, I will always treasure our special night together. And you know I love you, too. But really, we don't even know each other that well."

I choked back despair. "I don't care that you're pregnant. *I don't care that it's his.*"

"Angel. That's so sweet. Nobody's ever said anything sweeter."

I broke down. I wept—for Camille, for my mother, for the loss of something for which I had no name.

Squirrels, tamed by generations of generous students and faculty, flitted about near our bench, their small black eyes probing and hopeful. Camille draped her arms around my neck, lay her head upon my shoulder. My tears ebbed. Nobody walking by even seemed to notice. On a major university campus like Southeastern, someone's tears fell every day upon its storied, red-brick walkways.

"This isn't how I wanted to get married," she finally said. "But Levon and I love each other, so it's the right thing."

"As long as you're happy," not meaning it in the slightest. "With an old codger like Kunk for a husband," I added, trying to wink and smile.

"Hush your mouth. Silly boy."

I wondered: had I been forty, would she have loved me instead of him? It didn't sound like it. The stuff of conjecture; a waste of time.

"So you do love him?"

"Of course."

With that, I said I felt satisfied, and wished her well. No greater lie have I ever told.

She informed me I would be expected at the ceremony. That Kunk said if it weren't for Max, I'd have been his choice for best man.

I felt touched enough to mitigate the pain. For about five seconds.

We walked on to the garage, chilly, damp concrete and the echoing of tires squealing and engines revving from above our heads. At Camille's yellow Mustang, I put my arms around her and leaned in for a kiss. She put up a hand. Instead, my dream lover gave me a peck on the cheek, a friendly squeeze of a hug, and said she'd see me at the wedding.

WHEN THE TIME CAME, however, I feigned illness and blew off the ceremony. Others who attended told me the service had been brief and lovely, and that Camille looked stunning.

Outside class the next week, Max chided my absence. Said that I'd been missed by all involved, particularly the bride and groom.

"One hell of a lakeside party. I'm still hung over."

"Believe me, Prof, I'll be beating myself up over this one for a long time."

Too *Far Gone*, in the last stages, a time of finishing touches: all three groups of filmmakers in Hedda's class traveled by van to Atlanta, to a post-house where we could do our final sound mixes.

Following a smooth editorial period we'd had picture lock now for over a week, and Connor had begun the tortuous process of conforming, which he said he'd do on his own if we didn't mind. Neither Brenda nor I wanted to touch the negative unless we had to, but we kept this from Hedda, who expected each group member to participate in all aspects of production and post-production.

The sound mixing session proved lengthy and difficult, but the veteran audio engineer working with us seemed amiable enough. Our work print kept slipping out of the projector, which had been embarrassing, but what could we say? The reel of film had been handled and spliced and run to death. Besides, it happened with the two other films as well, so we all looked like amateurs.

Nothing could compare to poor Opal's ordeal, however. She'd tried to loop in replacement audio for the unusable interview recording, with rubbery, terrible, at times laughable results. The entire time we sat watching her struggle to get the mix right, she appeared nauseous.

"Nice score." The engineer complimented our project as we were gathering ourselves to leave for home. "Suits the images just right."

"My friend's a professional musician."

"Classy and subtle. Which that picture needs," muttering to himself.

Uh-oh, I thought. Not classy or subtle, eh?

I chalked this aside up to the technician's cynicism; he said he'd been in the business over thirty years. I couldn't imagine what turning thirty would feel like, much less working at the same job for so long.

The last fight the group endured about the film had been over the crawl at the end, how I'd wanted three title cards for the three principals:

Written by Brenda LaRose

Photographed by Connor Rush

Directed by [REDACTED]

Connor had been fine with the idea, but Brenda declared an intention to keep the crawl short, insisting we all be listed on the same card.

"It's a student short," she said. "Not *Apocalypse Now.*"

I didn't put up a fuss. In the wake of Camille and Kunk's wedding, some of the fire had gone out of my belly. I managed a meaningless, joking defense, a comeback dragged out of my storehouse of trivia. "Bad example —the first release of *Apocalypse Now* didn't feature any end titles."

We went over the list of other credits. Score: Levon Kunkle. Sound: Darren Woczinski. Costumes: Camille Grahl. Makeup: Sally-Ann Rush (Connor's sister, who had done all of one afternoon's work). Foley: Darren Woczinski.

Darren, not even officially in our group, would be getting two credits.

On my movie.

What a gyp.

Connor left to take the credit copy over to a guy named Woodard in the Instructional Media department across campus, who pretty much shot titles for everybody's film, making himself a few hundred bucks on the side from all the needy MACM students.

By that weekend the conforming job was finished without incident, the titles were complete, processed and attached, and we shipped off our final film elements and mag track mix-down to the lab for the creation of what's called the answer print, the one we'd screen and give an answer as to whether the film presented as truly finished.

All together now: *exhale.*

The waiting began; this time we sprang for next-day FedEx, going and coming. Almost there.

DURING THE CLOSE-QUARTERS work of editing earlier in the semester, I'd gotten to know Brenda quite a bit better, and despite our last minute bickering over this and that, genuine friendship grew between us. She filled me in on some of her secrets, and I offered her a few of mine.

After a long session one afternoon spent hunched over the Steenbeck, trims hanging all around us like translucent gray snakes, we strolled up the hill to get sub sandwiches and coffee. Connor, off somewhere on another bit of business. We all had our other classes to juggle around the intensive, involved processes of our Mass Comm work.

A delivery truck trundled up the steep hill next to us. *"Nobody does-n't like Sar-rah Lee."* Brenda, singing in a cute voice. Noticing the iconic tagline painted on the side of the truck, she said seeing it made her feel wistful.

I opened the door for her at Pappy's, and we went in. "Warm memories?"

"Sara Lee cakes remind me of a more innocent time."

"I'm that way about those yellow Zingers—the ones that used to have Peanuts characters on the package, with the frosting on top?"

"I don't think I ever had a Zinger."

"You're missing out. After my mother started bringing those home, I broke up with Twinkies and never looked back."

Brenda laughed, stumbled, braced herself on my forearm. Warmth where her hand had rested would linger.

Sitting across from each other, our chins dripping mustard, oil and vinegar and with little strings of lettuce dangling from the corners of mouths, Brenda and I talked about ourselves. Sparing her the most intimate of details, I described my mother, our problematic relationship, and the lack of closure I felt over her death more so than outright grief.

Brenda seemed troubled. "You loved her. She was your mother."

"Yes—with reservations."

Brenda seemed to accept the definitive but vague nature of my remarks, moving on to her own issues. "Everything was okay until my dad lost his job at the shipyard. He was a pipefitter."

"A working man."

"Yeah, but he had a degree, in mechanical engineering. The job was more than it sounds. And he made decent money. He'd put in so much time. He seemed ashamed when they laid him off, and he couldn't get on somewhere else."

"He took it hard."

"He changed. Long story long, my folks split up, and my mom and I ended up leaving Charleston and moving into a fricking trailer park in West Columbia for a while."

"Yikes."

"You got no idea. It's why I ended up in therapy."

"I grew up in Edgewater County," I said. "I know all about trailer parks."

She told me about being sexually harassed, of drug and alcohol abuse among the poor folks who populated the neighborhood. The mobile home had been owned by her uncle, a free place to live until her mother got on her feet, which after a year or so allowed them to move into a house in a nicer part of town. Brenda, a younger sister, and her mother, all making it on their own.

Her story made me feel blessed and comfortable and privileged. Whatever my mother's issues, I'd enjoyed a comparatively stable life.

Then Brenda laid something really heavy on me: She went on to say that this experience, an outgrowth of an interest in photography, had soured her on working in media.

"I don't think filmmaking is for me. It's just—too much."

I told her I felt shocked. While I hadn't much enjoyed sharing so much decision making across the triumvirate of our little filmmaking brain trust, I thought the film had turned out all the better for having had collaborators I liked and trusted. I still planned to make movies one day, but I'd really taken to the writing, to be honest, and told her so—with my script *Night Driver* now all but finished, I felt quite accomplished. I thought my draft kind of rocked, as did the experience of sitting by myself to get the work done.

"Writing—a solitary endeavor. I get it." A range of emotion cascaded across her face; she chewed her lip and seemed faraway. "Maybe I should go back to poetry."

She'd already had a dual major, English and Mass Comm, and for her senior year next year, she declared, it would be back to the literary life.

We finished eating and cruised back down the hill to our cars. I paused at her Tercel, a beater; another car scene. I felt awkward, but still went to hug her.

Stiff, she responded only in the smallest of ways, a tiny patting motion on my shoulder.

"I'm glad you're my friend, Bren."

Her face, already naturally pink, had turned scarlet. "Yeah. This has been fun with both you guys."

I got her vibe—she didn't trust men. I didn't blame her, only hoped that she understood my gesture for what it was: one of affection, not putting the moves on her. I liked Jaime. I wouldn't do that to him. I'd already betrayed enough of my friends.

During the Grateful Dead's Spring 1988 tour, every hippie's worst nightmare came true: Neill got arrested outside Cleveland, where the band was playing a three-night stand at a basketball arena.

Bummer, man.

The story: my roommate had been tagged at a rest stop holding pot and LSD, but not distribution quantity, thank god. His dad, a lawyer, reacted with anger, but felt he'd be able to get the charges wheedled down to a manageable level.

None of it slowed Neill down one bit. He'd gotten bailed out of jail, hauled ass home to get a few fresh tie-dyes and set out again to Atlanta, where the tour was to end. Crazy.

During the brief time he was home, I eavesdropped on a phone call between Neill and his father. "Of course I'm going to the fucking Atlanta shows," he shouted into the receiver, held white-knuckled in one shaking fist. "If I let the pigs beat me, then they'll have beaten me."

Neill listened for a while, his face getting redder. At last he told his father to come and stop him, if he thought he could.

He hung up, cursing. "Old man thinks I ought to stay away from 'those people,' he keeps saying."

"The other Deadheads?"

"Who does he think I am? Who does he think his own son is? 'Those people,'" he said in disgust, shaking his head. "They is we, bro. All I can tell you."

I agreed more with his father, but kept it to myself. Sounded like asking for trouble, jumping right back into the fray.

But what did I know? I wasn't a Deadhead. It was serious business, this following them around. Maybe I'd check it out one day. Maybe not. Acid seemed endemic to the enjoyment of the experience, and for all the positives that'd come from my trip on Kunk's birthday, I was certain I'd never-ever want to take another dose. In retrospect, I learned quite a bit about myself that night. Maybe too much.

AS THE SEMESTER WOUND DOWN, I made the decision to continue working at the Enemas for another summer. The big anticipatory title coming for Memorial Day was *Willow*, a George Lucas-produced fantasy film with a dwarf in the lead role and directed by Ron Howard, who'd shed his TV child-actor image as Opie and Ritchie Cunningham to become a top Hollywood director.

Good for him, I thought. But what an advantage, having grown up in show business, appearing on not one but two iconic TV series—two of the biggest ever. Makes it a little easier to get your shot at directing.

As someone who'd grown up in my own version of Mayberry, I wondered about my own chances to make it in the biz. I wanted to believe my talent would carry me through, but in my heart I knew I'd need some big breaks, and amazing luck to get anywhere in Hollywood.

Over the course of the last year at the multiplex I'd moved up the food chain, from usher to candy counter to box office, the pinnacle of floor staff responsibility, the place where most of the money flowed. Hank Halvorsin trusted me; I got on well with my manager. Had gotten raises. Whole bit.

One day I got called upstairs to see Halvorsin. I'd been whiling the afternoon away on a plush stool leafing through a week-old *Variety* I'd picked up at the Capitol Newsstand, the only place in town to get the national weekly edition of the show business trade paper, and welcomed the break.

"You've been here a while," Mr. Halvorsin said. "Almost a year."

"Sounds about right."

"And you're almost finished with school?"

"One more semester."

"I see. Plans?"

"Grad school—New York, or L.A. Eventually, anyway."

"How's the film coming along?"

I explained we were waiting to get our answer print back from the lab. "We're pretty stoked. It came out—good."

Had it, though? Or was it simply finished?

Hank Halvorsin seemed excited for me. He loved movies. He hadn't gone to college, instead working his way up from usher, he explained, until offered a job as assistant manager at a 'plex in Augusta, and on to his current position here in the bigger market.

"Assistant manager," he said. "It's a lot of responsibility."

"So I've seen."

"What do you think?"

I had no idea what he meant. "About—what?"

He laughed. "About becoming assistant manager."

Taken aback, I sat with my fingertips pressed together. Assistant Managers pulled long hours, but received benefits and a decent salary—a real salary.

I'd been given an unanticipated choice: I could take the job, start putting away money for grad school in New York, and after another year or so, splitting the scene.

Or, I could ask if he'd hold off until later in the year. I'd looked into the summer school schedule, had realized I could take two courses each term and complete my degree without having to go at all in the fall—I'd be done.

I proposed all this; Hank said he'd talk it over with the district manager, see if they'd hold off on filling the position until August, only a few months away. The way I saw it, I could stand moving up from the bluecoat ranks into management for long enough to get a decent stash of cash together.

We shook on the conversation, with no promises made; the next morning I went to the registrar's office to check into summer school. Strange how in one day everything could change. I'd been through it with my mother's death; thankfully, these changes seemed far more benign.

ight Driver turned out okay, but no world-beating masterpiece had sprung, fully-formed, from the nimble intellect and fingertips of the world's next great screenwriting prodigy. At only 88 pages, it had come in on the low end of the feature length script scale, but then, I'd gone for economy in terms of the narrative, descriptions, et cetera. Who could fault me for brevity?

Only my teacher: "I didn't get a good sense of the visual nature of this 'movie,'" Max said upon reading the draft. "And I have trouble with some of the dialogue."

I cringed in the chair across from his desk, under the picture of 52nd Street, but tried to keep a smile on my face.

"But overall, I did find myself caught up in the narrative, and I'm not sure I can give a higher compliment than that. Bravo, Mr. [REDACTED]." He closed my screenplay, took out a thick red marker and wrote an A on the cover. "You've earned the top grade in the feature writing class."

The best I could say about my own work? The piece turned out better than I'd originally imagined the story way back in December.

By the time I turned in the final draft in the first week of May, however, I was sick of the script, and sick of sharing a classroom with Kunk, a friend I could no longer look in the eye. He'd spent the semester piddling with *Binges* instead of writing a new script, not to mention all his personal drama. Now he'd become distracted with lining up a job, his own "real" job, as he kept calling it with dread, after May graduation.

As for me, I was more than ready to move on to the next script, which I'd planned to write over the summer, but for which I hadn't yet settled on an idea. In the face of having so much classwork ahead of me during the next two and half months, though—I'd decided to go for it, to get the degree finished and take the management job at the Enemas for the next year—I wasn't sure how many screenplay pages I'd crank out. I would make time for it, somehow. I couldn't lose the thread. Not over having some ordinary job.

HIS LONG FINGERS TREMBLING, Connor started threading the answer print onto the Steenbeck, where we'd already watched our movie so many times. Brenda had run and left a Post-it on Hedda's locked office door with the news the answer print had arrived, and before we could begin our professor knocked, excited.

"It came?"

"*Yes.*" All in unison. We laughed, nervous and halfway giddy.

"Forget the Steenbeck. Let's do the work justice—let's project it in the classroom."

The thought hadn't occurred to me. "That would be fantastic," I said.

Blown up big, the film had flaws and little problems and sure enough, the story didn't seem all that interesting, but on the whole we'd crossed a dangerous, difficult, and expensive rubicon, one leaving us intact and with a decent film to anchor our professional reels. As the brief end cards flashed on and off, I felt happy. I felt successful. A weight off.

That night the three filmmakers went out, drinking champagne with our actors. I didn't call Kunk and Camille, who'd moved into a townhouse near campus. I knew the rent had to be enormous, but on the other hand, Kunk, as it turned out, would soon be stepping into a new job at a national insurance company with a headquarters located in Columbia, one that included a media department engaged in producing insurance-related video content.

Kunk would be the new head scriptwriter; the last time I saw him before the Student Showcase, he'd been on his way to pick up a suit from the cleaners, he said, and onto the campus not of Southeastern University, but the insurance giant where he'd endure a final interview.

"Everything's working out," I said.

"I guess it is. I guess so."

"You've gotten what you wanted, dude. You realize that?"

"Have I, champ?"

"Considering what you told me when we first met? I'd say so."

He snorted, nodded, seemed skeptical. "Time will tell."

I wanted to punch him. He got Camille, found a job writing scripts, and at a fat salary compared to what I'd be making at the multiplex.

Maybe his life *was* over, in a sense, but only an older iteration. The man said he wanted normalcy, stability, what have you; the opposite of his journeyman music career, the opposite of gigging in bars all night, seeing many sunrises, never quite knowing from where the next payday might come. Be careful for what thou wishes, yes; but indeed, all had seemed to work out to his specifications.

Beautiful young wife, that much for certain. Whatever Kunk's issues, that much you had to give him.

Camille, now six or seven months pregnant. On the off times when I saw her, she had acquired a radiance I'd never before experienced in a woman I knew with intimacy. In the years since, I learned this is a common trait among expectant mothers—two hearts beating, the glow of new life emanating from within fecund young bodies. Seeing her with Kunk's baby growing inside did little to quell the ache in my heart, the yearning. As I'd once heard, we want most that which we cannot have.

On the day of the public screening, the three filmmaking teams drew numbers out of a hat to decide the order. Freddie's badger opus would screen first, then Opal's punk doc, with our macabre murder movie going last.

Freddie, beet-cheeked with annoyance, nonetheless kept his the irritation to himself.

Opal's reaction? Pale, paler than normal all the time now. One evening at the Pizza Joint Too the week before, I had seen her and her lovely gal-pal Marcy from a distance; Opal, distressed, dewy-eyed and gesticulating.

A fellow traveler, I understood her strife without knowing the details; that she struggled to finish a problematic film was enough. My heart went out to her. Our technical problems, all minor. Hers? Enormous. Poor kid.

At last we gathered inside the projection booth in the student union theater where prints of second-run and revival movies played in the evenings. I'd managed to catch a number of films there I'd never seen before: Hooper's *Texas Chainsaw Massacre*, Truffaut's *Shoot the Piano Player*, Cox's *Repo Man*, Waters's *Polyester*, complete with scratch-and-sniff cards. Sacred space.

And now?

My own images, about to flicker.

Distracted and anxious throughout the other presentations, Connor, Brenda and I managed to become drunk as skunks.

My father, alone, sat downstairs among the crowd of parents and well-wishers and media students. I could see the top of his head, pink beneath thinning, cottony hair. Since Mother's death, I swore he'd aged ten years.

Footsteps came clunking up the stairwell. The door opened—Kunk, a thick manilla envelope under his arm.

"Thought I'd find you miscreants up here."

"Want a toot?" Connor had set up a makeshift bar the other filmmakers had also been using. We offered vodka and blended whiskey, cold beers in a small cooler, a few mixers. I'd been downing vodka tonics, fast and smooth and easy compared to drinking beer. As such, I felt potted. As I came over to Kunk, my legs wobbled.

"Got my store-bought right here." Kunk, producing the silver flask out of his jacket pocket. He gurgled the whiskey and went to pass the flask to me. "Broke out the good stuff."

I sipped, handed it back. He slipped it into his coat pocket. My friend looked so debonaire—a new suit, I thought, he'd bought for his new job. His new life, his new wife, his couple of paintings from Sears. Whole trip.

Winked. "Big night—eh?"

"A happier occasion than the last time we used this flask," I said.

Searching his memory. His big-blues widened in recognition. He put his arm around me. "Saw your old man down there. He looked a little uncomfortable."

"He's always hated driving over here in Columbia. I think he mainly wants to see what all that money went for."

Kunk, who'd screened the film while writing the score: "He's gonna be one proud papa. As am I, sir." He seemed to remember the envelope tucked under his arm. "Oh, and here you go. Turned this in earlier today."

I took his revised, polished *Binges* and stuck it into my book bag. "This isn't your only copy, I hope."

Kunk laughed. "Nah. But you owe me yours, now."

"I'll burn one off at Kinko's first thing tomorrow morning."

Connor and Brenda, sharing some private joke, burst into drunken laughter from the other side of the projection booth.

Cocking my thumb at them, I said, "Or whenever I manage to wake up."

"I hear you. You guys are screening last."

"Right."

He started to go, but stopped. "Oh—Camille said for me to tell you congrats."

"How is she?"

"She's beautiful. Before her, I never thought pregnant women looked attractive."

"Me, neither."

"But now we both do."

"Yes."

I reached out. "Give me the flask. Gimme another toot of the good stuff. Would ya?"

"Sure thing, champ."

THE FIRST TWO FILMS SCREENED. Thanks to inebriation—Hi, Mom!—I don't remember them that well, other than bits and pieces familiar from the screening of rushes in the classroom setting.

Freddie's, about a young man who believed he harbored an inner badger he'd later manifest physically, and which played so broad and flat both in it theatrical presentation and in the unfinished film we'd seen garnered major laughs; the sight of Freddie, who'd played the lead as well as directed, wearing that badger suit with its great lazily swishing tail going about the daily business of modern life in an office building— fixing coffee, watercooler chit-chat, the slapstick of getting on-and-off elevators—entertained the audience. And me too, for that matter. A success.

Opal's documentary, however? A drag. Interesting enough, but the whole punk scene proved much too much for this staid crowd of parents and alumni, in particular the music of the hardcore bands themselves— loud, grating, distorted. Her syncing issues hadn't helped. Snickers could be heard at some of the more egregious instances of rubbery looping in the interview segments. Opal sat in the corner of the projection booth with her head down until it was over. Tepid, brief applause.

The projectionist took off the print, gave it to her. She left without saying goodbye.

"Bless her heart." Connor, watching as the guy now threaded our answer print—there'd been no time to order a proper projection print yet —into the machine. "That was the sound of death out there."

"I thought it was fine," Brenda said. "Whatever its technical limitations, she captured the milieu."

"It could've been worse. I'll take punk over that noodling Deadhead nonsense I have to endure at home."

Connor, definitive. "I knew it'd be good when we saw the raw footage."

"That's the way I felt about our film," mixing a new drink despite starting to see double. "Anyone need freshening up?"

Both my partners held up full cocktails. "We're fine," Brenda said.

The last segment before our film screened had been a live performance from one of the feature screenplays, a scene selected by Max de Lisle. Alas, he hadn't chosen an excerpt from *Night Driver* or *Binges*, but rather Hoyt Bollard's untitled 'oater,' as *Variety* termed examples of the Western form. He'd had the biggest stones of anyone in the class—working in a genre all but moribund? The scenes I'd read in his script had rocked, though. A good writer.

Max, also suitably impressed, had chosen a midpoint monologue by the bartender character on whom Hoyt's story turned, a proud and resourceful ex-slave who'd foresworn violence only to be sucked back into its vortex to avenge the death of his family at the hands of recalcitrant Confederate soldiers unable to accept defeat, or so Hoyt had pitched the story back at the beginning of the semester.

Hoyt and Max had asked a trained thespian from the theater department to recite the soliloquy, in sonorous tones projected deep from the diaphragm as he cleaned glasses and wiped down a makeshift bar set hastily carted out and later struck. Hoyt's writing and the actor's performance gave me chicken skin.

On the whole, this would turn out to be the highlight of the evening for me. Gratifying to see one's ideas translated into filmic images, yes, but experiencing Hoyt's work performed with such immediacy made me remember my few high school theater experiences. Made me want to write plays. Made me envious with ambition.

The lights fell and Hedda Gamble stood on the small stage. "And at long last tonight, we close the 1988 Mass Comm student showcase with our final 16mm project, *Far Too Gone*. Oh—shoot. Or is it the other way? It is. *Too Far Gone*. Sorry, guys." After thanking the assembled crowd for their support, making two additional announcements and calling for a round of applause for all who had made the evening possible on a technical level, she walked offstage with a quick signal up to us in the projection booth.

The film began. Compared with Freddie's movie, which had been bright and airy and funny, and Opal's, which had been colorful and loud and impossible to ignore, a crowd made restless by the waning, lengthy evening sat in silent repose as our quiet, dark tale unspooled.

By the time Jaime Marzol struck his 'brother' the first time with the vodka bottle, however, it seemed we had them: they jumped and gasped.

But by the end, in which our psychopathic perpetrator manages to bury his brother's body and gets away scot-free, the audience offered only polite applause. To win them over, it seemed, evildoers still needed their comeuppance. In real life the perp who'd bludgeoned his girlfriend to death and buried her in the backyard got the death penalty. Our guy walks away, looking a little haunted. Not much justice. I get it.

In any case, our shared credit popped up on the screen and disappeared with shocking abruptness, *Directed by [REDACTED]* zipping by in an eye-blink. A ten minute film goes by fast.

IN THE CACOPHONOUS lobby of the student union afterwards, the crowd milled and hobnobbed. Sloshed and rubbery of gait, Connor, Brenda and I found our various family members, shook hands with professors, congratulated other students.

My dad tried to smile and gave me a good pounding on the shoulder, but seemed troubled.

"What'd you think, Pop?"

"I thought it was real good, son. Kind of short. I was expecting it would've been closer to a real movie."

"Real movies costs millions of dollars."

"Well, now—I reckon I'm glad it was short, then."

"But otherwise: did you like it?"

"That one old boy knocked the mess out of the other one, didn't he?"

"Yes. He did."

"That one bit, where he was looking down into the camera? That was right scary."

The infamous POV shot. "He was hitting my fist with the bottle," I mimed, "just out of frame."

"That must've hurt like the dickens."

"It did. Sometimes we suffer for our art."

"Son," he said. "You're acting like you might've had a bit to drink tonight."

I explained we'd been in a celebratory mood, which he understood, but with a caveat:

"I hope you ain't driving nowhere."

The statement hung heavy in the air, buffeted by all the chattering voices around us. "I'm not. I wouldn't."

"I would hope not."

I added words that for the two of us held portentous weight: "I've got more sense than to drive drunk."

I introduced Dad to my fellow filmmakers, Hedda Gamble and Max, who'd been off to the side conferring with Kunk.

My writing teacher beamed with pride. "Your son is on his way to great things," Max informed my father. "He's not only completed an accomplished film this semester, but written one damn fine screenplay as well."

I'd barely discussed the script with my father. We looked at each other. I felt embarrassed.

"Well, dang," he said. "That's my boy."

"A keen mind. An emerging voice. A fine young man."

Daddy tousled my hair, an acceptable humiliation. "He's always been real smart."

Out in the horseshoe-shaped parking lot next to the student union, I bade my father farewell. He asked if I'd thought I was up to the busy summer school schedule I had planned for myself.

I explained how I wanted to be done with Southeastern. That I felt it was soon time to move on. I hadn't told him about the job offer at the cinemas yet. At the moment, I felt the job offer wasn't of any lasting import, only the film and my screenplay.

He shook my hand again, pulled me close to him. "She'd be so happy for you tonight."

"You think?"

"I know."

My father drove away, the taillights of his Cadillac flashing as he negotiated the parking lot. My dad had always seemed older than his years. I wondered how much he'd enjoyed his life with my mother, and what he would do from here. I didn't have those questions. I only knew where I was going—somewhere. Eventually.

Only days later, fresh, abhorrent tragedy struck, forever tainting the entire experience of making *Too Far Gone* and our happiness at having screened it for an audience. In its suddenness, this catastrophe felt immediate and more horrible, somehow, than my mother's more commonplace traffic accident death:

On an ordinary Tuesday, Jaime Marzol had clocked out at McHaffie's, where he'd been promoted to bartender and had planned to work all summer and save money before moving to New York to become the next Eddie Murphy. He'd told coworkers he intended to grab a slice of pizza before going home to bed. His coworkers described him as upbeat and happy, wishing them all well and that he'd see them tomorrow.

But he never got his last meal, or worked another shift—a fight had erupted on the sidewalk outside of the Pizza Joint Too between alleged gang members and a group of college joes, two of whom were big-time football players out for an off-season carouse. Jaime, a natural mediator, jumped into the fray.

Right at the moment shots rang out, the crowd scattered. At first no one seemed to have been hurt, until the Samaritan wishing to the soothe the bestial anger of strangers collapsed onto the chipped, dirty granite of the curb. Jaime, bleeding out after the lone stray, hot bullet shredded the tender flesh of his neck, died in the ambulance rushing him to Palmetto General.

For months the headlines would scream about out-of-control students and urban gang-bangers rampaging in the Old Market, but no charges associated with the crime were ever filed; in the confusion of a bar brawl, no one could, or would, say from whom the single shot had come. In an instant, the college ghetto acquired a rep as a dangerous inner city neighborhood instead of a quaint urban village. This, however, far from the gravest injury.

ANOTHER EDGEWATER COUNTY FUNERAL. Jaime came from Red Mound, a rural bump in the road near the Pisgette National Forest comprising the western third of the county. He'd grown up only miles from me, but on the other side of the tracks, so to speak.

Jaime Marzol—charming and charismatic. Good with voices, jokes, routines. A helper, not a taker. Always ready to serve.

All gone in an instant.

Max, Kunk, and Camille, looking uncomfortably swollen and pregnant —downright miserable—had made the long ride out into the boonies together. We convened in the white clapboard church parking lot. I greeted them with warmth tinged by shock and sadness.

Max, gray and old. Kunk, red-eyed, seemed distracted. Camille, shiny and round.

She took me aside. "Look at my feet."

I did so. The sight of her legs startled me into remembrance of happier times, of impetuous, forbidden, ephemeral moments.

"They seem fine to me."

"They're so swollen I had to borrow my mother's shoes." An aggrieved hiss. "My *mother's* shoes."

As though it were my fault. "Your toes are still cute."

"Hush your mouth," but appreciative of my flirty compliment. Her voice broke. "This is just so awful."

I could but agree. "Unreal."

"It's killing me to see Brenda so sad."

"Me, too." But I didn't know how to comfort my filmmaking partner.

Grim and uncomfortable, we all filed inside the small, country church.

AFTER THE SERVICE at which a local preacher, the Rev. Duson Mire, eulogized Jaime from a set of notecards, I went with Connor, a broken Brenda and a couple of theater students I didn't know to the Marzol house, a small brick ranch sitting on a two-lane blacktop marked only by a state road number.

His mother, a stocky, visually miserable woman, had been the Caucasian half from whom Jaime'd gotten his pale eyes and paler skin. Such a good looking kid. I thought out of all of us—besides me, of course—he had a career in show business ahead of him. He knew how to take direction, knew how to run with it. Or so I felt after working with him.

Brenda and I stood beside another of those Southern family funeral spreads of casseroles, macaroni, and fried chicken. Latin American dishes, too—guava jelly, a greasy soup, a tray of enchiladas, chips and salsas and guacamole and *queso blanco* and black beans, also an enormous platter of refried beans with yet more white cheese melted on top. When someone died, people went apeshit with food. Food, the stuff of life. A way of saying fuck-you to death, maybe. Look at us, Mr. Death, still living and eating and talking.

Remembering.

But getting on with life.

Somehow.

Brenda, a wreck for days thanks to both the shock and the constant local media attention, took me aside in a backyard full of rusting, mechanical junk from Mr. Marzol's HVAC repair business. "Can you drive me back to Columbia?"

I said I'd be more than glad to, and went to gather Connor. We made our goodbyes. I avoided Jaime's parents, sitting on a couch in a near-catatonic torpor of grief.

Brenda asked if we could all sit in silence on the drive back. We said, of course. I didn't know how she'd gotten to the funeral, and asked her. She had come with her mother, who'd declined to attend the wake. "I told her you would bring me home."

"A little presumptuous, don't you think?" Joking, of course. "Maybe I wanted to hang out and party in Red Mound."

A shrug, after which she shut down and stayed that way.

I didn't turn on the radio. I figured if she wanted quiet, she wanted quiet. Connor sat in the backseat glancing through a wrinkled, torn *Premiere* magazine from the previous summer. Counting mile markers, I thought about Jaime being dead. It made my stomach hurt.

THE HILLS, hardwoods and pine barrens of Edgewater County gave way to the lake country, and farther south the streetlights of nighttime Columbia smeared the opaque evening sky with a glowing orange sheen. Familiar locales, including a side street where we'd shot Jaime walking along carrying a suitcase containing pieces of his dead brother. I felt sick and empty.

We dropped Connor off first. He wept and held Brenda. "This is just so fucked up," he kept saying.

I drove through the Old Market, passing the bar where Jaime had died. Brenda, her body heaving and shaking, wept in silence, holding in the tears as though seeking to contain a rage most sorrowful from becoming loosed unto the universe, like a rogue, rabid, stalking horse, unbridled and testing the limits of grief and confusion for its own deranged amusement.

I pulled up to the apartment house in which Brenda lived, a brick building set amidst the large houses of the Columbia movers and shakers who occupied the upscale neighborhood looming over the lower campus area and the Market—the Albert Apartments, as the building was known, but Brenda called it the Roach Motel. An old building, like my own duplex, and indeed buggy.

I didn't know what to say. "What're you gonna do now?"

"The million-dollar question." Peeping at me through red-rimmed eyes. Scathing. "How am I supposed to fucking know?"

I smiled, tender and patient. "I meant right now. I don't want to leave you here alone."

"I won't be." She held a hand over her chest. "Can't you feel him? His spirit's still hanging around here."

I felt only a yawning chasm inside, but a gentle lie couldn't hurt: "Of course I do."

"He was so much like you."

"Really? How?"

"He didn't like going back home to the country. Wanted to stay in the city. Dreamed of a bigger city."

"Now he's in the biggest city of all." It sounded stupid; was all the dialogue I had.

I held out my hand, which she took in both of hers. Held her cheek against my fingers. Sighed. "Thank you."

"I love you, B—we all do. Don't forget that."

Brenda smiled, the first I'd seen out of her since the tragedy. "I won't. Not ever."

Our hug lingered, but without the spark of romance, only a moment of grief assuaged by the tonic of human contact.

Sitting in the car, I watched Brenda lope slump-shouldered into The Albert. I wondered if I shouldn't have insisted on staying.

She's got to handle this in her own way.

"Like a grownup?" I asked the car, turning the ignition. "I'm starting to miss childhood."

As for me, I dispensed with the self-dialogue and met Neill down at McHaffie's for pint night. All the servers and barkeeps were in black; an 8x10 portrait of Jaime, surrounded by flowers, sat propped on the end of the bar.

Draught after draught beer slid down my throat. Shaking my head, smoking too much, pondering tragedies held close in my heart, I grew angry. I heard myself shouting, bitter and cynical. The next thing I knew, I found myself out on the sidewalk in the humid South Carolina night-air with Neill, tears running down my face, puking my way into the alley.

I don't remember going home, but I woke up the next morning in my bed, my throat raw and eyes swollen. I had to prepare to start school again. The classes I had left would be nothing compared to all I'd done. After seeing all the pain caused by Jaime's death—experiencing it, I forced myself to admit—all my ambitions now seemed terribly pointless and small.

A FEW DAYS LATER, Connor called to discuss the striking of additional *Too Far Gone* prints.

I asked, "What're three projection prints gonna run us?"

"We only need two more."

I asked why only two.

"Brenda says she can't afford it."

I knew the real reason. We both did. "She can have the answer print."

"If she'll take it."

"She'll want it," I said with certitude. "Maybe not right now."

"You want to hold onto it for her?"

As the director, I'd been accorded the honor of holding onto our only extant print, already getting a few scratches and broken sprockets from our various projections of it. "Yeah. That I can do."

When I had time, I went back to Tillman Falls to help my father around the house with minor repairs, yard work, and the like. A couple of times I stayed overnight in my old room, which delighted Daddy, as did a meal we shared at Louella's diner.

The restaurant sat catty-corner across the town green from The Dixiana, juking, jiving and honkytonking to beat the band. While we ate, we both managed to ignore the bar where my mother had so often imbibed.

"You think it'd be okay if I had seconds on that chicken?" My father, glancing at the buffet. "It's about the best I think I ever tasted."

I'd noted the relish with which he'd plowed through his meal. "It's exceptional, all right. Compliments to Lucinda," who'd run Louella's for as long as anyone could remember, and one day threatened to finally spring for new signage reflecting her own name. I enjoyed seconds as well, loving every down-home, greasy bite.

I'd brought Kunk's revised script with me, and later I lay in my old bed belching Louella grease and reading. The first scenes hadn't changed much, but the more I read, the more pleased I became—he altered the elements and details so that *Body Heat* now seemed like an influence, certainly, but no more than that.

Meanwhile, the last act had become a real pulsepounding thriller, ending with the protagonist in triumph—until discovering, that is, a betrayal he hadn't anticipated. The character, THEO, didn't wind up in jail like William Hurt's duped sad sack lawyer, instead merely alone. Alone, back where he'd started and down to his last dollar, the final, poignant scene depicted the guitarist trudging down a crummy rundown side street, carrying his battered instrument case. Kunk had made the guitar a key objective correlative, the axe getting battered and thrown around much like its owner, finally heading into a rundown Atlantic City pawn shop.

> Theo LINGERS outside with his guitar case as a
> GROUP of urban youth MOCK him — miming the
> playing of a guitar, laughing, et cetera. Hesi-
> tating, finally he goes into the pawn shop. The
> door CLOSES behind him.
>
> Cut to black.

THE END. Bleak; autobiographical. How low this protagonist had sunk—I thought about Kunk himself, and hoped he'd never been that destitute and broken.

Overall I loved this new draft and thought his script had matured, emerging whole from the nuggets and tidbits of autobiography mixed in with homage to other stories to become, instead, its own beast. Bravo, Kunk.

I called and told him so. He replied how he'd get to mine soon; soon as he could.

As far as I knew, he never did—or if so, he never reported how he felt about it. A year and a half would go by before we'd really talk again, when he called at the right moment I needed to hear his voice, at a time when I felt I needed rescuing. The call had been welcome, but, alas, the occasion would bear bitter fruit, becoming another exercise in trauma to our friendship.

Genetics had blessed Arthur Cameron Kunkle, born on August 1, 1988, with his mother's dimples and his father's crystal-blue eyes. I sent over a congratulatory card to Camille and Kunk, but I would not meet the child for quite a long time.

I held out hope Kunk had found a way to be happy with these developments in his life, feeling far from the unhappy manner in which he'd first characterized the news of her pregnancy. A knee-jerk, inaccurate reaction. Surely.

As for me, I'd come to terms with the struggles of my own heart. Camille, I tried to think of her as I might a crush in high school—requited, but over.

Lost to time and circumstance.

Moving on.

I didn't have room in my schedule to ruminate on such melodrama—all summer I'd thrown myself into school work, ten brutal hot weeks, then added the pressure of going through management training at the multiplex. Each daybreak I ran at Canal Park, finishing up before the sun crested the tree line. Finding the time to eat became a nuisance, and I lost more weight than I'd gained in college. Sleep, at a premium. I lived for Sunday morning, when I'd generously lie in bed until seven or so. College —but not for much longer.

Neill suffered ongoing legal difficulties stemming from his arrest in Ohio, but far from encouraging him to settle down, instead he went truckin' along on summer Dead tour, an entire month on the road, coast to coast. He planned to sell beer and bottled fruit juices, cases of which he had purchased at the new big-box discount club in the northeastern suburbs.

He also packed a grill and a wok, said he might sell plates of stir-fry or kabobs. "Keep the people fed and happy."

I felt relieved to hear he didn't plan to "sling doses" to make his nut on tour. I liked Neill. I didn't want to see him end up in jail. He was a gentle hippie English major. Prison—it would eat him alive. At least based on what I knew about prison from movies.

Meanwhile back down on planet Earth, I began my straight life and job, as I thought of my new position. Ironic: surrounded by movies, yet feeling as though I'd sold out and bailed on my dreams.

The wind—it felt like it had gone out of my sails. I hadn't been close to Jaime, but somehow his sudden death—and, I admitted, my mother's as well—had sent a chill through my bones.

At times I felt panic out of nowhere. Drinking liquor and smoking a small stash of pot Neill left behind only made matters worse. Sweating in the night. Bad dreams. Loneliness.

NEILL RETURNED from tour grappling with his own fresh, soul-searching identity crisis, which he resolved by quitting school and moving out of the duplex.

It was fine. As a working man, I could more than afford rent on my own, so in that sense his absence offered no great loss. I worried about him, though. He planned to split the scene, as they say, to go live with a girl he'd met on summer tour. Start a new life out on the golden coast, he said.

No big mystery; California, the Dead's home base. "I'll be able to see a dozen shows a year without even traveling. Fucking utopia."

"What about school?" I knew Neill needed another year to finish, though I had no idea in what shape his grades might be. "You ought to complete the degree. Get it behind you."

"Thanks, pal," in rank sarcasm.

"Well—shouldn't you?"

"Heard enough of that noise from my father, from all those stuffed shirts in the Humanities building. Fuck this shit. This is Babylon out here. I'm done. I'm out. I'm going to go live on the beach. And I do mean live, [REDACTED]."

I contemplated telling him I thought he was nuts. But I didn't. "Sounds like a real adventure."

"It's not me who should stay here and finish school, it's you who should burn that monkey suit you're wearing now."

"It's temporary. But anyway, to do what instead?"

"Climb aboard the magic express to the promised land. What could be more fake and phony than movies, bro?"

I laughed in his face. What Neill suggested sounded like kid stuff—like being at play. Me? I was ready to play grownup; playtime was for children. Childhood, for me, ended a long time ago. "What about money?"

His face hardened like I'd hurled an insult. "Let me ask you this: what if none of this—the jobs, the money, the cars, the way we live our lives like the people on TV tell us to—is the way it's supposed to be?"

I whistled the *Twilight Zone* theme. "You're high."

"What if it's all a lie, dude?"

I asked him what he meant; asked who was doing the lying. He said if I didn't understand, he'd never be able to explain. And so he didn't, and that was that.

Still, after he left I missed him. As it turned out, Neill would return to Columbia a few years later when his father, an otherwise healthy and robust middle-aged corporate legal guru with two houses and four cars and money stashed here and there, succumbed to an aneurysm; his son inherited a sizable headstash, as Neill himself might have put it, and for whatever reason, he never went back to California.

I still see him around sometimes. Still a Deadhead, too. Said it's not something you grow out of, the Dead, even after Garcia croaked. I thought of Neill that day in '95 when word came over the wire in the newsroom. Wondered how he took the news. Felt a little kicked in the gut myself. Loss of innocence. Some sentimental foolishness like that.

The weeks and months stretched into a year, my deadline for leaving and going off to grad school—except I hadn't applied anywhere.

Movies opened and closed, my only concern in matching drink cup inventories and counting money and reporting figures and chasing after recalcitrant teenaged ushers and cashiers to do their jobs.

Triumphal; a dream come true.

Not.

A couple members of the floor staff had worked alongside me during my prior tenure as One of Them, but who had not themselves been promoted. They behaved with cool animosity toward their new supervisor, until I turned out to be a decent guy who didn't bark orders; who only wanted to get the tasks checked off; who cajoled and hectored, but did so in an upbeat, cheerful, and movie-knowledgable way.

I felt, at times, like I was directing them, my actors in their plaid vests —the theater corporation had retired the blue blazers, and now both boy and girl floor staff alike sported bow ties and vests. As management, of course, I wore either of the two suits I owned.

I took the job seriously, of course. And yet I didn't. A stopover. I still told myself I wouldn't tarry around these parts. Working fifty to fifty-five hours a week, though, I didn't have much of a life outside of the multiplex.

But I had always lived and breathed movies. Right? Wasn't working in this job like exhibition heaven?

Be careful what you wish for.

DURING MY INFREQUENT downtime I tried to get going on new screenplays, but after a year, and the *Batman* summer of '89—the biggest opening weekend of all time, a mad house, four screens sold out show after show, the hardest work I'd ever done at the Enemas; I thought it would be bigger than *Star Wars*—I already felt enervated, burned out, and worst of all, not getting any writing done. Nor, as established, applying to grad schools. Not moving forward.

I kept having great ideas for cool opening scenes. Would pound out a couple of pages and scribble down the odd note, but hit the wall quick and bail.

I did manage to revisit *Night Driver* for about the fourteenth draft, and entered it into an MGM-sponsored scriptwriting competition, but didn't place. I had revised and tweaked so much the damned script had ceased to make sense, the scenes like obscure hieroglyphics carved onto copyweight, three-hole punch. I put it into a drawer. Shut it tight, away from the light. And there my only screenplay would molder. But not for too long.

BESIDES LANGUISHING IN A CREATIVE FUNK, whenever I got a new packet of information from schools like UCLA and NYU and USC, I felt daunted and frightened to apply. I didn't feel up to the challenge of the film programs into which I knew I'd need to enroll, at least if I wanted to get the big-time experience and contacts to make the move into the realm of top-tier film production. People from Edgewater County didn't do this kind of work. My own grandmother had told me so.

Maybe she'd been right. I didn't feel the fire in my belly anymore, or inspired.

For another problem: drinking too much. After closing shifts I had started partying out back with the ushers, like some kid sowing oats. They loved me for this interaction. Down to their level, and all.

"Just no drinking on the clock, boys. That's all I ask."

"Not even toking some weed, Mr. [REDACTED]?" Benj, a good old boy from a place like Edgewater County. "C'mon, dude."

"Shhh," I said, finger to my lips. And everybody laughed and went he's-all-right—for a management type, anyway.

A SEMBLANCE of a social life began to bloom: I palled around with my boss Hank Halvorsin, having dinner with him and his wife Clarice, who coded medical records from home, which seemed like a sweet gig. She had a rather large body, one I supposed came from so much sitting.

I envied her computer, one of the original desktop Macs, those tiny towers with monochrome screens like southwestern adobe art sporting a single pale, glowing eye. She was the first person I'd ever known who worked from home.

Like her husband and I, Clarice knew her cinema, had her own taste for inscrutable 1950s melodramas like Douglas Sirk and other campily overwrought pieces, movie titles I'd heard of, but hadn't seen.

I smoked pot with them, watched a VHS of a blaxploitation movie and a John Waters called *Desperate Living*, so filthy I got uncomfortable and paranoid, thinking that Clarice, and sometimes Hank himself, were sending out swinger vibes. Nothing happened, though. We shot the shit about esoteric cult cinema, drive-in movies, what they now call grind-house, ate food together.

Hank enjoyed better memories of those old drive-in movies than I did, but I'd gone to a few with my father—always just me and Daddy, that I recall—to see pictures like *Vanishing Point* (he'd covered my eyes when the naked lady on the motorcycle scene happened) or a *Godzilla* sequel (we both laughed at the man-in-suit effects, munching popcorn and swilling syrupy Cokes) or *The Towering Inferno*, which was so exciting when I was nine, and seemed so silly the last time I came across it on TV, in a letter-boxed version I saw on one of the premium channels, trumpeted as a "Widescreen 15th Anniversary Edition" also being issued on VHS.

So much that seemed important to me at a younger age now felt less than the sum of its parts. Movies. Writing screenplays. Even the love for Camille, a change for which I felt grateful and relieved. I now only thought of her once a day, and not all day long like I had for so long. Once a day I could handle. No other choice.

As 1989 waned and another holiday movie season loomed, I got a call from Max de Lisle asking me to perform a favor that carried with it much honor:

"I'd be thrilled, [REDACTED], if you'd agree to judge the Ten-Scene competition this semester. Some of the work is so good I felt reminded of you and Levon, a few others. May I count on your participation?"

What could I say but yes? Max's invitation made me feel back in the game, albeit for one shining, brief moment. The actual event, though, would end up causing more consternation and embarrassment than happiness.

GRATEFUL TO BE in jeans and my favorite T-shirt, navy blue with the *Aliens* logo, a garment that after three years in constant rotation had been worn soft and nearly threadbare, I climbed out of my car in a familiar campus parking lot. Felt back at home.

I drank in the smells and sights of the university, already nostalgic for what I considered golden days.

Was college over already?

Was I now an assistant manager in a freaking movie theater?

Not a career track. All temporary.

I strolled across the sloping, asphalt parking lot toward the auditorium building. Early, I wanted to get the lay of the land and get caught up with Max, who'd be swarmed with students the whole night.

A voice, familiar, called out. "Hey—champ."

Shifting the weight of my old backpack, brought out of a retirement that'd never happened—although I barely wrote anymore, lugging around legal pads and the latest scriptwriting textbook I'd bought around made me feel legit—I saw a shadowy figure waving at me.

Kunk, sitting in his car, an Olds, like one somebody's grandfather would drive. He grinned at me through the gloom.

"That's a real choice ride."

My old friend wore a crisp shirt and tie, slacks, a gray coat on a hanger in the backseat—he'd come straight from work. "Glad you could find it in yourself to dress for the occasion."

"Both of us in suits would be too intimidating for these whipper-snappers."

Kunk grinned at my moxie. "Get in. What we need is attitude adjustment."

Inside felt warm and plush, blue-green glowing panel lights, a cassette playing Sonny Rollins. Kunk clasped a quart of malt liquor in a brown bag between his legs and held a wooden pipe in his hand, one carved to look like a bass clef.

He sparked his bowl of weed. It smelled cheap and brown. Neill never had anything but what he called "kind bud" he'd bring back from the Dead concerts. He'd taught me the difference. Said buying what he called commercial grade marijuana not only didn't get you high, but supported money-grubbing, murderous Mexican gangsters.

I waved off the pipe. "Not for me. I wanna do right by these kids."

My old friend cut the sharpest eyes at me I'd ever seen. With his face pinched and mouth downturned he held in the sour smoke, which plumed from his mouth and nose as he spoke. He giggled, seemed a bit potted already. "Who you think you is, Mr. High and Mighty?"

"No, thanks—I'll just breathe the air," quoting one of the best laugh lines in Kasdan's *Body Heat* script. Kunk didn't seem to make the connection.

"Brewski, then? I've got another one of these in the back seat."

I declined that as well. "Later. Don't you think Max will want to grab a quick one?" I pictured the three of us—adults, peers, gentlemen—communing afterwards, maybe at Murdoch's on Main. He and Max didn't have the gig there anymore, given up last year after Kunk had gone to work at Fidelity Assurance Corp. "You know the kids will want to get hammered—I know I did."

"Kids." He chugged beer, gulping it like cold Gatorade on a hot day. "Fuck them."

Kunk had more of a gut than when we'd been students. I wondered how much he drank these days.

As if to confirm that the answer was "quite a lot," he produced the storied flask and took a nip—or rather, a glug-glug. I watched his Adam's apple bobbing a couple of times. This he didn't bother offering me, chasing the whiskey with another pull on the quart of King Cobra.

"How's that lovely bride of yours?"

"Fucking awesome."

"The boy?"

"Less awesome—he's a hellion. Walking now, getting into everything. Just paid a guy to come in and kid-proof the bathrooms and kitchen. He's got his mother's spunk and resolve, if you know what I mean. Christ—" He fired up a Camel, yet another nasty smell in the car. I was going to reek. "It's the American Dream made real."

"You really think that?"

The slit-eyes again. "Like George Carlin said, it's a dream, all right: you'd have to be asleep to believe it."

"Kunk? I'm gonna go on in."

"Suit yourself. I'll be along."

WITH KUNK BELCHING behind his hand and checking the time, we watched the students perform their masterpieces. One was a serious religious drama I didn't get, but I tried not to let my own irreligious beliefs color how I felt about the script. The dialogue wasn't bad, story not so good, acting earnest enough.

The next had a comedic setup, but with sensitive overtones—a farcical piece about two multiracial babies getting switched in the hospital. I thought it played well as sketch comedy. Lots of laughs.

The final piece came, and presented itself as the winner: A clever conceit, one that brought back cool memories—two guys tripping on acid in their dorm debate philosophical matters while abstract manifestations of their discussion are acted out upstage from the two principals. This knocked me out. Not a great script, but entertaining theater.

Strong applause followed as we were ushered out. The third judge, a stern-faced young woman named Ruby who'd graduated in the spring, had apparently had been quite the classroom standout. Before the performances, she'd intimated that her feature length had been a semifinalist in

the Nicholl Fellowship, the prestigious Academy of Motion Picture Arts &
Sciences sponsored contest out of which careers were made.

I sputtered, "That's—unreal. Are you serious?"

"Got me an agent, but he hasn't been able to sell it."

An agent.

A writer with an agent, a professional corporate scriptwriter and
producer, and a movie theater assistant manager. I prayed she wouldn't
ask me what I did.

"What about you?" she'd of course asked.

"Working on stuff," my only vague reply. "I'm on my fourth script," a
lie, "but haven't had any luck selling anything yet."

"Keep writing. Right?"

"Yep."

To deliberate, we sat in an ancillary classroom, three desks pulled
together in a circle. I'd made quite a few notes. Kunk came in and sat
down after a long disappearance in the bathroom, and didn't appear to
have made any notes.

"What do we think?" I asked.

Kunk, giving me a hard, unfriendly, smart-ass smile, made me feel self
conscious and defensive. "About—? Oh, the scripts. Yeah."

"The last one really was the strongest."

Ruby seemed shocked. "You—you must be *joking*. I ranked it third. 1-2-
3, just as performed."

"No kidding." Kunk, who'd narrowed his eyes, peered down his nose
at her. He slammed his hand down on the desk, making us both jump.
"Bullcrud."

"For goodness' sake." Ruby, upset, brow furrowed beneath a wide
headband holding back long, straight hair out of her face. "What's wrong
with you?"

"I agree with my man, here. Number three is the winner."

"But—"

"That's two to one," he said, glowering. "Or am I wrong on the
math."

Trying to dispel the bizarre energy I defended my opinion, which held
that it wasn't merely the content of the script—interesting, heady philosophical stuff—but also the exemplary staging, which to my senses made
the work walk and talk like the strongest piece.

"But I'm open to some discussion and arm-twisting, Ruby. If you feel
really strongly."

"It was a ridiculous piece of crap that those two stoners probably wrote the night before it was *due*."

"Whoa there, little sister," Kunk said. "Settle down."

"Don't tell me to settle down."

"Too late."

"And I'm not anyone's 'little sister,' ace."

"All right now," I said. "Like he said, two to one. Not trying to bully anyone—it's what I really think."

This agented scriptwriter looked at us both like we were poseurs. Like we were full of shit. "Whatever. Let's move on. If it's group three, it's three."

We also had to assign winners in acting categories, which ended up taking about fifteen minutes of further haggling. In the end, Ruby hated us both, and it showed.

Once we called Max in and gave him our results, he seemed satisfied, but guardedly so. "Well, that's fine. Just fine."

He led us out onto the stage. The audience of writer's groups and well-wishers seemed a restless murmuring cluster of gray and black and white, as Jagger once sang.

Someone belched from the back—these kids were drinking it up, I was sure, like we had. I thought of Connor and all that drama, and felt glad we had been able to go on as friends, and also work together. I hadn't heard from him since we'd gotten in the prints of *Too Far Gone*, had written the final check and closed the book on our project. A year and a half had passed. An eternity.

We delivered our results to the audience, which erupted with both disappointment and elation at the news that *Hipster Tripsters* had proven itself the best work of the evening.

Ruby, like a minority opinion SCOTUS justice, delivered a dissenting opinion, which we hadn't discussed her doing. Kunk's comments, meanwhile, came off snobbish and unnecessarily critical, making him sound like a pompous ass.

Rewarded by only scattered chuckles and uncomfortable grumbling, I tried to make a joke out of Ruby's notion that the winners had taken acid and concocted the script the night before it was due. The two lead actors, also the principal writers, slapped five and laughed—they'd put one over on everyone.

Kunk, who said he needed to get home, declined the drink afterwards with Max; Ruby and I accompanied the professor to The Parlor, a place giving Murdoch's a run for its money by featuring live jazz a couple of nights a week.

We took a table away from the music. Nursing beers, we all talked scripts, old times, and movies.

When Max went to the bathroom I apologized to Ruby for Kunk's behavior. Said I thought he suffered undue stress from being a new father, managing a career, yadda yadda.

"He smelled like a distillery."

"He likes a nip here and there."

I noted that she'd ordered only fruit juice over ice. "Very inappropriate."

"I agree."

On the way back to our vehicles, Ruby leaving first, I asked Max how he thought Kunk was doing. "Oh, quite well. I have to say, though, that I'm a little disappointed in both of you—smoking marijuana and drinking before this obligation shows a marked lack of character."

Max had never said anything to me so cutting and harsh. "But I didn't —honest. I only smelled like it because I was in his car with him."

"Now, now, Mr. [REDACTED]. Please. Best of luck to you." He shook my hand, dry and cool, and got in his BMW.

A shock of recognition flooded into me—Max thought me a flake.

Was he wrong? Not only couldn't I write any scripts, after that night I figured I couldn't judge a good one from a bad one, either. I'd certainly never be asked to do so for Max de Lisle again. What a disaster.

Every time I discussed with dad the idea of quitting my job, burning my slacks and sports coats and GCC name tag and leaving South Carolina, he became downhearted. How he wanted me to follow my dreams, even if it meant he'd be left behind, alone.

Now, more than two years after her death, he still seemed puny and shocked. He didn't date anyone, didn't go to church, didn't have hobbies other than taking care of the house and yard, which he did, he said, out of a lingering sense of obligation to his wife's memory.

"I know she's keeping an eye on me. After I get up there too, don't want her cussing me out for letting her yard go to pot."

I struggled to find the words. "It would be fine—if you—wanted—if you didn't want to be lonely anymore."

He shook his head. "I'm still married to her. I reckon I always will be."

I considered pulling up stakes and pulling a FEAR—Fuck Everything And Run. But instead, I ran smack-dab into a brick wall of reasons why I shouldn't: I hadn't saved much money, instead blowing whole paychecks on crap like a laserdisc player and expensive, LP-sized videos of movies that looked so much better than VHS resolution; and eating out every meal; and not writing scripts or planning to make movies or any other creative endeavors of note.

As my pants had gotten tighter, I started exercising again, which in retrospect offered my only real outlet other than getting hammered and occasionally laid by one of three women who drifted in and out of my life. All had been met through the cinemas, including a lonely middle-aged divorcee with whom I struck up a conversation one night at work. I'd gone to bed with her twice, all the while thinking of Cloris Leachman in *Last Picture Show* and wondering if this ridiculous sexual peregrination weren't pushing me further off track.

"I had fun," I told Marion. She'd been forty-eight, so gentle and giving and patient. Taught me a few things. "But it also seems a little weird."

"I know, honey. For me, too. I'll never forget you, though—my movie theater boy-toy."

I wondered how many other such toys she had had. I never saw her again to ask.

Over a weekend I went home to help my dad—while cleaning out gutters, he'd slipped down the ladder and sprained his back.

Drawn and pale, he seemed older than ever. Daddy had been an old guy all my life, though. I was a late baby.

And now that we'd lost mom, as it had begun to finally sink in, I'd have to care for him the way he'd always cared for me. But I didn't mind. What are we here for?

THE WEEKEND HOME with Dad turned into four days.

I called to let Hank Halvorsin know I'd need more time off, and he understood. His parents, too, were aging and infirm. Of course, I'd have to work a long stretch without time off to make up for being gone. Sigh.

During our conversation he hinted about getting kicked upstairs to District Manager—our multiplex, it seemed, represented one of the highest grossing in the whole of the Carolinas.

The rewards, too, would trickle down.

"You're the only one," of three assistant managers, the other two being relative newcomers compared to me, "who's ready."

"Ready?"

"Ready to sit in the big chair," doing a Captain Kirk impression. "Commander Spock, you're in line for a promotion."

Manager? At twenty-four?

A compliment; but I didn't know how I felt about taking the job.

I mulled: Good money. Bonuses when certain thresholds were met—not from ticket sales, however, rather of the snacks and sodas. The cases of candy were handled under lock and key, with far more security than the prints of the movies. I'd have to think, and drink, on such a proposition. I'd be getting further stuck, but I tried to tell myself it was all temporary.

That it was the movies, still.

Sorta.

The decade about to turn over, time, getting away from me.

But how much money could I save during a year or two of being a full manager? Thousands.

What then?

Decamping for L.A. Looking up Hoyt Bollard, who'd manned up and made the trek to the golden coast. Crash on his sofa until I got on my feet. Get back to writing scripts.

I needed to talk this out.

On Tuesday morning, Dad sat me down in the kitchen with coffee, Krispy Kreme doughnuts, and a stack of folders and assorted documents.

"This looks serious."

"It is."

He said he wanted to take me through some financial matters—his stocks, his pension fund, his this and that. Liens on the house all paid, owned free and clear, worth over a hundred thousand; a couple of pieces of property closer to the lake country, parcels he'd bought back during a real estate investing binge, all but paid for.

"You could build yourself a nice little house on this one," he said, pointing to a rhombus on a blueprint-blue plat. "It's set back, and the river's not but a hundred yards down that-a-way."

"A man could get some writing done back there in the woods."

I'd told him for a while now that maybe I only wanted to write instead of make films, that I could do so from anywhere; that it didn't cost much besides a typewriter or maybe a word processor, all of which sounded okay to him.

"Who owns the land to the river?"

"Power company." Meaning the Sugeree River Station upriver. Another aspect of Edgewater County from which I'd wanted to escape. Downstream from the plant maybe not the optimum locale. But nukes were everywhere now. Nowhere to run. "Nobody's likely to turn them woods into a subdivision—they don't need the money."

"Why all this today?" I asked.

"When I fell off that ladder, and I know it's what people always say, but my life flashed before my eyes."

"And what did your life look like?"

"I didn't see my life—I saw yours."

"Mine?"

"With your mama gone, all I could think about was making sure you're taken care of, best I can, anyway. It isn't much. But if something happens, now you know what you got to deal with. What you can expect. There ain't no better gift I give you than that."

"Knowing what to expect—that does sound like a luxury." I choked up. "You're not going anywhere anytime soon, pal."

"You don't never know, son."

Wincing at the effort, back still tender, he reached across the table. His widow's peak, high and thinning, seemed more pronounced than ever, lips and face puckered from the smoking that he'd supposedly given up, sagging jowls—a man who'd once weighed more than he now did. Dad had been a strapping younger man.

Weight loss. At the time, I didn't consider the implications.

Later that day, when he felt the strongest yet, and could get around without much pain, I said I probably ought to head back to the duplex, where I still lived by myself. Do laundry, shop for groceries, get ready to go back to work. I'd likely have to work eight or nine days straight now. Joy.

We hugged. "I appreciate you staying with me, son."

"It's what family's for." I meant this more than ever. I had no one else. "And don't worry about all that paperwork. None of it seemed complicated to me. I've made movies, remember?"

"I know you did. You surely did."

I OVERHEAD some of the staff at the multiplex about a big concert coming to town—REM. A one-time favorite, I'd barely listened to them for years. When I first saw them play, it had been in the student union ballroom at Southeastern, alongside only a couple of hundred music lovers. Now they'd be playing the arena, the building where I had taken most of my meaningful classes.

I told the youngsters about the SEU ballroom concert. How I'd been right up against the stage, watching droplets of sweat flinging off Michael Stipe's dancing face.

"You going to the show, Mr. [REDACTED]?"

It sounded ridiculous to be called "mister"—wasn't I still one of the kids?

"No," I said, nonchalant. "I saw them back when they were brand new. And, too many memories in that building. Y'all go and have a blast."

A mysterious call came from Kunk on a day already fraught with stress and decisions. After a delay of a few weeks Halvorsin had gotten the promotion, and while the manager's job hadn't yet been offered to me, he hinted that any day now, it would be.

I told Kunk all this news, also how glad I was to hear from him. Asked after the family. And so on.

Sudden: "Don't take that manager gig."

"I'm on the fence. But, why not?"

"Got a copy of *Night Driver* on hand?"

My interest, piqued. "What on earth for?"

He explained how moments in life occurred in which opportunity knocked, this being one of them. "I'd like you to come over tc Fidelity Assurance for an interview, champ. That's why not."

A new scriptwriting slot had opened up in the media department, it seemed, and I was the first person Kunk considered. And had already recommended to his boss.

I felt breathless—I could become a working scriptwriter, albeit a corporate one. "Do you think—I'm right for it?"

"Does it matter? They love me around here. I say hire this fucker, and they'll say, when can he start?"

My heart pounded in my throat. "Really?"

"All you got to do is show up."

Flabbergasted. I stammered and stuttered and asked when he'd like to see me.

The next day I slipped into my gray suit, shaved off a goatee I'd been toying around with growing, and grabbed my master copy of *Night Driver* to have printed at the copy shop.

"Would you like this single or double-sided?" The Kinko's clerk gestured up to the price menu. "Lots of folks are doing double-sided these days to save paper."

Scripts in Hollywood weren't printed that way. "No thank you—single-sided, three-hole drilled, with brads, if you don't mind."

"Sure. Whatever you like, sir."

But toward the end the toner had gotten low, giving the final, violent climax and brief denouement of my feature-length epic a ghastly, graying sheen. Neither clerk nor customer noticed. It wouldn't matter.

THE INTERVIEW with Kunk went as he'd indicated: no big deal. As he tongued a couple of Altoids, we sat shooting the shit like we had back in the lounge at school. I asked questions about the work, the office, the atmosphere, him saying yeah-yeah and waving me off.

"Time for all that later. You're a cinch, you know."

"I don't know that I'm prepared for this kind of writing."

"Nonsense. Now: let's go meet some folks."

Kunk walked me around the media department. Fidelity Assurance had its own small studio and other production facilities, tape machines, lighting rigs, whole bit.

This, I said to myself, would be like getting back in the game.

Game?

What game?

Max always said that, if you were a writer, be unafraid of calling oneself a writer. But I didn't feel like much of a scriptwriter. I kept a sporadic journal. Didn't write letters. No Great American Novels or epic movie scripts, either. Ideas half-formed. Scenes. Character sketches. All adding up to zilch.

Last stop on the tour: the head honcho, a diminutive, humorless department head named Carol Lamford, olive skin, a small hard severe acorn of a face.

Clipped and officious, she asked a series of questions—about the kind of work I'd done since acquiring my degree. Where I saw myself in a few years. How I felt about the insurance industry, which made me panic because I had no feelings whatsoever.

I tried to smile and discuss the management aspects of the movie theater job, which had given me invaluable HR skills. I characterized the position I held there, however, as a stopgap measure until a posting in my actual field came through.

"Not that 'movies' aren't my field," I joked. "Just more on the production side than exhibition."

"Understood."

Kunk displayed with pride the copy of *Night Driver* I'd brought. "This is one of the best scripts the MACM department ever produced."

What bullshit. I doubted he'd read it.

Lamford cracked a smile. I was afraid her face might break. "Well, now. I'll have to give that a read sometime."

On the way back to Kunk's office, he snickered and cursed his boss's name. "Would butter melt in her mouth?"

Not encouraging. "You tell me."

"Don't worry—you'll report to me. I'll run interference. You write the scripts, and I'll do the rest."

"Won't we both write the scripts?"

"What what *what*," he said. "Course we will. I'm a producer now, though."

I left with a wink and a nod; to sit tight and anticipate a call about an offer.

Kunk seemed steady and cheerful, much better than he had the night we judged the Ten-Scene competition. I noted a tremor in his hands as I handed him the script, though.

On the way to the Fidelity lobby, I asked him if he'd been working on any screenplays.

Kunk glared like he had back when we'd first started hanging out, when I must have seemed like such a child. "Are you fucking kidding me? *When?*"

I didn't know—I figured having a wife and kid still left you with a little time to yourself. To pursue hobbies, or dreams. "Weekends, I guess?"

"Keep guessing."

I said I'd wait to hear from him, offered my thanks.

On the drive to work at the multiplex, my stomach roiled and pitched and produced acid. The vibration at Fidelity felt wrong. But how could I turn down a writing job? I agonized over what ought to have been an easy decision.

I drove on over to the Enemas, where I parked and attached the Assistant Manager name tag to my lapel. I had a shift to work, a long one, in which to mull the rest of my life, and try to choose between two jobs, neither of which made my soul sing. I tried to remind myself that, while it wasn't directing movies, lots of poor folks like we have back in Edgewater County never get half the chances I've had.

NOW THAT THE manager position had become a reality, as well as the Kunk situation, I called to seek my dad's wise counsel.

"Insurance? Is it what you want to do? You ain't never said the first word about it."

"I don't have a clue," I said, truthfully.

"What about the money?"

As it happened, to go to work in the corporate world I'd probably take what amounted to an entry level position, even a pay cut from the potential salary I'd be making as manager of a bustling suburban multiplex that served thousands of patrons over the course of a busy weekend. Benefits better, of course—it was an insurance company, after all.

"As theater manager I'd be making twenty-eight as a base salary, versus twenty-two-five to start at Fidelity as a scriptwriter."

"Then there ain't no question."

"Is it only about the money?"

Dad may not have known from scriptwriting, but he understood financial matters. "You can't say no to the money. More'n that: At which company could you go further?"

I thought about it—where to go from there for me at Fidelity? The title of producer, which Kunk had earned, I supposed. And from there, creeping up into some ill-defined middle management position like Carol Lamford. I hadn't a clue what my life would be like in five or ten years—meetings and ties. Numbers. Nothing creative. Nothing meaningful.

"To be honest? I'm not sure I wanna be an insurance salesman."

"Thought you said it was a job doing your scriptwriting type-deal?"

I said while I might be working in media, I couldn't imagine a more prosaic and inscrutable business than that of insurance. A cog in a corporate machine.

A regular nine-to-five bloke in a cubicle.

Suddenly, the multiplex seemed downright glamorous.

In any case: "Not what I had in mind."

In the end he stood by his assessment—that a good salary with bonuses and room to grow in the corporate theater chain would be the prudent move, and hadn't I always loved movies so much?

By the time I hung up, however, neither option seemed correct. Multiple employment opportunities had transformed into one massive existential conundrum.

A nd so: I chose neither. Instead, I concocted a feint, a tangent, an angle to work.

I went back to school. But not to make movies.

The epiphany came while drunk and going through my high school yearbooks filled with reminders of Nicole, of childhood innocence and other affectations and interests I'd had, namely that of journalism: working on the school paper, writing different kinds of articles, learning to do layout. My favorite pieces, naturally, were a couple of movie reviews that the advisor had allowed, taking pity on me and succumbing to my pleading. How we'd gone to the *Edgewater Advocate* offices downtown and been shown the ropes by Bill 'Gooch' Wimmel, the publisher and editor of the paper.

The soft-voiced, white-haired Southern gentleman told the students that, for all the flaws brought upon it by its own practitioners, there remained no higher calling than journalism, which under the best and purest of idealized circumstances, he said, could be seen as truthtelling.

"But that's over yonder on Blueberry Hill in an idealized Land of Oz," he said, sucking on an unlit pipe like my grandfather used to smoke. "And god forbid, don't pay attention to men behind curtains. Not too close, anyways." A plaid sweater vest clung snug across his barrel-body, one he seemed to wear year round. "In the real world, it's a little messier. Maybe a little less noble, at times, than the notions of idealized muckraking that often launch us down the road to the newsroom."

At the time the journalism life sounded inscrutable but glamorous, and I considered it as a career pursuit. Until I found about the Mass Communications program, that is. Had seen the course descriptions like Scriptwriting and 16mm Film Production. A goner.

An issue of our high school paper—ours at James F. Byrnes High had been called *The Scholar*—had been tucked into the back of my senior yearbook. I skipped over the page full of Nicole's bubbly teenage girl hand-writing full of platitudes and affection and naughty double entendres, instead staring down at the byline with my name, and my review of *The Adventures of Buckaroo Banzai: Across the Eighth Dimension*, a movie that no one at my high school seemed to have heard of, one that I'd gone to see over at the very cinemas where I now worked, thinking it the funniest and most clever sci-fi action satire I'd ever seen—perhaps the only one. My praise of the movie came effusive and with certitude that it should be viewed as a modern classic of its unique genre, but the picture only ran for two weeks, flopped big-time. My review stands, however, and now it's a cult classic.

So, the grand idea sparked by my criticism, my published words, and nostalgia? I'd become a movie critic.

Right?

I had the media degree, and some small amount of journalism knowl-edge and experience, if only in high school.

No matter: I'd reenroll at Southeastern. Get a journalism degree. Many of the credits I already had would cross over.

Biggest, grandest idea I'd had in ages. Bigger than any story ideas, which had been few. And when they did come, felt phony and forced. Becoming a reporter felt raw, real and right-now. I started rehearsing what I would say to Kunk, as well as Hank Halvorsin, about turning them both down.

AFTER AGAIN TALKING matters through with my dad, he'd been upset at first about my not wanting the theater job, either.

However: "If you think this is what's best, what will make you the happiest, then I want you to do it."

"I'm sure it's right." A white lie. I hoped, maybe. But I wasn't sure about anything.

"Then go with your gut."

The two other father figures, however, were disappointed, downright angry, even. Hank Halvorsin took it better than Kunk; the theater manager could understand.

"The day I started in exhibition," he said, "I knew it was for me. But you're not me. Sometimes working here makes you almost not like movies very much."

"I wouldn't mind maintaining a shred of my innocence."

"Don't blame you a bit."

Furthermore, I said I'd stay on as assistant manager there for another year while I squeezed in my classes, and that made him happy. Told me that such an offer showed character, not cutting and running on the corporate family like that. A hearty handshake, and Hank called his boss to explain they'd need Plan B, probably a relocation of an existing manager from another multiplex property.

Levon Kunkle produced a different reaction. I called him toward the end of his workday, my evening shift only getting underway. Broke the news, nervous and stammering. Kunk still had that effect on me.

Cold and angry, a knife edge to his voice. "Why. The fuck. Would you do this?"

"Don't take it personally."

"Christ, champ—I need you here. Like back in the group. Remember?"

"Of course."

"And so that doesn't mean anything to you."

"I didn't say that."

"Fuck you didn't." He mumbled a string of epithets. Sounded like a Jersey mobster. Atlantic City seawater in his veins. "What a crock."

"I can feel in my bones that my path lies elsewhere than at Fidelity."

"Don't give me that hippie-dippy shit."

"It's the truth."

"You know what this is going to make me look like?"

I did. "I'm sorry."

"They were calling you first thing tomorrow with the offer."

"Well—let them. I'll break the news myself."

"Thanks for nothing." He hung up with a click.

BETWEEN THE DAY I turned down the job and the end of Kunk's life, I would run into Camille and her son more often than her husband. Always casually, and always in some random way, but the news each time the same, if not worse: Kunk seemed unhappy; he was hitting the booze and bars far too much; Camille, worried.

To which I could say what? Any outreach from this drunk—it's what I would become, as the years ground on—would have been rank hypocrisy. After I got out of school and went to work at the paper? In journalism? *In a political town*? I drank my weight until I looked like a pear.

On some nights I'd sit drinking at Beulah's until five in the morning, hearing the Silver Crescent pulling in, back when the Amtrak station was still downtown. Shooting the shit. Chasing down stories, I'd tell myself. And order another round.

More like a bullshit bullpen with drunks who'd been hanging there for years. Surprised Kunk wasn't one of them—he'd have fit right in. A million stories.

In the old days folks would sit at Beulah's on Thursdays getting drunk, this one oldtimer told me, and then hop on the Silver Crescent, grab a sleeper car, and wake in New Orleans twelve hours later where happy hour would be cranking up. Said folks used to do it all the time, then ride back in time for work on Monday. Nobody he knew did anymore, of course. "Everybody was young and full of piss and vinegar back then."

I was there the last night that train pulled in, before the station relocated down the hill to the new tracks laid through a ravine they called The Cut, freeing up downtown from train-traffic jams. Thought about hopping on that mighty machine like the revelers of old, going to New Orleans, getting a cheap room and writing a novel. But I didn't. What a ditherer, I've always been. Drinking, dithering, and watching the train come and go for the last time. But only watching.

As it turned out, I started back to school right as my old partner in creative crime Brenda LaRose, who'd gone on to pursue an MFA in poetry and prose, finished up her thesis: a novel.

We had lunch, got caught up. I didn't bring up Jaime at all. Didn't ask if she was dating anyone. Toyed with the idea of asking her out.

I didn't. Coward.

Again, too much history, but I felt comforted by her presence.

She bid me farewell that day by asking a favor. "Keep holding onto that print for me, will you? Don't lose it?"

"Safe and sound, for as long as you need me to."

"Maybe someday I'll be able to watch our movie again."

"Same here."

How I envied her creative output.

Maybe I'd write novels one day.

Plenty of journalists went on to write books.

Or screenplays.

Sure.

Two more years of college ground on without much excitement, nor would the next few years after that, at least on a personal level. I busted my ass and walked away with a journalism degree, and thanks to good recommendations from the Dean, wrangled a job at the *Columbia Record* as a fresh-faced newbie reporter, one given the crime beat.

The weekend I received my journalism degree, I had gone home to check on my Dad. I pulled around the long curving driveway to note with curiosity a small U-haul truck sitting in the driveway.

I found my father inside, surrounded by boxes. "What's going on?"

"Thought it was time to do some cleaning. Your mother's things—they shouldn't be left in closets to rot and be forgotten. Too many needy folks in the world out there."

I'd been after him forever to clean out the past, to stop living in it—it'd now been almost five years. Finally doing so had rendered him more energetic and happier than I'd seen him in ages.

Progress; this felt like overdue healing.

For the rest of the afternoon I helped my father load boxes into that truck, the best sweat I could remember having in ages—a lightening of the load, for both of us.

FOR A TIME I dated an attractive fellow J-school student named Janeen Kurtwood, until an old lover came up for air and stole back her heart.

She had been lovely and smart and wonderful; losing her made me angry.

She expressed regret, but the "other guy" had been the one who'd felt right; that seeing other people had solidified these feelings for both of them; and how, to be frank, she said it seemed like I'd never fully let her in on what made me tick, which I denied with vehemence.

I asked if we could make love one last time, and she said no.

I don't know why that part mattered, except that losing the physical intimacy hurt worse than losing the person herself, perhaps. I got over it by throwing myself into the work. Moving up the ladder. And watching the calendar pages fly away like in a montage from an old movie, faster and faster, a visual shortcut depicting a temporal gap in the storytelling.

I reported; I learned the ropes, made friends in the right places, wrote stories that Chief Carter of the CPD praised as being as accurate as any crime reporting he'd yet seen. I cultivated sources on the inside who trusted me. I earned the scar tissue on my reporter's hide.

All fine and good, all the while waiting for my chance to write reviews for the entertainment page. The media editor, an older guy not long from retirement, still wrote everything. People often complained about his reviews. That he didn't like any new movies. I thought to myself, it's because of his age. They need someone fresh and young.

Time went on, however, and once the editor retired, the paper started printing wire reviews. I pitched and pitched. Cutbacks, they said. I should have taken this turn as foreshadowing.

But I grew to love reporting, which could at times be downright exciting. By 1995 I was promoted to the State House beat and apprenticed with Ward Bentham, a regional legend for his political writing, and who liked me, seemed invested in my personal growth and success.

As established, I drank; I got laid quite a bit. The State House gang, a randy assemblage of old, white codgers with beautiful, young staff members. Enough interesting and scandalous stories came out of this period that I once started to write a novel about it all, but never got past the first couple of chapters. I drank too much in those days to nurture a nighttime creative outlet.

One day I enjoyed a serendipitous instance of running into Camille, this time at Canal Park. She'd taken up jogging; looked fabulous. I'd also started back up my own running, which I hoped would counterbalance an otherwise not-so-healthy lifestyle.

Side by side, the two of us set off at a modest pace around the curving berm of earth and trees separating the nineteenth century canal from the confluence of rivers. Herons stood regal and watchful; swifts darted every which way; turtles lay upon logs, sunning; the scent of honeysuckle in redolent bloom filled our noses. Idyllic.

"How's our boy?"

"Artie's a wonderful little guy," she said. "Smart as a whip."

"Like Mommy?"

Sardonic. "Well, I don't think it's from his Daddy."

"No?"

"Who knows where he got it from."

I felt a knot in my stomach—I'd worried about Kunk, wondered how he was, but not enough to call. I still felt guilt over how upset he'd seemed at my rejection of the job.

Bracing myself, I asked about my old buddy.

A shadow crossed her perfect features. She explained how her husband had become an alcoholic; that his life was becoming unmanageable; that theirs, a marriage in trouble. This rush of information seemed to lighten her load—the more she revealed, the faster she jogged. Hell of a workout.

I expressed concern. Asked how she'd been coping.

"We're interviewing World War 2 vets this week for a D-Day anniversary series. I'm busy as all get-out." As a producer at ETV, South Carolina's homegrown public broadcasting network—one of the finest in the nation —Camille had now achieved far more with her MACM degree than I ever had.

"You've got a lot going for you, angel-eyes."

"Except for an absentee husband, who's acting like he's a bitter old man. That isn't the end of the world for me. But it might be for him."

I asked her about his work—if he was writing. If Max had been in touch lately.

No on both counts. Camille reported that Kunk didn't write at all when he was home, only drank, and never hung out with Max.

"I don't let him drink in the house anymore, though."

"So where does he go?"

"Anywhere else. I tell you—well," she said. "I'm not a patient woman, [REDACTED]. I'm at the end, I think."

"Maybe I should call him up, see what's what."

"Which would accomplish what?

I said I didn't know.

"Good luck with that."

We finished the run making much smaller talk, how proud and interested about me being on the right track in my life, how she would see my byline in the paper and giggle.

"I always point to your name and say, we know him, Artie. He's our best bud."

She asked me twice, once in the beginning and once at the end of the canal, as though she'd forgotten the answer, if I'd been seeing anyone. I mentioned Janeen, and one or two others of lesser significance.

"I'm sorry, hon," giving me a sweet buss on the cheek. "Let's try to do better about keeping in touch. Don't worry about me, by the way—I'll be fine."

"None of it's your fault."

"Some of might be." Her face appeared on the verge of crumbling. "Maybe I just chose wrong."

My heart clenched the entire time I stood stretching and watching her drive away. If I hadn't known the reason for the raw discomfort in my chest, I'd have gone to the doctor. But no, not a cardiac event, only a welling of old heartache. Maybe anger.

I didn't call Kunk. Right then I didn't think I could stand to look at him, perhaps ever again. As it turned out, I would all but get my wish.

Another year on the [REDACTED] timeline would pass before I'd again see Kunk, well into the era when I'd started working as Ward Bentham's protégé.

Sakes alive—who knew this was the beginning of the last act of my career, one lasting the best part of another decade and a half? At the time, I never would have anticipated the ultimate, abrupt termination I would later receive.

As with my park encounter with Camille, the run-in with my old buddy had been casual and unanticipated: walking down the sidewalk in the Old Market on my day off, heading to the coffee shop with a new Toshiba laptop to work on an idea for a short story—I'd begun thinking about writing fiction in my spare moments instead of screenplays—and there he was.

And yet, it wasn't him.

Kunk came knocking down the sidewalk in jeans and a windbreaker covering a grungy, threadbare *Ernie Ball Guitar Strings & Accessories* shirt underneath. He'd gone more gray, looked thin—like he'd aged ten years—but still had the easygoing amble of a guy who had it going on.

Who was hip.

Who knew the score.

A young woman accompanied him, decidedly not Camille Grahl, neither in looks nor carriage: this girl had the disheveled look of a crack-head. Sallow skin, emaciated, missing a tooth—a rock star, as they call the cruisers over on Two Notch Road, ground zero in Columbia for vice and other crime.

Wait, I said. Maybe she was only skinny. A good reporter ought to wait on the facts, not leap to conclusions.

Kunk called out to me. "Am I seeing things? Or what?"

I grabbed his enthusiastic hand. "Your eyes do not deceive."

My old mentor pulled me to him, held on tight with one arm. He had that sour hangover smell. A hint of mildew wafted from his greasy jacket.

"Hey now, I'm Kaitlin," the girl said. She couldn't have been over twenty, twenty-one, I thought. "I'm Levon's main squeeze."

My eyes met his, a slight narrowing of both sets. "So I see."

Kunk indeed squeezed her close. "This gal's really something. Keeping me on the straight and narrow."

I didn't know what to say, other than ask a thousand questions—it's my line of work, after all. "I was ducking into Maxine's for a cup. Join me?"

"Nah, I gotta get back to my crib," the girl said, twitchy and scratching at one of her scabby forearms. "I'm—tired."

"Well hurry along, then. I'm gonna hang for a bit." To me Kunk said, "She lives just up the hill."

A reporter's deductive reasoning kicked in—unless she was a rich girl slumming, there was only one building 'up the hill' rundown enough to attract characters like her. "The Albert?"

"How'd you know?"

I shrugged. "Lucky guess."

Suspicion flitted across her face. "You coming?" she said to her main man.

He laughed, devious. "Soon as I get to your place."

"Better last longer than that," grabbing his narrow bottom.

"She's awesome," Kunk said to her sashaying backside. "A real woman."

My gut burned. I grabbed his skinny arm. "Where's Camille? Where's Artie? Huh?"

He yanked his jacket from my grasp. "They're at home, wise-guy."

"And so why aren't you?"

He cursed and fumbled in his pocket for the Camels. He packed the smokes against the old Zippo. "Because it ain't my place to be no more. Apparently."

"What the fuck are you doing?"

He gave me his what, what, *what* look.

After ordering coffee we sat down at the one of the outside tables. His hands shook like crazy; his eyes, once so clear and bright, now a lattice-work of red, and the sides of his nose not much better—the striated countenance of a lifelong drunk. Saw it every day up at the State House on all those corpulent good old boys from places like Edgewater County.

"You been drinking today already?"

He shrugged, answered like Kevin Bacon's drunken Fenwick in *Diner.* "So what? Big deal."

I answered with the next line from that screenplay. "But it's too early."

A sad smile, looking the way he used to when I'd blurt some naive notion that in no way matched up with his jaded worldview. "What it is, besides never too early, is none-ya."

"Pardon?"

"As in, none-ya business." Laughing like he'd come up with some witty *bon mot.* "Relax, pal."

"How's work?"

"I blew that popsicle stand." He explained how he kept butting heads with "that Lamford twat." That after seven years of service, he'd been laid off.

I imagined him showing up for work half in the bag like he had at the Ten-Scene competition we'd judged. "Laid off? Or let go?"

He tilted his head, looked disgusted. "Does it matter, champ?"

"I suppose not."

He told me a story about driving up to a corporate meeting in Charlotte, and having gotten stoned at a rest area on the way on some really good green dope one of the videographers had scored for him, next thing he knew he started panicking. Had to pull over on the side of the road.

"I walked around for a minute or two, trying to breathe. Thought I was having a heart attack."

"You went to the ER?"

"Shit, no. Went and had a couple of snorts—a bracer, that's all—and headed on to the meeting, which, eh, I don't remember too good. That was the last of me at Fidelity," he said, ruminative.

"Not very professional."

"I 'embarrassed' her in front of colleagues. So what. That cunt didn't have to be so pissy about it all. You believe that?"

"I can see how your boss might've been disappointed."

"That corporate shit wasn't for me anyway."

He went on to say that, after Camille kicked him out, he'd been gigging to make ends meet. That for the last few weeks he'd been staying with his "little piece of chicken" he'd met there in the Market at one of the college bars. Had been crashing up the hill in her apartment.

"I called Max about getting the old gig back at Murdoch's, but the old bastard said, 'his time for playing late into the night had passed'," in a mocking imitation of our writing teacher. "Said if I put my own combo together, he'd put in a word with Murdoch."

"And?"

"I rousted some players I knew, left Max a message. But I never heard back. Rotten old son of a bitch."

Kunk said he'd been gigging around with those cats in Charleston, and looking forward to moving down there for keeps. "We can play six nights a week in the tourist season. A motherfucker could just about live on that gig."

I fumed at Kunk's apparent disdain for Max. "Thought you'd had enough of that life."

"Maybe that's what I was supposed to be doing all along. Who was I kidding with this media arts crap?"

"When I first met you, you said you wanted change."

He nodded, shrugged. Kunk seemed to take no umbrage at my seething, supercilious tone—chewing his lip, fingering the coffee cup, he seemed lost in memories. *"Who was I kidding?"* as though to him the notion had come revelatory. "You can't teach a dog to change its stripes. Or however it goes."

"I can respect not having easy answers. But what about your family?"

Scoffing, he waved away my concerns. "Fuck 'em if they can't take a joke."

My teeth ground. I hissed my words in a breathy, aggrieved whisper: "What is that supposed to mean?"

"They want me gone? I'm gone."

"From your wife and son?"

"It is what it is."

"Maybe they don't want you gone—maybe they just want the real you back again."

"The real me?" His slack jaw indicated incredulity. "As though all you motherfuckers didn't know the real me. Like I said, fuck you cats if—if you can't—whatever I said."

I shook my head and sipped coffee, bitter and hot. Whatever his condition and circumstance, he'd made me hard pressed, for obvious reasons, to find sympathy for his purported plight. "You're married to the best woman in the world, asshole."

"What in hell would you know about it, kid?"

"You're right—nothing."

"Do yourself a favor: don't get fucking married." He pounded the table, rattling cups. His voice had risen. Passing shoppers turned their frowning heads. "It ain't worth it."

"Listen—I've got to bolt."

"Already? You haven't even finished your—" He stopped himself, held up a tremulous finger. "I know, here's what: let's get a real drink. You and me. Hair of the dog's just what I need."

"Thank you, no. Like I said—it's eleven in the morning."

Kunk looked at me like, so? "You always were a stubborn little prick."

"It's taken me this far."

"You still don't got a clue, do you."

"About what?"

"About anything. About me."

I told him this was the first thing he'd said I could agree with, though only in a manner grudging and dissatisfying. "I've got a few clues, old buddy."

He knocked back his coffee and shoved off, perambulating up the street as though he didn't have a care in the world. Hell of a note to feel revulsion for a person you'd once loved—a guy like a brother, or a father, even. But there it was.

I DON'T KNOW how much she appreciated the gesture—oh hell, I do know: it wasn't much, not much at all—but I called Camille to report on my visit with her spouse. I had had visions of Kunk picking up Artie for a dad's day out and going for a joyride with his new gal. To do god knew what. The idea chilled me to the bone.

"None of this surprises me," she said. "You do understand that I kicked him out not only because of the boozing, right? But the cheating?"

I could imagine what he'd been up to—the Wolf. Those eyes. Women fell for him, sometimes easily. She had been one of them. "I want to know what I can do to help."

"You can't—he's not rational. The last time I let him stay overnight—*for the sake of our son, and only on the promise of no drinking*—I came back early to find my son alone in the backyard, and my drunk, soon-to-be ex-husband struggling to get the cork out of a dusty bottle of cheap red wine that'd been sitting in the back of the pantry for three years. And do you know what he said when I walked in and started screaming? 'Oh, I wasn't gonna drink it.' He says he's out back with the kid, right? And noticed the grass was yellow? And that he'd just read an article saying that the sulfites in wine make good fertilizer. He was opening it just to pour it out."

"That story lacks credulity."

"How sad is that?"

I'd heard enough. "Now what?"

"There isn't a now-what."

"But—"

"You haven't been in on the attempts to get him straightened out. He doesn't want it."

She filled in details about a couple of detoxes and a rehab stint, as well as this period when he'd gotten a 'script for Valium from someone and had gotten hooked on *that* as well. He had a problem, she said. He had a disease, untreated.

"You want to help him? Go Christmas shopping with him for his little boy. He keeps calling me to come do it with him, but I can't. Won't."

Scribbling down the last number she had for him I agreed that I would. If I couldn't reach Kunk directly, I was sure I could use my mad reporter skills to determine in which apartment his young girlfriend lived in The Albert.

It didn't come to that. I got him on the horn and we agreed to meet up again, this time to hit the stores and get some holiday shit, as he called buying gifts. He sounded upbeat at the idea; I thought, this might work out after all. Maybe I can fix this.

S itting in my idling car in a parallel parking space along the Old Market retail strip, Kunk, in his denim jacket and sucking on a butt like a life-giving tube of precious oxygen, leaned against a tree and pretended not to notice me.

I rolled down the passenger window and bade him to climb in. We'd head to the suburbs and take the shopping centers by storm, I said.

Kunk balked at my idea to hit the malls, insisting that I suffered from pedestrian taste and a decided lack of inspiration.

I'd told him I had someone to buy for as well, a woman I'd dated a few times but nothing serious; how I wanted to nonetheless surprise her with a gift card from Vicky's or one of the department stores.

He appeared chagrined. "A gift card? Jesus, champ." He cocked his thumb up the block. "Get her a tchotchke from the Happy Accident. Kitschy. Campy. She'll love it."

The Happy Accident, a holdover hippie shop from the early 70s still stocking its bohemian selection of clothing and jewelry and whatnot, complete with burning incense and tarot readings and tapestries on the walls, was an Old Market mainstay. It also happened to be located next to a favorite watering hole from the old days where so much had occurred, another legacy business: McHaffie's Pub.

I relented, got out of my car and fed the meter.

"Let's duck in here first," he said when we reached to the tables outside the Irish pub. "For a quick one."

"Kunk—we're shopping, not partying."

"You resist too much." That voice of his, so steady and quiet, offered a whisper of authority like the day we sat together in the Upstairs West playing getting-to-know-you. "Go with the flow, tiger."

Without waiting for my response, he ambled finger-popping into the bar.

I followed, thinking that if I went with his advice and got him to let down his guard, I could eventually steer him in the right direction—toward sanity and responsibility. How wrong I was.

WE DRANK and talked and reminisced for what turned into hours.

After the first few rounds the knot in my stomach disappeared, and my plan to let Kunk be Kunk for a time before putting the hammer down and saying, this has got to stop, turned into the biggest drunk I'd had in years —perhaps ever. I pled helpless to the raging currents, the heat of the moment. For the sake of old times.

No—I was a coward and a naive fool. I didn't know what I had on my hands with Kunk. Didn't know how bad someone could get—I was only thirty at the time. Still a naive kid.

After dragging me out of McHaffie's and across the neighborhood on a tour of the worst dives the Market had to offer, our dialogue turned, at his prompting, to Camille and Artie and the whole family situation.

"Once I get my shit together, she'll take me back."

I asked him what constituted getting his shit together—he'd had a decent gig at Fidelity, fucked that up but good. "Why should she?"

"Cause she loves me, champ. I can see it in her eyes."

I thought back to my glorious night with Camille. How I'd exaggerated —or perhaps not, as the case may have been—Kunk's perfidy concerning girls on the side, and all for my own wrongheaded carnal intent. I flushed with guilt.

Here, however, I saw a way to force, I hoped, a moment of clarity on my inebriated friend. A judgement call I made, admittedly, under circumstances less than ideal, in a lousy hole of a joint on a bad corner in the worst part of the neighborhood:

"I hate to break this to you, buddy." I sat sipping a diet soda I'd ordered in lieu of yet another drink. "But Camille—she's moved on."

His lovely blue eyes, spinning with intoxication, seemed to wind down in the manner of a roulette wheel, slowing, slowing, and coming to rest on double-zero: my own set of peepers. "Excuse me?"

"She wanted me—to tell you—well. She thought you should know."

"That I should know. That she wanted you to tell me." Steam began leaking out of his ears. "I get it."

"So you wouldn't waste any undue time on her. And what y'all used to have."

"This don't surprise me a bit, [REDACTED]."

"No?"

No, he said. "You fucking little snake."

"It's—wait. I'm not talking about me."

He hooted with derision. "You think I don't know about you two?" He slid off the barstool, eased over until that beak was about an inch from mine, a tough guy about to put some dipshit's dick in the dirt. "*About what happened that night?*"

As the blood drained from my head, I'm sure my ghostly, blanched pallor spoke volumes of confirmation. Ten years fell away, and I again felt intimidated and chagrined at the thought of betraying and disappointing him. I shook my head. "I don't know what night you mean."

"Sure you don't."

"One question—was it all so terrible?"

Backing off, he put his forearms on the bar. Kunk leaned forward, head down. Muffled: "Was what so terrible."

"A straight, happy, normal life with her and the kid."

Looking up, he seemed more upset over the question than the fact I'd once fucked his wife. "Who're you to say what 'normal' is?"

"Look at me—it's because I *am* normal. I'm nothing but normal. I'm so normal, it's like I'm not even here."

"I don't see a wedding ring on your finger either, Mr. Normal."

"Yeah, well—I didn't get the chance. Not with you in my fucking way."

"At last—the truth."

"Yeah. Not that it matters now."

Drunk, I wanted to hit him. Wanted a moment like in a movie—the old friends fight, after which they realize how stupid it all was and how valuable their friendship, much more so than the petty dispute over which they've been clobbering one another. Walking away, arm in arm, laughing it all off.

But Kunk didn't have a fight in him. At my last comment he pushed back and dug a couple of crumpled bills out of a pants pocket. In that moment I saw age in the jutting bones of his face and body, wear and tear I realized had piled up in a cumulative fashion: before, I think, a part of me still saw the old Kunk, the handsome rake, the suave with-it dude who knew all the angles.

"So take her. She's all yours."

I watched him stagger-step out of the bar, flipping me off.

"Hold on, asshole," I called after him, but too late. It had been a half-hearted callback attempt anyway.

Outside on a mild, South Carolina December night, I nevertheless shivered as though chilled by an icy cutting wind—shaken, I supposed, by the occurrence of a moment I'd have sooner continued avoiding like I had for the last decade.

What a disaster. Not only had we bought a total of zero holiday gifts, I'd managed to let him get drunk and also dig his personal wounds deeper. Now, I realized, I'd displeased not only Kunk but Camille—I'd made matters worse, not better.

How much worse I couldn't know, not yet. But I'd find out, big time.

The holidays came and went with no further Kunk news, for which I was selfishly thankful.

Embarrassed by what had happened, I buried myself in work. Toyed around with writing a comedic novel about South Carolina politicians, but found their actual behavior stranger than fiction and impossible to satirize. I cut way back on the booze. Dropped some weight. Felt better.

Ah, the celebratory year-end season: I'm the person this time of year they talk about who's terribly lonely. I catch up on movies; I visit my people back in Edgewater County. My aunts, always trying to set me up with women; my uncles, wanting to talk politics and the newspaper business and how proud they are at seeing my byline so often in the *Record*. A routine.

I spoke with Camille once during this period. Ashamed, I'd avoided calling her or returning a couple of her messages, until one day before New Year's when she finally caught me.

"What the *hell* did you two talk about that night?"

"I thought if I ran with him, tried to speak his language, saw firsthand what the booze was doing to him—that I could get through to him."

"That's the dumbest idea I've ever heard. I mean, really, hon."

"Not the first time I've fucked something up."

She laughed, a sarcastic bark of disbelief. "In any case, since that night I've not seen hide nor hair of my husband, I'll have you know, Mr. [REDACTED]. Missed his boy's Christmas, he did."

With vigor and contrition, I expressed my deepest shamefaced apologies. Camille had never sounded more angry or upset with me. With everyone—with her whole world.

"Where is he now?"

"With his shack-up, I presume," she said with frosty, supercilious bile. "Try another bar crawl. You'll run into him eventually."

※

LIKE I'D FIGURED, it didn't take much detective work to find my old friend:

The four-story red brick Albert, situated in the midst of the well-to-do homes of what we joke around the *Columbia Record* offices as the 'landed gentry' of the neighborhood east of the University, stuck out like a sore thumb—it was as though the apartment building had been kicked out of its proper place in the nesting of student rental housing a quarter mile away, across the railroad tracks.

I knocked on the door of 3B, leased to a Kaitlin Barnhart. I could hear the muffled tones of a television—from the buzzer sound effects and applause, a morning game show. I knocked again.

I saw the peephole darken and heard Kunk's gruff voice: "What the fuck d'ya want?"

"Hey—it's me."

Unintelligible mumbling.

"Let me in, brother."

"Go get me something to eat, and you can come in." He suffered a spasmodic spate of coughing. "I ain't ate nothing in a couple days."

A fair trade. "What do you want?"

I heard him shuffle away. More coughing from deeper inside the apartment.

Retching sounds.

Twenty minutes later, I returned with sub sandwiches and coffee for both of us. But once he let me inside, I lost all interest in eating or drinking —the rank smell, too much. Trash everywhere, yes, but mostly vodka bottles, an army of them. Empty. Cheap stuff. You could smell it in the air.

Kunk, his skinny bones poured into a stained armchair, gestured to the couch, a horror of crumbs and rips and mysterious discolorations. "You're a real prince for getting me some grub."

"Least I can do."

Had lost more weight—drinking himself to death. A living corpse down to only subliminal flashes of the Kunk I'd known—in his eyes, his hands, the way he moved, the long delicate musician's fingers he said made typing easier, too.

"Here," unwrapping one of the sandwiches. "Let's get some decent food in you."

He gripped his stomach. "Mayo or mustard?"

"I got both."

He leaned over and struggled to handle the sandwich. I reached across, helped. His face contorted into a grimace, I think at the scent of the food. "Looks right tasty."

Chewing with deliberation, he ate a few bites. Struggled to swallow.

Sipping coffee, I asked what had happened with Christmas. Why he'd been in hiding.

Shrugging, his eyes glassy, face red and shiny. "Having more fun here. With my old lady."

"She's here?"

"Nah. Ain't seen her ass in a week or more. *Oh,*" he said, belching. "Shit."

"What?"

"I'm fucking sick."

Sudden and involuntary, Kunk heaved vomit into his own lap—the bites of sandwich, first, followed by a second expulsion of clear liquid.

I cried out, jumped up to grab a stained rag from the horrible kitchen. "You're—I'm—okay. We're going to the hospital."

He puked again, groaned. "No fucking way."

"There's nothing to discuss."

He started crying. "Don't call an ambulance. Take me. Drive me there."

"It's time, bub. Way past time."

Struggling to his feet, he grunted and gurgled. Kunk grabbed ahold of my arm, staggering forward and knocking our drinks over on the cluttered coffee table. His jeans now horribly stained front and back, I glanced at his chair. It clicked—not only had he puked on himself, but he'd been sitting there so drunk he'd shit his pants.

This man, whatever his issues, deserved more dignity.

On the way into the bedroom to get him cleaned up, though, Kunk crumbled to the floor like a sad, bigheaded marionette cut from its strings, and we ended up going to the hospital in an ambulance after all.

Camille and I stood in the ICU at the foot of Kunk's bed, on a quiet, sterile, spooky floor of one of the downtown hospitals. Bodies connected to hoses and tubes, machines making soft beeps and exhalations like lovers engaging in breathy platitudes. Actual conversations between humans came to us whispered and grim.

Pens scratching on clipboards.

The smell of disinfectant.

Fluorescent lighting.

A tomb.

I despised hospitals.

It wasn't about me.

Kunk, unconscious, his skin damp and thin hair plastered across his broad forehead, writhed before us. Besides an untenable saturation of alcohol, tests revealed the presence of a variety of substances as innocuous as cold medication and as serious as opiates; on top of all that, pneumonia in both lungs, a distressed liver and kidneys functioning at a low level of efficiency. The doctor said if I hadn't gotten him there when I did, he might have died. Maybe that same day.

I put my arm around Camille's waist, a gesture of support accepted and returned. "Looks like he's having a helluva nightmare."

"He's detoxing. On top of everything else, they've got him on an Ativan drip to deal with the DTs."

"Prognosis?"

"Responding to treatment. Kidney function looks better. His liver is next to shot."

I thought about the heroin, from his youth as well as the more recent past. "I hate to ask, but—HIV?"

Her mouth dropped open. "They didn't say. And frankly, I didn't think to ask."

Camille made a strangled sound, her face a mask of revulsion. I suspected she struggled with the notion that maybe it'd be better if he didn't survive.

I'd never seen anyone in such dire shape. I wondered if he wanted to come back. His, the behavior of a man who hadn't wanted to live.

"What did you say to him that night?"

"That you didn't want him anymore. That the two of you were finished."

She nodded, pulled away from me. "I wasn't using you for a messenger service."

"I thought he already understood."

"He did. But still, [REDACTED]—to hear it from you?" The eyes of Camille, flaring with anger. *Don't you think that might've hurt just a little?*

I told her I hadn't realized he had known about the fabled night.

"As far as I know, he didn't. Not unless you told him."

Had he tricked me into confirming a suspicion? Kunk, always a step ahead of a rube like me. "Like it matters now."

"Thanks for coming. But no need for both of us to stand around here."

"But—"

"Go home, hon. You've done enough."

I left the hospital that day at a low point, to say the least. With more to come.

Kunk, as resilient a mo-fo as there'd ever been, left the hospital, moved in with his brother for a time, and got his strength back. Pulled himself together, or so I heard.

He didn't call me after getting out, but Camille kept me updated. Not caring how sober he now seemed, she hadn't deigned to take him back. No animosity, but no more chances, either; an amicable dissolution to the marriage; a semblance of a normal relationship with his son, if possible. Or so she reported.

He managed to secure the Charleston gig playing standup bass in the jazz combo, moved down there. A mistake to live without any support, as it happened, for a man like Kunk—not out on his own again, in his element, the bass in his hands, and smack-dab in the midst of all that goes down in the milieu of the musician.

The late hours.

The clinking of glasses.

The vibe of the nighttime.

The lure of old habits.

Maybe Kunk, fated to fail. Still, I never expected it to go like it did. Never crossed my mind he'd take his own life, not in such a direct manner. Not Kunk.

Over the next year I managed to keep up with Camille, often checking on her and the boy. I also got reports about Kunk. Having dodged a bullet last winter, it seemed he'd gotten right back to pulling this or that inebriated stunt. How him moving to Charleston had been the best thing to happen to her in a while, but not for him, it seemed:

"I filed for divorce. We've been separated for over a year now."

"How sad."

"Not so sure about that. It's been an ugly ride. More than you know." I heard her choke off, collect herself. "I'm glad it's almost over."

I waited.

Finally: "What was I thinking?"

"You were in love."

"Maybe."

"He was bigger than life to all us back then."

"Coolest guy I ever met."

"Same here, sister."

THE NEXT TIME I CALLED, I found her in tears. Her erstwhile spouse had had a fresh run of bad luck—his second DUI, upon conviction to result in an enormous fine and potential jail time. In the process he'd also totaled his car, that ridiculous Olds he'd bought. Lost the gig in Charleston with the jazz combo at the fancy restaurant—he'd shown up drunk one too many times. Back in Columbia now, in a flophouse, to use her word.

In disbelief at his condition, I asked about helping her get him into rehab.

"I'll let some judge tell him to do that. He's never listened to me about anything."

"Where's he staying?"

"A room in some boarding house on Governor's Hill, behind the park. He came back here, he said, so he could be closer to his son," breaking down. "The asshole."

I drove over to the address, a weathered Victorian set on a steep hillside of downtown Columbia, only blocks from the Governor's mansion and Federal building.

I knocked, went into the foyer on a hardwood floor that creaked. Stairs, doors with numbers. Now what?

A short black dude popped out of a room down the hall, a fabric measuring tape draped across scrawny shoulders. "You picking up?"

I could see into his room—racks of clothes hanging behind him, a sewing machine: some kind of back room tailoring operation. "Looking for a guy named Kunkle. He around?"

The guy pulled the door closed behind him. A stoic mask dropped across his features. "Couldn't say."

I asked the tailor to play straight with me.

"Why, he in trouble?"

"No, no—I'm an old friend."

He snorted with odious skepticism. "Hate to get a man in trouble on a nice afternoon like this."

"I'm no cop."

"Serving papers, then."

"No, sir. Not even selling insurance."

"If you was, I bet I'd-a knowed it by now."

"Look—I admit to being a reporter, but it's not on the clock. I'm like family to him."

He relented, told me he'd seen Kunk leave about fifteen minutes ago, heading over toward the park. "He been hanging out over there a good bit —but you didn't hear *nothing* from me. No sir."

"My sources remain confidential."

I gave him a couple of bucks, which he nodded and took without question, disappearing back into his room. I could hear the sewing machine come to life. I supposed his business came from word of mouth.

I locked the car and walked up the steep hill to the park entrance, the topmost part of the hillside affording a picturesque view of our modest skyline. I walked over to the spiraling waterfall and surveyed the green expanse of the lower park, dotted with sunbathers and kids throwing Frisbees and old people strolling languid and unhurried around the elliptical paths.

I spotted Kunk's denim jacket and big head, sitting beside another male figure on a bench near the duck pond.

Dodging the occasional gust of spray from the waterfall, I hurried down the flight of steps, crossed a footbridge and loped across the open grass. The closer I got, I realized the additional figure on the bench was the statue of Mayor Finlay, sitting in a relaxed, ever-present pose in the park bearing his name.

Kunk, blinking and red in the face, noticed me coming.

"Hey pal, think you could spare—oh."

A drunk, panhandling in the park. I couldn't believe it.

Casual as hell, I said, "Kunk, baby. What's shakin'?"

"Just taking in the day. And you?"

"Same here. Grabbing a free afternoon for myself."

I explained how Camille had told me about his recent travails, and that I'd tracked him down.

"Why—do I owe you money?"

"Wanted to check on you. See what I could do."

"Mighty white of you."

My façade crumbled. "I could not fucking goddamn believe that, after surviving your last binge, you started up again."

"That's what drunks do, my boy." Furtive and watchful, he pulled a pint of vodka from his jacket and tooted it. "That is what we do."

"Doesn't have to be that way."

He offered the pint. I shook my head.

"Thought you were doing better for a while there, eh?"

Ignoring the substance of my inquiry, he gestured and ranted. "You know they feed people in this park every Sunday? Goddamn Sunday dinner, right up there on top, in the parking lot. I tell you, to make a difference like that? It's just a hell of a way to to make America a brighter place." He spat across the sidewalk into the grass, laughed. "Bunch of weaselly little piss-ant college fucks—Food Not Bombs, they call themselves. Saving the world one empty stomach at a time. You ought to write it up for the birdcage liner of yours."

"Not such a bad thing they're doing. Worth writing about."

"Eh, it don't change nothing in the end. Why bother?"

"You eat there much?"

"Every Sunday."

I wondered aloud how that could be preferable to having dinner with his own family. If not his wife and son, at least his brother.

"I don't got a family no more, champ. Doug kicked me out too."

"You've got a son. Nobody can take that away from you."

"She already did." He gestured and sputtered and cursed. "They've all wrote me off. Prob'ly for the best."

I squatted down in front of him. I took Kunk's hands, rough and scabby, in my own. "Stop this foolishness," I said. "Please."

He yanked his hands away, a violent, dismissive gesture. "Do you know why I had to get out of Atlantic City?"

I told him I remembered—the gangster's girlfriend. "They had the long knives out for you."

He pressed his lips together. Fought to keep water from spilling out of his eyes. "Well, it was all bullshit."

I didn't know what to make of this. "Which part?"

"I was just a junkie. That's all." Hanging his head. "Nobody had my number. I was just trying to get away from myself."

I told him he had nothing over which to feel shame, at least as far as his old tale-spinning went. "You've just bottomed out again. So that means nowhere to go but up—right?"

Hiding eyes gone cloudy and wet, he slipped on a cracked pair of aviators. "You know what your problem is, [REDACTED]?"

"Do tell."

"You never could mind your own business. Now get outta my face. Or I'll show you bottoming out like you ain't never thought of."

Metaphoric and chilling, his threat.

I sighed and stood up, my joints popping. Even if trying to settle down into some straight picket-fence, family man existence for which he hadn't been cut out had been the wrong turn in life, there were always alternatives. Second—check that—third chances.

How many, though? How much more cajoling and pleading is worth doing for an addict who doesn't seem to want the help?

"I feel like opportunities are slipping away," I said, not knowing exactly what I meant by that. "And I'm a busy guy these days. So, either let me help you, or not."

"Champ—you're embarrassing us both, now."

I tried to think of an appropriate movie line—my own real-world dialogue had been landing hollow and ineffective. "I'll have to turn my back on you," echoing the mob boss Pauly, a friend and benefactor now pushed to the limits of his tolerance and generosity, to his one-time capo Henry Hill in *Goodfellas*. "Take the hand that's extended, or I walk away."

Laughing at me. "Do what you gotta do."

"I have a choice in the matter—like you."

Unsteady, he struggled to his feet. "See ya when I see ya." He walked away into the evening without another word.

His bluster and denial, all an act. I'd gotten through. I was sure of it. He'll come around. Kunk would bounce back from this sad moment.

Newsflash: He didn't.

A fter discovering the odor in the basement, I had to make myself go back downstairs to collect Kunk's stuff, including the filing cabinet, a few VHS tapes of video projects he'd worked on, and a framed picture of the writing group from Max's class. The Empire State snapshot Camille he'd clasped in his dead hand had already been given to me, of course.

I lapsed into a deep depression. It began at his memorial, at which the tension flowed thick enough to make the church feel close and tight and uncomfortable; when I arrived, Camille stood outside having a furious argument with a man who'd been introduced to me as Kunk's brother Douglas, a man younger than him by maybe five or six years. Of course, as a healthy normal person, he looked twenty years younger than the alcoholic I'd seen in the park.

"You did this to him." These, the first tearful words I understood coming out of Doug Kunkle's mouth. "Kick a man when he's down, why don't you?"

"What I did was put up with his shit for almost ten years," her own voice coming brittle and on the verge of shattering. "You have no idea what I went through."

I strode up and interjected, pleading for calm.

"Who the hell are you," Doug barked in his Philly accent.

Camille took my arm. "He was Levon's best friend."

Her words caused me to burst into tears.

Camille, grabbing me and burying her face in the lapel of my coat. "Now leave us alone, Doug," muffled and aggrieved.

"Took away my goddamn brother." He moved away with clenched fists. "Bitch."

Weeping against my chest, my old love heaved and shook. I spoke to her in gentle, loving tones. "He's got his own burden to bear. His heart is broken, like ours."

"I will not be blamed for what happened."

"Hey." I made her look at me. "None of us were in that basement. The choices were all Levon's."

The service, brief and sad. Familiar faces abounded—many of my Mass Comm brethren had stayed here in Columbia, it seemed. I sat with Connor and Darren Wozcinski, who managed a recording studio. Hoyt Bollard had flown in from L. A. We all shot grim, knowing looks at each other like the cast of *The Big Chill* in the funeral scene.

Max, frail and weak, got up to deliver a eulogy. He concluded by paraphrasing from memory a poem by e e cummings:

"Buffalo Bill is defunct. He used to ride a watersmooth white stallion, shooting clay pigeons. Jesus, he was a handsome man." Max choked off, collected himself. "But how do you like your blue-eyed boy now, Mr. Death?"

I'd been asked to speak, but said I didn't have any words in me.

Afterwards we all went out to McHaffie's and got as plastered as decorum allowed. Max, seeming infirm and upset, declined to join us, as did Camille, for obvious reasons—she had to care for her grieving, confused, nine year-old son. He'd start his adolescent decade as a kid without a father, a role no one, not even "Uncle [REDACTED]" could fulfill, even if Camille wanted it. Which she didn't, and wouldn't. Not for a few years, anyway.

nd if one metaphorical father figure dying weren't enough, not long after the first of the next year my own dad passed away. He'd been sick for a long time, a slow progressive disease people get, one eating away at him until nothing left but a shriveled, desiccated body in a coffin, and looking nothing like the strapping man I'd called my father.

I said through my tears to an aunt, "That's not him lying there in that casket."

"No, honey, it isn't. Only what he left behind."

I felt as an isolated speck in the universe. I finally understood so well why folks had children—for most ordinary people, it's the only shot at any semblance of continuity. I'd always assumed I'd make my mark with a great movie or novel. That the name [REDACTED] would be carried forward by my work. Now, not even that felt possible.

Nagging thoughts like these led me these many years after Kunk's death, and so many more after MACM, toward writing my recent screenplay. How else to look upon my workaday writing career as anything but the production of ephemera?

The news?

Here today.

Gone tomorrow.

On the other hand, the news never stops, does it? One would think this job security. One would think.

Maybe for old time's sake, I'll write a movie. Yeah, that's what I thought one afternoon. That's the ticket. A movie script about my old buddy, who used to write movie scripts.

And about me—the young me. The dreamer. That's the only person I'm truly suited to write about anyway. The only person I've ever known.

After Kunk I continued at the paper, as we know eventually becoming lead political writer following Ward Bentham's promotion to managing editor; I started writing CityBeat, a weekly column focused more on human interest than state politics. My columns prompted angry letters, death threats, the whole bit. By then, everyone in town knew my name. At least the ones still reading the birdcage-liner.

But I never did get to review a single film for the *Columbia Record*; in a way, I wasn't qualified. Eventually they wouldn't run any reviews of movies at all, not with the rise of the web.

The modern information age has about killed off all the newspapers, at least what they call the dead-tree edition, which I think now goes out to no one but retirees and oldtimers who still prefer the tactile sensation of holding newsprint, of washing grime from their fingers. I know I still did for a long time, but now it's reading the news on my iPad, lying in bed in the morning.

All of which, of course, has cost me my job. It's not the end of the world. I'd pretend I didn't see it coming, but I did.

DESPITE AN ATTEMPT or two on my part, Camille and I never got together, but at this juncture of sagacious maturity, I no longer view this as a tragic misfire of fate. Not like I did as a starry-eyed, emotionally inchoate kid, learning about love and friendship and life. In time, I found that I was still in love with the idea of Camille Grahl, but probably not the woman herself.

Not really.

Maybe a little.

Which I try not to think about.

So I made it all into a fable instead of a memory, the stuff of myth: The legend says we had an amazing night together, and later, a strong mature relationship; who at this far remove knows the truth?

Me.

The sex, it had been so intense and perfect.

But relationships require so much more.

Issues of trust.

A fear I suffer holds me back: Of getting close, and the possibility of betrayal. A fear of loss.

Perhaps one day I'll realize why. Maybe someone will point out the reason. This reporter's investigation goes on.

Luckily, I'm still like an uncle to Artie, who's in college now and looks handsome with his deep soulful brown eyes, and there is friendship and warmth all around.

A couple of years later, Camille remarried. Not surprising. Camille Grahl, a catch. A decent, stable guy, Phil—an ordinary, unremarkable tax attorney, nice as all get out. After a spin on Kunk's Tragic Ride, who could blame her?

As for me, I've dated and romanced and screwed, a rut I've been stuck in for decades, now. There's an intimacy hindrance, a wall inside. Not quite as dramatic as the Roger Waters one. But an impediment nonetheless.

"When are you going to find her?" Camille will ask this at her house on Christmas Eve, where I usually attend the family dinner, after she's had a few too many glasses of pinot noir. "That special someone?"

"I thought I did," groping and tickling her in the kitchen while we clear plates. Stealing a peck on her cheek. "I'm trying to remember her name."

Scolding, but with a naughty, secret smile. "Oh, hush your mouth."

Before I left last time the talk between us turned, as it sometimes but not always does, to the old days—of MACM, and of Levon, as Camille still calls him.

"You both were always so cool."

"I was never cool."

"Do you think he'd have hung around you if you weren't?"

I'd never thought of it that way. "Truth is, I felt honored just to be his friend—his peer."

"I know. Me, too."

WHO CARES about losing my job. I've got some irons in the fire, ironic ones considering how I've felt about my hometown—old Bill "Gooch" Wimmel, who's been the publisher and editor of the *Edgewater Advocate* since I was a little boy, is trying to sell the publishing company.

Might sound crazy to want to own a small town newspaper in the era of decline, but on the other hand, what else will I do with myself? Write screenplays?

Probably not. One and done. For old times' sake.

I no longer think of Edgewater County like I used to, as a place from which to run away. Besides, it wouldn't be moving into my childhood house, after all—about a year after Dad died, I sold the property to a lovely young family who've made a home there.

I still own the other parcels of land he left me, however, and often think about building a place in the woods near the river. I've money to buy the paper from investments I made with what I inherited from my dad, whose own shrewd stock market eye never lost its keen insight. I could sell my longtime bungalow in Columbia for a decent profit, or else rent it out to Southeastern students needing a place convenient to campus. Then, build a homestead to my specs. To my singular bachelor-farmer needs.

Last time I talked with Gooch, I left the door open. Said I could be interested. He replied this was good to hear, because sure as shit nobody else wanted it, but wiser to put my money into gold bars or pork belly futures or some such commodity.

"But don't forget," he cautioned, "I'm an old, addled man, and not one whose advice should be given due consideration."

We both laughed and rang off with the promise that I'd keep him posted. That if the deal were to happen, I'd ride over one day and get a feel for the routine of putting out a small weekly community paper.

But by myself?

Is that how it's going to be?

I have more years behind than ahead now, at least going by the averages. This has been fun, sure. As fun as sharing the ride with somebody? Well, hell—I don't rightly know.

The wall inside.

A few weeks ago, I might have discovered a crack in that barricade. It's taken me some degree of effort to admit this. But I have. Especially after talking to Camille about the past.

And thinking about Brenda LaRose.

And what I ought to do.

On the drive home across the city from the copy shop, I've stolen glances at the cover sheet of my screenplay in the passenger seat, just as I stared out at Collegiate Coliseum across the wide avenue, the boxy over-sized building where I once made a movie, in an epoch that's starting to seem like a thousand centuries ago. In the spirit of nostalgia, maybe I'll frame the cover page of this magnum opus, hang it on my wall in the home office alongside my two degrees, the family photos I keep—including my mother's, a young innocent high school portrait—and of course the lovingly framed portrait of the writing group after our triumphant Ten-Scene win: Max standing amidst the five of us, his long arms outstretched, grins on all our faces. Kunk looked so young in the photo, but not as much as the rest of us, particularly me.

And of course the photo of the terrible trio atop the Empire State. That one the most special; that one to be kept close, always and forever.

Maybe I'll run off a few more copies of the script. Drop one off at D'Alessandro's, which Opal owns and runs, and where I eat lunch at least once a week. Or with Darren, who now owns a rigging and sound reinforcement business; he's also an adjunct teaching audio recording classes in Mass Comm. And of course Camille, whom I'm certain will appreciate what I tried to do.

Not to forget Brenda. She's been on my mind ever since running into her at the book festival.

Brenda.

Driving home I pass through the Old Market, skirting campus and motoring into Herndon Hill, my neighborhood of towering old oaks and wide streets. The waning light dapples ethereal, and the yards and sidewalks teem with residents—families doing chores, children at play, joggers, bikers, dog-walkers. Home.

Going into the house, I put down the keys, kick off the shoes, and toss the screenplay—the pages—onto the cluttered dining room table. It's musty in here. Needs a good cleaning and straightening and sorting.

My eyes fall upon the title page.

The Courier font causes all the years to come roaring back, a rushing raging river.

But navigable, now that I'm rediscovering my creativity:

```
RECONSTRUCTION OF THE FABLES


Original Screenplay by
Porter Bucknam


Final Draft
```

'Porter Bucknam'? Sounds like a pseudonym to me.

And, 'final draft'? A joke. You don't 'finish' a screenplay, or a novel, a memoir, or a life—eventually you just quit.

But quitting in a good way.

And this screenplay story, it's not like the real Kunk—this time I gave him a happy ending, the narrative details of which may seem germane to this telling, but aren't important. Let it be enough to know that in my version he went back to Atlantic City, got the gig, got the girl, and made all that was wrong right again.

He survived.

He thrived.

What more must we ask of our protagonists, the heroes of our mind-movies?

The movies—what was it about them, that made those darkened escapes so appealing?

The capturing of dreams, I think, are what make film special. Dreams made tangible. Dreams you can hold onto, like the flesh of a lover.

I dig around in a blue filing cabinet, come up with the film can containing Brenda's print of our movie. Put it on top of the script on the table. Contained within these objets d'art, I think, are multitudes.

I pretend I don't have her address; pretend I've forgotten how to use email. As an excuse to call.

On the street that day outside the book festival, what did I see in her eyes?

A question asked of the female gaze for a long time, now.

Yes. A call.

To Brenda.

I pace in a circle, waiting with a dead-silent digital phone connection until I get a pulsing, electronic tone. The sound bounces back clangorous and hollow, like the voice of a faint memory wailing from within the far deep well of the receding past. I listen, more anticipatory with each ring. Voice mail will do. For now.

But the prompt doesn't come. No menu choices or options. Only ringing.

And ringing.

And ringing...

ABOUT THE AUTHOR

James D. McCallister (middle), a 1988 graduate of the University of South Carolina's Media Arts program, is the author of eight novels, a short story collection, poetry and creative nonfiction. A lifelong South Carolinian, he lives in the midlands with his wife and beloved brood of cats, muses all.

RETURN TO

James D. McCallister's

"EDGEWATER COUNTY, SC"

in

King's Highway

Fellow Traveler

Let the Glory Pass Away

The Year They Canceled Christmas

Dogs of Parsons Hollow

Dixiana

Down in Dixiana

Dixiana Darling

Fables of the Reconstruction (Stories - 2022)